# LONGHORNS EAST

Center Point
Large Print

Also by Johnny D. Boggs and available from Center Point Large Print:

*The Killing Trail*
*Taos Lightning*
*Greasy Grass*
*MacKinnon*
*The Fall of Abilene*
*The Cane Creek Regulators*
*Buckskin, Bloomers, and Me*
*A Thousand Texas Longhorns*
*Matthew Johnson, U.S. Marshal*

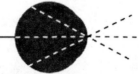

**This Large Print Book carries the
Seal of Approval of N.A.V.H.**

# LONGHORNS EAST

# JOHNNY D. BOGGS

CENTER POINT LARGE PRINT
THORNDIKE, MAINE

This Center Point Large Print edition
is published in the year 2023 by arrangement with
Kensington Publishing Corp.

The text of this Large Print edition is unabridged.
In other aspects, this book may vary
from the original edition.
Printed in the United States of America
on permanent paper sourced using
environmentally responsible foresting methods.
Set in 16-point Times New Roman type.

ISBN: 978-1-63808-900-1

The Library of Congress has cataloged this record
under Library of Congress Control Number: 2023940605

*For Jon Chandler . . .*
*And all the miles on the road*
*of fun songs, cheap hotels, better whiskey,*
*and laughs galore*

# LONGHORNS
# EAST

The cattle of Texas are a breed peculiarly fitted for that country. They are principally of the old Spanish breed, and the peculiarity which will first strike the attention of a stranger is their long, spiral-like horns, which, to speak a little hyperbolically, are not unlike 'Yankee seythe snaths' attached to the animals head. Their symentry and beautiful, stately appearance, I have never seen surpast and seldom equalled in any other cattle.

—E. E. E.,
for *The* (Elkton, Maryland) *Cecil Whig*,
June 10, 1854

# PART I
# 1840

Within the last few months the trade or traffic in black cattle has experienced vicissitude bordering on revolution. Previously prices had attained to a height which induced many to believe that black stock had become scarce in consequence of the lessened attention paid to breeding, and the increased introduction of sheep, stimulated by the growing extension of turnup husbandry. A feeling to this effect induced sellers to ask long prices at home, and buyers to calculate on remuneration still attainable in the markets of England. And for a time the hallucination worked passing well; but a day of reckoning lurked in the rear which overtook jobbers as well as drovers with a vengeance.

—*The Leicester* (England) *Chronicle: Or, Commercial and Agricultural Advertiser*, November 7, 1840

# CHAPTER 1

"I have been informed that you are a grazier."

Tom Candy Ponting took one step back to consider this stranger to Somersetshire. Guessing the wayfarer to be a gentleman, Tom had been wondering why a man of means would seek out the fifteen-year-old son of a stock farmer. Now Tom reevaluated his first impressions.

Granted, the man wore a top hat, but those weren't just for the upper classes anymore. Not even for those in the middle class. Coachmen wore them all the time these days. Why just Sunday last, Harriet Portbury said she had spotted one atop the head of Goolsby, the potter. True, the stranger's clothes were clean, but the toes of the boots showed their age, plus countless miles, and his face had been tanned by long days in the sun. Yet that cigar must have cost him eightpence at Ryland & Warwick's, while the glass of Madeira would have been another seven shillings. Then Tom recalled the man's grip when they shook hands. Gentleman or not, he knew hard work.

"We Pontings have been breeding cattle since we arrived with William the Conqueror," Tom confirmed.

The stranger sipped his wine, then dipped the end of the cigar into the glass before lifting weed to mouth for another pull. He blew out smoke and said, "I would not have guessed you to be quite that old."

Twinkling blue eyes punctuated that statement, and Tom failed to suppress a short chuckle.

"I turned fifteen last August," Tom said.

"William the Conqueror." The man smiled again. "Hastings, 1066." He looked around. "I supposed William got the better end of the deal."

Tom shrugged. "I cannot say. William went to the throne. But we Pontings found Somersetshire to our liking."

Which was true. True enough, anyway. Somersetshire was all Tom Ponting had ever known, and little of that. The Mendip Hills. Stone walls. Cattle. And this village called Kilmersdon.

Tom had left the farm that morning, sent on the monthly errand to pick up the month's post. Mail did not come often enough to the Pontings to make regular trips into Kilmersdon, and neither John nor Ruth Ponting, Tom's parents, could read or write. That was likely why they paid Old Lady Hallett a tuppence a week to teach eight Ponting kids, Ann being too young for schooling. If a post—with luck, an inquiry into the availability of Durhams or Herefords for sale—by chance arrived, Old Lady Hallett might read it aloud. She would have to. The Ponting brood had not taken to the alphabet any better than John or Ruth Sherron Ponting had.

This happened to be Tom's month to walk

to Kilmersdon. Brothers John, the oldest, and Frederick, three years Tom's junior, and Mary tried to buy Tom's errand, but none came up higher than a fourpence. Only Mary, seventh-born and five years younger than Tom, showed him coin, and had she gone up even just a penny or two, Tom might have accepted.

The post office stood in the postmaster's two-story stone house, where Squire Corbyn let two upstairs rooms to travelers since Kilmersdon had no hotel. No post awaited Tom, but that was no surprise. Under new regulations, a letter that weighed between a half ounce and an ounce cost fourpence to be carried fifteen miles or fewer from the post office; eightpence for up to fifty miles. People did not write so much these days. Sometimes, the Ponting child might be instructed to bring back flour, tools, or clothing, putting the payment on the Ponting bill, but not this trip. Tom's brothers would have been pleased to have escaped work on the farm, but Tom cursed his luck. Trodding six miles for nothing. With six miles to go, up and down those hills, back home.

Tom had walked outside, stared at the road that wound its way past the trail that led to the farm, but before he had stepped onto the street, the stranger had approached him and asked, "Pray tell, my good lad, but are you Tom Ponting?"

Now the man was asking: "What cattle do you breed?"

"Shorthorns," Tom answered. "They are known for their milk. One of Father's bulls is to be sold at the Boolk farm in Gloucestershire." Maybe the man would want to talk to Tom's father. Perchance, as a stranger would likely not know his way to the Ponting farm, the man had a fine barouche—even a gig would please Tom—and might let Tom ride with him.

"Black cattle?"

Tom thought about this. "Well, some are black. Black and white. Mostly we have Durhams and Herefords that are, well, red, I guess. Red and white. Some black, though."

"Ah." Setting his glass on the sill, the man dropped his cigar into the dregs. "My name is Sydney Ivatts. I have purchased fifty-three head of cattle from Daniell and Forrester. Black cattle. Black is gold today."

So much for a comfortable ride in a carriage back home. Tom tried to keep his face expressionless, though disappointment made his feet and legs ache. Tom's father had done business with those auctioneers several times, but had never mentioned that color drove up the price at market. When Tom got home, he would have to remember to ask his father or grandfather about that.

"Their cattle are black," Sydney Ivatts continued. "Aberdeen Angus and Galloway polled. The Scots did something right after all as black brings a good price in London markets. Good price in all markets today."

Again, the wayfarer reached inside his waistcoat. This time he pulled out a tiny piece of paper, and extended it to Tom.

"My card," Sydney Ivatts said.

Tom stared at it. He recognized some letters that Old Lady Hallett had drilled through his skull, and nodded as though he understood what the words meant.

"I can show you my badge." The stranger turned and tilted his head up toward the stone house's second floor. "It is number thirty-two. It just seemed silly to wear that piece of metal until I near London with my beeves. And, of course, my license is as a Smithfield drover. Not a country drover. Though I have a bit of metal for that, too."

He winked.

This Sydney Ivatts might as well have been speaking Latin, another favorite subject of Old Lady Hallett that left Tom perplexed. "Badge?" Tom asked, hating to show his ignorance.

"Oh, drovers have been licensed for years," Sydney Ivatts said. "But now we have even more regulations. I supposed the Society for the Prevention of Cruelty to Animals had a hand in getting this legislation passed. And merchants, as well. The residents of London want meat on their plates, but dare not wish to see their supper being walked down the city's streets. But as long as the market holds, I can live with a nuisance."

Tom nodded as though this made sense.

"I was told to seek you out," Sydney Ivatts said.

Tom might get that carriage ride home after all. "Do you wish to see my father?" Though Tom had no idea what business Sydney Ivatts would have with John Ponting—not having already purchased fifty-three head of cattle at an auction, and learning of the scarcity of black animals on the Ponting farm.

Sydney Ivatts's smile widened. "It is you, Tom, that I desire to hire."

The licensed drover explained before Tom could ask the obvious question, and that proved merciful to Tom, so shocked that he did not think he could form a coherent sentence for hours.

"I am driving this herd to market. I have hired George Croumbie as one drover. You came highly recommended as a second."

Tom recovered to ask: "Driving cattle to . . . Newport?"

Tom had never been to Newport, either. He would finally get to see the Bristol Channel. Would they take a ship across the inlet?

"London," Sydney Ivatts said. "I did say I was licensed as a Smithfield drover, did I not?"

Drawing in a deep breath, Tom fastened his eyes on the stranger. This must be some jest? But who would play a joke like this on Tom Ponting? The man looked serious. Maybe . . . Tom exhaled. London. Another city Tom had never seen. Back when Tom was only five years old, maybe six, his father had driven a herd to one of the London markets, returning with a puzzle for the children, and an India shawl for their mother, a hat for Grandfather Theophilus. And John Ponting never displayed . . . What was the word Old Lady Hallett used?

*Extravagance.*

Mostly, John Ponting sold his cattle here, or drove them to Bristol or Bath, forty miles at best.

Tom had only heard stories and seen drawings of London. A city of almost two million people—a number almost impossible to comprehend, and Tom knew his numbers. The greatest city in England, perhaps the mightiest city in the world. A city . . .

"That is one hundred miles from here." Tom's voice dropped to a whisper.

"Nearer one hundred and ten," Ivatts said. "Perhaps farther, depending on the graze."

Their eyes met, held.

Part of Tom wanted to shout out an immediate acceptance, but he also pictured his mother. She would worry herself sick. And his father had taught him to think first.

"What . . . ?" he started, but quickly remembered another of his father's rules regarding business.

*Don't bring money into the conversation first. Leave that to the other man.*

"When," Tom said slowly, "do you begin this drive?"

"Thursday."

The day after tomorrow. Tom sighed. "I would miss the ploughing match."

"Ploughing match?"

Tom nodded until he could speak without his voice cracking. "This year it is scheduled for next Tuesday."

"You have entered in this . . . ploughing match?"

"No, sir, but my grandfather, Theophilus Ponting, is umpiring."

A few seconds passed. The breeze cooled Tom's sweaty face and body. "I dare say that I have never seen a *ploughing* match," Sydney Ivatts said after a moment, "but, alas, I cannot delay my departure. It is a long way to London. The market for beef is strong now. Wait, and it might not be as strong." He sighed. "However, I am sure I can hire another drover. Times are hard. Men need work. And if not, I daresay one hired man and I can handle fifty-three head. I would just, well, rather not work as hard as I've been doing these past ten years."

"I am not declining your offer, sir." Tom spoke too quickly, and he had not been able to hide the panic in his voice. That might have cost him a shilling or two in what Sydney Ivatts planned to offer. "It is just that I must ask my father for permission."

That easy smile returned to Sydney Ivatts's face. "And receive your mother's blessings."

That might come a bit harder, Tom knew, but he nodded and mumbled, "Yes, my lord."

"I am neither your lord nor your grace, Tom," the man said. "I am a dealer in cattle. Much like your father." He reached inside his waistcoat and retrieved a silver watch, glanced at it, and slid it back into a pocket. "Talk to your father and your mother, lad, and your grandfather Theophilus. Let me know your answer by half past six o'clock this evening."

Half past six. Tom would have to run those six miles back to the farm. And race back.

"If your answer is yes," Sydney Ivatts said, "then you will be paid two pounds in London."

"Two pounds?" Tom had expected maybe a handful of shillings.

"Two pounds. It is what I shall pay Croumbie, too."

"But George Croumbie is at least twenty years older than I."

"You will be doing the same amount of work as George Croumbie, will you not?"

Tom could not stop his own grin, though it must have looked gawkish compared to that of Sydney Ivatts.

"You shall find me here. I hope and pray that your answer will be yes."

*I do, too.*

When Sydney Ivatts turned back to retrieve the wineglass and started for the front door, Tom cleared his throat and said, "Sir?"

Ivatts turned, waiting.

"By your grace, sir, but might you confide in me who recommended me for this job you have so generously offered?"

Names had been going through his head. The Reverend Henry Quicke? Robert Fitzpaine? Hugo Hannaford?

"I desire to know this so I might thank him should fortune and my parents allow me to accept this opportunity," Tom quickly explained.

The smile had departed. Sydney Ivatts turned into a solemn minister or jurist.

"It would be a breach of confidence to answer that inquiry without blessings from the man who spoke so highly of you." The drover spoke with formality.

Solemnly, Tom's head bobbed.

"But I guess, between the two of us, that I can at least reveal to you that his last name is Ponting."

# CHAPTER 2

Inside the barn, Grandfather Theophilus sat on a stool, milking Rebecca, the Durham that gave the sweetest milk in Somersetshire. Tom's father forked hay into the stalls. Without stopping or even glancing at Tom, John Ponting asked, "Any post?"

"No, Father."

"Took you long enough to get home." More hay sailed toward another Hereford.

Tom frowned. His feet and legs hurt from covering the distance in such remarkable time. Sweat pasted his shirt to his body. And he still had not completely caught his breath.

"A stranger in town, a licensed drover, stopped me outside the post office," Tom began.

His father forked more hay.

"He seeks to hire me as a cattle drover."

Grandfather Theophilus must not have heard, for he kept tugging on one of Rebecca's teats with thumb and pointer finger, sending streams of milk into the bucket. Tom's father, however, turned away from the stall and the mountain of hay, and stared hard, waiting, with great annoyance, for Tom to finish the joke.

"He has bought fifty-three head. At an auction. Daniell and—"

"A *drover?*" John Ponting turned to his father. "I have not heard of a country drover in these parts in ages. Have you?"

Grandfather Theophilus grunted, and kept milking Rebecca.

"Steamboats are used more today," Tom's father said. "Or a farmer ships them himself, negotiates a contract with a licensed drover who brings the beeves to some jobber."

His father started to smile at some ancient memory, but then his brain finally picked up what Tom had just said.

"He desires to hire *you?*"

Tom swallowed. "Well, he has engaged Mr. Croumbie for his services, as well."

For a great eternity, all Tom heard was Rebecca's milk splashing against the sides of the oaken bucket. Now, Tom's father placed the hayfork's tines on the hard-packed earthen floor, and set his right boot atop the iron.

John Ponting put his hands on his hips. "*You* desire work as a hired *drover?*"

His father looked furious. Tom stammered, then tried to blink away the tears that welled in his eyes.

"I was . . . re-re-recco-comended." He choked out the words. Tom never stuttered.

"Recommended? *You?*" His father roared. "A twelve-year-old pup. Who would recommend a lad like you for a man's job?"

The scene outside the stone house in Kilmersdon played through Tom's mind again. . . . *I can at least reveal to you that his last name is Ponting.* Maybe Tom had been played for a fool. It wouldn't be the first time. But who? Frederick was too young to be giving recommendations to a stranger in the village. Besides, Frederick had not been off the farm since December. At nineteen, brother John left on errands more frequently, but he was too mature to dream up such tomfoolery, especially something this mean-spirited—even for a big brother. Perhaps it was the gentleman calling himself Sydney Ivatts who had perpetrated this caper.

"Son, I recommended Tom for the job."

The sound of the milking had stopped, but Tom did not move. Only when his father turned toward Theophilus Ponting did Tom exhale and look at his grandfather.

"You?" Tom's father started toward the cow and old man but stopped, and his shoulders sagged. "But why? What on earth were you thinking?"

The old man stroked his beard. Tom tried to remember his grandfather's age. Seventy-five. That was one subject Tom picked up quickly. Arithmetic. Even Old Lady Hallett praised Tom's abilities. Sums. Differences. Powers. Progressions. Proportions. Roots. Tom mastered those faster than any student Old Lady Hallett had ever taught, and she looked more ancient than Grandfather Theophilus. "Why," the hired teacher had once said, "he can do sums in his head and without even glancing at an abacus."

"Two pounds is a lot of money," the old man said. "When I was a lad, and the Scots came down with their beeves, a drover would earn three, maybe four shillings, and get ten shillings for his return home."

Rebecca chewed her cud.

"Aye." His father sighed. "And when you were a lad a drove would have two hundred head of cattle, with four hired men working on foot and a topsman riding ahead to clear the road and make arrangements for lodging, meals, and a place to bed down the beasts." He shook his head. "Now we have one topsman hiring a drunkard and a child to work just more than fifty cattle."

"My days as a lad passed many a year ago." Grandfather Theophilus kept his voice level.

"Why Tom? Why not John?" Tom's father said. "He's the oldest."

"Ruth would never let John go. He's her favorite. Besides, John has dreams of America."

Tom's eyes fell to his shoes. America. John was not alone in those dreams. Quickly, he looked up.

"You are thirty-five years old," his grandfather said. "You need to think about who shall take your place when you can do little but milk cows and give recommendations—because *Ponting* remains a much-respected name—about cattle and cattle *men.*"

"Then mayhap William? Or Ann?" John Ponting's voice rose again.

But the old man remained steady. "Now, you are being silly."

William was seven. Ann, only three.

Grandfather Theophilus yawned and pushed himself off the stool. He tilted his head toward Tom. "I have seen the fire in this lad's eyes. And I taught you that the best way to learn the cattle business is to learn all there is to know about the cattle business. Getting a drove to market is part of that business. An important part of the business."

"He is twelve years old, Father."

Tom's grandfather chuckled. "He is fifteen. You were twelve when you went on your first drive. To Bristol. *Remember?*"

"Yes, but times were different in those days, as you keep saying. And we went there together."

"Aye. And do you remember how it made you feel? *Like a man.*"

Sweat stung Tom's eyes, so he closed them, and prayed, one of the rare times he prayed. When his eyes stopped burning, he raised his lids, blinked several times, and focused on his father. The wind carried a distant bellow from some cow in a pasture. Grandfather Theophilus began searching his trouser pockets for his pipe, his tobacco, and a lucifer. Tom's father's eyes bore through Tom's own.

"What is the name of this country drover?"

"Sydney Ivatts." Remembering the hard paper card that the cattle buyer had given him, Tom reached into his pocket and withdrew it. It was damp from sweat, but the ink had not run. He handed the card to his father, knowing that the letters would make even less sense to him. But it seemed to stamp Sydney Ivatts as official. Confidence men did not print up cards of introduction. Or did they? Well, no criminal would conspire to steal from Tom Candy Ponting.

"He has a badge, too. Number thirty-two." Tom did not forget numbers, but he realized that he was taking Ivatts's word that he was a licensed drover. Tom had not actually seen that particular item.

His father turned the card over and over, his lips moving as though he were reading the words, before he returned the card to Tom. John Ponting blinked, then focused on the cow.

"He drives to Bristol?"

Tom shook his head. "London."

*"London?"* The shout caused Rebecca to bellow, and Tom's father started to yell again, but drew in a deep breath instead. When he exhaled, he turned to Theophilus Ponting. "A licensed drover from London?"

"He is licensed. . . ." Tom fought to remember. "Smithfield," he finally sang out.

"Enterprising." Grandfather Theophilus nodded. "Comes and buys the cattle, takes them to London himself. He doesn't have to pay a Smithfield drover to get the beeves to jobbers." He drew on the pipe, and exhaled. "Though it always seemed a ridiculous notion to me that you need a license to get your cattle to market in any particular city, or market. Licenses, taxes. All graft if you ask me."

Tom debated his next move. He did not want to push his father too much, especially now. He forced out the words: "Mr. Ivatts says that I need to let him know by half past six tonight if I might travel with him."

John Ponting's face hardened, but quickly relaxed. "When does he desire to begin this journey?" The voice had softened to almost a whisper.

"The day after tomorrow."

"You will miss the ploughing match."

Grandfather Theophilus chuckled as he tamped his pipe. "By all that is holy, I wish I could miss that, too."

This time, Tom's father grinned.

The wind blew. After a full minute, John Ponting turned and nodded at his son.

"Take the milk to your mother, Tom. Tell her of your opportunity for employment."

"Mum will ask what you think," Tom told him.

"Aye. Tell her . . . tell her . . . tell her that two pounds is a tidy sum of money."

# CHAPTER 3

His mother looked old, though she had been born in 1795, as had Tom's father. But Tom remembered hearing Mrs. Gladys Reeves saying, "You're looking tired this afternoon, Ruth," and his mother responding, "Try not looking tired or old after you've birthed as many children as I have."

Ten. Though one, the first Mary, did not live out the year. Tom, fourth-born, came after her. Mum sat in her rocker, that worn India shawl—the same one Tom's father had brought from London all those years ago—over her shoulders, though July was seldom cold. Leaning forward, she tapped her pipe on the arm of her rocking chair. Mum had been using that pipe as long as Tom could remember. If anyone objected to the smoke, she pointed out that tobacco dissolved the evil humors festering in the brain of men and women.

When she smiled, Tom saw the brown stains in her remaining teeth and the valleys of her gums. "I suppose this is something you want to do, Tom."

Tom nodded. "Yes, Mum. And it pays two pounds. Father said that is a tidy sum of money."

"I suppose Frederick is too young for the job." Mum pulled hard on the pipe, blew out smoke, coughing slightly, and then shrugged her shoulders to get the shawl in a more comfortable position. "And John." Her head shook. "His temperament isn't like yours, Son. Don't know where you got it."

She sighed, shook her head, and started rocking again.

When William began bawling, Ruth Ponting shook her head, raised the pipe, then yelled, "Sarah. Quit tormenting that boy. If you cannot play nice, neither of you will get any supper."

The shrieks reduced to a whimper, and Tom heard his sister coaxing his kid brother.

Tom looked out the window, trying to guess the time. Half past six, he reminded himself. Half past six o'clock. It wasn't that late. He could still make it back to town.

"Is this something you have a strong desire to do, Tom?" Mum asked.

"It pays two pounds," Tom repeated. "A tidy—"

"You have bragged about your salary. I asked you if this is something you wish to do."

"Yes, Mum," Tom answered, bobbing his head. "It is. Very much so."

Ruth Ponting sighed. "Well, it'll mean I shan't need to cook as much breakfast and supper. How long do you suppose this journey will take?"

That was something Tom had not even considered. One hundred miles. The drover had called it closer to one hundred and ten. Make it a hundred twenty, for Grandfather had always said that one should always overestimate how long traveling anywhere would take. What? Ten miles a day? Fifteen?

He guessed. One hundred and twenty miles divided by fifteen. Eight days. Walking back home? Six days. No, quicker. Tom could be a mighty fast walker. "No longer than two weeks. But I should ask Father. Or Grandfather."

Mum sighed, though Tom wondered if she had paid even scant attention. "Well, two pounds would come in right handy. All right, Son, you have my blessing. When do you leave?"

"The day after tomorrow."

She breathed in, held it, exhaled. "You'll miss the ploughing match."

"Yes, Mum. I know." He painted on a smile. "You shall have to tell me all about it."

Mum spit again. "Like I'll be going to that confounded thing." Her head shook, she stopped rocking, and she leaned forward, setting the pipe on a side table.

"Kiss your feeble old mum goodbye."

"I'm not leaving till the day after tomorrow, Mum."

"That should not stop you from kissing your mother."

He smiled, came to the rocker, knelt, and kissed her cheek, which smelled like tobacco, too. When he straightened, he said, "Mum, I must hurry back to Kilmersdon to tell Mr. Ivatts that I shall be accompanying him and Mr. Croumbie."

She offered a nonchalant wave. "Off with you, then. If you are lucky, your brothers and sisters shan't eat everything I cook."

He did not stop until he came to Martin Buller's store and peered through the plate-glass window. Kilmersdon was too small to have a clock tower, and the store was closed, but all the clocks and watches displayed showed no more than five minutes past six. Tom wiped his face with the handkerchief he'd fetched before leaving home, and started to breathe a little easier as he walked to Squire Corbyn's house. The door was open to let in the breeze, but Tom knocked on the frame, and stepped back.

The small-framed postmaster stepped up, red galluses hanging down his tan trousers, his feet in stockings, his shirt removed, and half of his face covered in lather, the right side revealing a fresh shave with only two nicks. His right hand held a razor.

"Begging your pardon, Squire," Tom began.

"Aye. Master Ponting. Still no posts, laddie." He smiled. Squire Corbyn was the first good-natured postman the village had seen since Tom was old enough to fetch mail.

Tom grinned at the joke. "I know, sir. I am calling on Squire Ivatts."

The postman kept smiling.

Tom lifted his head toward the upper floor, then nodded at the staircase behind the jovial fellow.

"Did you know," Squire Corbyn began, waving the razor inches from Tom's nose, "that someone in your family makes shaving lather?" He did not wait for an answer. "Ponting's Shaving Cream. I saw an advertisement in some newspaper left behind at Wilson's Public House. A shilling for a bottle. Supposed to be quite soothing, from the testimonials." He touched the scratches on his right cheek. "I should buy a bottle sometime. Before I bleed to death." His grin widened. "Would you, perchance, be selling a bottle?"

Tom felt perplexed. "I . . ." He tried to think of the proper response. "It must be some other Ponting, sir. Father and John use regular soap. I think."

"I kid you, lad," the postman said. "Though I have been to Wilson's groggery."

Tom knew that already. The postmaster's breath smelled of stout porter.

"And there was an advertisement for Ponting's Shaving Cream. In a newspaper some wayfarer left behind after too much ale." Squire Corbyn lowered the razor. "What is it, Master Ponting, that I can do for you?"

"I seek an interview with Mr. Ivatts. He is letting one of your rooms. Mr. Sydney Ivatts. The licensed cattle drover."

Now Tom's heart began racing. What if Sydney Ivatts had left the village? What if he had found another man to hire? What if this had been a mean-spirited joke after all?

"He is not here, lad," the postman said. "He desired an interview with Randall Triniman."

"Triniman?" Tom wanted to make sure he had not misheard. "The scrivener?"

The jolly—likely inebriated—Corbyn let his head move up and down.

"Do you know when he is expected back?" Tom swallowed and stepped back, glancing down the street at Buller's clock and watch shop, half expecting all of his wares to start ringing or chiming the half-past signal.

"No, Master Ponting, by the grace of God, I have had no business with Mr. Triniman or any professional scribe. But you may wait, lad. Or walk over to Mr. Triniman's office." He pointed the razor down the street.

"Thank you, sir." Tom moved down the steps and onto the cobblestone path. "I guess I should wait for him here."

"You are welcome in the parlor."

Tom shook his head. "Outside will be fine. It is a nice day." The air, after all, was turning cooler. Plus, he could see Triniman's office from here, and, with luck, Mr. Sydney Ivatts could see him when he left that office.

He had just sat on the street's stone banks when

the door opened, and Sydney Ivatts, licensed cattle drover, stepped out of the office, holding a parchment in his left hand, and crossed the street toward Wilson's Public House. Ivatts must have spotted Tom, for he stopped, turned, and made his way toward the stone house. Rising, Tom walked toward him. They met in the street. Sydney Ivatts's eyes sparkled.

"I was not certain if you would return, but as you have, might I guess that you have decided to join my enterprise?" Ivatts still held the parchment loosely, as though letting the wind dry the ink.

"Indeed, sir," Tom said, bowing slightly. "If the position has not been filled."

"It has been filled, lad," Ivatts said, "by Tom Ponting."

They shook hands. "The day after tomorrow, just after dawn, meet me and George Croumbie on the hill above the brook." Ivatts pointed, blew on the paper, and began to fold it.

"I shall be there, sir." Tom's eyes fastened on the paper, which Ivatts started to stick into the inside pocket of his waistcoat. Seeing this, the drover smiled.

"Just a precaution, my lad. A last will and testament. It is one long journey to London, Tom, and many hardships and dangers might arise."

Ivatts stepped back, put his hands on his hips, and said: "Would you like to reconsider your employment, Tom?"

When Tom shook his head, the licensed cattle drover smiled.

"Excellent." Sydney Ivatts extended his hand, and they shook again. "A shake is good as a contract, lad. I will see you bright and early Thursday morning."

# CHAPTER 4

Holding out the old India rubber galoshes, John Ponting looked down at Tom's feet.

"Thought these too big for you," Tom's father said, "but I might be mistaken." Still in his nightshirt and cap, the wiry, hard-muscled man looked his second-oldest son up and down. "You have grown."

Tom's mouth wouldn't open. He took the galoshes, and might have managed to mumble a soft "thanks" to his father, who gestured toward the wooden rack by the door.

"Take my macintosh. Rain is likely, and your mum would be mad if you returned with a cold."

"Here," his mother said, a cotton sack hanging at her side. "Likely, you shan't be stopping at any inns, and I know of no man who can make a decent biscuit, so I baked these for you—and I guess Sir Sydney Ivatts."

"Don't load the lad down with sausages and the likes," John Ponting said. "They will not starve."

" 'Load the lad down,' he says." Ruth Ponting shook her head, and put her hands on her hips. "I give the boy biscuits. You give him galoshes that weigh more than an anchor and a rubber coat that is even heavier than taxation."

"Balderdash," his father said.

From the weight of the sack Tom held, he knew his mother had given him more than biscuits.

He had to set shoes and sack both down to don his cap and throw the old macintosh over his left arm. He shook his father's hand, then hugged his mother, who whispered in his ear, "And my heart is heavier than any taxation in our country." She did not want to let him go, but he made himself pull away.

Brother John, the only one awake at this hour, shook his hand and smiled, whispering, "Lucky, Brother, leaving us with all the chores to be done."

Tom smiled and returned to his mother's sack and his father's shoes. The door opened, and Grandfather Theophilus walked out of the darkness. Tom had wondered where the old man was. He held a long-handled whip in his left hand.

"Take this, lad," the old man said. "Cattle will be deaf to your commands, but they shall hear this."

Tom wondered how he would manage to carry his plunder to the meeting place at the brook, let alone all the way to London. He threw on the macintosh, though he would be sweating to death by the time he reached the fifty-three head of black cattle, and since his mother was sniffling as she shuffled off to bed, he dropped the rubber boots inside the sack of food. Finally, he slung the sack over his shoulder, holding it with his left hand and the whip with his right.

Grandfather Theophilus grabbed the hat off the rack and shoved it atop Tom's head.

"Good luck," his father called, and walked to the bedchambers.

"Aye," said his brother. "Bring me back a pack of London playing cards, and don't lose all your wages in some alehouse."

Tom's grandfather opened the door, and Tom stepped out. He looked up, then at his hand holding the whip.

"You best start walking, Tom," Grandfather Theophilus said. "No need to shake my hand. Shake it when you've returned." He smiled, and Tom tried to keep the tears from rolling down his cheeks.

Quickly he turned, and started for the trail.

"Tom."

He stopped, looked back at the house.

"A word of advice," the old man said, "since I do not know this Sydney Ivatts, just met him when he asked about drovers in the area. . . . When you reach a river, and the water is low, cross it. Do not wait. Rivers can be as fickle as a woman, and thrice as treacherous."

Tom heard the bawling cattle before he spotted the fire. He shifted the weight of the sack, sighing with relief when whatever tune Sydney Ivatts whistled reached Tom's ears. His feet and legs did not hurt so much, and Tom headed toward the orange glow.

Smelling coffee, he stopped a few land rods from the fire, and called out, "Mister Ivatts." That was another bit of advice his father and grandfather had given him. Announce yourself before entering any camp, and enter that camp with your hands in clear view.

"Tom?"

Tom smiled. It was Sydney Ivatts's voice.

"Yes, sir."

"Come in, lad. Come in. There is coffee to be shared."

Approaching, he saw Ivatts pouring coffee from a pot into a cup, which he lifted and held out. Then the man laughed.

"You are well laden, lad, but I dare say rain is not likely on this day."

Tom knelt to relieve his load, and quickly shed the weight of the macintosh.

"Mum sent biscuits, and I do not know what else."

"Your mum is an angel." Ivatts approached and when Tom took the proffered coffee, the drover knelt and reached into the cotton sack. He pulled out one of the India rubber galoshes and held it up.

"Your mum bakes interesting biscuits," he said, laid the boot on the grass, and found the matching one.

"Those are from my father." The coffee was strong, but hot.

Sydney Ivatts next pulled out the crumbs of a biscuit.

Tom swallowed the black brew, and frowned. "Oh, I did not think."

The cattle drover licked the crumbs off his palm and laughed. "The rubber of the boots gives it a remarkable taste." Ivatts backed his way to the fire, dragging the sack with him, and retrieved his own cup. He searched the bag for inventory.

"Looks like two sausages. And a cheese." He held the latter to his nose. "Well aged, it appears." The foodstuffs fell back in the sack, and Ivatts rose, holding a less damaged biscuit and pointing toward the paling sky in the east.

"Daybreak, said I, and here you are, Tom. Good. We can start our day early. We will load your macintosh and galoshes on a pack saddle I have put on a sturdy bullock. I dare say you shall have need of these on the journey east and north. And the whip I believe will pass the Smithfield clerk's muster. The food your mother has sent along will go to good use, as well." He popped the thin biscuit into his mouth and spoke as he chewed. "Even these biscuits. But the whip will be most useful."

He lifted his cup.

"Let us drink our coffee and be on the trail. The quicker we make London, the better."

Tom swallowed coffee, and looked around the camp. "Where is Mr. George Croumbie, sir?"

The brief laugh held little mirth. Ivatts tossed the dregs from his cup into the weakening flames and shook his head. "A lesson I should have remembered, young Ponting. Never advance even a shilling of your promised salary to a stranger. When I left that fine alehouse, Mr. George Croumbie promised he would have just one more whiskey with his friends and see me on the morrow. By the time I had my belongings and had paid dear Squire Corbyn, Croumbie was being dragged out of Wilson's Public House after perpetrating some dreadful maliciousness and being locked in the stocks."

Now he began kicking dirt onto the fire.

Tom looked around. "But you have no horse, sir."

Sydney Ivatts pushed a final mound over the embers. "An expense I do not need. Besides, we have only fifty-three head, and this drove is not coming from the Scottish Highlands."

He stepped away and adjusted his hat. "Yet I must warn you, lad. Your bed, as well as mine, shall be on the roadside. The cattle will sleep and eat with us. No inns for the two of us, no stables for our drove. Scottish I'm not, but a miser I am."

Tom breathed in, exhaled, and asked, "And if we meet someone on the road?" He knew from stories from his grandfather and father than the topsman usually rode ahead to warn travelers of the approaching herd.

"They will give us the road." Ivatts smiled. "Don't you think?"

By now, Tom did not know what to think.

"It shall be the two of us, but a fine adventure we shall have," the drover said. "As we reap our fortune."

They made good progress that long first day. Ivatts found it best to push the cattle fast and far to begin the drive. "Tired cattle," Ivatts said, "do not wander about. Nor do tired drovers." On the second day, they crossed the River Frome. It took Tom those two days to figure out how to use Grandfather Theophilus's whip without leaving his shirtsleeves, forearms, and back of either hand in tatters. Sydney Ivatts carried just a stick.

By then, the cattle moved easily, and Ivatts said that walking slow, after two hard days, would be the perfect pace from here to London. "Fatter the animal," he explained, "the higher the price." Though their temperament tended to be docile, sometimes these Aberdeen Angus and Galloways showed a stubborn side. Neither breed had horns, but the bullocks weighed around fourteen hundred pounds, and a small lad and a grown man could have a hard time making a Galloway or an Angus move until the beast wanted to move.

Ivatts had been right about other travelers,

too. When they saw the approaching herd in the country, pedestrians and equestrians gave them a wide berth, stepping well off the path and watching with curiosity and sometimes amazement as man, boy, and black beasts trudged past them.

A few cheered. Some cursed. Most just stared in silence. The cattle did not care one way or the other.

Villages were no different, though whenever he could, Sydney Ivatts skirted around the bigger towns—especially after one, whose name Tom never caught, where the drover paid a fine of six shillings for the deposits bullocks left on the street.

Which Tom had to shovel and carry to the fly-invested, malodorous manure pile behind the livery.

They camped underneath the shadows of a towering, grassy hill near Warminster. Sydney Ivatts said that they should rest here for another day, let the black beef fatten, and he left Tom in charge of the cattle while he walked into town. He returned the next morning with two sacks of corn, which he fed to the black cattle, and a blackened left eye.

Tom made no queries into the injury; Sydney Ivatts offered no explanations.

The next morning, they resumed their trek,

fording a stream twice that day. By then, Tom lost track of how long he had been walking. They crossed the River Bourne—at least, that's what Ivatts called it—more brooks and streams, and rested at Basingstoke, where again Ivatts left Tom in charge and returned without another injured eye but with a headache the following morn.

"We have traveled seventy miles, lad," Sydney Ivatts managed to say.

That night, the rains began.

# CHAPTER 5

As far back as Tom could remember, July and August had always been the wettest months, but these raindrops did not just sting when they struck. They bruised. Tom's cap offered little protection. The path they traveled turned into a stream, water flowing downhill, above Tom's ankles—the India rubber galoshes providing scant protection now. He could see three black animals head of him, but no more.

He raised the whip, let it down hard, neither knowing nor caring if the leather cord struck the Aberdeen Angus that had stopped in its muddy tracks.

Lightning flashed across the sky, immediately followed by deafening thunder. The earth seemed to tremble from the fury. Still, Tom raised the whip again, sent it slicing. He spit out water, wiped his mouth and nose with the sleeve of the macintosh, which felt heavier than the armor of one of King Arthur's knights.

"It's no use, Tom."

He spun around, shocked to find Sydney Ivatts standing next to him. At least, it sounded slightly like the drover. Tom blinked blinding water out of his eyes.

"There's a tree on a hill a few rods away."

Ivatts's right arm pointed off to the left of the road that had become a channel.

Thunder rolled somewhere behind Tom.

"Leave the cattle here," Ivatts said. "They shan't go anywhere in this blow." He pointed again. "Come."

Tom could not stop his mouth. "Are you daft? Take shelter under a tree? I shall not be cooked by a bolt of lightning."

Water rolled off Ivatts's hat.

"Lightning can strike a cow as certain as it can strike a tree." He pointed again. "The tree. The tree—"

"The tree," Tom interrupted, "is higher that these cattle. I shall take my shelter here, sir."

He turned, squeezing between two bullocks, and setting underneath one on his left. They had been traveling uphill, and water flowed down with vindictiveness. Tom figured he might not be cooked by a bolt from the skies, but he sure enough would catch his death on this afternoon.

The animal next to him began to urinate.

Tom shivered.

Then the sky lit up again, and the thunder roared so close, so loud, Tom's ears ached. The cattle seemed deaf. Or maybe they were worn out more than Tom.

He thought about that tree Sydney Ivatts had mentioned. The branches would be full of leaves, and trees did not urinate. He smelled something, and looked to his left.

"Or crap," he said aloud.

He pictured home, the fire his father might have going. He tried to remember some song Elizabeth, an alto, and Mary, a soprano, might be singing, with Grandfather Theophilus slapping his thigh in rhythm. He longed for coffee, and one of Mum's biscuits. And he could smell the pipe Mum would be smoking as rain danced on the roof, and the stone walls stopped the wind.

A moment later, he realized that Sydney Ivatts sat across from him underneath a somewhat larger Aberdeen Angus bullock.

"Well, laddie," the drover said as he pulled a flask from his coat pocket, "how do you like the cattle-driving business now?"

The thunderstorm turned into a slight mist, and they slogged through mud and misery, up and down hills, through muck that reached almost to their knees before the sky stopped shedding water. When the country flattened, Sydney Ivatts stopped the lead beasts and walked back to Tom.

He pointed his whip at the grass, then turned and gestured at the hill.

"By all that is holy, Tom, if I shall tread another mile on this day. We shall cross the Loddon tomorrow. Take off your clothes. We shall take advantage of this brief appearance of the sun to dry our clothing."

Ivatts kept talking, but Tom heard nothing except the first part. About crossing the River Loddon. When the drover began removing his hat, India rubber poncho, and shirt, Tom cleared his throat.

"My grandfather says always cross a river when you can," Tom said.

"The Loddon is not the Thames, Tom. We shall be fine." Ivatts tossed his shirt onto the grass, and sat down, where he began struggling with his boots.

"But the rains, sir," Tom said, hoping he was not jeopardizing his promised salary.

"The rain fell on us." Ivatts held out a boot that pointed southwest. "That way is where there shall be concern of flooding."

Tom looked off to the northeast, where the sky remained dark, ominous.

Ivatts dropped his boot, and began working on the left one. "Tom," he said without looking up, "I am sure your grandfather was a fine drover in his day. But this is not his day. We shall have no trouble on the morrow at the Loddon. Now shun yourselves of those soaking clothes, lad, before you catch your death."

The next morning, no longer feeling like codfish, and finding patches of blue in the dark clouds, they started the herd again, popping whips, and reaching the Loddon and the tavern that stood next to the river. After a drizzle here, a mist for several rods, finally the sun broke through with blinding whiteness.

"Get the cattle across, Tom," Sydney Ivatts said as he began whistling and walking toward the stone building. "I shall meet you on the other side after I warm my innards." He stopped at the door, turned, and smiled. "Do you think you can cross the Loddon by yourself?"

Tom gaped at the three-arched stone bridge. When he turned back, his grin matched that of the drover's. "I shall give it my best, sir."

"How about some brandy with your coffee this evening, Tom?"

Sydney Ivatts held up his flask.

Smiling, Tom shook his head. "Thank you, but I think not."

They had continued past the Loddon, pushing closer and closer to London, seeing more cottages, more farms, more roads.

The country was, as Sydney Ivatts put it, "crowding up."

"It will fight off any cold, lad, and you have been sniffling since God decided to give us a glimpse of what Noah saw."

Tom sniffed, swallowed. He tried to guess how long they had been gone, and figured he had underestimated—not the distance, but how often Sydney Ivatts would stop to rest the drove, or sleep off a night of too much brandy. For a man who said it was imperative to reach the Smithfield market before the prices of black beeves dropped, Ivatts found public houses more inviting than driving cattle.

"The brandy is all for you, sir." Tom forced his smile.

The drover nodded, and raised the flask to his lips, but stopped, and rose quickly. "What in the name of . . . ?" He stopped.

Turning quickly, Tom stared at a cow trotting down the path.

"It's not one of yours, sir," Tom said. That much was obvious. Ivatts's herd consisted of black bullocks. And this was a Hereford, red and white, with short pale horns pointing downward over its white face.

Ivatts set his flask against a stone, and pushed himself to his feet.

The cow kept trotting. The black cattle of Sydney Ivatts's herd considered the newcomer with little interest and returned to eating or dozing.

"Shall I stop it, sir?" Tom asked.

"No." Ivatts started for the road. "I shan't be accused of stealing some farmer's milch cow."

They watched the animal, never breaking stride, as it moved down the road.

Near the River Hart the next morning, more

Herefords grazed on both sides of the lane. Sydney Ivatts stopped the lead bullocks of his drove, stepped off to one side of the road, and called out, "Tom. Let us take the cattle into this pasture." He pointed to the right. "Then we shall investigate. This looks quite suspicious."

The road did not differ much from others they had traveled. Puddles and bogs everywhere, pools of water in low places, deep tracks in the mud, drying now that the sun came out of hiding.

Chewing their cuds or the lush grass and wildflowers, Hereford bullocks, cows, and heifers showed little interest in the man and the teen. Tom searched both sides of the road for a cottage or barn, but found no sign of a stock farm. Then he stopped, swallowed, and coughed to clear his throat before he could call out to Sydney Ivatts.

The drover turned, and Tom raised his right arm and pointed.

Ivatts walked back until he reached Tom. They looked up the slight incline. Ivatts found the flask from a pocket, drank swiftly, then said, "Come with me, Tom," and he started toward two dead cows and a blackened patch of ground. There, Tom spun, dropped to his knees, and gagged.

Dead cattle he had seen many times. Dead human beings, too, but always in coffins, always looking peaceful, if pale, and as though asleep. This man before him scarcely looked human.

Tom retched until his chest hurt. His stomach felt halfway past his lungs. He sweated, trembled, coughed again, and leaned forward, his hands in the burned grass covered with his own acrid vomit.

Something warm, bitter, and smelling of grapes came into his nostrils as his knees pressed deeper into the scorched earth.

"Breathe through your nose, lad," a kinder voice reached him. "Now, straighten up." An arm wrapped around his chest and pulled him. "Drink."

Tom hesitated. His eyes finally focused, and he spotted the flask.

Tom shook his head.

"Just rinse your mouth out with this, then," Ivatts commanded. "Come, now." The flask came up, Tom coughed, but he caught the hand at the bottom of the container. Together, Tom and Sydney Ivatts brought the whiskey to Tom's lips. The liquor burned his mouth, but he swished it around, feeling the cleansing, the healing powers of the alcohol, then spit it out. He coughed, swallowed, sighed, shuddered.

"I . . . have never . . ."

"Nor have I." Sydney Ivatts released his hold on Tom and took a drink himself, but he did not spit anything out. "Stanley Leicester. I knew him well."

Tom pictured the blacked corpse and hair,

scorched but whiter than sheep's wool, the skin charred, holes in the man's retinas, mouth wide open as though frozen in a scream, teeth so white and . . . gold. Yet the clothes seemed untouched, just wet from rain, except for the pewter buttons that had melted on his shirt, and another melted heap of something on the sleeve of his macintosh. "How could you . . . ?" He could not complete the question. Nor could he forget that horrible face.

Ivatts drew again from the flask, then screwed on the lid, and let the container disappear in the pocket of his jacket. "Stanley was the only drover I knew with gold fillings. The hair confused me, for Stanley's was blacker than any of those we take to London. I have seen hair and beard burned by men struck by lightning, eyebrows, too. But . . . never this. It must have been the shock . . ." Chuckling, he shook his head. "*Shock.* Isn't that a lark!"

The drover rose and looked down the lane, then back at his herd of cattle. "But where," he said, "is Philip Hume?"

Tom dropped his head, thought he might gag again. When he didn't, he asked, "Who?"

"Another licensed cattle drover. He partnered with Stanley. Not like Hume to leave a mate behind. Certainly not like him to leave behind a drove bound for market."

Sydney Ivatts stood, towering over Tom, and

held out his hand. "Come, lad, there is work to be done, an investigation to engage. Stanley will keep. And a stretch of the legs will help you."

The River Hart flowed high and deep. No three-arched bridge of stone crossed these waters, but Sydney Ivatts nodded at the boot prints that led into the torrent. Then he pointed to the far bank.

"See the prints?" Ivatts asked.

Tom made out something, but what he still mostly saw was Stanley Leicester, and he wondered if he would ever forget that nightmare.

"He forded the river," Tom heard himself whisper. "Maybe to seek help for . . ." Again, the face of the dead man returned.

"No prints leading out of the water on this side, though." Ivatts shook his head. "My guess is that Philip went to scout ahead, see if they could ford the Hart here. Got caught in the current. Swept downstream."

He started down the bank. "This way, Tom."

At a bend two miles downstream, they found the body, caught among logs, branches, weeds, trash, and one busted wagon wheel.

Water came up their thighs, mud to their ankles, but they dislodged the body and pulled it to the banks, climbed out of the Hart, and dragged the corpse from the river.

Tom sat down, panting, sweating, fighting

to keep the bile from rising any farther up his throat, while Sydney Ivatts went through the man's waterlogged coat and trousers. Burying his head in his hands, Tom tried to remember why he ever thought herding fifty-three black cattle to London might be an adventure.

"The gods smile upon me at last, Tom." Sydney Ivatts's voice thundered over the Hart's roaring current.

Lifting his head out of his hands, Tom blinked and saw the cattle drover holding up some badge, stamped with raised brass letters. Tom recognized the "D" at the beginning and the "O" near the center. There was also a shield of some kind, and a small, streaming banner with more letters. A coat of arms maybe, and a number. Tom knew the number. Fifteen. His age.

It was a fairly big badge, with a leather strap to fasten it to . . . an arm, perhaps.

"His license," Ivatts said. "As a cattle drover in London. And now it is yours, Tom. Fortune shines on Sydney Ivatts for the first time in forty-three years. Quick now, laddie. Rise. Let us get back to our herd."

He grabbed Tom's shoulders and pulled him upright.

Tom started to look at the drowned man, but just tilted his head toward the corpse.

"But what of . . . your friend?" he managed to ask.

"He'll be looked after, Tom. Fear not. Philip Hume shan't be the first hapless man to be buried in utter oblivion with his sorrows and nothing more."

*But,* Tom thought, but did not say, *we aren't even burying him.*

"It's the commissioners' doings, Tom," Ivatts said that evening after they had managed to ford the Hart and move down the lane five miles before camping alongside the road.

"The commissioners of London. And the men and women and children, the businessmen and noblemen, who don't mind eating beef—love beef—but detest the drovers that bring the meat they so dearly love into their city."

Tom tried to pay attention, but the two dead men kept interrupting. A man bloated by water. A man burned into a ghoul.

Last year, if Tom heard correctly, new regulations went into effect in London. No dogs could be used to herd the livestock through the streets and to the markets.

Ivatts held the big badge toward Tom.

"There is no need for the time being to worry about this identification, but once we enter London, you must strap it on your arm so that those peelers who think they are God Almighty can see it. Following certain thoroughfares—no more than twenty head of cattle after nine o'clock in the morning. We shall enter the city before nine, get our beef to market, sell, and celebrate." He beamed with delight. "Oh, yes, when we reach a main street, we must keep the herd on the near side."

"Sir . . ." Tom struggled to find the words. "I am not a licensed drover. I . . . this . . . well, this badge does not belong . . ."

"Tom," Ivatts said, "Philip Hume has no need of his. And Stanley Leicester's was melted like a cake's frosting on a hot day. I am an honest man, Tom. I did not steal any of their cattle. Lord knows, fifty-three head are more than enough for a man and a boy to handle. I did not take any coin or rings from the deceased, and I—with your help—dragged poor Mr. Hume out of the roiling river so that he might be buried as the Christian he was not, and not feed turtles."

He lay back down, hands supporting his head, staring at the darkening sky.

"But mayhap we can make even more money. Buy some more cattle when we get closer to London. Black cattle, of course. I bring in this herd, and you bring in another."

Tom thought he might vomit.

Ivatts kept talking. "Not a big herd. Ten, twenty. Enough for you to bring in yourself. Black beeves that are fat, will likely sell quickly. For that herd, we'll split the profits evenly, sixty-forty, less what I have to shell out to buy them."

Tom opened his mouth to correct Ivatts's arithmetic and to let him know he wanted no part of this fraud, but the man kept right on talking.

"Poor Stanley and Philip." The drover clucked his tongue. "We came up with the idea in a public house near the Smithfield market. Buy a herd outright from some grazier, bring beeves to London, sell them. A bit more work, but a fine deal." He drank more whiskey. "I wonder where they found their beef. Not in Somersetshire, that's for certain. And not black beef, either. The fools were young drovers, new to Smithfield, but hard workers. Just not as smart as I. And did you see that herd, Tom? Mixed. Cows, bullocks, heifers, and one bull. A mixed herd, Tom, can be a jinxed herd. They are harder to handle. Bullocks. They are much easier to handle. All men would be much easier to handle if they went around with their balls snipped off."

He laughed.

"Again, lad, no need to strap it on your arm till we reach London. Just do as I say, and you shall earn your two pounds and more. And, by all that is holy, what a time I will show you in London. It is a city like no other. Heaven for we sinners. Hell for everyone else."

Then, Sydney Ivatts began to snore.

# CHAPTER 6

Sydney Ivatts was right.

London was like nothing Tom had ever imagined, and he had not even crossed the River Thames into the heart of the city. Following Ivatts's orders, Tom herded the cattle to the lair, a patch of open pasture in what Ivatts called "Regent's Park." Tom's father would not have labeled this patch of waste a pasture. Grass barely rose above the soles of Tom's work boots. He expected sheds or some bit of shelter, but not a tree grew here, and the only water trickled in a miserable ditch reeking of foulness.

He did not know what Sydney Ivatts paid the man to lease this patch, which Grandfather Theophilus would have said is "is fit to hold the two ends of the earth together and nothing more." Whatever the drover had paid, it was too much.

But beyond the worthless lair, London rose higher than mountains he had imagined. How the buildings towered. And the people. Hackneys rushed past, whips snapping. Silent men led burros laden with wares. Fine horses pulled fancy carriages, while men, women, and children filled the streets and sidewalks. A horn blew, and a team of four white horses drew a coach that sideswiped a peddler's cart, sending tomatoes, potatoes, and cucumbers bouncing across the road. The old man rose to his knees, shaking his fist and pleading for assistance, but the coach did not stop, and soon the peddler began cursing boys and men who picked up as many vegetables as they could, then leaped out of the way of more horsemen, hackneys, and carriages, and took their plunder with them.

Voices sang out, words too fast, accents so strong, that Tom thought perhaps the people of London spoke a different brand of English than they did in Somersetshire.

Heart pounding, and head almost spinning, he found his gourd and emptied the last of the water down his throat.

On one hand, Tom felt lucky. Sydney Ivatts had bought no more cattle to bring to the Smithfield market. The drover had stopped at two stock farms but found the cattle lacking in weight, looks, and, mostly, color. None of the cattle he examined was black, and black, he kept saying, was gold in London.

Tom started wiping his mouth when across the muddy street, a man with a silk hat and fancy cane appeared. The wind blew the tails of the green coat as he waited on the other side of the street for a carriage to pass. He wore a fine tan waistcoat, too, Tom observed, with a cravat of green silk, and tan pants stuck into tall brown boots with pointed toes.

He crossed the street and into the pasture, heading directly toward not Sydney Ivatts, but Tom.

When Tom's and the stranger's eyes met, the gentleman stopped, fetched a monocle from a waistcoat pocket, and brought it to his right eye. He squinted, and the face, polite though pockmarked, changed to dour. Tom couldn't help but stare, not at the man's face, but at the waistcoat. Ink bottles lined the coat, though Tom could not determine how they were attached. And now Tom noticed quills stuck in the grosgrain hatband, and pens over the stranger's ears. Yellow papers popped out of the waistcoat's pockets like flowers.

The stranger kept his mouth closed, but Tom read disdain across the face. The gentleman returned the monocle and brought out a tin of snuff, which he opened quickly, put a pinch in his right nostril, then his left, but soon spotted Sydney Ivatts.

"I saw the shield on his arm and thought he to be in charge," the man said as he approached Sydney Ivatts. "But, by Jove, he is a mere boy. Are they issuing badges to pups these days?"

Tom turned to pet a docile Black Angus.

"He does the work of two men, Pearse," Ivatts said. "He's earned the badge, and the respect of every licensed drover in London."

They might know one another, but the tone of

the voices revealed they were not friends. The water in Tom's stomach began to feel as though it came out of the ditch near his feet. He sure hoped this Pearse did not know Philip Hume. Without realizing he had moved his arm, Tom looked to find he was touching the badge, and he began shoving it until the number was closer to the inside of his arm than in full display for anyone to read the raised *15*.

"Ivatts," the man said, "you remain licensed for Smithfield, am I correct?"

"Indeed."

"I did not know you were licensed as a country drover, too?"

Ivatts laughed. "Nor did I. But my partner, Stanley Leicester, is. 'Tis a good business, is it not?"

Tom stopped breathing.

He did not wear Stanley Leicester's badge. He had the one taken off the drowned Philip Hume. What if this Pearse knew Stanley Leicester?

Pearse shot Tom only a passing glance, however, and then, still holding the tin of snuff, sniffed. "Black cattle," he said. "And they look well fed. You should not need to graze them long."

"I don't have long," Ivatts said. "By my reckoning this is Saturday. We will move them to Smithfield Sunday night."

"I can save you trouble and expenses," the man said.

"Make your offer," Ivatts told him.

The man pulled a quill from the hat brim, and spun on his heels, studying the fifty-three head carefully now, squeezing his nose with thumb and forefinger on his left hand, moving his lips sideways, and eventually withdrawing a piece a paper from one of the pockets, unscrewing the cap to one of the ink bottles, dipping in the quill, then scratching the ink-doused end against the paper that fluttered in the breeze.

He waited just long enough for the ink to dry before extending the paper toward Ivatts.

"My first, best, and final offer." Again Pearse rubbed his nose.

Sydney Ivatts crumpled the yellow sheet after scarcely a glance, and pitched it over his shoulder, letting the wind carry the paper toward the herd Ivatts and Tom had driven from Somersetshire.

"I thank you, sir, for providing some roughage for my drove."

"Your cattle are so poor, they will not even entice the Saturday buyers." Pearse seemed to have forgotten he had praised the herd's looks just minutes ago.

"My cattle are not as poor as your offer."

Pearse snorted. His right hand withdrew the tin of snuff, which he extended toward Ivatts, who never took his eyes off the cattle buyer's face.

"The only thing that goes up my nose," Ivatts said, "is the air I breathe—and my finger."

The tin returned to the pocket, and the man stepped back. "You are nothing more than the pigeon-livered ratbag you have always been. I shan't do business with you. Good day, sir."

He spun quickly, and walked back toward the street, but had to wait again for a hand-pulled cart and three horsemen to pass. That gave Sydney Ivatts enough time to call back, "At least I am no malmsey-nosed hornswoggler."

Pearse kept walking.

Cupping both hands over his mouth, Ivatts yelled, "The only job you're fit for, Pearse, is jakes-farmer."

Tom did not know what a jakes-farmer was, but the lady with the parasol in the back of a hackney turned beet red as the coach passed the lair and disappeared into the maze.

Sydney Ivatts laughed, and crossed the pasture, examining the herd. When he reached Tom, he cackled again. "You're as pale as linen, lad. Brandy cures all ailments. Why don't we find us a jagger, buy a fish that shall feed the two of us, then celebrate our arrival by tipping a few glasses?"

The only thing Tom could manage for the moment was to blink repeatedly.

Ivatts removed his watch, checked the time, and glanced at the cattle in the closest lairs. His smile broadened, and as he dropped the watch into a pocket, he said, "We shall do well in Smithfield, lad."

Tom recovered the power of speech. "I thought all the cattle are sold in the Smithfield market."

Ivatts studied the boy before he understood. "Ah." His head tilted toward the busy street. "You mean Pearse. Sometimes jobbers conspire to get ahead of the game. Pearse tries that kind of deal every year. Every year he winds up paying a pittance for a pitiful drove, and I have never sold anything for a pittance. The market—*the money, Tom*—that awaits us in Smithfield."

A woman screamed, and Tom and Ivatts turned back toward the street, watching a woman dive out of the way of a speeding coach that must have held ten men atop the roof, six in the back, and an army inside. Pedestrians on both sides of the road laughed. The woman pushed herself to her knees, her red blouse now covered with filth, and spit out saliva and profanity at the nearest wayfarers.

"Is it always this . . . ?" Tom couldn't figure out what word he wanted to use.

"Busy?" Ivatts shrugged. "It is Saturday, but this is incomparable to anything I've seen. Do you reckon Victoria has died?" He laughed. "God save the queen!"

Wiping mud and anything else off the front of her dress, the woman made it to the footpath, and joined the procession into the vast city.

Sydney Ivatts let out a whoop. "All these people. They shall be hungry, laddie. And that could drive up the price per stone for these fine-looking, black-hided bullocks we've brought to sell."

Ivatts bought a fish—what kind, Tom probably did not want to know—from a peddler a few blocks over, and they returned to camp, where Ivatts left Tom in charge to clean and fry up the meat while he went to a public house to find brandy and bread. He returned with the former, but must have forgotten the latter.

The licensed drover chugged down brandy. Tom sipped tea. They ate with their fingers, which they licked with relish.

"Sir?" Tom summoned a tiny bit of courage. "What if an inspector or buyer sees my badge and knows I am not the late Mr. . . . ?" He could not recall either of the dead drover's names.

Sydney Ivatts chuckled, then licked his fingers. "Fear not, young Tom. Stanley and Philip were new to Smithfield. Besides, buyers, peelers, jobbers, and jesters like that see only the number on a badge—unless they happen to admire my handsome face. They focus on bullocks, not drovers. And I shall always protect you, lad. For I am your friend."

He turned toward the street, and sighed. "Look at this city, lad. Look."

People still filled the streets. Some left town, peasants from their looks, but now and then a barouche, the hood folded back, or a phaeton would leave the city. Tom wished he had started counting the people he had seen heading into London. He would be in the thousands by now.

"It's all changed than it was in my father's day. And his father's, too."

Tom turned as Sydney Ivatts shook his head.

"Father would say that all his father had to do, being a Smithfield drover, was walk to the lairs, let them fatten up on water and graze, strike a bargain and bring them to Smithfield, and always get the best price, a fair one."

He sipped from his bottle.

"Dogs could be used then. No dogs anymore. And it is hard for any drover to make a profit anymore. That is why I decided to buy my own drove. Be a country drover and a Smithfield drover. But on Papa's soul, I should never lower myself to become a butcher's drover."

He burped. "So this year I aimed to bring a drove to London myself. And we have done it, lad." He finished the bottle and tossed the glass over the back of his head. It smashed on cobblestones.

Ivatts stood, wobbling, and pointed at Tom's arm.

"Your drover's badge." He shook his head. "Philip Hume's, I mean. What was the number?"

"Fifteen." Of course Tom could recall a

number. He would much rather think of that than the condition of the drowned drover's body. Or, worse, Hume's partner, Stanley Leicester.

But now that he had thought of Hume's partner, he swallowed down bile and made himself ask: "Why did you tell that man, that man named Pearse, that I was . . . Mr. Leicester?"

"Leicester." Ivatts smacked his lips and sat down, then lay on uncovered ground, bringing his right forearm over his eyes. "Bread pudding. That would hit the spot, lad. Or a fancy woman. Stanley Leicester. Country drover. Went all the way to Wales once. He and Philip Hume were good drovers."

Tom sighed. Ivatts was worthless in this condition, and Tom really didn't need to care to know what rascality this licensed Smithfield drover had planned.

"Ivatts."

Still sitting, Tom turned, saw the flame of a torch fast approaching, and heard footfalls of its carrier trotting.

The torch carrier stopped near the campfire. "Is that ye?"

Sydney Ivatts pushed himself into a seated position, though how he managed that Tom could not fathom. The flame lowered, and a tall man knelt, pitched the torch into the dying cookfire.

"Right-oh," the man said. "It is ye, Sydney. In

ye cups." He was an older man, Tom saw, the flames illuminating a savage face with a brown patch covering the left eye, white hair hanging to the shoulders, and a hat that had been battered into something unrecognizable. The man's one eye locked on Tom.

"Give ye a fright, I did, young man, and I apologize. The name is Jardine."

"Jardine," Ivatts sang out. "You old ankle beater."

The man looked sharply at the drunken drover. "Ivatts, have ye heard about Philip Hume?"

"Hume." Ivatts cackled. "Why, Philip's right there. My partner. Well, my hired drover."

Tom almost vomited.

"No." Ivatts shook his head. "No, no. That's not Philip. That's—"

"Hume's dead, Sydney," Jardine said. "And so is Stanley Leicester. Hume drowned. Leicester." The man made the sign of the cross, and shook his head. "Struck by lightning."

Ivatts kept shaking his head. "No, Stanley's not dead. He's right . . ." He lost the thought. Or something more important came to Ivatts's mind. "Fiddlesticks, now, Eddie, my dear old friend. Might you have a dram to share?" He pointed across the pasture. "Or a few shillings. I know of a fine little public house."

"Ye've had enough for a platoon, Sydney." Eddie Jardine rose. He looked at Tom, nodded,

71

and said, "He'll be fine, lad. Once he passes out." He stared down at Ivatts, who stretched back out on his back near the fire. "I'll speak with ye on the morrow, Sydney."

Jardine extended his hand. "Edward Jardine." His hand swallowed Tom's. "Ye're working for a good drover. But a lousy drunkard." The shake, though firm, did not crush Tom's bones.

Jardine had taken just a few steps when Ivatts pushed himself up and said, "Why are all these people coming to London? Was Her Majesty called to Glory?"

"Victoria was living and breathing when I saw her Wednesday last," Jardine said.

Tom hardly found the words. "Mr. Jardine, you saw Her Majesty?"

"Right-oh." Eddie Jardine laughed. "Taking an airing with her royal consort, she was. In the parks that evening. Without a military escort. And, Master Tom, call me Eddie."

Tom wanted to hear more, but Jardine's next sentence jarred Tom into a state of speechlessness.

"They're here for the hanging, most likely."

That roused Ivatts. "A hanging." The drover rolled over, and tried to clap his hands. "When does the poor sap drop?"

"Monday." Jardine did not sound happy. "And it's not just one soul dropping. It's five."

"Good." Sydney Ivatts laughed, and lay back down. "By Jove, Tommy, we sell our drove and celebrate with a hanging."

A moment later, Ivatts began snoring, and Edward Jardine disappeared in the darkness.

# CHAPTER 7

His eyes and mouth jerked open. The ground trembled.

*The cattle are stampeding.*

Tom almost screamed—till he recognized Sydney Ivatts leaning over him, shaking Tom savagely as though to snap him out of some nightmare. Only Tom realized that the particles of his dream had been lovely, wonderful, not one bullock, nor one drunkard, not pounding rain or dead cattle drovers. He had been back home in Somersetshire. Now Ivatts's putrid breath and wild eyes brought Tom out of that peaceful sleep and into the reality of the rancid ditch, the stench of cattle and Tom himself, and the smoke from chimneys, campfires, and factories that burned Tom's eyes and made fresh air in London nonexistent.

"Let go of me," Tom cried out.

But Ivatts kept both hands clasped to Tom's shoulders, jerking him up and down.

"Tom," the man shouted. "Tom. Tom."

"I am awake." That's not all Tom told the drover. Profanity flew out, words that would have had him tasting soap back home.

Ivatts's wild eyes caused Tom to gasp.

The hands quickly released Tom, whose

head struck a rock. He cursed again, and Ivatts slowly pushed himself to his feet. The fool had been straddling Tom, jerking him up and down, screaming his name. Tom's ears already hurt, as the fingers on his right hand sought out the back of his skull. He felt no blood, but knew for certain that a knot would rise from the stone he had struck.

"What has . . . gotten . . . into . . . you?" Catching his breath, Tom pushed himself into a seated position.

"Tom."

That's all Sydney Ivatts could say for a few minutes. The man's face had turned a ghostly white.

"Sir?" Concern replaced Tom's anger. Sydney Ivatts had consumed vast quantities of ardent spirits on the drive, but he had usually awakened with cheerfulness. Now he breathed heavily, and his face glistened with sweat.

Tom tried again. "Sir?"

Ivatts wet his lips with his tongue. He sank into a squat, swallowed, and whispered, "Tom . . . do you have . . . ?" He struggled to say the name of Philip Hume. "His badge. Do you . . . ?" He cursed himself and jerked his head toward the street, swallowed, and looked behind him. Only the black bullocks could hear what he was saying.

Tom's head tilted toward his mother's sack.

"God be praised." Ivatts relaxed. "I must drop it in the Thames. I fear my loose tongue has aroused suspicion."

Now Tom began to pale. He felt as though he had begun to perspire as horridly as Sydney Ivatts.

"Cursed brandy." Ivatts pounded his right thigh.

The streets already bustled with activity. Horsemen, carriages, pedestrians. Church bells began sounding in all directions.

"It's Sunday," Tom said.

Sydney Ivatts blinked. He drew in a deep breath, and let it out almost immediately. "What else is in the sack?" he whispered.

The biscuits, cheese, and sausages had been depleted days earlier. Tom's right hand reached for the sack, but Ivatts grasped it tightly.

"I'm just getting my galoshes, sir," Tom cried out.

"Galoshes." Ivatts kept blinking. The fingers loosened, and the drover used the back of that hand to wipe his brow. "Yes. Take your rubbers, lad." He began gathering stones that circled the ashes from the cookfire. After Tom had removed the heavy boots, leaving only the drowned drover's metal badge and strap inside, Ivatts dropped the heaviest stones in the sack. He needed Tom's help to stand.

"Wait here," Ivatts said, and was gone.

Tom looked at the black cattle, at the men,

women, children, dogs, cats, horses, asses, and wheeled vehicles that filled the nearest street. The last of the church bells echoed, and Tom wondered that if he ran as fast as he could, how soon would he be back at the Ponting Stock Farm and away from this nightmare.

Instead of running, he reminded himself that he had done nothing wrong. He had made it this far. He had two pounds—*a tidy sum*—coming to him. God had determined that the time had come for two drovers Tom had never seen alive. Sydney Ivatts was right. They had stolen no cattle. No man could be blamed for a drowning or a poor soul struck by lightning. As long as Ivatts managed to drop that sack with Philip Hume's badge into the river . . .

Tom busied himself, checking the drove. There was little work to be done for the cattle, though. He couldn't make the water in the ditch any cleaner, or less pungent, nor could he make grass grow in this barren lair. He remembered passing a well on the way into London, though as he looked down the street, he doubted if he could figure out the way there or back. Cattle lowed piteously, so he found his gourd, and Ivatts's canteen, plus the coffeepot and teakettle. He summoned up enough courage to walk toward the street, deciding that he could surely find a spring or well nearby. If not, he recalled overhearing some talk of water at the Tideway. All these travelers. Someone in London would kindly supply directions.

He didn't make it to the street.

"Master Tom."

Turning left, he spotted Edward Jardine pushing past two beggars and a fat man.

Tom breathed easier. The one-eyed drover turned back to respond with a few words at whichever of the men had said something Jardine found rude, before the drover continued toward Tom.

"Do not tell me that Sydney has gone off to find another public house at this time of day." Jardine was not smiling.

"No, sir. He's . . ." Tom couldn't think of a lie.

"At this point, he doesn't have enough coppers for a Corinth."

"No, sir," Tom said, as though he knew what a Corinth was.

Jardine waited.

"He went to the river."

To Tom's surprise, Jardine accepted that. "Right-oh, we could all use a bath, but I'd prefer mine with soap. And that shall come on the morrow, with good fortune. And where might ye be off to, Master Tom?"

"To find water for our drove, sir."

Jardine seemed to have turned mute. The one eye blinked repeatedly, then looked over Tom's shoulder and studied the black cattle.

"Right-oh." After Jardine nodded slightly, his eye hardened, the jaw squared, and he smiled. "Ye come from a good family, don't ye, Master Tom?"

"Yes, sir," Tom answered slowly.

The man breathed easier. "And ye be a smart lad. But that drove has been well fed, and not pushed hard. Haven't ye seen how the rest of the cattle in these lairs look, Master Tom?" He laughed. "Even mine be thirsty and half starved."

Tom could not think of anything to say.

"Master Tom," Jardine said softly, almost smiling, "with good fortune for Stanley—and ye—and especially those fine bullocks—they will be in the market tonight and sold to a butcher come morn. They will be out of their wretched misery, and feeding London's gentry for weeks."

Tom thought of this. "And the poor?"

"God bless ye, Master Tom. Ye be a wonder." Jardine tilted his head back and laughed. When he looked back at Tom, he smiled and shook his head. "The poor, me good lad, get their meat on Fridays. Whatever is left."

"Oh." Tom felt he had to say something. He still ought to water the bullocks, something better than the stinking water from the ditch. Besides, his own mouth and throat hurt. The shaking he had endured from Sydney Ivatts certainly had not helped.

"How about some coffee?" Jardine asked. "And a spot of breakfast?"

Tom sighed. "We are out of coffee, sir. And not even a murphy to bake or boil."

Jardine laughed again. "Master Tom, I was asking if ye'd care to join *me* for breakfast." He pointed. "My lair is just down that crowded pike."

Spirits lifting, stomach anticipating food and drink, Tom felt his face brighten. He started to shout his thanks and acceptance, but a voice called out from the back of the lair.

"Don't let that rapscallion hoodwink you, lad."

"Speak of the devil," Jardine said, and Tom turned to see Sydney Ivatts walking briskly. Tom exhaled with relief. The sack with Philip Hume's badge was gone, but a man walked alongside the drover.

"Luck be with ye, Master Tom," Jardine said. "Or with Sydney, though why God favors him, I do not know. But that gent with him?" Jardine nodded at the stranger. "He's no rozzer, though some time in a jail might help your boss. Let's see what the verdict is, but the way Sydney is smiling, I'd say ye troubles will soon be a bad memory."


"This young man is your drover?" the uniformed stranger asked in a fast, harsh accent that Tom found hard to comprehend.

"Indeed, sir," Sydney Ivatts answered, smiling at Tom. "And a better drover you've never met."

"Rubbish." The man handed a slip of paper to Ivatts. "He works for you, don't he?"

While the drover looked over the paper, the man turned to Tom.

"I do not know you, youngster, but watch your language. Drovers are a blasphemous lot, but filthy talk upsets the decent people of our city— especially when they are returning from evening services on the Sabbath. Do you hear what I'm telling you?"

Tom couldn't find his voice, so he nodded rapidly.

"Good." The man turned back to Ivatts. "You have paid your toll, I hope."

"Of course," Ivatts said. "A drover can't get this far without being taxed to death. I'd show you my receipt, but as you cannot read . . ."

"Enough with your insults. I can read enough to slap you with a ticket that'll keep you and your stinking beef out of Smithfield for a week."

Ivatts nodded slowly, but the smile never left his face.

"Your badge. It must be on the upper and outer part of that arm, as well you know. Visible at all times." He waved his short, black club toward Tom but kept his eyes on Ivatts. "You will tell him the route he takes, and both of you will keep these mad bulls under control. A nine-year-old girl was crippled three weeks ago, run over on her way from church. Miracle, it was, she weren't gored to death, but the poor lass is still at St. Bartholomew's."

He tucked the club underneath his right armpit, and pushed back his tall hat.

"Any questions?"

"None, Your Highness," Ivatts answered. "Except this: When's the hanging?"

"Yours," the officer answered, "won't come soon enough for me."

"Right-oh!" Edward Jardine clapped his hand. "Now, sir, would ye like to see a drove that is managed by a gentleman, sir? Right this way." He bowed graciously and pointed down the street.

"He'll see your drove sooner, Eddie," Ivatts said, "if you show him a downer or two."

"I said no more insults, Ivatts." The man took his club, softly prodded Tom out of the way, and walked to Jardine.

"Lead the way."

Jardine bowed. "See ye boys in Smithfield." He and the official walked away.

When the two had neared the street, Ivatts put his arm around Tom's shoulder, and turned him till they both faced the fifty-three black bullocks.

"All right, lad," he said. "We're sixth in line. A good place, but not the best. We'll be entering under torchlight, of course. Before we get to Blackfriars Bridge, you'll see the timber wharfs on the left. Don't let the cattle leave the street.

Cattle aren't used to bridges. We crossed only a few on the journey here. So keep them going. But not too fast. Keep a good distance behind the herd in front of you. And on the near side of the street. Understand what I'm telling you?"

Tom did not know how to answer.

"The streets are wide enough, and shan't be many people traveling at that hour, but when you turn at the shoemaker's shop, then it's a tight fit. Just keep your eye on the torch ahead of you. Don't let any wagtail lure you inside Milford's. You'll never be fit for a virginal lass in Somersetshire or even the worst dollymop in all of England. They will turn us down Water Lane, most likely. Hungersford's Tavern is on the corner. If they keep us on Bridge Street, watch from Potts's haberdashery on the right."

Ivatts's head tilted back as he laughed.

"Be that as it may, when they lead you to Old Bailey, the streets widen enough to give the Lushingtons and mug-hunters enough room so they shan't be gored. But don't let the cattle run down toward St. Paul's churchyard. And Paternoster Row is nothing but a den of thieves. Gilt-Spur and you are practically there. Church on the left, Coleman's Inn on the right. Then through the gates and you'll be in Smithfield. Leave the bullocks standing free as long as you can. I like to sell them that way. But those that police the market are apt to . . ."

Ivatts stopped, and his eyes narrowed.

"What ails you, lad?"

Tom couldn't stop breathing in and out, deeply. He was sweating, his heart pounded, and he thought he might faint.

"Sir," he finally said, fighting back the tears. "Kind sir, but, I cannot read."

# CHAPTER 8

For the longest while, Tom fought off fainting, though dying of apoplexy would be better now than just passing out. Sydney Ivatts stared, not blinking, uncomprehending.

An instant later, laughter sent the drover doubling over. His hat toppled off, landing near the shallow ditch. After righting himself, he smacked Tom's back hard.

"By Jove, lad, that's wickedly clever. Wickedly clever, I say." Ivatts slapped Tom's back again. "Cannot read. You had me at a fright, Tom. A fright, I assure you. Cannot read. Bully good. You should be appearing at Adelphi in the Strand. Bully for you."

Tears welled in the drover's eyes, but just as quickly, the chortling ceased. Sydney Ivatts picked up his hat, started to put it on, then let it tap against his thigh.

"This is no jest?" Ivatts's voice dropped to a whisper.

"No, sir," Tom whispered.

After holding his breath for a few seconds, the drover exhaled, shook his head, wiped his mouth with his free hand, and finally donned the hat. "Tom," he said, "you don't battle with or insult the Queen's English when you talk. In fact, you speak the language as well as or better than anyone I know who has been graduated from the Rugby School. Or, as in my case, boast the honor to have been expelled by the Reverend Thomas Arnold, headmaster and pompous jackass. Surely you must read and write."

Tom's bowed head shook. He sniffled. "No, sir." The words came out in barely a whisper.

An Angus bellowed. A pedestrian insulted a beggar on the sidewalk.

"But the way you speak . . ." Ivatts kept shaking his head as his eyes bore through Tom.

"Oh." Tom's head dropped and he stared at his pitiful work shoes, noticing how much manure appeared to be permanently mortared to the sides. "Old Lady Hal— . . . Miss Hallett, our teacher, she tells us all about diction and presentation and how words should be used and pronounced. I take to that quite well, though John, my older brother, and Elizabeth and Mary, two of my sisters, speak much better than I. Mary in especial. Old . . . Miss Hallett . . . she says Mary's voice is musical. I'm much handier at arithmetic. But . . ." His lips trembled. "I just . . . I try . . . But . . . well, neither Mother nor Father know their letters."

Not that Old Lady Hallett ever tried to teach the Ponting youth. Tom remembered asking that witch what some letter was, and hearing her say, "If you don't know, I cannot help you." Sometimes he wondered if she knew all of her letters.

"Father," he continued, trying to block out those memories, "says the only word that matters is the word you give to another soul, and you do not need to read that."

Across the street, a minstrel began singing a bawdy tune.

"Your father is wise in many ways," Ivatts said after an uncomfortably long pause. "But he is asinine in that way of thinking." He sighed and shook his head.

Tom had no reply, and several seconds passed before Ivatts spoke again. "Can you read or write anything?"

Tom nodded. "My name. T-O-M. Though I often mistake the last letter for . . . that . . . other one."

" 'N'?"

Tom's head bobbed again.

"How about 'H'?" Ivatts asked. "And 'A' and 'S'?"

"Sir?"

Ivatts laughed again. "T-H-O-M-A-S. Thomas."

Tom wiped his eyes. "No, sir. My name is Tom. Not Thomas. The reverend wrote it down that way in Mum's Bible. Miss Hallett used Mum's Bible to show us how to write our own names. My brothers and sisters complained that wasn't fair. I had an easy name. Frederick was much displeased."

A policeman slapped a beggar down with his

club, and pressed his boot against the bald man's head. "I've told you, Witherspoon. . . ." But the bugle of a coach drowned out the rest of the officer's threat.

"I am sorry, sir," Tom said, still looking down. "I should have told you before you hired me. I just did not think it mattered. Reading. Writing. They never mattered to we Pontings."

There was no long silence now. "They should," Ivatts said.

Tom swallowed. "I understand, sir. I am sorry to have caused such a muddle." He breathed in deeply, exhaled, and turned toward the street. "Thank you for your trust. Thank you for all that you have taught me about being a cattle drover. I shall find my way back to—"

"Hush, Tom. Hush." Ivatts sighed, and finally laughed. When Tom looked up, the drover put his hand on Tom's shoulder and squeezed it tightly.

"A bullock knows his letters more than most drovers know theirs, Tom, so you are ahead of many." He drew in a breath, exhaled, and patted Tom's shoulder. "I shall take the point, lad. You bring up the drag. The rear. Just keep your eyes on the torch ahead of you. And don't let the bullocks push hard. Steady pace. Not too fast. We shall get to Smithfield by the grace of God or the curse of the Devil, but what a grand adventure you will be able to tell your folks and friends in Critchill."

"Kilmersdon, sir," Tom corrected.

●  ●  ●

If he ate anything that evening, he would throw it all up on his pantlegs and shoes. He wasn't even sure the tea would stay down, but Ivatts insisted that it would settle Tom's stomach and nerves. The drover then emptied the kettle's contents over the fire, which he then covered with dirt and manure by kicking mounds over the circle. The kettle disappeared inside Ivatts's pack. He threw that over his left shoulder, tugged his hat down tightly, and offered an encouraging smile.

"You'll do fine, Tom," he said softly. "Let's get these bullocks onto the street."

That proved easy enough. Ivatts explained that the drove was trail broke by now, but cautioned that driving fifty-three bullocks to Smithfield could prove troublesome. "London is not for the faint of heart," he said. "The towns and cities we drove through were nothing like what you're about to see. Just follow the torches, Tom. Steady the pace. Steady the nerves. The taverns don't close near the market, lad, so there's your motivation not to get lost."

Tom waited under torchlight. The black cattle stood idly, half asleep, while Tom paced back and forth, counting his steps, just to keep his mind occupied, and not thinking of getting this drove to the Smithfield market.

He could smell the River Thames, or what

he thought had to be the river. Smoke from chimneys, torches, factories, campfires irritated his eyes. Now he wished he had eaten something.

Footsteps on the cobblestones behind him caught his ear. When he turned, he drew in a sharp breath, but relaxed once Edward Jardine's face came into view underneath a streetlamp.

"Master Tom." The drover smiled. "How ye be faring this evening?"

"All right, sir." Tom's voice cracked.

Jardine made a vague gesture down the street. "I be three droves behind ye, Master Tom. Are ye ready?"

"I guess so, sir." No one would mistake that creaking voice for confidence.

Jardine studied the black bullocks. "Don't push them too fast or they will bunch up. Bruised meat don't sell as quickly or for as good a price. Try ye best to keep them off the sidewalks. And, for God's sake, don't let them trample a poor girl. Ye want to be at Newgate for the hanging tomorrow evening, not inside that dreary prison awaiting the hangman to offer a hood before he drops ye into eternity."

Tom stared blankly.

Jardine laughed. "I kid ye, Master Tom. Ye'll do a fine job. Right-oh, ye shall. And I shall see ye and ye partner on the morrow. After we sell our droves, the first arf and arf shall be on me." He held out his hand.

The shake felt strong and firm. "Good luck, Master Tom."

"And to you, Mr. Jardine."

The drover turned and took a few paces back into the darkness before he stopped. He did not turn around but asked, "Master Tom, it be none of me business, but what has Sydney agreed to pay for ye work and troubles?"

After a brief, internal debate, Tom answered honestly. "Two pounds, sir."

"Aye." Tom could just make out the head bobbing. "Good pay that."

Jardine started walking away, but Tom called out, "Sir, may I ask you one more question?"

The drover stopped. "Of course."

"How will I know when I reach Smithfield?"

Jardine chuckled heartedly. "Master Tom. When ye see nothing but misery and wretchedness, ye shall be in Smithfield."

All he heard were cattle. Bellowing right in front of him, far behind him, blocks ahead of him. That noise, so common to Tom, blended with the peculiar sounds of London. Whistles blaring. Songs, badly out of tune, echoing down alleys and off walls. Bells tolling. Laughter. Screams. Curses. The sounds of bedlam.

This close to the River Thames, the night air felt cool, but Tom kept sweating.

Suddenly, a familiar voice called up from

ahead. "Tom Ponting. We are off, lad. Get them moving, lad. See you at the market."

*Criminy. My whip.*

He had left it leaning against a lamppost. Ahead, he heard the hooves of Aberdeen Angus and Galloway polled clomping. Tom started for the post across the street, stopped halfway there, and remembered that he had moved the whip. The bloody thing lay right where he had been standing, propped against an abandoned, empty cart, its left wheel missing, on the sidewalk.

By the time he had grabbed the whip, a bullock had turned around, started trotting toward the drove behind Sydney Ivatts's herd. Tom slashed. The cord popped like a pistol shot. The hornless Galloway turned, and Tom slashed the whip again, popping it over the backs of the bullocks. They started forward. Tom's heart pounded. The drove was moving. He raced after the cattle, then slowed, remembering to keep the pace steady, not too fast.

He smiled at his success.

He walked across the Blackfriars Bridge, over the Thames. Not one bullock had tried to disappear in the timber wharfs. He glanced to his left, thought he saw a barge in the middle of the wide river below. No, no, that might be the City Gas Works. He could smell the water, but couldn't see it.

Past Chatham Place. Well, he had heard that Chatham Place lay immediately after the bridge. The Thames behind him. The immense sprawl and filth of London stretched ahead. Buildings towered above him, though most windows remained dark. He felt the buildings, more than saw them. Voices mingled with the clopping of hooves and lowing of cattle. Dogs barked, but not dogs used by cattle drovers. Those had been outlawed by the city's lawmakers.

At least this street was wide enough.

Lampposts shone ahead, and he breathed easier. His head lifted toward the towering buildings, and he felt as though he walked through a mountain valley.

"Up cattle. Move cattle. Get along, cattle." His voice sang out, and he tapped the whip's handle against the streets.

He had found a rhythm to his motions. Walk. Snap the whip. Tap the handle on the street. But now, he moved to his right, to a new street, narrow, and not well lighted.

Something smashed ahead of him.

A door partly opened from a noisy tavern, and a man screamed harsh profanities at Tom, waving his fist.

Tom popped the whip over the closest bullock. He yelled at the cattle, but did not respond to the man's curses.

· · ·

An infant bawled from a darkened window two or three stories up. A cat, or some wild animal, screeched down a black alley. A pennywhistle played at an intersection with a street that was even narrower than the one the cattle moved down.

He lost track of time. Had no idea how long he had been in the thickness of the city, but he soon felt darkness surrounding him, no lanterns, no torches, and the hooves echoed, as did voices ahead of and behind him. He was in a tunnel. Maybe going through some gate.

A moment later, brightness all around him practically blinded him. Torches and lanterns and campfires. Lights from taverns and inns and, most likely, bordellos. He smelled excrement, knew he waded ankle deep in manure and urine.

The square went on forever, surrounded by buildings, some as high as four stories—he could tell from the lighted windows—maybe even taller. Cattle bawled piteously, accented by the sounds of sheep and pigs. Horses neighed. Asses brayed. Human voices shouted curses, and from the taverns and brothels came songs.

"Tom."

He spun, spotted Sydney Ivatts walking toward him, still holding his torch though the lights from posts and fires and buildings lit up this part of the square like breaking dawn.

"Let the cattle stand loose, lad," Ivatts said.

A policeman pounded his club against a pen. "Nay, you don't, drover." The officer wagged the club under Ivatts's chin, then glared at Tom. "These stinking beeves of yours will be put into ring droves. They shan't be left wandering around this market like stray cats."

" 'Ring droves,' he says." Ivatts dropped the torch in a puddle of urine, and put his hands on both hips. "What do you know about cattle, you ignorant beagle? You think I can sell bruised meat or cattle with hides torn off? And if London didn't want cattle to be loose, Smithfield would put up more pens."

An ewe darted past, causing the officer to crash into a stack of filthy hay.

"You'll do as I say," the policeman said after he had recovered. He waved his club. "Or this drove won't sell, I promise you that, and you can wait till Friday to bring your bloody beeves back."

The officer brushed the straws of hay off his britches. "And you know I can do it." He turned, and walked away, pounding his stick against the fence posts and hitching rails.

Ivatts walked to Tom, spit in the street, and sighed. "Well, lad, we're here," Ivatts practically shouted, though Tom stood just a few feet away. "But I guess we shall have to get these beeves into ring droves. Facing each other as the copper says."

"Pray tell," Tom whispered, "what's a ring drove?"

Ivatts brought a finger to his lips. "That ass will have his hands full, so don't worry about a ring drove," he whispered. "It's the worst thing for cattle, and drovers, having the bullocks facing each other, beating them to keep their heads down. Punching them with a staff or the handle of your whip in their flanks. Abuse them, they'll be impossible to control. Or sell." He sighed. "Just keep them steady and quiet. It's a long time till the market opens." He pulled out his watch, glanced at it, and sighed. "A bloody long time."

Morning dawned slowly, but even after a church bell rang out eight times, the copper did not return. And as the sun rose above the buildings and its rays fought their way to the earth, Tom knew why. Torchlight and glowing lanterns weren't enough for anyone to realize the enormity, and insanity, of the Smithfield market.

Voices boomed over snorting pigs, bawling cattle, bleating sheep, braying asses, neighing horses, barking dogs. Whistles blew. Bells rang. Curses filled the sky almost as thick as the flies and other biting bugs. Smoke obscured the sky and much of the sun, while drovers whistled, or cursed, to keep their ring droves steady, and hawkers screamed out whatever they wanted to sell.

Tom felt dizzy. He had been standing all night, and since the sun rose, he had tried to comprehend everything he was seeing, hearing, feeling.

"It must be four acres," Tom whispered.

"Nigh six. When me pap first came, 'twas only three."

Tom whirled to find Edward Jardine approaching him, that one eye beaming, and his hands filled with greasy sausages, which he held out in his left hand. "Here's a couple of bags o' mystery for ye, Master Tom." He looked around. "Where's Sydney?"

That smell of the steaming meat almost made Tom pass out. The emptiness of his belly made him reach to jerk the meat out of Jardine's hand, but Tom stopped himself, remembering his parents, his grandparents, and Old Lady Hallett. He also saw his own hands.

The filth almost made him vomit.

"I . . . I . . ." He looked around for a washbasin, then realized the absurdity of finding one of those anywhere outside of a peddler's cart.

"Ivatts?" Tom turned, looking behind him, over the black drove, then wheeling around toward Jardine. "I don't know, sir. He was here just. . . ." But Tom had no sense of time.

He focused on the meat Jardine still held, and swallowed. "Let me find someplace to wash my hands, sir?" he pleaded, and when the drover nodded, he hurried to a trough several rods away, praying that Edward Jardine was not as hungry as Tom Candy Ponting.

The hands started to plunge into the trough but stopped, and Tom spun around, gagging. The drover in charge of the nearest herd laughed. Tom spit, wiped his mouth, coughed, and spit again. Excrement floated in the water in that trough, but not the feces of cattle, pigs, or sheep. That foulness came from a man.

He hurried away, choking down the bile that rose up his throat. Tom's head spun at the stores alongside the nearest walls. Catgut factories, horse knucklers, bladder blowers, tallow renderers, taverns, an inn, buildings that appeared to house banks. He almost stumbled into the horn of a red bullock, would have if a drover with one of those badges on his arm had not pulled him aside.

"Have care, boy," the man said. "Watch your way."

"Thank you," Tom whispered, and gasped, not at the closeness he had come to having his guts ripped open, but because for just a moment he thought the number on the drover's badge was fifteen. He blinked, fought the dizziness again, and made himself understand that the number was seventy-five.

A man with a horn read bits from newspapers.

Tom walked past him, tried to recall where the drove of black cattle might be, wondered if he were losing his mind. Or just lost in a mass of humanity and livestock. He kept walking, smelling manure, stepping in rivers of urine and climbing over mounds of foulness. He walked. Walked. Walked.

A rough hand jerked him around.

"Don't ye want these bags o' mystery, Master Tom?"

Tom's eyes managed to focus.

"Oh, Mr. Jardine." He saw the two sausages, which somehow smelled like those his mother made.

"Eat, lad. Before you drop dead from starvation."

He didn't care about the filth on his hands. He didn't care about anything. He took one of the greasy things and shoved it into his mouth. Nothing to wash it down but the grease that poured into his mouth. He hardly chewed. Then forced in the second sausage. He scarcely tasted either and, when he later thought about it, decided that had been a blessing from the Lord. *Bags o' mystery indeed.*

"What say you now, my fine friends?"

Tom could not answer Sydney Ivatts without spitting out meat of some kind. He chewed, and his eyes locked on the two mugs of steaming brew the cattle drover held in his hands.

"If I had known you were visiting, Eddie, I would have used my third hand." Ivatts held the mug toward Tom. "Drink up, lad."

99

Tom did not need another invitation. He drank, stopped, turned, and coughed. This was coffee like none he had ever tasted. Burning hot but with a sweetness and a heat that did not come from fire.

"Just a splash of brandy to make it palatable, lad," Ivatts said.

"Oh," Tom started.

"It'll do ye good, Master Tom," Jardine said. "Just don't guzzle it down. Sip it. And let it cool." Jardine turned to Ivatts. "Where have ye been?"

Ivatts took his time sipping from his mug. "Making a deal, of course, Eddie. For seventeen and a quarter percent above the market average." He pushed open his coat and pointed at a paper in the upper pocket of his waistcoat. "All I need to find now is a cattle banking house."

Jardine laughed. "Take ye pick."

"An honest cattle banking house." Ivatts winked.

"That will be harder."

"Sold yours?" Ivatts asked.

"I will."

"Well, don't wait till after ten or you'll be waiting till Friday. Worse, you'll miss the hanging. The drop, I'm told, is two this afternoon."

Tom coughed up brandy-laced coffee.

"I have managed to get us inside Newgate— seeing that I have the poor and only son, about to become an orphan, he being child of this doomed murderer named Postle. You're Tom Postle till we get kicked out, lad, but, fear not, for I also have a ticket to get us into a place at Old Bailey with a grand view of the party this afternoon."

# CHAPTER 9

Sydney Ivatts spent no more than fifteen minutes inside a shack between a coffeehouse and a grocery. Tom sat on the bench on the walkway, still sipping brandy-laced coffee. He started to stand when Ivatts came out the door, but the drover waved his hand and sat next to him.

Tom wanted to ask if Ivatts had his money, but he just couldn't sound rude or greedy. He was ready to get out of London and make his way back home.

Ivatts patted Tom's shoulder. "Feeling better?"

"Yes, sir," Tom said. "The coffee has settled my nerves."

"More like the brandy, lad." Ivatts stared at the vast market, still bustling, still noisy, still incredible and insane. "Tom," he said, still looking at the men and women and livestock. "Do you know how to play vingt-et-un?"

"No, sir. But I have heard of it. I think."

Ivatts reached into his coat pocket and withdrew a deck of cards. His fingers flexed and he shuffled the cards. Tom blinked in amazement. Then the drover turned over a card.

"How many diamonds on this card?"

"Ten," Tom answered quickly.

"Are you sure?"

"Yes, sir."

Another card turned over.

"What's this card?"

"It's a man."

Ivatts laughed. "It's called a jack. Jack of hearts."

"Jack," Tom repeated.

Another card flipped. "And this . . . lady is . . . ?"

Tom paused. "A . . . queen?"

"Smart lad." Tom beamed, but Ivatts tapped the card. "And that . . ." He looked up at Tom. "That is what we call a spade."

The next card was a man, but Tom needed no hints. "This must be a king. King of diamonds."

"You are smart, lad. You'll be winning a fortune at vingt-et-un in no time, Tom. No time indeed. Now, let us try this."

He gathered the cards and put the ten of diamonds beside Tom's left leg. Quickly he flipped another card, the seven of spades.

"How much are these two cards worth?"

Tom's face paled. "How many diamonds and spades total?" Ivatts quickly rephrased the question.

"Seventeen," Tom answered.

"Smart lad." The drover gathered the cards, except those with people on them. "These cards are all worth ten points. But this one . . ." He flipped over a new card. "This is the ace. The ace of clubs. That's a club. Clubs and spades are always black, diamonds and hearts are always red. The ace can be worth eleven points or one point. And vingt-et-un . . . does your hired lady professor teach you French?"

"Latin," Tom said, shaking his head. "Or tries to."

"Well, *vingt-et-un* means 'twenty-one' in French. The object of the game is to get as close to twenty-one as possible, or at least higher than the dealer of the game."

Tom nodded, but he had no idea why he would need to remember anything about vingt-et-un. Ivatts picked up all the cards, shuffled them, slapped a card near Tom's leg, facedown, a card near Ivatts's leg facedown, then the king of clubs beside Tom's down card and a ten of hearts partly atop Ivatts's down card.

"Look at your card," Ivatts ordered.

Tom picked up the card. "I have—"

"Don't tell me what you have. But do you think you're close enough to twenty-one to beat me?"

"But I don't know what you have, sir," Tom pointed out.

Ivatts grinned. "That's why we call it gambling. What do you think?"

Tom looked at his card. "I would like another card, sir."

Immediately, the three of hearts slapped atop his king.

Tom frowned. "Another."

The nine of spades fell down, and Tom sighed. "If I am over twenty-one?"

"You bust. You lose. Lose whatever you bet." When Ivatts reached for Tom's down card, Tom said, "I did not know we were betting, sir. I—"

The drover laughed. "We aren't betting, lad. I'm just teaching you the game."

Tom breathed easier, and Ivatts turned over the two of clubs. "Well, not much you can do with those cards, Tom, but you played the hand nicely." He flipped over his down card, the ace of diamonds.

"That totals twenty-one." Tom grinned.

"Yes, it does." Quickly Ivatts gathered up the played cards, put those on the other side of his deck, shuffled remaining cards four times, used his fingers to flip half the cards on the bottom of the deck, and dealt again, jack up for Tom, eight up for Ivatts.

When Tom started to reach for his bottom card, Ivatts asked, "Tom. Do you remember what cards were played our last hand?"

Tom looked up, closed his eyes, tried to recall. His hand was easy enough, at least the numbers. Three, two, and nine. And . . . a man. The king. Ivatts's hand was simpler. An ace and a ten. When Tom answered, Ivatts's grin widened.

"Tom, there are four sets. Spades, clubs, hearts, diamonds. Two through ten. Then jack, queen, king, ace. Fifty-two cards. What do you have now?"

"Twenty." Tom turned over another jack.

"You want another card?"

Tom shook his head. Ivatts turned over a three, then dealt a queen face-up.

"You win, sir," Tom said. "Twenty-one."

Ivatts gathered the cards. "I win, Tom, because I cheat." Now he pointed diagonally at a stone building. "But over there, I don't have to cheat. You don't have to cheat. All you have to do is count. Count the cards. Play the percentages. You won't win every time, but I think you will win more than you'll lose. And remember all the cards that have been played. Think you can do that?"

"Gambling, sir?" He picked up his mug and finished the coffee laced with liquor. "But I have no money . . . just the two pounds you will pay me."

"And I will pay you, Tom, but first we must celebrate our success. If you lose, you'll be losing my money. I shall bank you, Tom. I'll play the way I always play, and between my skills and your genius, we shall expand our profits, lad. Now, drink up, lad. The day has just begun."

Tom reached for the glass near him, dragged it over the rough table. So much smoke filled the room, Tom's eyes burned, but he could still see the cards in front of him and in front of the dealer with the thick red mustache and black hat. The glass felt heavy, but it came to his lips sure enough, and whatever it was Sydney Ivatts kept ordering went down smoothly. The brandy didn't burn so much this time.

"A card," Tom thought he said, laughing as he added, "my good man."

The four of spades landed atop Tom's king of diamonds. He nodded. "I am good, my good man," he said. The red-mustached man reached over and turned over a seven of diamonds.

"Vingt-et-un," the dealer said.

The other four men in the game, including Ivatts, had busted.

The dealer turned over a jack of clubs, matching his jack of hearts. "Twenty," the dealer said, and his eyes hardened as he nodded at Tom. "The winner."

Tom finished his brandy, hoped he might get another, but another man stepped behind the dealer. He had a dark mustache, a dark coat and tie, and one reddening face.

"Drover." The newcomer looked at Tom. "Nobody takes a hit on seventeen. So, you bloody hoggard, get out of my sight, and if you stick your head in this hall again, your head will get cut off." He pulled open his dark coat to reveal a massive knife in a massive scabbard belted on his waist.

"You don't have to be insulting. . . ." Ivatts stopped talking when the man with the knife glared at him.

"You two blokes came in here together. And you'll leave together. One way or the other."

Ivatts forced out a laugh, squeezed Tom's nearest shoulder, gathered his coins and paper money, and rose. "Come, lad," he said, and pulled Tom out of the chair. "It's getting close to hanging time, anyway."

"One day they shall hang you," the man with the knife said. "And that is one execution I shall gladly witness."

He did not remember entering the prison, but now he stood—swaying, actually—in front of a cold, dark stone wall. A man played a violin atop the long, dark, ominous scaffold in front of the crowd, five nooses hanging from a long wooden bar.

Two women danced a jig underneath the gallows. A boy kept jerking one of the nooses till a guard threatened to hang him.

Something was missing. Tom turned, found Ivatts, stein tilted and the Adam's apple working. Foam lathered his upper lip when the stein lowered, and Ivatts winked at Tom.

"You ready for another arf and arf, Tommy, my boy?"

Tom glanced at the big stein in his right hand.

"Jordon. He's supposed to buy . . ." He forgot what he was trying to say.

"You mean Jardine. That fool likely hasn't sold his drove. Maybe he'll get here before we see some killers dance." Ivatts handed what was left of his beer to a woman with a wooden leg next to him.

"Thank you, gov'nor," she said, and finished the mix of ale and porter.

"Tom?"

Ivatts's right arm was over Tom's shoulders. "See that?" He nodded toward the scaffold.

The dancers were gone. So was the boy testing the nooses. Now two lads, maybe older than Tom, maybe younger, were punching each other. The prison guard who had scolded a boy for swinging on nooses now watched with glee as a dirty waif slammed fists into the face, stomach, and chest of a lad five inches taller.

"They're . . . fighting . . ." That's what Tom thought he said.

"Prizefighting. For honor. The code of honor."

When another guard walked over as though to break up the fight, someone yelled, "Let them beat each other's brains out. A hoggard and a cattle drover? They're both bound to die on the gallows eventually."

The guard laughed, and stepped back, turning to the watchers, then saying, "My money's on the pig drover."

The pig drover's fists flashed like lightning. The cattle drover soon yielded.

"Tom." Ivatts pulled Tom closer. "This is for the honor of all cattle drovers. We can't let an Irish whelp be crowned champion of the ring. Show everyone your pugilistic skills."

He shoved Tom toward the ring.

"I hit him good?" Tom heard himself asking as another wet rag covered his face.

"You bloody well came close to tearing his head off, lad."

Tom thought about laughing, but just saying "I hit him good" hurt like blazes. Someone handed him a bottle, and he drank, but that burned like the fiery pit. His lips had been cut cleaner than a butcher working on one of those black bullocks. Blood still seeped out of his nose, and he could not open his left eye.

"What happened then?" he tried to say.

Sydney Ivatts answered: "The pig drover hit you harder."

"About twenty times more, too," a stranger's voice said.

"Shut your traps." That was a woman's voice.

Tom turned his head to the right as far as he could. The gallows were gone. No, he wasn't in the prison anymore. He was . . .

Old Bailey came to mind.

He felt Ivatts lifting him to his feet. "Work

your legs, lad," the drover instructed, and Tom thought he did, but his work shoes dragged across a rugged floor, then he stood, or was held up, in front of a window. He looked down into the prison grounds, found the gallows.

The window was open. The wind revived him.

Curses came from inside and outside Newgate's cold walls. Vendors on the street below hawked their wares, food mostly, and newspapers.

Beyond the walls, a man began walking up the steps, assisted by a robed man who held a Bible and prayed loudly, until they reached the first noose.

The crowd quieted. Those inside the prison. Outside, even the hawkers quit yelling, and the bawdy song blaring from a tavern ceased. All Tom could hear inside the room was heavy breathing.

"Thank God for a good sleep last night," the man on the gallows said.

"You'll sleep even better tonight," someone called out to him.

The second person started up the steps as a black hood was pulled over the first man's face. The priest or preacher turned to the second condemned killer and began a new prayer.

"Lord have mercy," whispered a woman's voice behind Tom. He tried to turn but couldn't, and not just because of the pounding he had taken from a pig drover. This small room on an upper story of a building in Old Bailey was suddenly packed tight with men, women, and at least five children. He tried to look down into the street below. Whips of drovers cracked.

"That is a jaded lot," another woman's voice whispered.

"Most horrible jests," said a man. "Drovers are not unfrequently demonical."

Tom hoped the wet rag would stop his blood from dripping onto the hostess's rug. A third man ascended the scaffold. Then a fourth.

"I am the resurrection and the life, saith the Lord." The preacher's voice rose from the gallows. "He that believeth in me, though he were dead, yet shall he live, and whosoever liveth and believeth in me shall never die."

The woman near Tom leaned forward and whispered, "The hangman's name is Calcraft. He always works with coolness and precision."

Tom could think of no reply.

"That's Mr. Cope." The woman pointed. "Worthy governor of the prison." Tom couldn't tell which figure she meant.

"For God's sake, give me rope enough!" The hood over the man in the middle did not diminish his voice. The panes of glass seemed to rattle from his cry.

Calcraft—at least, Tom guessed the massive man to be the hangman—moved over and adjusted the rope.

"There's the woman." Ivatts raised his drink as in toast. "They say she is quite pretty."

"Wasn't pretty what she did to her man," a woman said. "Or her three children. Her soul is filled with the grossest depravity and immorality."

The doomed woman stood on the far right. The hangman came to her, shoved a hood over her head, and began fitting the noose.

Inside the room, a man recited a poem or song.

> *All you that in the condemned hole*
>     *do lie,*
> *Prepare you, for tomorrow you shall die;*
> *And when St. Savior's bell*
>     *tomorrow tolls,*
> *The Lord have mercy on your souls.*

"Tomorrow has come for these five." Ivatts laughed.

Tom's face remained swollen, but it seemed impossible to close his eyes. Four men, one woman, now stood on the scaffold, faces covered. One of them began to wail, "God have mercy. God have mercy. God have mercy."

"She's a cold wench," Ivatts said, looking at the woman who had murdered her husband and children. "The only one of the lot who shows nerve."

"He'll pull the bolt now," a woman whispered to Tom.

And the five hooded figures dropped out of Tom's view.

The crowd cheered below and in the room where Tom stood.

# CHAPTER 10

Rolling over, Tom pushed the upper half of his body up with his arms, and vomited.

At least, he tried to, but by now, nothing remained in his stomach to throw up. Though he felt like he would soon see his stomach, his intestines, his liver, and anything else inside his body spill onto the dirty emptiness of the lair. The same barren wasteland that probably wouldn't even hold the two ends of the earth together.

"Easy, son."

Sydney Ivatts giggled.

The laugh Tom recognized easily enough. But the voice. Well, that was hard to place as Tom wretched and gagged and coughed and spat.

"How much brandy did ye pour down the boy's throat, ye blackguard?"

"I didn't pour anything down anyone's gullet but my own," Ivatts fired back. "Tom did it himself. All himself. And a man's job he did, too. You'd be proud, Eddie."

Tom cringed. Some fiend was pulling the skin off his forehead. Burning pain shot from his left eyebrow to the back of his skull. "Laddie, ye shall have yeself a scar, me thinks."

Ivatts chortled with contempt. "Compliments of a bloody pig drover."

A firm hand locked on Tom's left shoulder.

"Master Tom." The voice dropped to a whisper. "Do ye think ye can sit up?"

"I want to lay down. . . ." Tom caught his breath, and swallowed down whatever wanted to come up again. "And die."

The grip tightened. "Right-oh. And if ye keep it up, me young friend, ye surely will . . . all too soon. But I need ye to sit up. Sit up and drink something down."

Thought of drink had Tom heaving again, heaving air and what little saliva remained in his mouth.

Sydney Ivatts laughed heartily. But the strong arms forced Tom into a seated position on the empty pasture. Tom turned, realizing his mistake. There was no stinking ditch with little water flowing. The grass here was thin, but not barren. This camp wasn't near a ditch, but a small pool of water. It had to be the camp of . . .

Turning, he looked, waited for his vision to clear, and found the brown eye patch and rough face of Edward Jardine.

The drover held up a steaming mug.

Tom fought down the bile.

"Drink this. Else ye'll be shaking yeself to all ye joints pop loose."

"I drank too much brandy and arf and . . ." He almost vomited his guts out again.

" 'Tisn't brandy. Butter and hot rum. Ye needs

116

it, Master Tom. Drink it down now. It be good for ye."

Tom shook his head, only to realize he now held a warm mug with both hands. The heat soothed his aching and scarred knuckles and joints. The butter smelled fresh, like something Mum would have made.

He didn't remember drinking. He didn't remember anything. But when he woke up, Edward Jardine did not stand over him. Again, his vision focused slowly, and when he saw the face of Sydney Ivatts, Tom wanted to cry.

"You're alive, Tom. Bully for you."

He remembered the chunk of meat Jardine had bought at a market, found the warm steak, and eased it over his blackened right eye. Jardine had joked that the steak might have come from one of the bullocks Ivatts had sold at Smithfield.

Ivatts squatted. "We sure had a fine night on the town, did we not, Tom?"

A new mug came into view. "This is coffee, Tom. No brandy to sweeten it, though."

Tom removed the beefsteak from his eye and took the porcelain cup but could not bring it to his lips. He blew on it.

"Tom." Ivatts looked across the lair toward the street. "Tom, I know I owe you ten shillings for your work, but, well, lad, I am short on funds after our fine night celebrating. But . . ."

"You owe me two pounds," Tom said.

"Aye?" Ivatts cocked his head to the left and let his eyelids arch. "Two pounds? For a hired drover?"

Tom set the mug down. Oddly, he did not think like he was going to vomit again. He just stared at Sydney Ivatts until the drover looked away.

"Two pounds," Tom said, but softer this time.

Ivatts managed a hollow laugh. "And do you have that in writing, lad?"

Tom breathed in and out. His ribs hurt, but not so much now. "You told me: 'A shake is good as a contract.' "

"But not as legal." Ivatts turned and shrugged. "And I also called your father daft for trusting a man's word. Remember that?" He did not wait for an answer, but sighed. His voice dropped to a whisper. "The sad truth of the matter, Tom, is that—"

"You sold that drove for seventeen and a quarter percent above the market average."

Ivatts waved his hand. "Gabble and twaddle, blarney and balderdash, I said—"

"I make lots of mistakes," Tom said, "but rarely when it comes to arithmetic. Seventeen and a quarter percent higher than—"

"Well, if I said, that it was to make Eddie think—"

"You still owe me two pounds."

"Tom." The drover rose now, adjusted his hat, and lifted the sack that he threw over his left shoulder. "Tell Eddie to pay you the two guineas I owe you, and that I'll pay him back the next time we see each other. You did well at cards in that first den, but luck abandoned the both of us after that glorious hanging."

Now bits of memories came back to Tom, only remembrances he would prefer to forget. He had started drinking for the fun and excitement, then to ease the pain after being pummeled by that tough little hoggard. And after the hanging, he had kept drinking to forget all that he had seen and heard.

"You're a fine drover, lad." Ivatts kept talking. "In fact, the finest drover I've worked with in some time. Tell Eddie to make it twelve shillings. You've earned that. I shan't be back in Somersetshire, me thinks. But I do know I need to begone from London as some issues have come up, and rumors of a warrant of arrest." He touched the brim of his hat. "Good day to you, Tom Ponting. And good luck."

Tom watched Sydney Ivatts walk to the street, turn right, and vanish in a sea of pedestrians.

"How ye feel?" Jardine asked.

"Like a bloody fool."

"Aye. I feared Sydney's bad habits would be resurrected when ye told me he was paying ye two pounds." Jardine stirred the soup in a pot with a stick. "This be warm enough. Time for supper, Master Tom."

"I can't eat anything." It hurt to talk. He wondered how he would explain his bruises and cuts to his mum.

"Oh, ye shall eat. For we have a mighty long walk ahead of us."

They spent the night in the lair, and a kindly peddler agreed to let Tom ride in the back of a mule-drawn cart while the merchant and Edward Jardine talked as they took the Kent Road all the way to the Grand Surrey Canal.

From there, Tom and Jardine walked till London fell out of view. For that day and two more they traveled, slowly, taking frequent rests, Tom regaining his strength, using the staff of his whip as a crutch when needed. He soaked biscuits in coffee or tea so he could manage to swallow them, sucked on fruit Jardine had bought at the Covent Garden market. His strength slowly returned. At least his legs and feet had not been injured.

He had a long way to walk till he reached home.

Late morning on the third day, Jardine stopped where the road forked.

Tom had fallen a few rods behind, but he forced himself to move faster and caught up. Jardine swung the pack off his shoulder and gave Tom a hard look.

"Eddie," Tom said, "I can walk faster and farther. You don't have to slow your gait or stop to rest." Still, he found the gourd, uncapped it, and drank.

"Master Tom." Jardine pointed at the road that turned south. "Home . . . me wife . . . me baby girls . . ." He laughed, shook his head, and looked back at Tom. "One's older than ye, Master Tom." He sighed. "That be me way home." His jaw jutted toward the other road. "And that leads west."

It took a moment for Tom to remember how to breathe.

"Oh," he said.

"Do ye know the way?" Jardine asked.

Tom tried to laugh, but that just hurt his teeth and opened up one of the cuts on his bottom lip. "There should be enough dung to mark the trail." He kept looking down the road, letting the wind dry his face and his eyes.

"I'd like to go with ye, Master Tom," Jardine said. "But . . ."

Forcing a smile, Tom extended his right hand.

"Thank you for all your kindness, Mr. Jardine."

"Call me Eddie."

"Stop calling me Master. My name is Tom."

They shook. But neither turned to walk away.

After half a minute, Jardine reached into a shirt pocket and withdrew a piece of paper. He handed it to Tom.

Tom stared, finally took it, and just stared. He

wet his lips before looking back at the drover. He had an idea what he held, but wasn't certain. "What . . . is . . . ?"

"It be a note. A five-pound note." Before Tom could protest, Jardine sang out: "I'll get me money back from Sydney Ivatts, mark me words. One way or the other."

"I can't."

"Ye can. Ye will. Ye cannot even whup a puny Irish pig drover when ye be healthy. Thinks ye can best me? Take the note. Ye earned it. Earned it and more."

Tom looked at the paper, then again at Eddie. His head shook, but the drover stepped back.

"One thing ye should know about Sydney," Jardine said. "He's a good cattle drover. One of the best. He stinks at everything else, but he knows his cattle. And cattle drovers, too. And he told me—mind ye, this be no balderdash . . . he said that ye be the best drover he ever hired. Worth two men, he said. He be right."

"I can't . . ." Tom tried again.

"I'll brook no more of that talk. Ye take the note so I can see me family. And ye can see yours."

The banknote disappeared into the pocket in Tom's britches. The right hand raised again, and this time they shook.

"I can never repay you, Eddie."

"Ye do not have to. I've been paid by ye friendship."

"I'd admire to meet your family one day."

Jardine grinned. "And I would be honored to meet the rest of the Ponting brood. But ye will keep ye dirty eyes off me oldest daughter. And the little one, too."

They laughed, and Tom looked down the trail. He drew in a breath, which still hurt his pounded ribs, and exhaled. "Farewell, my dear friend."

"Tom." This time Jardine did not use *Master*. That might have been the best compliment Tom had ever gotten. He and Edward Jardine had become equals.

When Tom looked back, the drover said, "Might I give ye some professional advice?"

"I could use some, it sure seems like," Tom said.

Jardine grinned. "Learn ye letters. Know how to read. Know how to write. It's harder to hoodwink and cheat an educated man. And here's a lesson I think you known when you was birthed. When ye take a job, see it done. See it done no matter the cost."

Tom nodded. "I'll do that, especially the learning part. Old Lady Hallett will start earning that tuppence she gets."

"One more thing."

Tom waited.

"If ye wants to be a drover, ye might learn how to better defend yeself. Not that ye ought to set out to become some celebrated pugilist, but surely ye ought to be able to lick some miserable hoggard."

They laughed, started to shake, but Jardine pulled him into a hug.

"Eddie," Tom gasped. "I'm greatly bruised and shaken."

Jardine laughed, released his hold, grabbed his sack, and walked down the road. He did not look back. Tom did not pick up his pack and whip until the drover disappeared on the far side of a hill.

Tom thought about using the banknote to let a room in some inn, but he slept on the ground that night. He had enough food in his pack to get him almost home. The less he ate, the more his teeth would have time to settle back in the gums.

He could say that his face got battered by a wild bullock. Or let them think that without actually telling any falsehood. He stared at the stars, saw one shooting across the dark skies. And he imagined himself standing before his father and grandfather, shaking hands, Tom handing the five-pound note to his father.

He could hear Grandfather Theophilus saying that Tom had found a career. Maybe his father would agree.

But they'd both be wrong. Tom Ponting knew the truth. He had not found a career, or adventure, or a way to make his livelihood. He had discovered his calling.

# PART II
# 1852-1853

I believe Texas has the capacity to supply the world with beef cattle; and I hail this prospect for a profitable and extensive market as a subject of the greatest interest and promise to her citizens. I trust that it will receive due attention from them.

—Thomas Butler King,
quoted in *The* (Victoria, Texas)
*Texian Advocate*,
May 17, 1850

# CHAPTER 11

Milwaukee was dead.

Tom Candy Ponting didn't have to read the *Weekly Wisconsin* to figure that out. Oh, the exhibition of the Wisconsin State Agricultural Society had a fine display of cattle and sheep, and Tom had enjoyed the fair, sampling farm and dairy products, studying all those newfangled agricultural implements. And the city had certainly been growing over the years. But as a market for selling cattle?

The contract from Frank Chapman told that story. Hardly worth bringing a drove nigh three hundred miles for this price.

Sitting out of the surprising October heat in a groggery on Chapin's Block, a cup of black coffee now cold, Tom kept reading, letter after letter, word after word, sometimes going back over a sentence two or three times just to make sure he didn't miss anything.

"Confound it, Ponting," the pot-bellied butcher said at last. "It's the same contract you've been signing for years. You ought to know I treat you fair."

Tom put his finger on the period so he would not lose his place. He did not lift his bent head, just his eyes. "And you ought to know I read everything before I sign." He smiled briefly, dropped his gaze, and kept reading.

Slowly. Letter by letter.

Washington Malone, Tom's business partner, once said it took Tom four hours to read a four-page newspaper. Tom had not disagreed.

*When a man learns to read so late in life, he doesn't want to miss even one little word.*

He turned the page.

That caused Chapman to sigh, and he called out to the beer-jerker for another pint of pilsner, before adding, "Buy you a beer, Tom?"

"Thank you, no." Chapman might be honest, but he could also be a nuisance.

Tom finally came to the part of the contract where he did not struggle with letters. Numbers he understood quite well.

Malone returned from the privy, sat on his stool, and picked up his stein, pointing it at the bar.

"Müller was just telling me that he lost forty head." Malone sipped beer and waited for Tom to mark his place on the contract and look up to hear the story. Chapman muttered an oath.

"Loaded them on a propeller on the Ohio," Malone said. "But the fools pushed the cattle too far to the water side. The boat careened, almost sank, and all forty head went over. Drowned."

"That," Chapman said, "explains why Müller is

drinking ten-cent gin instead of his usual German wine."

Tom started to tally the figures, but Malone had another bit of gossip.

"And Kelley at the bar said some lady drove her cattle two miles, where there was a low swale. She had a tin cup, and that's what she used to dip and water her cattle with."

"Lord," Chapman said, "send us rain."

Tom started to look back at the figures, but Chapman had more to add.

"I read that a cattleman in Racine dug fifteen feet in what for years has been a wet slue. All he got was dry earth. And I . . ." Chapman must have read Tom's face, for he fell quiet. The bartender brought the new beer, and Chapman raised his stein and nodded at Malone.

The drought and unseasonal heat should have driven up the price of beef. Especially Illinois cattle. Yes, there was no question now. Milwaukee was dead.

Malone and Chapman drank their beers. Tom began ciphering. Neither would take long.

"How long have you been in America, Tom?" Chapman asked.

*If people will shut up.*

He knew what Chapman was doing. Trying to distract Tom. Rush him. The butcher ought to know better, but Tom looked up and smiled.

"Five years," he said.

He had sailed out of London with brother John, traveling with a most pleasant couple returning to America.

"Two weeks of fair weather on a lovely ship," Tom said, "and four weeks in between of throwing up everything I put in my stomach."

Tom had learned to ride horses like an Illinoisian and had adopted many of this new country's customs. His accent, however, remained unmistakably western. Western England.

"Aye. I once sailed across Lake Michigan. Sick as a dog, I got," Chapman said. "Bet you never been that sick before or after." He pointed the stein at Tom.

"Oh, I was sicker once," Tom said, but offered no details. Memories took him back, and he sipped more coffee.

Mr. and Mrs. Winfield Baxter, the couple, lived in Ohio, so John and Tom traveled with them to America. A boat on the Hudson to Albany, the railroad to Buffalo, boat to Cleveland, footing it to Wooster. Brother John still lived around there, but Tom kept pushing on. Ohio had some good stock farms, but Wisconsin beckoned. Then Chicago. And finally Central Illinois. He bought cattle, sometimes hogs, and drove them to the markets.

Tom set the cup down, and focused on the contract. Chapman turned his conversation to Malone.

At length, Tom raised his head, and slid the papers across the table.

Chapman drained his beer and stared. "That's the best I can do." He placed the stein on the table and folded massive arms across a broad chest.

"I understand." Tom nodded politely. "But Crump can go one-and-a-half cents higher per pound."

The butcher frowned. "I did not see Crump in the pens today."

"It is much too warm today for Crump," Tom said with a smile. "But I passed by his house on the way to the pens."

Their eyes held for a moment before Chapman retrieved a gold pen from the upper pocket of his waistcoat. Chapman turned the document to the final page, removed a cap from the pen's tip, fiddled with the instrument, and began scratching out the figures, then scribbling. Tom had used quills and dip pens since he had gone into the American cattle business. He had heard of these newly patented fountain pens, but Chapman's was the first he had seen.

The butcher blew the ink dry, and slid the papers back across the table. "Two cents more. Initial the changes, sign your name, and we're done."

With deliberation, Tom pushed the papers back. "You sign first."

Shaking his head and sighing heavily, Chapman

worked the pen roughly. He did not blow the ink dry this time, and shoved the papers back in front of Tom's coffee cup. Slowly, the butcher extended the pen, which Tom took and studied.

The cap that had been on the bottom now set atop the pen.

"Turn the cap this way." Chapman made a brusque motion. "That releases the ink." His face turned a deeper shade of red, but not from the heat. "Then make your mark over mine and sign it."

Tom scratched *T C P* over the new figures, and smiled. Methodically, he wrote his name, and brought the pen back up.

"Ordered a dozen from a place in Buffalo." Chapman reached out for the pen, which Tom handed over. "Better than a pocket inkstand."

The butcher returned the cap to the bottom of the pen and the pen to his vest pocket. "You can buy your own fountain pen, Tom, for what I'm paying you." Rising, he reached down and snatched the contract, shaking it dry, found his hat, and shoved it on his bald head.

"Pay you at my office on the morrow?"

Tom nodded.

"There's a game of twenty-card draw poker tonight," Chapman said. "Rochester House. Corner of Reed and Florida in the Fifth Ward." The smile seemed unenticing. "Give me a chance to win my money back?"

Tom's smile was genuine as his head shook.

"You're a cattle dealer," Chapman said. "Surely you gamble."

"All the time," Tom said. "But I have learned that I can control cattle. Not cards."

"You don't like ardent spirits, either." Shaking his head, the butcher sighed. "I don't know why I even do business with you."

Rising, Tom stepped away from the still-sitting Washington Malone and extended his hand again toward Chapman. "I like spirits. Too much. That's why I don't imbibe."

The butcher turned to Malone. "The invitation goes to you, as well. Your credit is good. Any partner of Tom Ponting's credit is good in Milwaukee."

Malone considered the invitation, but soon shook his head.

"Perhaps it's for the best," Chapman said. "I would probably wind up signing over my shop to Ponting and Malone." He shook Malone's hand, and extended his to Ponting.

"I always enjoy doing business with you. I haven't said that about most foreigners."

Tom liked the butcher's grip. "I don't consider myself a foreigner anymore," he said. "And I know why I've done business with you these past four years. When I brought that small herd up in '49 . . ."

The big man's face lightened, and the lips

almost curved upward. "And you bought those three fine bulls for your stock farm and some hogs to sell in Chicago," the butcher said.

"I had not a farthing to my name," Tom said, "and the bulls were worth more than the cattle I sold. But you trusted me enough to tell me to send the money when I got it."

Now Frank Chapman smiled broadly.

"Only money in town back then was Mexico dollars and francs," Chapman recalled.

Tom smiled. "And only five francs."

"But you could buy whiskey for fifteen cents a gallon."

Tom laughed aloud. "Good days then."

The butcher stuck the contract in another pocket. "You know," he said, "I would have gone up to two-and-a-half cents."

"I know." Tom held out his hand again. "But the price we agreed on was more than fair."

As they shook, Chapman asked: "Will I see you again next year?"

Tom's head shook, and the smile flattened.

"I do not think so. Milwaukee has gotten too crowded. Too many sellers. Not enough buyers."

"You ought to go west, Tom," Chapman said. "California. Those miners would pay well for beef. Or Texas. Why, the stories I've heard of that wild country—and wild men. Or the Western territories. Ask me, that's where the future of American cattle lies. West."

"I have considered it." Tom's head bobbed. "But I do like Illinois."

Chapman started for the door, stopped, and glanced over his shoulder. "Good luck to you both."

"And to you," Ponting said.

"Aye," Malone concurred. "It has been a pleasure."

After the butcher left, Tom sat down next to Washington Malone and drained the cup of coffee.

"Are you mad at yourself?" Malone asked. About to turn twenty-two, Tom's partner was six years younger, and twenty pounds heavier than Tom, but Malone was honest, a Freemason, a Christian, and a good judge of cattle. But maybe not so much a reader of businessmen.

"Why would I be mad at anyone?"

"Because you could have gotten another half cent."

Tom grinned. "He would not have gone up a quarter of a cent more."

"But—"

"He said that to make us think we came up short." Tom turned, raising his empty cup so the bartender would send a boy over with the pot for a refill. Not that the coffee was good, or even strong, but it was wet. ". . . And mayhap to make him think he got the better of this deal."

After considering Tom's statement, Malone chuckled.

"Tom?"

"Yes?"

"Did Crump really offer you one-and-a-half cents over Frank's first offer?"

"He would have."

Malone's smile matched Tom's.

"You lied?" Malone suggested.

"I did not lie," Tom said. "I said Crump would up the price. And I did walk past his house this morning."

Waking to Washington Malone's snores, Tom tried to recall the dream.

He and brother John were walking in New York City, trying to find the boat that would take them up the Hudson River. Walking past all the beggars. The blind. Cripples. Widows. Children in rags. Even that postmaster from Kilmersdon. Holding out their cups, pleading for money. But they weren't in New York City. It was London. The London Tom remembered from 1840, not the city he visited seven years later to sail to America. The accents were all British. Sydney Ivatts was begging—underneath the gallows at the old prison. And one-eyed Edward Jardine was on the scaffold, a noose being pulled over his head.

"Do you know where the dock is on the Hudson?" John asked a waif begging on the sidewalk.

The boy pointed across the dirty street. "Ask the Texian," the kid said.

That was all Tom remembered. And in a few hours, he would not even recall that.

He knew what had caused the dream. Talking to Chapman in the grog shop. And the newspapers he had brought upstairs.

Tom and Malone were staying at the City Hotel. It was brick, and every year Tom came to Milwaukee, the hotel seemed to grow. But one thing had not changed. The ground floor held the hotel offices, a post office, and a barbershop. The dining room was on the second floor. So was the room Tom and Malone shared. The newspapers came from the barbershop, where the self-proclaimed "tonsorial artist" had trimmed Tom's close-cropped mustache and beard and long, dark hair. Sitting up in the bed, Tom struck a lucifer to light the lamp on the bedside table.

Beside him, Washington Malone snored away. That man could sleep through anything. Tom adjusted the pillow, threw off his sheet, and reached down to lift the two newspapers off the floor.

Hotels and barbershops always had newspapers handy—though rarely was any periodical timely. This first paper was from May 11. *The Louisville Daily Courier* out of Kentucky. Tom turned to page three and folded the paper over, scanning till he found the item he had read hours earlier.

## CATTLE MARKET.
## JEFFERSON CITY, TUESDAY EVENING,
## MAY 4.

BEEF CATTLE—There are but few head of Western Cattle left on sale, with about 85 Texas Cattle received this evening. We quote Western at 6½@7c, and Texas at 4@5c per lb. net.

The second paper, New York's *Albany Journal*, was even older, from January. Tom rarely scanned a newspaper, but he had already read most of this one, and he just wanted to make sure he had not misread those figures. He found the small headline.

## NEW-YORK
## CATTLE MARKET—JAN. 12.

His eyes fell to the figures for the drove yards.

Washington's reported "dull," but Browning's had seventy cows and calves selling for twenty-five dollars to forty-two fifty. "All sold." And Chamberlain's had fifty cows and calves selling from twenty-five to forty-five dollars.

Tom hadn't misread anything.

After dropping the newspapers to the floor, he found his pocket watch on the side table and checked the time. 4:21.

Malone continued to snore, while Tom sat in the bed, calculating figures and estimating miles while wondering if he were losing his mind.

# CHAPTER 12

Frank Chapman walked with Tom to the bank in Dickerman's Block, where Mitchell himself greeted the two men as soon as they stepped inside, leading them to his office with his short arms over both men's shoulders.

Milwaukee would never hit the depths of New York City or London when it came to crime, but any growing city—especially on the Western frontier—had what Mitchell labeled "growing pains." That's why, the banker said, he hired the two men armed with shotguns who stood next to two large strongboxes in the corner of the suffocatingly hot room. Neither guard paid any attention to the three men, and the heavyset bank president motioned to two chairs in front of his curtain desk. Mitchell eased himself in a well-cushioned chair, found his spectacles, and lifted a sheet off a six-inch stack of papers.

Chapman didn't look away from the two guards, and Tom couldn't blame him. The men appeared to neither blink nor breathe. They reminded Tom of the wax figures he had seen in London when he went with his brother to Madame Tussaud's before they sailed for America back in '47. Kings and popes and generals, even Jenny Lind, the brilliant soprano. How lifelike they seemed.

But the two guards weren't made of wax. Tom studied their faces briefly, glanced at the well-worn boots that did not fit with their woolen trousers and black coats that made them look like businessmen.

*Except not many merchants carry double-barreled shotguns.*

He turned toward Mitchell. The banker's eyes—enlarged by the thick lenses—shot left to right several times, his lips twisting as he read silently. He laid the paper back atop the pile and removed his eyeglasses.

Tom marveled: *It would have taken me ten minutes to read that.*

Mitchell cleared his throat to get Chapman's attention.

The butcher turned his head, but gestured toward the silent guards.

"I know you got a vault," he said.

The banker sighed. "Yeah, we have a vault. And I also know that I've read of three or more banks being robbed. Including one last Saturday night out west in Mineral Point. Broke in at night, blew the vault open with gunpowder. Made off with six thousand dollars."

"Catch them?" Chapman asked.

"Caught one. Course, he denied it, though they found two thousand dollars' worth of notes from that very bank. He says they were counterfeit— least that's what I read in the Madison paper. Says he's a criminal, a scoundrel, a counterfeiter, and guilty of many things, but not that. Fears they'll lynch him. And the *State Journal* says they ought to. Besides, a bank in Richmond, Virginia, was looted of seventy-five thousand dollars one night this past January."

"Surely you don't expect anyone to try to rob you in broad daylight."

Mitchell grinned. "Not as long as I got Chew and Powell and their double-barrel shotguns . . . all day, all night."

"When do they sleep?" Chapman asked.

"They don't." He laughed. "Better not be, for what I'm paying them." He gestured at the men in high boots and cold eyes. "These boys come up from Texas, and you know what Texans are. Half alligator, half bear. Best of all, they don't talk much."

When Chapman opened his mouth again, Tom cleared his throat. The butcher shot Tom a sideways glance, smiled, and settled back in his chair, hooking his thumb toward Tom. "Guess someone's ready to mosey back to Illinois. Malone says Tom's got a sweetheart there."

Mitchell picked up the paper again and turned to Chapman.

"You bought all three hundred head?" He glanced at the paper quickly. "Three hundred and seven head."

"I did indeed."

The banker's head shook. "Are Milwaukeeans eating that much beef these days?"

Chapman laughed. "When they want good beef, they'll be coming to my butcher's shop to get it—for the rest of this year and well into next. Including you."

"I prefer mutton." Mitchell picked up the paper in his left hand, grabbed a quill in his right, dipped that in an inkwell, and began scratching figures in the margins.

*The banker uses a quill,* Tom thought, *and the butcher owns fountain pens. That says something about Milwaukee.*

Finished, Mitchell pointed the tip of the quill at the numbers and checked his arithmetic.

"Three hundred seven head." He looked up. "You both agreed on an average weight of seven hundred and fifty pounds per animal?"

"Yes, sir," both men answered.

"Four dollars and eighty-five cents center-weight," Mitchell said.

It wasn't formed as a question, but Tom and Chapman answered with nods.

Mitchell raised the paper. "That's thirty-six dollars, thirty-seven and five-tenths of a cent per head. Meaning you owe Mr. Ponting . . . ?" He looked over the paper at Tom and grinned, waiting.

"Eleven thousand, one hundred, sixty-seven dollars, Mr. Mitchell . . ." Tom paused. "And twelve and one-half cents."

The banker tilted his head back and laughed so hard the heavy desk seemed to shake. Tears formed in his eyes, and he wheezed until he could stop shaking from the laughter. "By thunder, Ponting, if you would become my teller, I could fire the two I have now and have no need to balance the books at the end of each workday." Turning, he yelled through the open door: "Smithcors."

A moment later, a timid, pale man with balding gray hair stepped inside. Mitchell did not look up. "Mark a withdrawal of seventeen dollars and twelve-and-a-half cents from Mr. Chapman's account. Bring that sum to me posthaste."

The teller was gone after a meek "Yes, Mr. Mitchell."

The banker opened a drawer, withdrew a key, and moved around the desk while the two men with shotguns slid about a half foot from the sides of the two boxes as Mitchell knelt in front of the box nearest the office door. He grunted as he lifted the curved lid open.

"Chew," he said a moment later, and the guard on the right, a narrow-eyed man who reminded Tom of a North Devon bull, shifted the shotgun to his left hand, and bent to pull Mitchell to his feet.

Smiling, the banker walked back and held out his closed fist in front of Tom. When the fingers unfolded, Tom saw the octagonal, gleaming gold coin.

"Ever seen one of these?" Mitchell asked. "Go ahead, take it. It's yours." He winked at Chapman. "Compliments of my former wealthiest depositor."

"I'll earn back that money before you can count your interest." But the butcher too stared at the gold piece.

One side showed a circular spiral design, practically hypnotic when the light from the office window caught it. Turning the coin over, Tom studied an eagle, wings spread wide, serpent in its beak, and claws gripping arrows, olive branch, and a shield, with words UNITED STATES OF AMERICA circling the engraving, and 887 THOUS just below STATES OF. And, at the bottom:

FIFTY DOLLS

Atop the eight sides read a man's name, AUGUSTUS HUMBERT, and his title: UNITED STATES ASSAYER OF GOLD. And at the bottom, the year 1851.

"Started minting these in California last year," Mitchell said.

"Heavy," Tom said. He had the urge to bite the coin, just to make sure he wasn't being cheated. Washington Malone would have already done that. Tom couldn't think of anything else to say. He passed the coin to Chapman, who whistled.

The teller returned with bills and coins for the banker, who laid those on the edge of the desk, and left.

Mitchell cleared his throat. Planting his elbows on the desk and putting his fingertips together, he leaned forward, bracing his chin on this thumbs.

"Tom, you've done business with me for a number of years, but you've never done anything for this much money." He was serious now.

Tom smiled. "We never brought three hundred head of cattle here before." He thought he could explain that despite the profit, he expected the market would drop substantially as Milwaukee continued to grow, while other cattlemen brought herds in to sell. But that wasn't the point Chapman was making.

"That is a large sum of money—especially carrying those slugs—all the way back home. Highwaymen have become a problem. In Chicago, men will cut your throat for three cents."

Tom waited.

"Do you have a gun?"

Tom shook his head. "But Washington has a smoothbore rifle," he said. "English made."

"Carbine," Malone corrected. "It's shorter than a rifle. Short, but heavy."

"So are those slugs." Joining the conversation, Mitchell pointed at the gold piece. "You would be wise to spend that on a pair of the new revolving pistols in one of our gun shops or hardware stores."

"Washington and I will consider that, sir."

"No, you won't." The words came out as a cough. "You are too bullheaded, sir." He sighed, turned toward the open door, and bellowed again, "Smithcors."

The teller returned.

"Count out two hundred and twenty-two more of those slugs, and give them, and a receipt, to Tom Ponting here. Then mark the withdrawal from Mr. Chapman's account. Does he have any money left with us?"

"Yes, Mr. Mitchell."

Chapman chuckled and passed the coin back to Ponting. "Like I say, people eat beef in Milwaukee."

"I prefer mutton," Mitchell repeated.

Tom caught up with his partner at the livery stable on Spring Street, where Washington Malone was settling the bill.

Rawboned George Oakley looked up and smiled. "Understand you two birds are flying south before winter," he said. "Pulling out today, eh?" He turned back to the pad in his left hand and began scratching with his thick pencil.

"Tomorrow," Tom said.

Both men looked up.

"Maybe the day after. Will that work for you, George?"

The livery man laughed. "I ain't turning down business. Trouble?"

Tom shook his head. "I wouldn't call it trouble." He nodded at Malone. "I am not sure I would call it even an inconvenience, but additional time is suddenly required."

When they left the livery, Tom pointed toward the nearby American House and crossed the street. But he didn't stop at the store. Instead, he slipped into the alley.

"What's the matter?" Malone whispered.

Tom withdrew the gold coin from his pocket and let Malone take it.

"We have two hundred and twenty-three of these to carry home," Ponting said. "Well, not quite that many once all of our accounts are squared. Some paper money. Some other coins."

Malone bit the coin, nodded, and whistled. "Heavy," he said.

"Yes," Tom agreed. "What do you think it weighs?"

Malone shrugged. "Two or three ounces."

Ponting nodded. "That sounds right."

"Where's the rest of the gold?"

"Still at Mitchell's. He agreed to keep it till we depart. The fewer people who know about it, the better." Tom read Malone's concern. "Don't worry. Those coins aren't going anywhere. Mitchell's made sure of that."

After a moment's thought, Malone said, "We

could trade the gold coins in for banknotes."

Contempt filled Tom's laugh. "From a Wisconsin bank? I think not." An exchange broker or an Illinois banker would take out a percentage, most likely, or not even cash the notes at all.

"Well," Malone said as he returned the gold to Tom. "Our pack mule can carry thirty pounds with ease."

"He can." Tom pocketed the coin. "But he shan't."

Chandler's shoe shop was their next stop. Over the years, the master cobbler had patched and resoled Tom's boots two or three times, repaired bridles and pack saddles, and outfitted Tom with a new saddlebag just last year. So when the bell rang above the door, the tall man in the leather apron instantly stared, a habit of shoemakers, at Tom's and Malone's feet.

After setting a thick piece of leather and a pair of massive scissors on the counter, Chandler brushed his hands on the back of his pants, and called out, "Those boots don't looks like they've traveled all the way from Illinois, boys. What brings you two here?"

They were shaking hands when Tom said, "We both need money belts."

Chandler looked eager to hear the rest of the joke. When he realized Ponting was serious, he chuckled and shook his head. "The American

House oughts to have some. That place be bigger than Ashby's barn and the City Hotel combined. Gots everything. The wife comes home two weeks ago with a kitchen settee table. Just folds the back of the seat down, and you gots yourself an ironing board. And the seat is actually the top of a chest. She put some blankets in that part. Damnedest thing you ever seen."

"We need special money belts," Tom said. "And you are the only one who can do the job quickly and perfectly."

The cobbler scratched his ear, found a pad he used to trace a customer's foot, walked behind the counter, and rummaged through a drawer until he found a sharpened pencil. He licked the tip, and nodded at Tom.

"What exactly you gots in mind?"

Tom leaned on the counter. "The belts have to be buckskin." Chandler started scribbling.

"I want compartments to hold coins. With wadding of some kind to keep the coins from moving about."

"Cotton oughts to do the job," Chandler said.

Tom nodded. "They'll need to be held up with suspenders—"

He stopped and stared until Chandler finished chuckling. The cobbler stuck the pencil over his left ear, shook his head, and laughed again. "A belt . . . that needs suspenders, too." He slapped the countertop hard. "By golly, Tom, you had me.

A belt. With suspenders." His face turned cherry.

"The suspenders," Tom said, and Chandler's smile vanished, "and belt will go over our undershirts. Cotton undershirts. Our shirts will be pulled over that, so no one can see the belts."

After blinking a few times, Chandler cleared his throat.

"You ain't fooling." It wasn't a question.

"Have you ever heard me make a joke?"

The cobbler found the pencil and resumed writing.

"How much weight your belts gots to carry?" he asked.

"Let's say eighteen, twenty pounds per belt." It likely wouldn't be that much, but Tom didn't want to underestimate.

Nodding, the cobbler scribbled some more. Without looking up, he asked, "What size will these coins be?"

"About an inch and a half in diameter."

When the interrogation and Chandler's scribbling ceased, the cobbler found a cloth tape measure and stepped around the counter. "Hands up, boys," he said, laughing again, and after Tom raised his arms, Chandler wrapped the cloth around Tom's waist. He measured Malone, returned to the counter, found the pad and jotted down a few more figures, shook his head, scratched through a mistake and corrected it, and let out a long breath.

The pencil returned above his ear, and he nodded at the two drovers.

"Give me three, four days, boys, and I'll have something for you."

"We need them tomorrow," Ponting said.

"Tom . . . Tom . . . Tom . . ." Chandler shook his head until Tom reached into his pocket and withdrew the California slug. He held it out between thumb and forefinger.

"This is yours," Tom said, "if those belts are ready by noon tomorrow—and your promise not to mention this to anyone."

The cobbler's leathery finger and thumb pulled the coin free from Tom's grip. He brought the gold closer to his blue eyes, twisted the slug around, turned it over, and closed his fist over the fifty-dollar piece.

"I'll see you boys tomorrow arounds dinnertime," he said.

# CHAPTER 13

"I have to remind myself that I'm not as fat as that banker." Washington Malone sounded old and tired.

Tom knew exactly what his partner meant.

Only their fourth morning on the trail, and already Tom and Malone had to question the wisdom of money belts. Oh, Chandler the cobbler had done an excellent job, and the cobbler had explained that both men needed to go over to the American House and buy flannel undershirts.

"I knows it's warm now," he had said, "when it shouldn't be. But if you two wants nots to have your shoulders rubbed off clear downs to the collarbones, you'll shuns those cotton ones for something that'll protect your skin."

Despite the heavy cloth, Tom already felt both shoulders chafing. The buckskin was supple, yet every day Tom's back and sides turned rawer where the money belt rubbed through the flannel. Still, those fifty-dollar pieces did not rattle, and no one would suspect that each man carried a bit more than sixteen pounds of California-minted slugs under their coats. But Tom dreaded squatting by the fire just to fill his cup with coffee.

Kneeling wasn't so tough. Standing proved challenging.

The first two nights, both men removed the money belts, hiding them underneath their saddles. Last night, neither wanted the hassle of strapping that weight to their bodies again come morning, so they slept—not well—with belts still secured around their waists and shoulders.

Just sitting up this morning hurt. Saddling the horses and loading the pack mule left both men sweating, despite the cool breeze off Lake Michigan.

"This shall get easier." Ponting sure hoped what he told his partner would come true.

"Well, I'll be needing a stump to help me in the saddle this morning." Malone grinned, shook his head, and sipped coffee.

They had camped off the road near in woods that had been thick four years ago, but now thinned by settlers. Stumps were easy to find. Tom had already picked the one he planned to use to make it easier mounting his horse.

He was fingering a piece of greasy fish out of the skillet when the head of Tom's roan jerked up, and the horse whinnied. The mule brayed and turned north, while the ears flattened back on the head of Malone's chestnut.

On the Military Road, travelers were not uncommon, especially just a day's ride from Chicago. This part of the country had started to crowd up, too. Rich soil had started attracting farmers, and no one would ever go thirsty with Lake Michigan in view.

But carrying more than ten thousand dollars in gold slugs made both men nervous. Yesterday they had passed through St. John's and Port Clinton, stopping at a tavern called the Green Bay House for supper. That's where they had bought the fish to fry for breakfast. No one had given them more than passing glances, though, and Tom had paid with a small note from Mitchell's bank. Food came cheap in this part of Illinois.

Malone set down his cup, stood casually, and moved to his horse, cooing at the gelding as he walked softly, and began rubbing the horse's neck with his left hand while reaching for the Paget carbine in the scabbard.

Tom swallowed the fish, and poured the rest of his coffee on the fire.

"Halloo the camp," a voice called from behind the timber in an unusually thick drawl. "I smell coffee, if you're neighborly and have a cup to spare."

Malone kept his hand on the stock of the .66 caliber, and looked back at Tom.

"We would welcome company and conversation," Tom said cheerfully, while his sober nod warned his partner to keep his hand on that smoothbore.

The horses and mule remained alert, as a big man leading two saddlehorses came out of the trees. His left hand held the reins, while his right carried a shotgun, barrel pointed down. He wore trail clothes, tall boots, a duster, and a grain sack over his head with holes over both eyes.

"That'll do, boys. Stand real still," a voice called from behind Tom.

The lake wind no longer felt cool.

"Let go that long gun, buster, step away from that hoss, and the both of you turn around."

Tom moved slowly, keeping his hands wide apart, and found another big man with a sack over his head with slits cut so he could see. He held a big Colt's Dragoon in his right hand, and Tom spotted the walnut handle of a smaller revolver tucked inside the road agent's waistband. His bowed legs carried him about two feet from Tom, and he waved the cannon-like barrel of the .44 underneath Tom's nose.

"Shun them clothes, cattleman. And take off that fancy belt." He shot a quick glance at Malone. "You do the same."

Malone's wide eyes focused on Tom.

"Don't look at your pard, buster," the man leading the horses said.

Suddenly Tom smiled. "Chew and Powell," he said.

That stopped both highwaymen.

Tom pointed at the nearest one's feet. "Your boots. I remember them from Mitchell's bank. And the drawl, and despite that you two didn't speak a word in the bank, however, I have heard that Texians possess a peculiar colloquial—"

"How did—" Powell began. Chew had to be the closest one. Tom remembered the brown boots. Powell's were black.

"Shut up." Tom didn't know if Chew's words were meant for his partner or Tom.

It had to be the two guards. Those money belts had been filled inside Mitchell's office, while the guards stood next to the strongboxes. Only four men in Milwaukee knew about the belts. And Tom trusted Mitchell and Chandler.

"Besides," Tom said, "you are not Smithcors."

Chew pushed the barrel of the Dragoon closer to Tom's forehead.

"Tom . . ." Malone's voice creaked.

Wind rustled the trees.

The roan began to urinate.

The bandit kept the .44 inches from Tom's head, but his left hand reached up and slowly pulled off the wheat sack, revealing the cold blue eyes, the thick face, and the ruby-colored mustache, beard, and slicked-back hair.

"You just signed your death warrant," Chew said. "You'll be at the bottom of that big pond over yonder."

Tom laughed. "Oh, you can't shoot us. Don't you hear that squeaky wheel on a wagon?" He nodded toward the road about fifty yards from where they had made camp in the forest. "This part of the country is crowding up. You should have made your play the night before."

The pistol barrel slowly lowered. "Fetch your knife," Chew told Powell as Chew's left hand reached for a massive bowie sheathed in a scabbard on his right hip.

That was all Tom needed. His long arms flashed. A right fist slammed into Chew's jaw, turning the man's head perfectly so that Tom's left smashed the nose. The heavy Dragoon dropped onto leaves and moss. Chew straightened, and his eyes tried to focus but a combination of left and right jabs dropped him to his knees. Quickly Tom turned. He had hoped Malone would have taken advantage of the surprise attack, but Tom's actions had likewise startled his partner. And Powell, still masked, had covered the distance like a falcon. His skinning knife came up as Tom started to swing, knowing he was too late.

The blade slammed right into Tom's stomach.

Tom grunted. While Powell screamed, clutching his right hand with his left, and dropping to his knees. The man blubbered. "My fingers. My fingers. You cut off all my fingers."

Tom's left hand instinctively went to his belly, but he felt no wound, no blood, yet knew he would have a nasty bruise around his belly button. The masked Powell fell to his side, still clutching his right hand. His knife lay in some briars, the curved blade spotted with blood. Had the knife's handle been fitted with a guard, Powell likely would have not been maimed. Instead, he rolled over, one way, then the other, cursing savagely.

Ignoring him, Tom turned back to find Chew reaching for the Dragoon he had dropped. The Texian was trying to bring the gun up when something flashed to Tom's left. It was Washington Malone, holding the carbine like a battle ax. When the heavy stock came down on Chew's right shoulder, the road agent's scream could not drown out the sound of the collarbone breaking.

Falling away from both men, Chew swore savagely. Malone dropped to his knees, gripping the Paget to remain upright, his chest heaving, face already beaded with sweat. Powell sobbed and rolled left and right, still clutching his hand.

Tom looked at the ground, found no dis-membered fingers, stepped back and knelt over the cursing Chew. He grabbed Powell's knife first, threw it deeper into the forest. Chew's bowie followed. Then Tom picked up the Dragoon, which had to weigh close to five pounds. He didn't throw that weapon into the woods, but he kept it aimed at a teary-eyed Chew and used his left hand to remove the smaller revolver out of the Texian's britches. Tom pitched the little pistol toward the horses and pack mule.

A newcomer appeared just off the Military Road. Malone stood, and started to raise the carbine level, but Tom whispered, "He means no harm."

For one thing, the stranger carried no weapon, just a walking stick. And no sack hid his face. Through the trees, Tom spotted a donkey-pulled cart on the side of the road.

"You folks got troubles?" the traveler asked uncertainly. He wore canvas britches, a muslin shirt, and a slouch hat.

"My partner and I do not, sir," Tom answered, and pointed the pistol barrel at Chew, then Powell. "But they have found some."

The man took in the scene. He nodded soberly.

"Could you be kind enough to go back to Port Clinton and fetch the constable of that township?" Malone asked.

Considering that briefly, the man said, "Yes, sir. I can do that for you gentlemen. Should I bring back a doctor, too."

Malone looked again at the two Texians.

"Yes. That is a most excellent idea."


Once the stranger began to lead the donkey and cart back north, Tom reached down and jerked the canvas sack off Powell's head. The road agent kept whimpering. "Wrap this around your fingers." Tom dropped the coarse sack. "I believe your digits remain attached to your hand."

Next he squatted by Chew, who had stopped his groans and curses while his eyes shined with hatred. Tom aimed the Dragoon.

"By my estimation, it shall take that man twenty minutes to reach Port Clinton. How long it will take him to find the local constabulary is uncertain, but you two could be well on your way to Texas, Canada, or the nearest groggery for all I care. Or perhaps, the Sisters of Mercy in Chicago. They did a fine job, I have been informed, with that poor drover who was gored by a bull last year."

Chew's eyes became questioning.

Even Malone looked confused. "Tom, what—?" But a raised hand silenced the interruption.

"But first, I need you to tell me everything you can about Texas," Tom told Chew. "And those longhorn cattle I have heard so much about."

Even Powell stopped whimpering as he wrapped the sack over his bloody fingers.

"What?" Chew asked.

"Texas. You two do come from that state. Or was that just braggadocio or rubbish from Mr. Mitchell?"

Behind Tom, Powell let out a little yelp, and said, "What . . . what . . . you want . . . to know?"

"Cattle." Tom repeated. "Texas cattle. Your longhorns."

"They're . . . cows," Powell whimpered.

"Yes. And where do we find them? Hundreds of them. For purchase? What are they like? How much do they weigh? How healthy are they? How sturdy? What do Texians do with these longhorns? And how much does one sell for per head?"

"Chew . . . ?" Powell pleaded.

Tom focused on the man with a busted collarbone.

"Go to hell," Chew said.

"Chew . . ." his partner pleaded. "You know 'bout cattle. You—"

"He's lying, you idiot. He—" Pain caused the ruby-haired man to flinch.

"Were you a stockman?" Tom asked.

The man just glared.

"I have never broken my word," Tom said. "To anyone."

"You sent that fellow—"

Tom cut him off. "My partner sent the man on his errand." Finding his watch, Tom turned the open face toward Chew. "That peace officer could be closer than Port Clinton."

Tom spoke evenly. "I do not know the penalty for attempted robbery and murder in the state of Illinois, but I do remember Mr. Mitchell talking about that man in Mineral Point. You remember our conversation. You and Powell were there, armed with your shotguns with nothing to do but listen. Remember? About the bloke who was found with the banknotes after the robbery, the ones he says he counterfeited. That poor, perhaps innocent, felon admitted to being a scoundrel and guilty of many things, but not robbery. And he feared he would be taken from his cell and lynched."

The Dragoon waved a bit again, though Tom kept his pointer finger on the outside of the trigger guard, and the big .44 wasn't cocked.

"Westerners seem to have their own sense of justice, whereas, back in my home country of England, my countrymen would hang anyone for even a trifling offense—legally."

Malone cleared his throat. He nodded toward the road.

"Getting later in the morning," Malone said. "More and more people are heading south to Chicago."

That pleased Tom. His partner caught on quickly. "Chicago is a big city. Easy for a man to disappear."

Malone pointed east. "And we passed lots of boats on the lake. Even with a bum shoulder and a mangled hand, between the two of you, you have two working arms."

Tom picked up where Malone stopped.

"I sincerely doubt if a peace officer from a new settlement like Port Clinton would even think to look on Lake Michigan for a couple of malicious road agents with murder on their minds."

"You would not dare let us go," Chew said.

His partner cried out, "Don—don't be—"

Tom cut them off. "Have you ever seen a man hanged?"

Powell focused on his bloody hand. Chew just stared.

"I have," Tom said. "Five. Well, four men and a woman. In London. The hanging was legally done, carried out by an experienced executioner. *Ghastly* does not even begin to describe it."

The trees rustled in the wind. A horn of some type sounded over on the massive blue lake.

"Texas?" Chew finally whispered.

Tom smiled. "And longhorn cattle," he said.

# CHAPTER 14

After signing his name on the paper pressed against the saddle, Tom stepped away from the roan, returned the pencil to his inside coat pocket, and moved to the nearest tree. Washington Malone was coming up from the road when Tom picked up the skinning knife and pushed the blade through the top of the paper and into the tree.

"What are you doing?" Malone asked.

"Explaining to the marshal, sheriff, justice of the peace, or whomever our Good Samaritan went to fetch that we decided they had paid enough for their crime." He stared down at the two revolvers, shotgun, skinning knife, and bowie they had collected from Chew and Powell that lay at the base of the tree. "I do not think that is enough," he said, and turning toward Malone, asked, "Do you?"

"Enough what?"

"Payment. We cost that peddler part of a day of selling his wares, sending him all the way back to Port Clinton. And a peace officer's time is not worth wasting on piddling affairs such as ours."

"I would not call robbery and murder piddling affairs," Malone said. "Especially when we very well could have been robbed and murdered."

"But," Tom said, "we were not murdered, and now we have more knowledge about Texas and longhorn cattle."

"You are dead serious about buying cattle in Texas," Malone said.

Tom's head shook. "My investigation is not complete, but the idea intrigues me. Give me a five-dollar banknote."

"What for?"

"As amends to that poor peddler and the peace officer."

"Why do I have to pay them five dollars?"

"It was you, my good friend, who sent the man back north. Not I."

Malone sighed. "But . . ."

"And this plunder and five dollars might appease them enough so they shan't pursue us."

Malone shook his head, but reached into his coat and withdrew a rawhide pouch from which he withdrew a colorful banknote.

"Where did you leave Chew and Powell?" Tom studied the note, then knelt, rolled up the currency, and stuck it partly into the barrel of the Dragoon.

"Last I saw them, they were walking south along the banks of Lake Michigan."

"They might make it," Ponting said. He sighed and held up his right hand.

"Be a good sport, and help your partner up."

Both men grunted as Malone pulled Tom to his feet.

"We should make haste, too," Tom said, and headed for his roan. "We are getting a late start today."

Tom led his horse to the stump he had picked out earlier and managed to get into the saddle. Malone picked a fallen log to help him climb onto his horse, and Tom rode to the pack mule, grabbing the lead rope, and let the roan carry him toward the Military Road.

"Do not be upset about that five dollars," he called back. "I shall treat you to supper at Nockin's French eatery in Chicago tonight."

Seven days out of Chicago, they reached the store at Mount Auburn around midmorning. Mrs. Roberta—Tom never caught her last name because everyone called the snuff-dipping, fat woman nothing but Mrs. Roberta—had taken over the store after her husband, who had opened the store two years earlier, cut an artery with an ax while chopping wood and bled to death. Tom always liked to stand on the porch and look off to the southeast.

Which is what he was doing when Mrs. Roberta brought him a mug of steaming tea and a plate of cornbread, apparently the only thing Mrs. Roberta knew how to make.

"Make you homesick, hon'?" she asked as Tom took both plate and mug. She called everyone *hon'*; it took Tom three visits before he figured out what she was saying, and another night passed before he realized that *hon'* was short for *honey*.

"Not homesick, ma'am, but it reminds me of where I grew up." He tilted his head toward the view. "Of course, the land was proved up more than here."

"Because you growed up in England, hon'. That's an old country." She spit a stream of brown juice over the railing. "This here be young country. New country. But it'll get proved up before you know it. And won't be fit to live in."

Tom sipped tea. He had lost track of the days, but the store was busy that morning, filled with farmers, traders, and wayfarers like Tom and Malone, who had stepped inside to play whist.

"What made you leave England?" asked a newcomer named Gale who had moved in from Kentucky.

Tom debated answering while he drank more tea.

"There was an outbreak of foot-and-mouth disease," he said. "And after the repeal of the Corn Laws, farming in England became tougher. It was hard in the best of times for our parents to feed nine children, so my older brother and I sailed for America in '47."

"They say the only time that foot-and-mouth rot hits a herd in America, it's because of English cattle," said a man who had been sharpening an

168

ax blade. "Maybe you brought that disease to our country."

Tom smiled, though he sensed the man wanted to fight. "I only brought my older brother with me. He was in fine health according to his last post. And all the cattle I have raised, bought, or sold have been American cattle."

The man, on the far side of the porch, set the ax down and began tapping the file he had used as a sharpener against his flat palm. "I read that there've found pleuropneumonia in New York herds."

That came as news to Tom.

"England has done brought that nastiness to us, too." The man punctuated the end of his sentence by slapping the file hard against his huge palm.

"New York is a long way from Mount Auburn, boys," Mrs. Roberta said. "And if you boys are thinking that a go at fisticuffs would be fine entertainment on a cool autumn morn like we're blessed with this fine day, and whupping on this here man who speaks funny on account of where he got born, you ought to know that you won't be fighting just him." This time, she spit onto the floor. "And I don't think there's a one of you here that I can't whup."

"No offense, Mrs. Roberta." The man picked up his ax, set it on the railing, and started to use the file again. He stopped, though, and nodded at Tom. "No offense to you either, stranger."

"None taken, sir," Tom said. "And I appreciate the news of the pleuropneumonia. It is sad to hear, and I was not aware of that outbreak."

"What is pleuropneumonia?" Malone asked as they rode along Mosquito Creek. "I've never even heard of it."

"We had not heard of it in England, either," Tom said, "till shortly before I came to America."

But he hadn't forgotten. The epidemic went all through Cheshire in '44. A stock farmer said a few cows were suddenly attacked with delirium. They had been grazing, then they were dead. He sent for the veterinary surgeon, but before that fine gentleman could arrive, seventeen of his cows fell prostrate in their stalls in ten minutes on the second day. Other stock farms were struck.

"One called it a 'monster of destruction,'" Tom told Malone. "There was no treatment, no cure, but if you could separate the sick from the healthy, spread could be contained."

Malone sighed. "I guess that ends your dream of taking a herd of cattle to New York City."

"On the contrary, I find it imperative."

Malone reined up quickly, and Tom had to stop his horse and turn in the saddle.

"Tom . . ." Malone spoke in a whisper. "I find feasting on one's misfortune—especially a fellow cattle breeder—improper if not immoral. To make one's fortune—"

"I am not thinking of the misfortunes of any stock grower. I am thinking of how hungry half a million men, women, and children might be."

"I see."

Tom kicked the roan into a walk. His partner caught up alongside him.

"I know it sounds perverse, considering our conversation," Malone said, "but I had hoped to eat dinner at Mrs. Roberta's—however, we left in a hurry. And it's a long ride to Taylorville."

Tom let his reins drop over the roan's neck. Twisting, he opened a saddlebag, reached inside, and pulled out a hunk of Mrs. Roberta's cornbread wrapped in wax paper. He let the flap fall back over the bag, but did not bother fastening it. Instead he held that out for Malone while gathering the reins in his free hand.

"You didn't eat Mrs. Roberta's cornbread?" Malone cried out. "Why, she makes the best cornbread I've ever had."

As the cornbread vanished from Tom's hand, he smiled.

"That is one taste I have never acquired," Tom said. "All that wheat you can thresh, and you Yanks grind cornmeal and call it bread. A man might as well be eating sawdust."

He couldn't understand exactly what Malone said as he chewed and tried to talk, spitting out yellow particles that looked very much like wet sawdust, but it sounded something like *"dontknowhwatyermissin."*

"How would we eat?" Malone asked as they rode south.

Tom had been studying the country. Fires had burned much of the tall grass on the vast prairie while they were gone, but in this part of the world, prairie fires came like taxes in England. With a healthy dumping of snow during the winter, come spring, the grass would grow tall. Lightning or one of those fool wayfarers heading west in a wagon who didn't know how to put out a campfire would send the fires raging again. Winter would return. And 1853 would be more of the same.

"I said," Malone repeated, " 'How would we eat?' "

"We shall be in Taylorville directly," Tom said with irritation.

"That's not what I asked. If we were driving cattle from Texas, how would we eat?"

Tom stared at his partner. "The way we've been eating every time we took a drove to Chicago or Milwaukee. Stop at a house, pay for food and lodging."

The chuckles annoyed Tom. He turned in his saddle, frowning, and said, "What do you find so bloody amusing?"

"We'd have to push the cattle through the

Indian Nations, Tom. And after that, much of Missouri is not what we would deem civilized."

That's why it paid to have a partner like Washington Malone. Tom nodded.

"You aren't much of a hunter." Malone patted the stock of the Paget carbine in his scabbard. "And I'm not exactly Davy Crockett."

Tom realized he had more things to consider.

So did Malone.

"And how many cattle would be in this particular drove?"

"Several hundred," Tom answered. "To make it profitable."

"We started out this year with one hundred and seventy-five," Malone pointed out. "We bought sixty more from that Davis fellow in Clinton. Had to hire that kid to help us from then on. Then I bought fifty head from that skinflint on Short Point Creek."

They rode thirty yards in silence.

"Filled out the herd in Elk Horn because the diphtheria had called that poor man's family to glory," Malone said. "Few calves born on the drive . . . But it was all the three of us could do to keep that drove together."

"Mixed herd," Tom explained. "Not just bullocks, heifers, cows, calves, but different breeds, and from different stock farms. Droves such as that are much tougher to handle."

"Three hundred miles, or thereabouts, to

173

Milwaukee. Do you know how far it is from Texas to New York City?"

Tom's face brightened. "I pretty much walked and rode that distance after I got off the ship in '47."

Malone wasn't amused. "A thousand miles. From here. But Texas? I don't know. And Texas is a mighty big state."

"But our friend whose collarbone you broke said we could get all the cattle we needed just on the other side of the Red River. We don't have to ride all the way to San Antonio."

Malone sighed.

A mile passed in silence. Then it was Tom who spoke.

"The way I thought we would work the drive is like this. We ride to Texas next spring. Buy as many head of cattle as we can handle. If we need additional men, we hire them on. Bring the drove back home. We pay off our employees, winter the cattle, then push them on to New York City. We can hire Illinoisians to finish the drive. Illinoisians know cattle. I have no idea what a Texian knows."

"Other than try to steal cattle," Malone said.

"They were not efficient about that."

Malone laughed out loud. They rode another quarter mile before Malone spoke again.

"It's still a gamble."

Tom grinned. "Indeed. But we are not playing cards."

The Eighth Judicial Circuit had to be in session in Taylorville. Nothing else could explain the crowd on any afternoon. Horses and mules were tethered to every post and rail as far as Tom could see. Children ran down the streets as though the schoolmaster was chasing them. Women huddled together, and most of the men circled the front of the courthouse.

"Ponting!"

Turning to his left, Tom found James Morrison waving him over to the courthouse. Morrison had the fanciest house in all of Christian and Shelby counties, and he had built it himself. He ran a big farm and had made the red bricks himself, then carved the walnut railing on the stairs that led to the second story. He had also built the first jail in Taylorville, in Christian County, ran a ferry, a tannery, and you wouldn't find a more respected man in this part of Illinois.

Tom and Malone eased their horses to the court-house. Someone had freshened up the whitewash. Yes, the district court had to be going on.

"How was the market in Milwaukee?" Morrison, who also raised cattle, had to shout over skin-crawling squeals and rough grunts.

"We did fine," Tom answered. He cleared his throat and shouted the same three words again, adding: "But it took us longer. Lot of people moving in to that country."

Morrison turned away and yelled, "Cannot anyone quiet those infernal pigs?"

"That, my good man, is what I have requested from the judge." The lanky man—ugly as sin and twice as tall—ducked as he stepped out of the courthouse's front door. Tom and Malone, both still in their saddles, had a good view, but Morrison had to stand on his toes and still couldn't see over heads and hats.

"The squealing is so raucous," the lawyer said, "I have requested that Judge Davis issue a writ of quietus."

Tom laughed with the rest of the crowd.

"But as the noise has not abated, I fear the judge has yet to figure out how to spell *quietus*."

The courthouse stood two stories tall, and the lower floor rested on stone pillars, which raised the floor about eighteen inches off the ground. That's where the hogs had gone to find the shade and whatever fell through the cracks in the floor. Tom counted at least eight hogs, and something had excited them.

"But, you good people of Taylorville, perhaps we—and my client—have a chance of due process after all." The lawyer from Springfield was staring, and now pointing, directly at Tom.

"For if my eyes remain strong, I believe I spy that good man, Tom Ponting, one of the finest drovers to call Christian County his home—even though he speaks a language of which I lack familiarity."

"It is called English, Mr. Lincoln," Tom said with a grin. "Yet I have never figured out if I live in the county of Shelby or Christian, as Moweaqua lies on the border."

"You speak a different kind of English than I hear and speak, and I will defer the question of which county claims you to a governmental surveyor. But perhaps you could use your expertise and drive this drove off the Cliffs of Dover."

Tom touched the scar above his left eye. His head shook. "I am a drover of cattle, sir. Swine I leave to . . . hoggards."

Abraham Lincoln chuckled and shook his head. He didn't resemble most lawyers Tom had met. He looked more like a farmer, a tall farmer, and his arms and shoulders revealed that he knew how to swing an ax. Tom liked him a lot, though they didn't know each other well. They made each other laugh.

"Swine have been the bane of my legal career in this fine city." Lincoln was speaking to the crowd now, not just Tom. That was another thing to like about the lawyer. If Tom didn't have a lawyer down in Shelbyville, he would probably have taken the Springfield stagecoach from Decatur.

"Back in '42, some of you might recall—I

certainly have not forgotten—Old Masterson lost seventy-five pigs because a boy's carelessness let four hundred of those noisy little critters break out of the pen. You can't sue a young lad, of course, so I filed for three hundred and fifty dollars against the boy's father. Alas, the jury saw things differently—"

Two hogs began fighting under the courthouse, drowning out the lawyer's closing argument. Tom waved at Lincoln, shook Morrison's hand, and turned the roan around.

# CHAPTER 15

"I remember," Malone said as they rode northeast toward Stonington, "when I could stand at my cabin door and shoot turkeys. Can't do that anymore. Might wing a neighbor."

Tom nodded. Simon Spears had started a grist mill two years ago; not long after that, old Sanders had opened a trading post on Flat Branch to the southeast. But since Tom and Malone had left for Milwaukee, Uplanders had been busy, tearing up the land with their mole-board plows, planting corn.

Children walked back from the new Stonington schoolhouse, and Tom wondered if the schoolmarm looked or taught anything like Old Lady Hallett. He sure hoped she got paid more than two pence a week.

Four miles out of Stonington, they crossed Brown Branch, and Tom urged the roan into a trot. He kept a faster gait until they came into Moweaqua—another new settlement.

"Ask me," Malone said, "Moweaqua is just more of it."

"More of what?"

"Ruining the country."

Tom chuckled. "You are mighty young to be a curmudgeon."

179

The roan turned skittish, though, when something whined toward the new settlement. As Tom took a firm hold on the reins, the screeching racket melded with a mechanical buzzing.

"That's more of it," Malone said. "You know what that is?" He answered his own question. "A sawmill."

Which is what Tom would have guessed, but it did not sound like the mills he had seen and heard. And this one had not been in Moweaqua when Tom and Malone departed for Milwaukee.

Once the whines and buzzing stopped, a mechanical belching started up, but that noise did not spook their horses. Still, Tom kept the reins tight in his hands.

Malone pointed at the big house and barn off to the right. "I suppose this is where I leave you. Besides, my rheumatism is acting up." He dropped his voice into a whisper. "What do you want to do about those gold coins?"

Ignoring the house, Tom kicked his horse into a reluctant walk toward the new town. "I want to see this mill first," he said.

He remembered muley saws. Water pushed a turbine around, which caused the vertical blade to move up and down. This was new to him.

A whistle screeched, and the whines began as chains pulled a log from the millpond to the upper floor of a new wooden building. This time

Tom and Malone had to dismount, or risk being bucked off, and led their mounts to the nearby flouring mill, tethering and hobbling both horses behind a five-plank fence. The flouring mill, which had been here for a few years, wasn't nearly as ear-splitting as the sawmill.

Tom removed his hat, slapped it against his thigh, and found Cowle, one of the owners of the quieter mill, dipping a brush into a can, then painting something on the oak sill walls. Walking over, Tom read:

This mill erected in 1

"You any good at drawing an eight?" Cowle asked without turning around.

"No, sir," Tom answered. "Not after riding all the way from Milwaukee."

Cowle made a decent enough *8* with the black paint.

"Eighteen fifty," Malone said.

"Thank you, but I haven't forgotten when we built this son of a—"

A whistle screamed again from the saw mill's steam engine, and Tom whirled to make sure the horses didn't pull down the fence.

Cowle spit tobacco juice to the ground, and leaned down to wet his brush.

"You probably don't recognize Moweaqua now, boys," Cowle said as he deftly made a five and a zero, laid the brush on a rock, and walked over, shaking both men's hands, and wiping his mouth with the back of his arm. He looked back and nodded at his marker.

"That's for the historical record," he said. "So that our children will know who come here first."

"A historical record is good," Tom said.

Malone pointed at the mill over the creek. "It makes a tremendous commotion."

"Chester Wills's doings. Cutting ties for that Illinois Central Railroad." He hooked his thumb toward the flour mill. "We pulled our engine out of a Mississippi sidewheeler. Chester ain't said where he got his. But it cuts wood like a son—"

This time, the whining saw interrupted the miller.

"It's all Snyder's doings," Cowle yelled over the noise. "Gifted the land to Chester for his mill. You boys know what we paid for this land? Shay, Goodwin, and me?" He didn't tell them, but spit out juice and nodded again at the new store. "That's the town square. Or will be. Snyder platted the town. Give a patch of land for a gristmill, too, and I don't know what all he promised to that railroad. Must've been a passel." He pointed. "Over yonder will be a livery. Ezekiel will be running that."

Cowle shook his head. "When Zeke and me first got here, t'weren't nothin' more than four houses here." He sighed. "Two of 'em were frame, though. Guess I should have knowed it was bound to get uppity and civilized."

The miller wiped his mouth. "How was Wisconsin?"

"Good," Malone answered.

Cowle nodded. "Must've been. You boys put on some weight." He shook hands, turned, saying something about it being quieter inside his mill, and started walking to his paint can.

Tom and Malone returned to the fence, suddenly aware of how heavy their money belts felt. All that riding, they had finally gotten used to the weight, and the aches from carrying California gold coins almost three hundred miles.

Malone stepped closer to Tom and whispered again, "What about our money?"

"Keep your half for now." Tom kept staring at the clearing that must be what was to become the town square of Moweaqua. "It does not look like Moweaqua has a bank."

"I would not trust a bank with this much gold," Malone said.

"Do not forget where you bury it," Tom said.

The whining stopped again at the mill, but smoke belched from the pipes and the rhythmic pumping of that engine reminded Tom of the steamships at New York Harbor.

"You going to see the sawmill?" Malone asked.

Tom turned and looked westward down the road.

"I might see it later."

His partner chuckled. "You'll want to see that store they've put up." He pointed at the new log cabin.

"Maybe later."

"Oh," Malone said. "You'll want to see it now. I just saw someone peeking through the curtains. And I don't think she was looking at me."

Michael Snyder was one of those Germans who seldom smiled. His pale eyes usually reflected fire. His nose was straight, the mouth flat, no mustache but a beard that came down to his heart. If he really had a heart.

He glanced up from a register on a counter inside the newly constructed cabin, saw Tom in the doorway, and looked right back down, found a pencil, and checked something. His three oldest sons—though William probably was no older than ten—busied themselves putting items on shelves. Two hunters Tom knew slightly played some kind of dice game on a barrel by the window.

Tom saw no sign of Snyder's only daughter.

Maybe Malone had been playing a joke. Tom didn't see Mrs. Snyder around, for which he felt thankful. That woman was tougher than pretty Margaret's father.

A loud oath turned Tom's head toward the dice rollers, but one of the men had just been sputtering something about luck. If Tom didn't move, he would take root here, so he nodded at the Snyder boys and made himself walk to the man behind the counter.

"Drove sold?" Snyder asked without looking up.

"Yes, sir. Took a while."

Snyder scratched a number, then barked at one of the boys in German. All of the boys muttered something before they resumed stacking items on shelves, while their father eyed the ledger.

Tom's boots were about to take root again unless he could figure out something to say. Another thought struck him. *Just turn and run out of here, find the horse, and gallop home.*

"Tom Candy Ponting." That voice frightened him almost as much as standing this close to Mr. Snyder. For different reasons, though.

He spun around, started to remove his hat, only to realize he held it in his right hand. He quickly switched the hat to his left as blond-haired, blue-eyed Margaret Snyder, all five feet, four inches of her, stood in front of the blanket partition on the cabin's east side.

Her brothers giggled while Tom shifted the hat from hand to hand, and finally just dropped it on the floor.

Margaret put her hands on her hips.

"When did you get back?"

"Ummm. Today. Just a few minutes ago."

"Did Mother tell you I was here?"

Tom shook his head. "No. Washington and I just rode here." That explanation didn't sound right. He added, and pointed toward the open door, "To see the sawmill."

"Sawmill?" She shook her head, then told her laughing brothers to shut up. "You wanted to see a *sawmill?*"

He opened his mouth. Closed it.

She waited.

Tom opened his mouth again.

He blinked.

Shaking her head with a sigh, Margaret thrust the sack she was carrying in her left hand. "Take this, Tom Ponting," she said. "The least you can do is help me pick hickory nuts."

He found himself holding the sack in his right hand.

"Father," she said. "Tom and I will pick the hickory nuts Mother wanted. We will meet you back home. Is that all right, Father?"

"*Ja.*"

She smiled. "Come along, Tom. We have chores to do."

He watched her walk to the open door. She stopped, turned, and put her hands on her hips again. She wore a green dress. Her chest heaved as she drew in a deep breath, which she held, waiting, before her head shook and she sighed.

"Are you lame, Tom Ponting?" she asked.

The dice rollers laughed. So did her three brothers. Behind Tom, Mr. Snyder grunted.

"No," Tom whispered. "No, ma'am," he corrected a bit louder.

One of the dice rollers whispered something to his partner, who slapped the keg's side, tilted his head back, and howled with delight.

Tom stared at his left boot. It managed to move toward the doorway. Then the right leg followed suit.

"Your hat," Margaret reminded him.

He remembered, turned, picked up the hat, and walked toward Mr. Snyder's daughter. When he reached Margaret, she took his arm and led him into sunlight.

Tom stopped under a tree, leaned down, and fingered a nut, which he held out toward Margaret. She put her hands on her hips and shook her head.

"That's a maple tree," she told him. "Not a hickory." She pointed deeper into the woods. "And over there, that's a locust tree." She looked at the branches directly over her head. "This is a hickory tree, Tom Ponting."

He studied the tree. He couldn't tell much difference. Those that still had leaves looked real pretty.

"I fear that I am not much of a nut drover, Miss Margaret." He started to fling the nut he had picked off the ground deeper into the woods, but she shrieked at him.

"You can eat maple nuts." She rushed over, held out her left hand, palm cupped upward, and he let the nut fall.

"You just have to take care of these whirligigs first," she said. "Then boil them, peel the pod, and roast the seeds." She tossed the pod away. "But maple nuts are best in the spring or summer. They're too bitter this time of year." Looking up, she smiled. "And stop calling me Miss Margaret. I don't call you Mister Tom."

"Yes, ma'am."

"You don't have to ma'am me, either."

He started to speak, forgot how, and let his head move up and down.

He could just dive into those blue eyes. And he couldn't swim worth a fig.

"The hickory tree's over there," she said.

"Yes, ma'am." He didn't look away.

"Mother is waiting at home. Father and my brothers will be walking home soon. You need to shake the limb first, but don't stand underneath the limb. Hickory nuts can hurt when they fall."

"Yes, ma'am."

"Do you want to gather those nuts?"

He had used up all his vocabulary. So he just nodded.

"So do I," she said. "But I want you to kiss me first."

# CHAPTER 16

"Can I trust you with a secret?"

The sack of hickory nuts, with a few nuts from locust trees, hung from the saddle horn. Tom led his roan with the reins in his right hand. His left hand held Margaret's right hand. Amazing how their fingers slipped into each other's perfectly.

"Tom Ponting, are you deaf?"

He blinked, looked to his left, saw Margaret Snyder staring at him. For a moment, she glared, but that faded away and she smiled. "I asked if I could trust you with a secret."

"Yes . . ." This time he managed to choke back the *ma'am*.

"Absolutely." Maybe he ought to be adamant.

"Mother whipped me after you left that first time you rode to the farm." She smiled when she said it. Tom had never smiled over any of the whippings he had received from his father or mother. Not that those had come frequently, but one was all you needed to remember.

"Why did she whip you?"

"Because when you rode away, I ran to the window and watched you go. Said I was being *frech*."

"*Frech*." He tested the word.

189

"*Frech.*" She giggled. "You know . . . brazen . . . naughty?"

"Oh." He matched her smile. How would Frau Snyder react if she found out her only daughter had kissed a cattle drover? On the lips? More than once? Unchaperoned? In a thicket of trees thirty yards off the road. Which reminded him. There had been nut trees closer to the road. Why had Margaret taken them . . . ? Suddenly he smiled.

"She also said if she knew you were serious when you said I was the prettiest girl you ever saw and that she, *die Mutter*, should take special care of me because you were going to marry me someday, that she would not have been so kindly toward you."

Tom almost tripped in a hole in the middle of the road.

"I said that?"

"Father heard you, too." Margaret frowned and turned up her nose. "So did Michael. And even Valentine, *der Schwachkopf.*"

He tried to remember, but couldn't. He just remembered blue eyes.

She lifted his left hand to her lips, and he felt the kiss. Kissing his hand. His entire body started tingling. But she dropped his hand, sighed, and nodded at the road.

They had reached the lane to the house, just off the track, the big barn, the big house, the big trees.

"You better not be caught holding my hand," she whispered. "If you want to keep yours."

They produced tough stock in Baden-Baden, wherever that was, Tom thought as he led the roan back to the growing village of Moweaqua. And likely none tougher than Margaret Kautz Snyder. Margaret the daughter had expected that since Tom had helped gather those nuts, he would be invited for supper. But Frau Snyder had thanked Tom with a nod and some hard-sounding German word before sending him on an errand. *Tell her husband to leave that store and come home for supper before the food got cold.* Margaret started to speak, but her mother turned with a look that froze the blue-eyed beauty—until her oldest brother, back home from the store, said something underneath his breath, then yelped and hopped, grabbing the toe of his left shoe.

"*Halt den Mund*!" Margaret's mother roared at her children, turned to Tom, pointed the spoon she held toward the door. "*Gute Nacht*," she told him as he headed through the door and toward the roan.

The day's work had ended at the sawmill, but the smell of supper drifted from the frame houses and wooden cabins. Moweaqua still didn't look much like a town, but Tom knew that would not last. The door remained open to Snyder's store, and he heard laughter and curses as he tethered the roan to a post, took off his hat, and stepped inside.

Mr. Snyder had joined the two men at the barrel in their dice game. He was shaking his right hand, and then let the dice bounce across the top of the keg. The man with the coonskin cap groaned. The one with the cap turned and hit the nearest log with his left fist.

"*Ich gewinne*," Snyder said, laughing as he held out his left hand. The one with the coonskin cap reached into the pouch hanging around his neck, pulled it open, stuck his fingers inside, and withdrew a beaded bracelet. The one now holding his left hand swore, and brought the skinned knuckles to his lips while his right hand jerked a crucifix off the rawhide thong that held it around his neck.

Michael Snyder was still laughing as the two men walked through the door. He looked at the trinkets, shrugged. "They sell. Someone buy." He rose, crossed the room, and stepped behind the counter, dropping the bracelet and the crucifix into a rawhide pouch before lifting a jug from beneath the counter. He held it out toward Tom.

"No," Tom said, shaking his head, "but thank you, kindly, sir." He cleared his throat. "Frau Snyder says—"

"I know what she says." Snyder pulled out the cork, lifted the jug, and took two swallows before setting down the jug. Tom figured then that this was some sort of conspiracy. The merchant—the man who had platted the village of Moweaqua and was bringing the Illinois Central Railroad to this town that really wasn't even a town— nodded. "Come, Tom Ponting." He said the name as if it were one word. "We talk."

Tom leaned against the counter, and Snyder pushed the jug closer. Again Tom shook his head and looked the big man in those cold eyes. If anyone tried to dive into those eyes, he figured, they'd come out with busted bones, bloodied lips, and broken hearts.

"Five sons have," he said. "All will be successful. Michael. Second Michael. William. Valentine. Adam." He grinned. "Adam. He just two. Baby when you first came by house to look at cattle. Maybe I have another son. We see." He took another pull, and set the jug closer to Tom's reach. "*Meine Jungs*, they grow to be good men. Businessmen. Know business. Know what father do to be . . ." He didn't want to say rich, or powerful, so he just shrugged. "This I know."

"I imagine you do, sir." Tom stared at the jug. He sure could use a snort right about now, but . . . he remembered England. He cleared his throat.

"But daughter." Sighing, he shook his head. "Women not know business. Women not men. Women cook. Give husband good, strong children. Boys become men. Smart men. Businessmen. Daughter no businessman.

Daughters must marry. I make sure that Margaret
. . . daughter Margaret . . . marries right man."

Tom tried to recall exactly what he had said
about Margaret to Frau Snyder that year or two
ago. He couldn't remember, but he certainly had
been captivated by Margaret's grace and eyes.
She was—still was—the most beautiful girl he
had ever seen. He thought: *Why didn't you keep
your dumb trap shut?*

"You," Snyder said, "gambler. *Meine Tochter*
not marry gambler. I not gamble."

Tom blinked, tried to make sense out of the
absurdity. His eyes fell on the dice on the counter.
Snyder laughed as he picked up the ivory squares,
tossed them a few inches, and caught them. He
pointed at the keg where he had won the trinkets.

"That not gambling. Bet sure things. Dice.
Gilbert and Nye? Sure thing. You work cattle.
Cattle gamble."

"I think I have done all right in the cattle
business." Tom felt he had to say something.

"Cattle not business. Corn. Wheat. That
America needs. Black dirt. Good dirt. Grow
things." His eyes turned colder. "*Das Vieh?*" His
head shook with finality.

Tom wanted to pull his shirt over his head
and show this fool the money belt that held five
thousand and more dollars. Most of it in freshly
minted California slugs. He could see the look
on the man's face, but also knew that would be

like bragging. He had more money right now, he figured, than Michael Snyder.

"Land," Margaret's father said. "Land sure thing. Everyone want land. I have land. Bring railroad to Moweaqua. Railroad future. Canals." He barked a laugh. "Canals will . . . dry up. Ha!" He slammed a palm flat against the counter.

"You good man, Tom Ponting," Snyder said. "Margaret like you. Daughter Margaret. Mother, *Meine Frau*, like you not much. But you work hard. But work at wrong thing."

He hid the jug underneath the counter, found his hat, his coat, and stepped around, guiding Tom to the door, which he closed behind him.

"I like you. You visit . . . here . . ." He tapped the log wall. "Any time. Credit good. For now. You friend. Good friend. But husband?" His head shook. "Not with cows. Maybe like run store?"

Tom shook his head. "Come spring," he heard himself saying, "Washington Malone and I will be traveling to Texas. There, we shall buy a herd of cattle. I do not know exactly how many. We shall buy cattle cheap. And then we will drive that herd here. Winter them. And take them to New York to sell. I have a vision, too, Herr Snyder. And that is what I will do."

The big man laughed, clamped his right hand on Tom's shoulder. "You make good joke, Tom Ponting."

"It is no joke, sir."

The man's hard eyes blinked. He released his hold and stared hard at Tom, stepped back, and opened the door. "Come," he said, and went inside. When Tom just stood there, he came back out, waved his hand. "Come. Come, Tom Ponting. I show you."

Reluctantly, Tom stepped onto the planking and followed the weaving man back to the counter. Light was beginning to fade, but Snyder lighted a candle, and used it as he searched on shelves in the far corner. He motioned to the counter. "Drink. Good whiskey McCutcheon make." He must have forgotten that he had put the jug underneath the counter.

So Tom just leaned against the wood, and watched the German look on top shelves and middle shelves and finally found the right shelf. "*Ach.*" He blew out the flame, grunted as he went to his knees, and withdrew what at first Tom thought was a bolt of cotton or something. But as Snyder returned to the counter, Tom realized it was a large map, rolled up. The German laid it atop the wood. "Unroll. I get better light."

Tom looked at the parchment, wondered how old it was, and then began carefully unrolling it. It covered the width of the wooden counter. A match struck, light flared, and Snyder returned with a lantern, which he held over his head. The map was beautiful. Like a painting.

Margaret's father tapped a spot on the map.

"This Illinois," he said, and ran his finger at an angle toward Tom, stopping at an enormous patch of green, gold, and brown about eight or nine inches from what the German had called Illinois.

"That Texas," Snyder said. Then his hand came up a foot or better and jabbed at what could have been the long neck of some dragon-like creature. "That," Snyder said. "That New York." He ran his finger back to Illinois. "You think you go from here to there." The finger came back up. "To New York?" He laughed again and set the lantern near the map.

"No, Tom Ponting. *Unmöglich.*"

As Snyder began rolling up the map, Tom said, "I will do it, sir. You can bet on it."

Those big hands stopped atop the parchment. "You gamble."

"I do not gamble," Tom said. But his stomach began twisting. "Not with cattle."

*Have you lost all your reason?*

"Make bet?" The light of the lantern flickered in Mr. Snyder's eyes.

Tom swallowed. He drew in a breath, started to shake his head.

"*Ja.*" Snyder laughed. "I know. You—"

"How much?" Tom asked.

The merchant, the land speculator, the dice roller studied Tom again.

"One hundred dollars?" Snyder wet his lips.

"Five hundred?" Tom countered.

The man straightened and said: "Much money, Tom Ponting." Which Tom found unnecessary.

Outside, an owl hooted.

"How much cows?" Snyder asked.

Tom didn't understand.

"Much cows." Snyder looked at the ceiling. "Many." He nodded, satisfied with his English, and asked slowly, "How . . . many . . . cows?"

Shrugging, Tom offered, "One hundred?"

The big head with the beard shook instantly. "And fifty."

Tom nodded, and he held out his right hand.

But Margaret's father was not quite done.

"Must be deadline. And cows must be in one . . . one . . . *ein* . . ."

"One drove," Tom finished. "As far as when I get that drove to—"

Snyder cut him off. "July four. Independence Day. Eighteen and fifty-four. *Natürlich*! Me. You. Now Americans."

The Fourth of July. A long winter could make that problematic, if not impossible. But he heard himself saying, "Agreed."

The man's blue eyes suddenly sparkled. He said something in German, then translated. "Bet thousand dollars?"

Tom had gone years not seeing that much money. His father probably never made more than a hundred pounds in a year. *Why don't you just pull out twenty California slugs and pay off this fool bet now? You can't win.* But there went his hand to shake and again he heard himself saying, "It's a bet, sir."

The big hand squeezed Tom's. "You come home," Snyder said. "*Mit mir.* Least I do for fools. *Meine frau*—she feed you. She like to feed *dummkopf.*" He picked up the dice and rattled them in his hand. "I like take *dummkopf* money."

*I've been hoodwinked,* Tom thought.

# CHAPTER 17

"You bet what?"

Tom nodded at the two rawhide pouches on the rough-hewn table in his cabin. "A thousand dollars," he told Washington Malone. It came out as a weary sigh.

"Tom." Malone's head shook slowly. "Tom, Tom, Tom. You pitiful fool." He drew in a deep breath and let it out slowly. "We might need that thousand dollars."

"I know."

"You let that rich Hun get to you."

Tom's head bobbed. "I know that, too."

"Have you ever seen or heard of Michael Snyder losing a bet?"

"No." He had grown tired of answering that question.

"Because he hasn't," Malone lectured, as if Tom didn't know that, either. "He's also the most powerful man in the county. Maybe this part of the state. Maybe all of Illinois. He's bringing the railroad here. He has created a town. I would not be flummoxed if Moweaqua changes its name to Snyder City or Snyderville. It may well rival Chicago."

Tom left his doubts about the latter unspoken.

"He is a man of vision."

"I have a vision, too," he told his partner.

Their eyes held for a moment, until Malone's lips curved into a cynical grin. "Does it look like bankruptcy?"

That led to a round of laughter before Tom turned to the fireplace to fetch the teakettle. They sat at the table, and Tom outlined his plan. He even told Malone where he would hide the twenty slugs in the event something happened to him, leaving Malone to pay off the bet. Tom, alive or dead, would not be known as a man who did not pay off debts or bets.

"If I win," Tom concluded, "five hundred dollars goes to you. We are partners."

"Then I should pay half—"

Tom cut him off. "No. This was my doing—or my undoing. But should we somehow complete this mission, I shall not have succeeded without help from you."

"We will need help from others."

"Who will be paid."

Malone's expression soured. "We will need assistance from . . . Texians."

Tom turned mute.

"The last Texians we worked with were not . . ." He tested the last word. "Amicable."

*Another unnecessary reminder.*

That winter, he read as much as he could.

A story in the *Alton Weekly Courier* informed

Tom about "A Texas Bear Hunt" in which Tom learned that Texas boys were equal to most men in other parts of these United States, but by the time he had finished the article, he determined that the author was attempting to be humorous. On a trip to Springfield, Congressman Richard Yates told Tom to, at all cost, stay away from Texas.

"God Himself abhors Texas," Yates railed, "because Texians are slave-owning demons and a curse to American democracy. They are dangerous and unreasonable, and no abolitionist would eat a Texas steer. Even if Texas would divide its immense land and become two states, one free, one slave, I shall always damn my congressional colleagues who voted to bring that fiery fiefdom into our precious Union. If I were you, Ponting, I would never venture into that savage, evil place."

Dry rot had destroyed much of the cotton crop in Texas. Tom overheard that when he let Sanders cut his hair. What he didn't hear or read about was anything related to Texas cattle.

"It appears Illinois will go for Pierce," Washington Malone said after Tom dined with his partner.

"Pierce?" Tom looked up.

Sitting on the slab that served as a bench, Malone folded the newspaper and stared hard. "General Pierce." Tom blinked. "Our next president."

Tom looked back at the map Mr. Snyder had loaned him.

"Well, this might interest you more," Malone said. "Texas went the whole swine for Pierce. Every county voted for him."

Tom's head shot back up at the mention of Texas, but when he realized the article had nothing to do with the country, trails, or cattle—just that presidential election—Tom focused on the map.

Forking hay to keep the cattle fed. Breaking ice in the stream and pond with an ax so that the cattle could drink. Trying to thaw out himself with hot tea or coffee, and sleeping in his bedroll next to the fireplace. One of these days, he would buy himself a bed. When he wasn't trying to learn as much as he could about Texas or trails to Texas, 1852–1853 was no different than most winters. Except that he had a thousand dollars buried beneath a stone fifteen paces from the corral's northernmost post, and a money belt filled with fifty-dollar coins and other currency under the loose plank next to the south-facing window that had greased paper instead of glass.

Flat Branch was a long way to ride in February just for an unannounced visit, but the clouds hiding the sun did not appear threatening, nor did the wind bite wickedly hard. Isom Adams had killed a deer—on Tom's land while passing through—and, good Kentuckian that Adams was, he brought Tom more smoked venison than he could eat. So Tom decided he ought to be as neighborly as Isom Adams, even though Tom had closer neighbors.

Captain Alfred C. Campbell arrived in Moweaqua around the same time as Tom, but Campbell was a native of the state, born on Lick Creek near Springfield in 1819. He called himself the third-oldest white man in Illinois. Since settling here, he had cleared his land of much of the timber, replacing hardwoods with crops. But what interested Tom was that the captain had served in the late war against Mexico.

The farm impressed Tom. Four hundred acres and more, though much of it had yet to be cleared. Smoke belched from the fine cabin's chimney as Tom reined in the roan.

The door opened, and the captain stepped outside. He looked a bit like Michael Snyder, that same style of beard, no mustache, but Captain Campbell's hair was lighter, his eyes friendly, and his smile broad.

"Pontin'," he said, turning to hand his Mississippi Rifle to one of his sons.

When he looked back, Tom hooked his thumb to the sack tied behind the saddle. "Isom Adams downed a good-sized buck on my place while passing through on the way to Prairieton

Township," he said, "and brought me more deer meat than I could eat in a month of Sundays. I figured you might like some."

"Lots of neighbors closer to you would have liked it, too."

Tom nodded. "Yes, sir, Captain, but you have more mouths to feed."

The strong man laughed as he walked outside, inviting Tom to light down. When they shook hands, Campbell whispered, " 'Bout to have another mouth to feed, if the Good Lord's willin'."

"That'll make . . . five?" Tom guessed.

"Six." The youngest couldn't be much older than two.

"John Peyton," the captain called back to the cabin. "Come fetch this deer meat and take it to the smoke shed for the time bein'."

A strapping young man of maybe twelve, thirteen years hurried outside. After Tom helped Campbell's oldest son with the sack, the captain, as Tom had hoped, invited the visitor inside for coffee and . . . cornbread.

Somehow, Tom managed to smile. "I have not tasted cornbread in some time."

"Polly makes the best in the county," Captain Campbell said.

"You'd be wantin' to hear 'bout Texas," the captain said with a smile after Polly topped off Tom's cup of coffee.

Tom looked up.

Campbell shrugged. "Moweaqua ain't big enough to keep secrets." Then he grinned, rocking his chair's rear legs.

"I joined up in '46, Company D, Fourth Illinois, got elected lieutenant, and we left Alton for Jefferson Barracks. Took a steamboat down to New Orleans, then another ship to the Río Grande. But all of our fightin' was done south of Texas—Matamoros, Victoria, Veracruz, Tampico. That's where I become capt'n 'cause ours got kilt."

Tom nodded, but he wasn't interested in war stories.

"Did you see any of those long-horned cattle?" he asked.

The captain found his uncorked jug, and nodded at it. When Tom shook his head, Campbell grinned. "I heard that about you. But figured I ought to show good manners." He took a swallow, but just one, then laid the jug on the floor and pushed it away.

"Ugly critters. Lean, leathery. Some of those horns must have stretched ten feet. Heard folks say that the meat is lean, tasty, but, well, I had the misfortune to be in the Army—and the Army thinks all a soldier needs is beans that are hardly cooked and crackers that is either moldy or so stale they'll break your teeth."

Tom sipped his coffee.

"But here's one thing I heard 'bout Texian beeves," Campbell said, and Tom set his cup down. "Texas rancher told me this. They call them ranchers, not stock farmers. Anyway, this Texian he told me that if you get yourself a good leader, a good steer, the rest of 'em critters will follow that boss man for as long as you need them to go."

"How far did they drive them?" Tom asked.

"Can't say. Nearest market, I suspect, was in Louisiana. For meat. But the Texians I met seemed more interested in the hides than the beef. Drive 'em to tanneries is what one soldier boy tol' me." He glanced at the jug, but reached instead for his coffee cup. "Now, some folks might call that talk about a herd followin' one ol' steer nothin' more'n Texas brag, but I got a notion it's one of the few true things I ever heard from a Texian. Just from seein' some of 'em long-horned devils bein' drove by what 'em Mexicans called *vaqueros*."

"*Vaqueros*." Tom tested the word.

The captain nodded. "Mex—Spanish—what-ever you want to call it. Those are what they call the men who work the cattle. Sorta like the drovers you and Malone are. Except they dress up real pretty. No offense. Farmers dress for farmin', drovers dress for drovin', but both of us dress up for church, weddin's and funerals. But that's one thing I'll say about Mexicans. They like fancy duds. Well, maybe not the farmers. But those *vaqueros* sure do. And those *caballeros*. That's a Mex name for a horseman—'bout the only Mex words I recollect—well, that I can say in polite company."

Tom smiled. "And the country?"

"Like I said, Tom, most of what I saw was in Mexico. Now, the country on both sides of that creek they call a river looked like nothin' more than burned-up desert. Dry as a lime burner's hat." He finished his coffee and shrugged. "The coast was just god-awful ugly. Swampy thing. Mosquitoes the size of blackbirds—and the blackbirds down that way was huge. Sand was just nasty. Heard tell that there was thick piney woods north of there. But this fellow I met in New Orleans, he bragged about the country up north, on the Red River. Said it was finer than frog's hair cut eight ways. That's a Texian for you."

Polly Campbell, heavy with child, walked back with the pot of coffee, but Tom put his hand over the cup and smiled. "No, thank you, ma'am. But the coffee and the cornbread were heavenly."

He spoke honestly about the coffee.

She smiled, topped off her husband's cup, and asked if Tom would be staying for supper. Tom said he regretted that he had to return home before dark.

"Ain't been much help to you," the captain said after Polly had left.

"On the contrary," Tom answered honestly. "I will leave here knowing more than I did before I arrived." Both men stood, and Tom shook Campbell's hand, found his hat, and let the captain lead him to the door. The roan stood patiently, tethered to a fence rail.

"You're a smart whippersnapper, Pontin'," Campbell said as Tom untied the roan and swung into the saddle. "I might look up that hard-rock Snyder and place a bet that you win your wager. Get the money back I lost on that tree-fellin' contest last year."

"I thank you for the compliment, Captain." Tom started to wrap the muffler over his neck. "But I would not want you to lose a wager and have your regiment go hungry." Another question came to him, and he pulled down his hat and looked at the stocky Illinoisian. "What about Texians, sir? Generally speaking?"

Captain Campbell snorted. "Some of 'em— most of 'em, at least them I met—they ain't hardly human." He didn't appear to be joking, but Tom recalled the two Texians he had met in the Milwaukee bank and then on the road north of Chicago. " 'Course, we was fightin' a war, and Texians had some hard grudges against 'em Mexicans. But I would hate to tangle with one— Texian, I mean—but if it come to a fight, I'd surely want a Texian on my side."

"Well, I am looking for cattle drovers. Not soldiers, Captain."

The laugh startled Tom. Captain Campbell shook his head, his eyes bright.

"Son, you ever been to Missouri?"

"No, sir."

"Well, I have. And trust me, Pontin'. I'd sure want a Texian ridin' with me if ever I was to run into any wild Missourian."

# CHAPTER 18

"Bids fair for an early spring, Mr. Tom," John Peyton Campbell said.

"I hope you are right." Tom led the roan out of the barn.

The captain's son looked nervous. Tom reached into the pocket of his coat and pulled out one of the gold coins. He held it out to the young teen.

"No, sir." The boy shook his head. "Papa told me to take no money from you."

"You are not taking, John," Tom said. "You are earning. How long I shall be gone is uncertain, but I can assure you it will be no sooner than midsummer and, perhaps, early fall. You will have need of things. And you are doing me a service by looking after my cattle and cabin."

The boy stared at the coin.

Tom smiled. "You can use it if you need it. I have plenty of hay for the cattle, and there should be enough beans and coffee for you to get by. I certainly hope so." He had been shocked at the prices Mr. Snyder charged—little wonder that old miser had so much money—and had found better deals at the Flat Branch trading post.

The boy could not take his eyes off the gold coin.

"Maybe you could even buy your new brother a present. And your mother, too."

"Baby ain't been born yet," the youngster said. "I kind of hope it's a sister, though. Got enough brothers already."

Tom nodded. That was one reason, he figured, Captain Campbell had suggested that his son look after Tom's place. There were enough mouths to feed at the Campbell farm already, though Tom made certain that both John Peyton and the captain understood that the boy should be free to go help out at his real home whenever needed. Tom's cattle could look after themselves for several days, especially if the warm spell held.

The boy still did not take the slug.

"Tell you what, John. I will leave this piece on the hearth inside. If you need it, take it. Fifty dollars will buy a lot of necessaries." He moved back inside the house. "Providing you are not dealing with Michael Snyder."

He met Washington Malone at the fork, where they turned their horses toward Moweaqua.

"I thought we were going to Shelbyville," Malone said.

Tom nodded. "We shall. But we have been invited to dinner."

Malone reined up, and it took a few moments before Tom, his mind occupied on another matter, realized his partner no longer rode alongside him.

He looked back, saw how pale his partner's face had turned, and stopped the roan. "I have not even informed you of where we shall be dining," he said. "But I do not think Frau Snyder will poison us—certainly, not you—and not me, either, until her husband can collect his winnings."

"It's not that." Malone kicked his chestnut forward, halting next to Tom. He drew in a breath, exhaled, and said, "I traded some of those gold slugs for paper money from Mr. Tolly."

That wasn't necessarily a bad thing. Cornelius Tolly was a fine man, and, like most men in the county, honest. But . . .

"What kind of notes?" he asked.

"Missouri," Malone answered.

Tom felt his lungs and heart working again. "Missouri paper is good as gold," he said.

"I know. But I thought that now you are carrying more weight than I am and that perhaps I should—"

Laughter cut off his partner. "You forget, my fine friend," Tom told him, and wiped his eyes. "I left more than three pounds of slugs under my floor."

Slowly Malone managed a smile. They rode toward the trees that lined the lane leading to the Snyder home.

"I suppose we shall be forced to eat sauerkraut," Malone said.

"As long as it is not cornbread," Tom whispered.

• • •

Mr. Snyder looked delighted when he opened the big front door, and the smell of sausages and onions made Tom's stomach remember exactly what it had been digesting all winter. Removing his hat, Tom shook the big man's hand. "Hang your hats, coats there," Snyder instructed, and offered a warm greeting and similar instructions to Malone.

Closing the door, Snyder walked past them as they hung coats and hats, and he slid a door into the wall, stepped back, and pointed his big right hand into the library.

"Smoke," he said. "Good cigars. Brandy if you want."

Tom and Malone eased into the room. Tom stood by a bookcase, admiring titles, trying to grasp what the German letters meant. Malone put his finger on one spine and whispered, "It's a McGuffey's Reader." He chuckled slightly. "A *First Reader* at that." He found another title and shook his head. "And a *Ray's Arithmetic*."

Mr. Snyder stepped inside and closed the sliding door. He motioned to two leather chairs with legs and sidearms made of horns, while he took a large, cushioned couch and opened a cherrywood case. "Cigars," he said. He found one, bit an end, spat into a brass cuspidor, and struck a match. "Smoke," he said once he had

I would not be a worthy suitor, let alone a good son-in-law. The bet stands, sir." He waited till the old man's brow smoothed and the blue eyes twinkled. "The bet stands," he repeated.

Michael Snyder did not smile, but his face changed. Maybe Tom had finally gotten the old man to respect him.

"The bet stands." Not a trace of a German accent that time, and now Snyder grinned. "I enjoy when I collect."

"As will I, sir," Tom said. "As will I."

"*Komm.*" Snyder opened the sliding door. "*Essen wir*. We eat."

No sauerkraut. But enough sausages, onions, and sourdough bread to stuff Tom's stomach for a week. Frau Snyder kept filling his plate, as though she hoped his gut would bust and he would succumb to a ruptured intestine. She even made a joke, saying that for a bachelor he sure had eaten well during the winter, making Tom keenly aware of the weight of his money belt. They brewed tea for Tom, while Malone and the Snyders drank wine, even the youngest of Margaret's siblings.

Frau Snyder and her daughter cleared the dishes, the boys went about their chores, and Mr. Snyder led the guests back to the library for another cigar, more tea for Tom, and more brandy for Malone and the big German. Tom kept looking at the closed door, and the smoke became thick in the small office, but finally Tom found a pause in the conversation and said, "I hate to leave such refinement, but Texas is a long way from here. We should take advantage of the weather. And hope this is not a false spring."

"*Ja.*" Snyder crushed out his cigar and again heaved himself out of the sofa. He pushed the door into the wall. "You get horses from the barn," he told Tom. His English, Tom realized, had improved over the winter. "Malone and I say goodbye to *meine frau.*"

"I should like to thank Frau Snyder, too," Tom protested. "I—"

"*Nein. Nein.* You get horses from barn. Malone tell thanks. Remember. It is long way to Texas."

Snyder stepped out into the foyer, and his massive frame blocked the way to the winter kitchen and dining room, leaving Tom only one exit—the front door. Once outside, he turned toward the steps, and saw her on the swing.

Her face shined. Margaret Snyder glanced at the window, swallowed, and her shoes stopped the swing from moving, and squeaking. The curtains were closed. Mr. Snyder had helped formulate this conspiracy. His eyes locked on Margaret's.

Yet the first words he told her were: "I have to get our horses."

She stared. Then laughed. Tom's face flushed.

Her head tilted toward the hitch rail. "Do you mean . . . *those* horses?"

He saw them, saddled, lounging sleepily, the roan pawed the earth a couple of times. The chestnut's tail swished back and forth.

"Oh," Tom said. He looked at his right foot, urging it to step toward the swing.

One leg finally moved, then the other. The wood did not creak beneath the weight of himself and his money belt. He stopped at the swing, and studied the window just to confirm no one peeked through the curtains. Then looked again at Margaret Snyder.

"How . . . ?" No, that was not the way to talk. Not with him about to leave for a long, possibly dangerous, journey. Probably dangerous. Undoubtfully dangerous. And likely resulting in a rather large depletion in his finances.

She held out her hands. "Help me up?" she requested.

How could he refuse?

"May I write you?" he asked.

"You had better." Her stern countenance vanished in a wide grin. "Can I write you?"

"That . . . I must find a place, with luck in Missouri, where the postmaster will hold my mail till I return from Texas. You can write me there. I will let you know where."

A door opened in the rear of the house, and she

pulled away from him, sighed, and tilted her head toward the steps. "I am supposed to be gathering eggs for supper," she told him. "I fear I must lose sight of you now."

"I will never lose sight of you."

He blinked. Tom C. Ponting, who had never read one book completely through in his life, had said something like that.

"Oh, Tom," she whispered, and leaned her head against his chest. She pulled back from him, touching a mark above her right eyelid.

"What are you wearing underneath your shirt?" she asked.

It must have been the clasp on his suspenders.

"Turn your head," he said. "And close your eyes."

Her lips tightened. Those pretty eyes narrowed. Again, Tom made sure those shades remained closed, and glanced toward the front door. "I shan't shame you or me, my dear," he told her.

"You have loved me to distraction," she told him, and faced the whitewashed planks, the heavy curtains, closing her eyes.

When she turned upon his request, he held the octagonal coin between his right thumb and forefinger.

"They are worth fifty dollars," he told her, turning his hand over and letting the gold rest in his palm. "Minted in California."

She started to reach for it, stopped, and jerked

her head up to make sure that he would not mind.

"Take it," he said. "And keep it."

Suspicion narrowed her eyes once more, but he smiled. "Hold it for me, then," he said, smiling. "There is a good chance I might need that coin upon my return."

# CHAPTER 19

Tom guided the roan to the hitch rail and looked at the shingle hanging above the Shelbyville barbershop.

DONOVAN GRAD,
ATTY AT LAW

"I didn't think you needed a haircut or shave," Washington Malone said. "But a lawyer?"

Swinging out of the saddle, Tom walked to the hitch rail.

"Just a precaution," he said. "And a lesson I learned many years ago in England." He smiled at the memory and looked back at his partner. "It is a long way to Texas. And many . . ." He fought to try to remember the words Sydney Ivatts had told him that evening all those years, all those miles, ago. ". . . many dangers and hardships might . . . arise."

"A will." Malone pushed his hat back as though contemplating.

"Solicitor Grad's fees are reasonable," Tom said. "I am sure he can accommodate you."

His partner dismounted the chestnut, stepped to the rail, smiling. "I think a haircut and shave will suffice. I detest shaving on a trail, and believe

221

that tonsorial parlors shall be infrequent until we reach St. Louis."

They traveled light. No valises. Not even Malone's carbine, which had misfired in December, splitting the barrel, but, luckily, not Malone's left hand and arm. Just saddlebags holding coffee and crackers, tin cups, a skillet, a change of socks and a change of shirts, India rubber ponchos rolled over their whips and strapped atop bedrolls behind cantles, and canteens hanging from the saddlehorns.

It took a while for Tom and Malone to become reacquainted with the weight of their money belts. Suspenders dug through the flannel undershirts, and the belts bit into their sides. On cloudless days, they sweated, then shivered when evening came. But neither man ever looked back toward Moweaqua.

They aimed to cover a hundred miles every three days, not hard to do riding southwest through Illinois. Springlike weather held. They never stopped for dinner, and took their supper early. Sometimes, they found a farm and asked to sleep in a barn. Most folks were glad to share coffee, tea, bread, eggs—but mostly conversation—with them, and few would accept any payment. Even corn, grain, or hay and water for the horses went gratis. Tom always chopped firewood before he left, or forked hay to the milch cow and any livestock. Malone would help, when his rheumatism wasn't on the prod, carrying firewood or gathering eggs.

In Vandalia, a blacksmith reshod their horses while they sat down to a fine meal across from the old state capitol. The big building still stood, though Springfield had taken over as the capital back in '39, while part of the big building now served as the county courthouse, and the other part, Tom guessed to be the jail. Malone shook his head. "Schoolhouse," he said. "Jail would be much quieter."

It felt like spring when they rode out of Vandalia.

But this remained part of Illinois. Winter greeted them that night, and stayed with them to the Mississippi River.

The gold felt heavier in the freezing wind. A woolen scarf held the hat on Tom's head, pulling down the brim to help keep his ears from breaking off. His right heel slammed into the ice. Again. Once more. He lifted his head as much as he dared, for breathing in air hurt his throat and all the way down deep into his chest.

Turning, he looked up the bank at Malone.

His partner shrugged, and led the chestnut down.

Both men stood on the Mississippi River.

"The ice is thick enough here." Tom regretted

speaking. That hurt his tongue, his teeth, and burned his lips, which he dared not wet.

He drew in a deep breath, regretting it immediately because the cold blistered his nostrils, maybe even his lungs.

"It's not exactly flat like the frozen ponds back home," Malone yelled over the wind.

Tom nodded. Chunks of ice loomed up, like waves from the Atlantic Ocean at high tide, only frozen solid. And he spotted glimmering pools where the Mississippi still breathed. Mist rose from those pockets of frigid water. *Just stay away from the mist.*

He shot Malone a glance.

Malone smiled without humor. "I suppose crossing at New Orleans is out of the question!" Then Malone took a step toward the Missouri shore. Tom followed, head down, gloved right hand holding tightly to the roan's reins.

Twice he slipped. The second time he had to grab a stirrup to pull himself to his feet. Once the chestnut slid onto its haunches, precariously close to a steaming pool of icy water, jerking Malone facedown on the sharp, ugly ice. He pushed himself up, fell flat again, cursed, rolled over, and by then Tom had the roan near. Malone grabbed the far stirrup, managed to get to his knees, at last his feet, and turned and found his horse, already moving toward the western bank.

As the sun dipped behind clouds and trees far

off to the west, both men draped the reins over their mounts' necks, moved back, grabbed the tails, and let the chestnut and roan lead the way. Horses, Tom knew, had better eyesight than humans.

They did not stop when they climbed up a wooded slope. Just kept moving toward the lights of the city of St. Louis.

Still no snow, just a terrible wind. Now Tom and Malone led the horses. The trail Tom followed— if it indeed were a trail, or a path, or a road— moved toward the flickering lights of a city that might rival Milwaukee, perhaps even Chicago. That would be St. Louis, but what was that fireball off to his left?

The sun rose in the east, but Tom didn't think the sun had set that long ago. And that glow appeared to be more southerly than easterly.

The roan stopped him. Like an anchor. His right arm jerked back, and he groaned. His gloved hand still clutched the reins, and he flexed the fingers just to make sure they had not frozen off. Turning into the wind, he glared at the gelding, which just snorted. Behind him, he made out Malone, who tilted his head up the trail, past Tom.

Tom strained to see. He could just make out the shape of a man with a furry hat and thick coat. The roan had seen the figure. Otherwise, Tom would have walked right into him. While the wind howled, Tom tried to clear his throat. Finally, he moved toward the man, who heard, or sensed, his presence.

Tom nodded and held up his free hand. His right felt like it had frozen to the reins.

The stranger stepped off the path a bit to allow the two horses passage. Tom stopped when he reached the man.

When Tom opened his mouth, he thought layers of his lips were peeling off. His brain told him that it was too cold to talk, but curiosity made him ask: "What is it?"

The shout came out like a whisper. He inched closer. The man glanced at him. This time, Tom pointed at the bright glow. It had to be a fire, but that could be no building, no structure in St. Louis. It lay too far away from the flickering lights off to the southwest.

"The *Jean McKee*," the man yelled. "Capt'n Russell's sternwheeler. Laid up for the winter." His big, bearded head shook. "Told him he never should have give up masonry."

A steamboat. Burning in all that water. Water frozen solid. Tom made out the smoke now.

"That river," the man said, "she'll break your heart." He sighed a frosty sentiment, and nodded at the trail. "Best get out of this norther, boys. Follow the trail. Be careful along Point Breeze." He gazed again at the inferno that resembled an oil-on-canvas, frozen in the gloaming.

• • •

His brain had not succumbed to the cold. Tom understood all the mistakes he had made. Counting on spring temperatures to last was the biggest. He had been in England back in '39, but he had heard the stories from Zeke Prescott, Captain Campbell, Thomas Bradley, and other old-time Illinoisians about that Manitoba wave that froze ponds so fast, frog heads were seen above sheets of ice. He had not made arrangements for lodging in St. Louis, either. Point Breeze, Tom figured, lived up to its name. Down bluffs and over gullies, the wind howled. While the lights of St. Louis still looked far away.

"Sinkhole."

Now walking ahead, Malone stopped, turned, and pointed to his right, guiding the chestnut around a dark opening in what passed for a road. Tom pulled the roan away from the deep pit, and back on the rough road. He made out a tall fence off to the east, silhouetted by the glow of the burning *Jean McKee*. A moment later, another light grabbed his attention. Malone must have seen it, too, for he stopped and pointed.

A moment later, a man cursed, then yelled. "Fire. By God, the stable's afire!"

Tom stopped. The spark had exploded, and Tom made out the stable. Hay fueled the flames, and the scream of horses carried over the freezing wind.

"Tom . . ." Malone's voice came out as something less than a whisper. "I can barely move."

That rheumatism. "Can you hold my reins?" Tom asked.

"I . . . think . . . so."

Tom heard his knees pop as he bent. He laid the reins on the ground near Malone's right foot. "Just stand on them," he said.

He waited till Malone's left boot planted hard against the leather. The flames were a good twenty yards away, off where the road curved, and Tom figured the roan and chestnut were too played out, too frozen, to spook. As long as the wind blew the stink of smoke away from them. As long as that fire did not spread.

Stiff legs, numb from the norther, somehow managed to carry Tom to the blinding fire. Flames licked up the stable's walls, devouring through hay, harnesses. A man in some sort of uniform whirled around, raising a stick over his head. Tom read fear in the man's eyes. That fool held a club, and that club came straight down toward Tom's skull.

He stepped aside, surprised his frozen muscles could react so quickly. The club whooshed past his shoulder, momentum bending the man toward the ground as he cursed, grunted, tried to straighten. Tom did not remember hitting the man. He blinked, and saw the figure on the street, trying to get his own limbs to work.

Another man raising a big stick started toward Tom, but a voice stopped him.

"Look at him, Stubbs! Does he look like he belongs in the workhouse?"

Tom found the voice, moved toward it.

"I am Tom Ponting," he said. "Of Illinois."

"Peers," the man said. "Superintendent of the workhouse." He cursed, and spit toward the singeing flames.

Tom's brain worked despite the cold. Workhouse. A prison. Debtors' prison. That would explain the guards. And possibly that fence he had seen.

A woman hurried out of the darkness with a teakettle. One of the guards tried to stop her, but she dodged him and threw the contents of the kettle into the blasting wall of flames.

She slipped and slid her way back to find more water.

Peers cursed and nodded at a neighboring stable.

One guard swatted a blanket at the fire. Another stepped toward it and spit.

Inside the burning stable, a horse screamed.

"We must do something," Tom said. "Quickly."

"Most of the water is frozen," Peers said. "We must wait for the engines to arrive."

The woman was back with the teakettle. No one tried to stop her.

Another horse screamed.

Tom stepped forward, passing the woman as she ran back for more water.

"What are you doing?" Peers yelled.

Tom kept walking toward the blaze, but he pointed at a neighboring stable. "Get the horses out of there before it catches fire, too."

From icy cold, he stepped into hellish heat. He held up his right arm, as though that could protect him from the smoke and flames, moved to the side. Hearing raw cries from more horses, he sprinted. Smoke stung his eyes. The fire roared at the entrance to the stable, turning the night into midday. He moved to the side, past the flames and smoke, looked up, saw the opening. He spotted what must be a pulley, probably to bring hay or feed to the loft. No rope or chain. No luck. Smoke belched out of the opening, but not yet flames. But where was a ladder?

Hearing the screaming horses behind the wooden walls, Tom gritted his teeth. Those horses would die hellish deaths. Then he saw another one of those guards carrying one of those ugly sticks.

"You there."

The big man, with a thick mustache, looked stronger than many mules Tom had owned. When he stopped, Tom pointed. "I need a boost up there."

"Huh?"

*Dumb as some of those mules, too.*

230

"Get me up there." Tom pointed.

"You're loco."

Maybe he wasn't so dumb after all.

"Just get me up there. It is the only chance we have at saving those horses inside."

"Who cares about dumb horses?"

The haunting cries of the horses must have gotten to the big man, too.

"I can get an ax," he cried out.

"After you get me up there."

The wood felt hot against his hands, as the behemoth grunted, cursed, groaned, and eased Tom, boots pressing down on the guard's shoulders. He heard the strained voice say, "You weigh more than a mountain of gold."

An oath almost slipped from Tom's mouth. He should have removed the money belt. No, that would have taken too much time. He raised his hands upward.

"Can . . . you . . . ?" Sweating now, and Tom had removed his coat. "Tiptoes?"

The guard swore savagely this time, but Tom felt himself rise another few inches.

"Wall . . . hot," the man moaned. "Can't hold . . . much."

Tom managed to get his right forearm on the loft's flooring. His left hand shot up, and a second later, Tom realized he was dangling. The guard had slipped or fallen backward. Tom used his arms to pull himself up. He sucked in a breath and immediately coughed. Smoke filled his lungs. Burned his eyes.

*Just drop down to the ground. You tried your best.*

Horses screamed. Their pounding hooves shook the stable.

*Bloody idiot. The building is shaking because it's about to collapse.*

Then he was coughing. Somehow he had managed to pull himself into the loft. Smoke blinded him. He rolled over. And dropped through an opening that was much closer than where he would have put it.

# CHAPTER 20

He landed on hay, just not a whole lot of it. Coughing, cringing, rolling over, he tried to blink sight back into his eyes. Pressed his hands against dung and straw, pushed himself up, surprised he could still breathe. Smoke churned above him now. But flames whipped closer.

Crouching, he crooked his arm over his mouth and nose, and moved to the first stall. A horse—color and sex indeterminable—crashed at the hard wood with its forelegs. Tom saw the latch, a steel bar holding the gate closed. He gripped it, screamed from the burning iron. Whipped off the scarf he thought he would need to keep from choking on smoke. Used the wool as a mitten. The bar came out, dropped, hissing onto the ground. He barely stepped aside before the horse bolted, crashed into the far stalls, fell on its side, righted itself, and ran to the fire, then galloped off to the far wall.

Tom moved to the next stall, empty, crossed the barn—dodging the horse that ran to the inferno, then away from it—used the scarf to unlock this gate, releasing a pale horse.

He did not remember much else, until he led a big draft animal, maybe seventeen hands, deep-necked, short legs. He must have found a rope, because he used it to pull the giant red roan to the wall. Turning the horse around, he stared ahead at the blinding fire. The small patch of hay that had moderately broken his fall from the loft was gone. Flames leaped toward the horses he had freed. And himself.

Something slammed into the outer wall. The planks thumped. He could scarcely hear over the roaring flames, but a thud sounded again. Maybe that ugly guard had found an ax. Tom sure hoped so. A wall of hell blocked the stable's only entrance.

But a wolf pelt hung on the rear wall. That might help. He backed the bay toward it, and howled. He tried again. The red roan remained shockingly calm, and Tom suddenly knew why. The draft horse was blind. The thump of the ax whacked nearby. Tom removed the lead rope, hurried to the rear, tied the rope below the horse's thick right fetlock, rose, and jerked the rope. Once. Twice. He coughed, spat out the foul taste of smoke and death, pulled the rope again. This time, the big horse kicked, the hoof landing just underneath the pelt. The leg came down, and Tom pulled the rope again. The red roan responded, with both legs this time, maybe now sensing the panic of the other stampeding horses. Both rear legs slammed into the wall. Then again. On the third time, the board loosened.

He watched the smoke shooting up through

the opening in the loft. Flames drew closer to him. Another horse slammed into the wall. Tom let the red roan kick once more, loosening another board. Then Tom stumbled toward it. He saw rough hands grabbing the planks from the outside.

Suddenly a man's head appeared, then his hands, holding . . . a large rope.

"There's a . . ." It was Peers. The superintendent coughed. Pointed. "Hole. Knot hole. Push the—" The man cursed. "Rope through it." He disappeared, but Tom understood the plan. He moved along the wall, stopped while one of the wild horses rammed into it, spun, and raced back toward the fire. The red roan kept kicking, too. Tom found the hole. He tugged more rope. Reached up, began trying to thread the rope through that hole. Someone must have taken hold of it and jerked, because Tom realized he was on his knees, shaking his hands, looking at the ripped fingers of his gloves. Had he been gloveless, the rope probably would have sawed off his fingers.

Behind the wall, someone yelled, but roaring flames consumed the words.

He coughed again. Then something caught his attention. In another stall. On the far side. A movement between the slats. Closer to the fast-moving wall of hell. Tom ran right for it—just as the back walls, like Jericho, were ripped down.

That sucked heat and flame and smoke past Tom, who dived, hit the ground hard. But it was cooler down here, and he could breathe.

Even in this maelstrom, he recognized the sound from the stall. He came to his knees. There was no bolt locking the gate, but the metal burned his fingers again. The gate swung open, and Tom fell in.

He laughed when he came to his knees. Walked on those knees, bent down, and lifted the struggling animal in his arms.

"I stand corrected," he heard Washington Malone say in the freezing night. Malone must have willed away his rheumatism to help fight the conflagration. It was the last thing Tom recalled. Or maybe he just dreamed it.

"I thought you were bringing out a calf. Never figured you'd risk a fiery death to save a sick filly."

Superintendent Peers brought Tom and Malone to the Planters' House and instructed the staff that the city would foot the bill for as long as both men desired to stay in St. Louis. Ten horses had been saved, eight of which belonged to the city, and one owned by Peers.

Most newspapers and hotel employees blamed the fire on prisoners from the workhouse. A few pontificated that sparks from the *Jean McKee* landed in the hay, but those theories were denounced, and Tom concurred. The wind had been blowing from the northwest.

"The *Daily Missouri Democrat*," Tom said from the couch in the suite, "is filled with advertisements for steamboat insurance. And news of all sorts of fires. I find it a miracle that this city is not rubble and ash. And they list the names of hotel arrivals. My goodness, I never knew of a city with so many hotels. City Hotel. American. Virginia." His eyes found Malone. "How far away are we from the state of Virginia?"

"It could be a woman's name," Malone said, and returned to sipping his brandy.

Tom nodded. He had not considered that. There was a Missouri Hotel, the United States Hotel, and the Monroe House. And, of course, the Planters' House. He read the names of the new arrivals, but found no Malone, nor a Ponting.

They rested for three days, when Tom could bend his fingers without grinding his teeth, when the blisters on his palms had burst and the wrappings no longer stung, when he could breathe and not feel like he was sticking his head down the stack of those steamboats waiting out the winter in the Mississippi.

When Tom and Malone walked down the stairs to the lobby of the Planters' House, workhouse Superintendent Peers was waiting. He barked some rough name that Tom could not catch, and a thin man of color stepped from the entryway, hat in hand, eyes staring at the rug.

"Off to Wiles's stables," Peers ordered. "Fetch their horses." He waved toward Tom and Malone. "Tell Peter to bill the mayor. And don't you dare tarry. These gentlemen have a long way to travel yet." He looked back at Tom. "You sure you don't want to stay another night?"

Tom grinned. "It is a long way to Texas, sir."

"Well, fine. But you might take a bit of advice, my fine Illinois comrades." Moving closer, Peers lowered his voice. "T. J. Albright is a friend of mine. Has a shop on Chestnut Street. You cannot miss it. Look for the gilded gun on the roof. T. J. says he has more than five thousand guns—shotguns, rifles, pistols. I believe that is no falsehood." His voice dropped another octave. "Boys, carrying iron is a good idea in this state."

"Thank you," Tom said softly, "but we—"

"If you don't want to go to Albright's, Dimick has a fine shop on Main Street." He pointed out the door. "Army rifles and Army muskets. And Colt's and Allen's revolvers. I fancy Colt's newest models myself."

"We have made it this far," Tom said. "Neither Washington nor I have much of an aim, and, well, we have had no need of muskets and the like. The people we have met have been incredibly generous, though none as unstinting as you."

The superintendent shook his head. "Thieves in

this city will cut your throat for the buttons on your coat, boys. And the road to Springfield is filled with demons and dangers."

Tom glanced at Malone, who shrugged and smiled at Peers. "I would likely shoot my foot off with a revolving pistol."

"There are men who would shoot your head off." He sighed. "But, this is your own choice. I made my plea. And I shall pray for your deliverance." He moved toward the desk counter. "Allow me to settle your accounts, and I shall meet you out of doors."

"Washington and I would gladly pay—"

"Nonsense." Peers cut Tom off. "As I said, the city of St. Louis is paying for everything. And the money you save here will come in handy at your funeral."

The last part did not sound like a joke.

Malone grabbed his saddlebags, and Tom, throwing his bags over his left shoulder, followed his partner out the door and onto the bustling sidewalk.

The air had warmed, though the skies looked threatening. Or maybe that was smoke from the steamboats, though Tom doubted if the river's ice had thawed enough for any ship to move.

He spied the man of color leading the roan and chestnut down Fourth Street, and Tom reached into his trousers pocket, found a one-cent piece, and stepped onto the street. Malone followed, taking the reins to the chestnut. Tom accepted the roan's reins and held out the penny, wondering if that was an insult as a tip in a city like St. Louis.

"What in heaven's name do you think you are doing?"

The Negro stepped back with a gasp, and Tom turned to see Peers charging, raising a walking cane in his right hand. The poor man who had brought the horses from the stable dropped to his knees in the filthy street, and covered his head and neck with his arms and hands. "Please," he begged. "Please."

Comprehension sickened Tom. He stepped in front, blocking Peers, whose eyes reflected a savagery Tom had never seen.

"It is my fault, sir," Tom heard himself saying. "I thought he was an orderly, a porter, an employee of the Planters' House. I did not know . . ."

His words faded. His heart skipped. His stomach almost turned over.

". . . that he was . . . *yours*."

The workhouse superintendent's eyes slowly focused. The red of his cheeks began to fade. His breathing remained hoarse, but the quirt slowly lowered until the leather tip touched the boardwalk.

Men and women stopped on the boardwalk, waiting. Behind Tom, the . . . *slave* . . . sobbed and begged for mercy.

A moment later, Peers howled with delight.

"An orderly. Or a porter." The cane popped against the hitch rail. "By thunder, Ponting, you are a foreigner indeed. Ha." He stepped to the side, and touched the slave's side with the toe of his boot. "Up, boy. Stand up. And don't sob like your poor ol' mama. Up, I say, or a thrashing you will get that shall leave welts on you for months."

Peers turned, grinning at the penny Tom still held. Then he looked into Tom's face, and the fire returned to his eyes. But he must have fought that down, for he held out his free hand, nodding at the coin.

"May I?" he asked.

Tom glanced at the penny, and let it fall into Peers's palm. The prison official turned, and held it out toward the slave. "Take it, boy. Don't say your good old master Peers never gave you nothing. Take it. Tom Ponting wanted you to have it, so, by God, you shall have it. Like I say, I treat my darkies right."

Union, the next village they would see, lay fifty miles to the west. Tom did not think he and Washington Malone spoke ten words over the day and a half it took them to reach that town.

Next, they camped on the Meramec River, and Tom was glad they did. The limestone hills were heavily wooded, and the river shallow and peaceful. A settler on the road said that the river had some healing powers. Tom wasn't sure

241

he believed the bearded man, but he soaked his hands and feet in the cold water. The hands felt better, but he still did not sleep well.

"It is as though we are in another country," Malone whispered.

*We are.* But Tom kept that thought to himself.

"Will Texas be worse?" Malone asked.

Tom had no answer.

The Gasconade River revived his spirits. The Meramec might have done the same, had the newness, the shock, of what he had seen in St. Louis been more distant. But here on the Gasconade, they saw turkeys. Dozens of them. Feasting on acorns.

"Now I wish I had taken Mr. Peers's advice and bought a shotgun," Malone whispered. "Roasted drumstick would taste fine."

"Not as fine as watching them," Tom said quietly.

# CHAPTER 21

6 Apr 1853
Springfield, Missouri

Dear Miss Margaret Snyder:

I take pen and paper to let you know that Washington Malone and I remain in good health and wish and pray that the same surrounds you and your family.

We arrived in this town—by our estimations 250 miles southwest of Saint Louis—on Monday the 4th, and are having our horses shod, for the road from Saint Louis was very hard and rough. It is a fine town, and I have been told that the population was 500 before "California fever" took a fair number west. Coffee is 12¢/pound; sugar, 10¢. There is talk of building a branch of the Pacific Railroad to this town, but our landlord tells us that there is a better chance of getting a railroad to the sun than to Springfield.

Many slaves we have seen, more here than in Saint Louis, while the latter was a much larger city. It shames me to tell you that on our arrival in Springfield, I saw men and women of color preparing our supper in the kitchen and when the victuals arrived in the dining room, I told our hostess, a Mrs. Harvey, that I would only drink coffee. Our gracious landlady asked if I were not feeling well, and I honestly answered that I just could not eat food cooked and prepared by colored people. Ever gracious and understanding, she escorted me to the kitchen and the quarters where the slaves—six of them, three women, two men—one quite old— and a boy of maybe twelve—lived. Everything appeared neat and clean, and she, Mrs. Harvey, had all of her slaves show me the palms of their hands, which were clean, if rough, and not as dark as their faces and their eyes.

Thinking, I was struck by the truth that while I have seen Negroes in England and America—two, I recollect, worked as sailors on the ship that brought my brother and me to America—I never paid much attention to them. A sad fact, I understand now. I should pay more mind to these discussions and heated debates about abolition and the expansion of the bondage across this new country.

Reluctantly, I ate what was served, but to my surprise, found the food more than satisfactory.

I will confess, however, that I am glad we live in a state without men and women in bondage and servitude.

Never have I much considered this peculiar institution, but never have I seen slaves, and I find it disconcerting that these men, women, and children cannot—or will not—look me in the eye. They speak softly, if they speak at all, and while their masters—is not there but one Master who loves us all?—here in Springfield have generally acted kind to these chattel, it sickens me to say some of these "lords" that I have seen since crossing the Mississippi River and into a slave state believe in the rod and the whip.

I should not trouble you with such sadness, yet I thought you would be one person who might understand what I write, and how it affects my troubled heart, mind, and soul.

Let us move on to cheerful subjects.

We have been told to turn south and ride into Arkansas as to avoid the Indian Nations to the southwest. The road will carry us into Louisiana, and from there we will journey northwest into the state, and formerly Republic, of Texas. The man who informed us of this route is named Marney. That is the only name he has given us, and our landlady told us that in these western regions, it is impolite to inquire any man's name. This Marney, however, is herding one hundred mules to Shreve Town, which he says is now called Shreveport but he likes Shreve Town better, and is in Louisiana on the Red River. He has extended the invitation that we travel with him, where, upon reaching Shreve Town or Shreveport, we may follow the Red River northwest and into Texas, where we should find plenty of Texas cattle around a place known as Honey Grove. He is an amiable man and we have accepted his invitation.

You may, if this be your desire, write me in Springfield, Missouri, as Postmaster Holland says he shall gladly hold our mail until our successful return from Texas. The post office is in a finely constructed, one-room cabin. The mail comes twice a month, on horseback, from Harrion's Store in Little Piney, and has been for 20 years.

I close with you on my mind and in my heart.

Till I see or write you again, I remain

Your obt servant,
Tom C. Ponting

He signed the letter, then closed *An American Dictionary of the English Language* by Noah Webster, published just three years earlier. The only dictionary he had seen in years was at solicitor Donovan Grad's office in Shelbyville. That one was two volumes, but it had been printed in 1841. Mrs. Harvey had allowed him to borrow the big leather book, which must have contained every word known to the world as of 1850. Her husband was a scrivener, and she sometimes taught school. Tom guessed that she was better at that job than Old Lady Hallett. Should he be successful in this venture, he vowed to buy a dictionary for himself. One volume would be enough. He did not need to know all of those words. But on the other hand, if he could get a really good price for those Texas cattle . . . a two-volume version would be fine.

After addressing the envelope and sealing it with wax from the candle, Tom rose from the table, found his hat, and left the cabin, where he groaned, realizing all the information he had left out of the letter.

He wanted to tell Margaret how four bits and sometimes two was all two men needed to spend for lodging, and that price included not only meals, but even feed for the horses.

He had left out details of their crossing the white, treacherous, bitterly cold, and mostly frozen Mississippi River, and wondered how his adventures compared to that Manitoba wave everyone in Shelby and Christian counties, Illinois, remembered—even those who were not around back in 1836.

The turkeys on the Gasconade River—how beautiful they looked, and how that feast of acorns reminded him of picking nuts in the woods off the lane with her.

Well, he could include those in another letter. Surely, Shreveport or Shreve Town or whatever it was called, had a post office.

He saw the roan and the chestnut lounging in the corral, crossed the street, then walked down the alley between two cabins, let a mule-drawn cart pass, and crossed the next street, or what Springfield called a street, and entered the post office.

After a fine chat with the postmaster, Tom stopped at Law's store. He desired to present the Harveys with a present for their hospitality.

The man with the bushy mustache that Tom presumed was Law smiled and said, "You come to the right place, mister."

Tom blinked. The man did not even know why Tom had entered this particular establishment.

"That shirt is done for."

Tom looked down at the woolen shirt. It seemed fine. He had another shirt in the saddlebags back at the Harvey cabin, but he had been wearing this one for only two weeks. When it got too filthy, he would wash it in a stream and let it dry, and wear the spare shirt for two or three weeks. Nor did this shirt stink, for Tom had bathed upon arriving in Springfield, and before that, he had soaked in the Meramec.

"Got cotton drills and woolens, Swiss muslins, bed tickin's. Got blue denims, Scotch plaids, checked tweeds. Got striped duck and black tabby velvets. Fine linseys and Georgia stripes. Got the most varied and richest hues you'll find west of Saint Louis. I got—"

The noise outside stopped him. The shopkeeper frowned, stepped around the counter, and headed to the window. Tom made out a foul curse. A woman shrieked. Someone cried out, "God save us!" The shopkeeper moved back to his counter, ducked below it, and came up with a heavy revolving pistol. Tom stepped outside.

Eight men, and two women, marched down the street. Three men, and one woman, carried torches—although the sun shone bright overhead on a cloudless day. Four men, and the other woman, held shotguns. The last man waved a revolver in his right hand and swung a Bible in his left.

One man, clean shaven with long white hair that hung to his shoulders, stood in the center of the street, facing the approaching mob.

The door behind Tom squeaked, the merchant swore softly, then called out: "Doc, you best get off the street. That's one fierce bunch."

The white-headed man nodded, but he cupped his hands over his mouth and yelled, "There is no need—"

A stout man with a torch in his left hand bent without breaking stride, came up with a rock in his right and hurled it toward the doc, though the stone sailed wide to the right and well over the old man's head.

Doc did not blink. "There is no need for this," he repeated.

"What's going on, Doc?" Law, the merchant, asked.

"Smallpox," the old man whispered. "At the Millers' place."

"Gawd," Law said.

Only ten people. Tom had seen larger gangs formed after word of smallpox hit communities—on both sides of the Atlantic.

Tom turned to the merchant and asked in a whisper: "Where is the local constable?"

Whispered Law: "He's the one that throwed the rock at Doc's head."

The eight men and two women kept walking. Doc just stood there, trying again with "There is no need for this." When that did not work, he yelled, "Stop, you lunatics. Stop and listen to me."

The rock-throwing constable stepped out to the front of the line, yelled something over his shoulder, but to Tom's surprise, the rest of the mob halted, though one of the men raised a shotgun to his shoulder and pointed the long barrel at the doctor.

"We got to burn the Millers out," the constable said. "You know that."

"Burn the Millers, too, you mean," Doc said calmly.

"It's them or us, Doc. You know there ain't nothin' to be done ag'in' the pox."

"I know they are sick, a good farmer, his wife— who carries a child—and two children. But the smallpox is contained. As long as they remain in their home, there is no danger of it spreading. This is the only case we know of. No one else has shown symptoms. It is *contained*."

One of the woman shouted a profanity.

"My Homer died of the pox," she told him. "It ain't killin' me, too. Or my kids."

"They'll die if they don't get care. Food. Mostly water. And—"

"We'll burn 'em out," one of the men yelled.

"No one survives the pox, Doc," the constable said. "You know that."

That's when Tom stepped into the street. Even Doc turned toward him. So did shotguns and the revolver.

"I survived smallpox," Tom said calmly.

Angela, the fierce woman, blinked. Her mouth hung open.

Tom looked at the woman. "Did not you

survive the disease when it also struck your late husband?"

"'Course I did. I'm here, ain't I?" Her voice became a whisper. Then she straightened, put her hands on her hips, and said, "The Lord spared me. Because I am a fine Christian woman. He took Homer on account of Homer's sinful ways."

"Burn 'em out," shouted one of the torch carriers. "Burn 'em to hell."

"Homer died because of the fever," Doc said.

"He died because he face was et up with scabs," the widow said. "Because he wasn't holy enough. And because he et too many peppers."

"The Millers need someone to care for them. That's all," Doc said. "They have a good chance—"

"There ain't nobody fool enough to care for those unlucky folks," another man bellowed. "We got to burn 'em out afore—"

"I'll look after them." Tom walked in front of the doctor, then turned, maybe ten yards from the woman and constable, fifteen yards from the eight others.

"Step closer," Tom said, bringing both hands to the close-cropped whiskers on his cheeks and the thicker beard on his chin. "The scars remain. I was just a boy in England. I survived." He swallowed. "Lloyd Dickens probably brought the pox to me. Lloyd survived, too." Now, he took a bigger gamble. "The pockmarks are easier to find on the backs of my shoulders, but I can show you those if you are curious."

"You're a freak," called the man with the pistol.

No one asked to see the scars on his back. That relieved Tom. He would have had a hard time explaining the suspenders holding up the belt.

"I read," the merchant said, "that one tablespoon of yeast, a good brewer's yeast, mixed with two tablespoons of cold water, taken three to four times, will cure the smallpox in an adult. Lesser quantities should go to kids." He made a slight gesture. "I got some yeast."

Ignoring him, Tom asked the doctor: "Do you have vaccinations?"

"No," the doctor whispered. "And even if I had them, convincing these folks to have cowpox injected into them would likely lead to me being burned as a warlock."

"Doc," said the woman who had not spoken. "We got our own families to protect. We got—"

"Sure," Doc said. "I know that. So you go right on, burn down the Millers' cabin. Then you tell Leo, Alice, and Jedediah Junior why Samantha and Lois aren't in school anymore."

"I drunk red wine and ate old bark," another torch holder called out. "Cured me." He sounded drunk. Probably was.

The man appeared to pout when nobody

commented on his information. Maybe because Doc's words had finally reached something inside the Millers' neighbors.

Tom turned to the doctor. "What all do I need to do?" he asked.

# CHAPTER 22

He burned the shirt two days later, but Law gifted him a new one, even britches and unmentionables, and Tom was glad to have them. He soaked himself in Wilson's Creek, let the sun dry himself before he pulled on the new undershirt, and then that gut- and shoulder-bruising money belt and suspenders, and finally slipped the blue shirt over his head.

"You done us a favor, Ponting," Doc told Tom back in Springfield. "More than a blessing."

"Balderdash," Tom said.

"Well, folks aren't scared as much of the smallpox."

They shook hands, Tom thanked Law, grabbed the horn, let his foot find the stirrup, and pulled himself wearily into the saddle. Across the street, Washington Malone waited on the chestnut. Tom waved to the doctor and the merchant before turning the horse to his partner.

"I figured they would give you a parade out of town."

Malone sounded and looked serious, but Tom chuckled. "More likely they wanted to parade me out of town on a rail."

"You did good work."

His head shook. "I just sat with some sick folks,

gave them food and water, medicine, kept their spirits up, read to the little ones, which must have been torture seeing how slow I read. That doctor— and the Lord—they deserve the credit. But I am surely sorry, partner. Surely sorry indeed."

"About what?" Malone genuinely looked surprised.

"About Marney," he said. "We had an escort all the way to the Red River. A man who knows the trails and the country. And a man with a hundred mules."

Malone laughed. "Still have them. He's camped south of town."

Tom waited for the joke, but Malone clucked his tongue and kicked the chestnut into a walk.

"He thinks you're a doctor," Malone called back. "And he has all sorts of ailments he would like you to look at."

Marney said he was older than Methuselah, and he looked it. Smelled like he had not bathed since he had been born, either. He had a bruise on his thumb he said wouldn't heal, and asked Tom if he could do something about this crooked thumb. While Tom was of little help with those ailments, he did say that hot tea with honey in the morning might help that hacking cough, and it did, though Marney added more whiskey from a jug than honey.

A big man with silver hair, balding at the top,

and a dropping, brushy mustache that had rarely seen scissors or comb, Marney dressed in greasy buckskins and wore a hat made from a mangy coyote. Every fourth word uttered while herding the string of mules came out as a bellowing profanity, but in camp, Tom was glad they rode with him.

He sat in a saddle as though he had been born to it, and did most of the work pushing the many mules on the narrow trails.

"I always found mules to be stubborn," Tom said one morning as he rode alongside Marney at the rear of the drove while Malone, far ahead, led the way.

Marney spit out tobacco juice. "Naw. Not as muleheaded as me no how."

"They herd easier than cattle," Tom said.

Marney laughed. "Well, they probably knows that most folks ain't all that fond of eatin' mule meat. Cows ain't stupid."

Tom chuckled. "I guess I never thought about that."

The country, like much of the land they had traveled from St. Louis to Springfield, was steep, thick with woods, and hardly any settlers. They journeyed south and easterly, and the air warmed, so much that Tom and Malone changed their flannel shirts to cotton.

"How would we get cattle up this trail?" Tom asked over coffee one evening.

"How many head?" Marney asked.

"Seven hundred."

Tobacco juice sizzled in the fire. Marney wiped where Tom reckoned his lips to be with the buckskin sleeve, laughed, and shook his head.

"You won't." He gently pressed two dirty fingers on his left hand against his stubbled right cheek, sniffed, and worked the tobacco in the left side of his face. "You sure you ain't got no whiskey?"

Tom's head shook. "Coffee or tea?"

"Them don't do no good for no toothache." He shrugged, spit again, and this time coughed out a big glob of brown tobacco that he flicked into the fire. He spit again, wiped his mouth, and said, "I grain the mules. Just enough so they don't look like skeletons and I can sell 'em in Shreve Town. But you can't grain no seven hundred head of cows. And there just ain't enough graze in these hills. But you'll be in Texas. Just take 'em north across the Red."

"But that is Indian country," Malone said.

"Don't I know it. Had to go through it when I went to Californy in '50. Come back with money, and like a dad-burned fool, I spent it all on mules. But there's a military road—"

"Are there soldiers?" Malone interrupted.

"Yeah. Fort Gibson anyhow. But 'em Indians in the Nations is mostly peaceable. Pay 'em a beef or two, or a calf that gets birthed and ain't likely to keep up."

"Pay an Indian?" Malone sounded shocked.

"It's their land, ain't it?" He laughed, touched the cheek again, and spit into the fire. "Well, land we give 'em after we took what was theirs."

"Pay a toll, you mean," Tom said, nodding in approval.

"Uh-huh. There's enough graze in that country—unless you gets a prairie fire—that can feed that many cows. Be friendly—be right—to 'em injuns, they'll be right by you. Cherokees up north. Cricks 'n' Choctaws down south. Them's the tribes you'd run into. After that, you get into Kansas Territory for a bit, clip right across it, and find the road to Saint Louey."

A mule brayed. Marney brayed back, cursed, and told the mule to shut up.

"Where is it you say you be takin' 'em cows to?"

"New York," Tom said. "The city of New York."

He nodded slightly. "Heard tell of it." He leaned forward. "Now, I been talkin' 'bout 'em Civilized Tribes. But I best warn you that Comanch', and Kiowa, they roam around 'em parts, too. Some of 'em can be friendly if they feel generous. Not always. Fact, hardly ever. They might ask for a cow or two to let you pass, too. Give' em what they want, just don't give 'em all that they want. Do that, they'll think you is yellow. Besides, they had that land first, too. They's all honorable people, no matter what soldier boys, fool gov'nors and congressmen says. But give 'em somethin'. Or they take it anyway, take your hair, too. Good chance they'll do that anyhow."

On the Buffalo River, Marney asked, "What will you be doin' for vittles?" He snorted, cringing at the pain it caused in that tooth in his upper right side, settled that down with a snort from his jug, and added: "Don't reckon you'll be eatin' beefsteaks."

Tom smiled. "I don't reckon," he said, then answered: "We know that paying for meals the way we have been doing shall not be efficient."

"Won't be possible in most places, on account there won't be nobody to take no payment or cook you no breakfast."

Nodding, Tom said, "We shall hire a cook."

"Reckon that's smart. I ought to have hired a cook."

Tom shook his head. He had been cooking breakfast and supper since they had left Springfield.

"Seven hundred cows." Marney frowned. "I can handle a hundred mules. When they ain't bein' ornery. Can you handle seven hundred cows?"

"We shall hire an extra drover or two."

Marney studied on that till the South Fork of the Little Red, where he told them: "I'd hire me more than two."

"Two what?" Malone asked.

"Drovers," Marney answered.

It took Tom a moment to recall the previous conversation. "Washington and I delivered cattle successfully to Chicago and Milwaukee assisted by only—"

"Tame critters," Marney interjected. "I been to Illinois. Cows up that way be tamer than a baby kitty cat. Ever seen a longhorn?"

Silence provided the answer.

"And you might need some extra gun hands with you."

"You said that the Cherokees—"

"I know what I said, but I ain't talkin' 'bout no civilized injuns. Or uncivilized injuns. I taken this here path south out of Springfield on account that I have traveled through 'em hills betwixt Springfield and the Injun Nations. For a good reason. The ruffians that live in that country, they's meaner than a stepped-on rattlesnake or a hydrophoby wolf."

They did not talk much until they ferried across the Arkansas River in Little Rock, and turned southeast. The rains came then, slow, steady, cold, and a heavy frost chilled them as they rode. They stopped in Washington, where a blacksmith put new shoes on the chestnut and roan, while Marney went to refill his jug with corn liquor, and got in a fight that broke off part of the tooth he had been favoring since leaving Springfield.

Tom paid the fine—a dollar plus court costs—and asked about a dentist. "Try Shreveport," the constable told him. Tom bought another jug of liquor from a man in a barn, they gathered the mules, and moved on.

When they reached Fulton, Marney stopped the mules and pointed to the black smoke belching from steamboats on the Red River. He stepped off his horse, and Tom and Malone followed suit.

Marney spoke softer now. "Boys, ain't no need in y'all followin' me all the way to Shreve Town." He pointed toward the road that led to the bustling little city. "That's Fulton. Louisiana ain't far south from here. And Shreve Town ain't that far, neither, and 'em mules is trail broke. I've herded more mules in my day, so this, I reckon, is where we ought to part ways, though I'll shorely miss you two boys."

"I thought we were to cross the Red River at Shrevepor—Shreve Town," Tom said.

"Might as well cross 'er here." Pain flashed in his eyes with every syllable. "I mean you two boys might as well swim 'er."

"I can pull that tooth," Tom offered.

"You ain't pullin' no tooth of mine. Ain't got that many left. This one stays. It's a good tooth. What's left of it anyhow." He found his jug of liquor and took a healthy swallow. Nodding at the clouds over the town, he continued. "Water's risin'. There's a ferry here, but you boys can swim her all right, not have to pay no fee. Wait till we get to Shreve Town, and you'll be payin' Shreve Town prices—and they gots a new operator on that ferry, and he wants to be richer than your king."

"Queen," Tom corrected.

Marney must not have heard. "Ask me, all 'em ferryboat captains, they ain't nothin' but pirates. River pirates. And look at 'em big boats, burpin' all that smoke up on the river. That was one thing I'll say that I surely did love whilst I was forty-ninerin' myself 'cross the west to get to 'em Californy gold fields. Weren't no black smoke. Not much of rivers, actually. Hardly no people till we hit the gold camps. Real pretty country. Not enough people out there to ruint it like they done here."

Tom reached into the coat pocket and withdrew a scarf. He walked up to the behemoth, looked up at him, and smiled. "Take off your hat, sir."

When the man did, Tom reached up and wrapped the scarf over his head, tying it beneath the chin, carefully adjusting it so that it fit over the busted tooth. "That should help a bit," he said, and stepped back.

To his surprise, Marney reached over and pulled him into a choking bear hug.

"You been the best pards I ever knowed," Marney said, releasing Tom so brusquely he almost tripped and fell. The man staggered over to Malone—causing the chestnut to shy away, leaving leather burns on Malone's left hand as he dropped the reins, and Marney crushed the Mason in a clenching hug.

"You 'specially," Marney told Malone. "You got the most gentlemanly nature in a man I ever seen. You is the picture of a real gentleman, a pard for certain sure. I ain't never gonna forget you."

When he turned back, Tom saw tears in the big man's eyes.

"Won't forget none of y'all. Best pards, I ever had." He wiped his eyes, readjusted the scarf, and held out his right hand. Reluctantly, Tom let Marney's paw swallow his, and shake it hard. Again, Marney wiped his eyes, found the reins to his mount, and whistled at the mules.

Once in the saddle, while Tom tried to shake feeling back into his hand, Marney retied the jug of whiskey to his saddlebag, and nodded at the two drovers.

"I'll tell you boys one more thing that might come in handy. Don't trust no Texian. Lyin' is in their nature. Don't trust nothin' no Texian tells you. Not even a Texian she-male."

"How far is Texas from the river here?" Tom asked.

The big man shrugged. "Ten miles. Fifteen." He pointed. "Once you swims across, just follow'er on the south bank. It's mostly piney woods. Ticks'll suck till you ain't got no blood left in you. There's a trail you'll pick up, lessen you go blind, and that'll bring you to Clarksville. Ain't nothin' there but Methodists, but them's easier to swallow than Baptists. I don't know nothin' 'bout no Honey Grove, but someone there's bound to give you good directions. Likely, it's around Bois D'Arc. Though 'em Texians done renamed that place again. Had changed it to Bloomington or somethin' like that, I don't rightly recollect, and up and decided they ought to call it for one of 'em fools who got kilt at the Alamo. But it ain't Crockett or Bowie."

He whistled at the mules, and rode off.

Tom felt an unexpected sadness as the man and the mules rounded the bend and disappeared.

Malone cleared his throat, and Tom turned.

"What an odd fellow," Malone said. "He calls me one of the best gentlemen he has ever known when I dare say that I hardly spoke a dozen words to him in the nigh two weeks we have been traveling together."

Tom laughed, and eased into the saddle.

"He does not let one get many words into a conversation," Tom said.

Malone mounted the chestnut.

"Do we really swim across this river?" he asked. "It looks treacherously high and vile."

"Mr. Marney gave us much countenance on

the journey ahead," Tom said. "But I side with you, partner. I would like to see Texas and not be swept to the depths of that river. Let us find the ferry and pay the ransom."

# PART III
# 1853

The cattle in Texas have as many claims to our patronage as those of the Attakapas. They are living in a half savage state on broad plains and wide prairies, attaining to great size and strength whilst acquiring such qualities of that fine-grained, tender flesh that feasts the eye of the amateur and enables us to dispense with stalls and stall-fed animals. We have often seen, in the depth of winter, on the beautiful prairies of Western Texas, droves of beeves, each of astonishing size and splendid proportions, in as fine condition and with as glossy hides as any that ever asked the Northern farmer's incessant care. Yet only the nourishment our Texas live stock had before them for months at a time was the short dry stems and diminutive seeds of the winter-blasted musquite grass.

—*The* (New Orleans) *Daily Picayune*,
September 29, 1851

# CHAPTER 23

"We must be in Texas by now," Malone said.

Tom swatted a mosquito bent on whining for eternity outside his left ear. By his reckoning, they had traveled nigh twenty miles since leaving the Red River ferry opposite Fulton. This probably was Texas, but it looked no different from Louisiana. No, Arkansas. They had not made it into Louisiana. He sighed. Another mosquito became fascinated with the back of Tom's neck.

"Tom," Malone said maybe an hour later.

His head shot up. He must have fallen asleep in the saddle. The pines towered above him, behind him, all around him, and Malone trailed him on a road that was nothing more than a deer trail through the forest. Yet as clarity returned, and Tom blinked away the sweat, and wiped his eyes, he saw the man ahead of them, on a dun horse, a long rifle cradled in his arms.

*Maybe,* he thought, *we should have taken Mr. Peers's advice about bringing firearms with us.*

The rider had reined in the dun. Now he lifted his right hand away from the rifle, and held it high.

Tom breathed again. He raised his own hand, and whispered: "Wave. So he knows we are friendly chaps."

"I am. But he does not look friendly."

No, he certainly did not. He resembled a slimmer, dirtier version of Marney, with a black beard that touched the second button of his greasy muslin shirt.

"Howdy." The man lowered his right hand to the saddle horn. The rifle, held by his left hand, rested across his thighs.

"Salutations," Tom said. He let the horse cover a few more yards before stopping. Removing his hat, he wiped the sweat off his forehead. "My, but it is one hot day." He pulled the hat back on.

"Nah." The man had dark eyes. "Don't get hot here till June. Name's Wootton."

"I am Tom C. Ponting." He hooked his thumb behind him. "This is my partner, Washington Malone. We have come to Texas to buy cattle."

"That so." Not a question, but Tom replied:

"Indeed, my good man."

Wootton studied both men long and hard, his jaw shifting right and left as he considered the strangers. "Don't reckon you'd find much beeves in these woods."

Tom grinned, though he did not think the rider had been making a joke. "We come from Christian and Shelby counties in Illinois. We were told that your long-horned cattle could be found in the Red River country near a settlement called Bois D'Arc at one time but has since been renamed."

The bearded face relaxed, the man shifted the rifle casually, and nodded.

"That be Bonham." He tilted his head down the trail he had traveled. "Right long ride from here."

"We have traveled far already."

"Illinois, huh?"

"Indeed, my good man. Have you been there?"

The big head shook. "Hardly even heard of it. But welcome, travelers, to Texas."

He jerked his thumb up the trail.

"Yeah," he said, "there be plenty of beef up yonder way. You'll come out of these woods three miles or so. Find the crick and follow it. That'll take you to White Sulphur Springs. You boys gotta stop there. Finest water there is. Cure all that'll ail you. Even if you ain't ailin'. Now, don't stop at the first two-three places you see. Just ride till you see the big corral, the barn that looks like a tornado whipped through it, more dogs than you can count. Place don't look like much, but that's old Erskine's place. They treat visitors right. And Erskine, he can give you the names of folks you can seek out to buy your beeves. But Bonham, boys, like I done told you, that be a right far piece from here."

"You have been generous with your time and information, Mr. Wootton. We shan't forget you." Tom urged his horse forward, stopped it at the man's side, and extended his hand.

He regretted it, because the man reeked of

grease, sweat, and rancid awfulness, but the shake was brief. Wootton nodded, clucked his tongue, and rode to shake a shocked Malone's hand, and then continued through the forest, letting the woods swallow him.

*A right far piece from here.*

The stranger in the woods had not exaggerated. Tom and Malone quickly learned that stories about the size of Texas were not exaggerations. Two-and-a-half days later, they rode into the settlement, passed the fine cabins until they saw the wind-blown barn, the big corral that held only two horses, and a cabin that looked as though it might have been at the Alamo.

Malone shot Tom a frightened glance, but Tom shrugged. The sun was setting, and they had not slept under a roof in days. About a dozen coon hounds and puppies barked and snapped as they rode up, but they were smart enough to keep a safe distance from the horses, and both roan and chestnut, while wary, tense, and ready to kick if the dogs got too close, were as hot, tired, and as miserable as their riders.

The door opened, and a young woman stepped outside.

Tom swept his hat off. "Ma'am, my name is Tom C. Ponting, and this is my partner, Washington Malone. We hail from Illinois and are bound for Bonham to buy cattle. A fellow wayfarer we met days ago said that we must stop here, for the water is the best to be had, and that you are generous and offer lodging, comfort, and conversation to travelers. For which we shall gladly pay as we would at any hostelry."

She pointed. "Put your horses in the corral yonder."

Jerked her thumb in the opposite direction. "Spring's that way. Hundred and fifty yards or thereabouts."

She cursed the dogs to be quiet.

"My man ain't home," she said. "Will be directly. I'll have fixed our supper by the time you two is settled and soaked. Welcome to stay. Fresh straw on the floor for your soogans."

The door closed. But the dogs had shut up, except for some growls, and now settled in front of the cabin.

Malone eyed Tom with suspicion.

"It should be fine," Tom said without much conviction.

"What is a soogan?" Malone asked.

"My guess is it is our bedroll. Come. Surely, Wootton knew what he was saying and this will be a fine respite."

"Surely," Malone said, but he did not dismount until Tom had done so first.

The water in the springs smelled awful, but Tom felt rejuvenated. He had wrung out his clothes in the water, too, letting them dry on the rocks as he sat to his chin, and let the water soothe most of the pains.

Reluctantly, Washington Malone slipped into the water, too.

"That Wootton," Malone said, "told us the water was for drinking. But I do not think I would care to drink water that smells worse that a fart."

Tom smiled.

"I do not even like bathing here."

A moment later, Malone closed his eyes and smiled.

When they returned to the cabin, the dogs ignored them. Tom spotted another horse, a big bay, in the corral, and guessed that the husband had returned. He knocked on the door, and somehow managed to hide the shock and disgust when a thin, leathery man opened the door.

Tom had seen sore eyes before, but never a case like this. Both eyes were inflamed—how the man managed to see through the redness, or the oozing puss, Tom could not even try to fathom. At least two of the six children in the cabin also suffered from ophthalmia, though not quite as horrible as their father.

The woman—much younger, even thinner than her husband—had clear eyes, but Tom could not fathom how long it had been since she had combed her hair or taken a bath.

The man had no interest in cattle or conversation, but he took fifty cents from Tom and pointed at the straw.

When the woman began cooking supper, the stench from the meat soured Tom's stomach.

"My word," Malone whispered, "that meat has not been cured."

"We shall take our meals outside, if that suits you." Tom forced a smile as he took his plate of some kind of greasy meat, bread that was hard as a rock, and half-cooked beans. "To enjoy the gloaming."

"The what?" the woman asked.

"Evening," Tom translated. "And, well, with your many children, there is not much room inside as it is."

"Suit yourself," the woman said. "I'll have coffee for your breakfast."

The coon hounds had no problem devouring meat, bread, and beans. Tom and Malone drank the stinking water.

"I think," Malone said the next morning as they rode northwest, "that Wootton miscreant sent us to that wretched place as a jest."

Tom shrugged. "And I believe that Mr. Marney warned us about trusting anything we heard from a Texian."

Malone grew weary. He complained about the heat, swearing that this still must be spring but the wind and the sun made him feel as though they traveled toward the gates of hell. Tom, however, felt a newness to this country, and now that the thick piney woods lay behind them, he could see why people flocked here. It was a big land with a massive sky, full of small hills, plenty of water, and grass that could feed hundreds, thousands, perhaps millions of cattle. And the few Texians they met on their travels soon washed away the memories of the family of a severely sore-eyed man and his poor children and unkempt wife.

North to a settlement called Clarksville, then west to a place named Paris. But as they traveled, the heat, the land, and the rheumatism plagued Malone. Tom had to help him out of the saddle, and practically carried him to the door of a cabin in a place known locally as Honey Grove.

A woman answered the door, and immediately pulled it open. "Bring that sick man in here now," she snapped, lacking any trace of the drawl Tom had been hearing since he reached Texas.

"Betsy!" she barked.

Tom turned, and saw the black-skinned woman come through a side door. He drew in a deep breath, holding it, realizing he was seeing another slave. "Get as many quilts as you can, and put them there." She pointed to a fireplace. "Hurry." Malone leaned against Tom's left side, so she rushed to Malone's right.

"What ails him?" she asked.

"He suffers from rheumatism," Tom said.

"Betsy," the woman shouted. "Hurry, please. This poor man's stiff as a board and I can feel his swollen joints just standing next to him."

"I am Missus Clutter," the woman said, bringing Tom a cup of steaming coffee.

"Ponting, Missus Clutter." Tom smiled as he took the cup. "Tom C. Ponting. I come from Christian and Shelby counties in Illinois."

She grinned over her own cup of coffee, and motioned to the chairs around a table. "I would daresay you come from a place farther to the east than Illinois."

Tom let a weary grin crack his face. "Somersetshire, England. But Ohio and Illinois since '47."

She sat across from him. "I was born in Evansville, Indiana," she told him.

He gave her a curious look.

"We are practically neighbors," she said.

"Indeed."

"The man I married brought me to Texas," she said. "What brings you?" She nodded at the sleeping Malone. "And your sickly friend?"

He told her about the cattle. She sipped coffee, and nodded. "That might explain how heavy that little partner of yours is."

Tom swallowed the coffee, set the cup on the table, and looked into her dark eyes. She smiled. He sighed.

"Missus Clutter," he said, and felt relief as he finally told someone the truth. About the cattle. The California coins. The money belts.

"It is a cumbersome business carrying that much money around," he said. "I beg of you not to tell your . . ."

"Her name's Betsy," she said, and shrugged. "That's my husband's doings. He comes from Alabama. We treat her right. Unlike how some people treat theirs."

Tom could think of nothing to say. She smiled again. "You were talking about cattle."

"Could you keep our money belts, Missus Clutter?" he asked. The words rushed out. "Hide them, say, underneath your mattress. Tell no one. Not Betsy. Not even your husband. Keep them safely until I have found the cattle to buy and have need of that money."

"You would trust me, a stranger in this strange land?"

He smiled. "If an Illinois drover by way of Somersetshire could not trust a Hoosier, who could he trust?"

"You have my word. The belts will be safe, and untouched, until your return. And Betsy and I, and John, my husband, will see your partner through this time of peril."

"I thank you. I will pay—"

"You shall pay nothing." Her smile warmed him again. "We have no cattle to sell."

He already felt lighter, and he had not removed the money belt.

She pointed out the window. "You follow that road to the fork. Turn left. You'll come to a . . . well . . . a tavern. Ask for a man named Rusk. He's the man you'll want if you're after cattle."

"Whenever I have found a place where men are drinking whiskey, I have left those places," he told her.

"You're not a drinking man, I take it."

He shrugged. "I learned my lesson years ago."

She sipped coffee. "That's fine. I wish Mr. Clutter and most of the men around Honey Grove did the same. But if you want cattle, and you want a man who can get you that cattle, you'd be wise to call upon C. W. Rusk."

May 15, 1853

My dearest Tom,

This time last week, I wondered if you had reached Texas, if you had bought your cattle, if you were, I prayed, beginning to bring your herd, your dream, but mostly yourself back to your Illinois home.

It is strange to say this, but often I do not miss you. How can I miss you when you are right here? How can I miss you when I see your face, and those eyes that burn with an intensity and a thirst. How can I miss you when you are part of my soul, part of my well-being, part of me? And yet, I do miss you, miss you so much. Mostly I miss your voice, even when I hear it on the wind. If you do not appear tonight in my dreams, you will always be in my thoughts and prayers.

Your dearest love,
Margaret Snyder

# CHAPTER 24

He was reluctant to leave the next morning.

Washington Malone's breathing turned even more ragged, he felt feverish, and Tom had never seen any living man that pale. Rheumatism often plagued Malone, but for the first time since they had known each other, Tom worried that his partner might die.

"We'll look after him," Mrs. Clutter said.

He wanted Malone to wake, just to hear his voice, just to tell him . . . anything. But the man seemed to have trouble just breathing. The door opened, and John Clutter stepped inside.

"Got your horse saddled, Ponting. You think you can find that tavern all right? Be glad to show—"

"You have work to be done here, Husband," Mrs. Clutter informed him.

John Clutter winked, but the grin faded as he nodded at Malone. "Get your business done, Ponting. My woman, she'd put most pill rollers to shame. Your pard will be fine."

Tom found his hat, reached for his coat, but quickly realized he would have no need for it. He spoke his thanks to Mrs. Clutter, shook hands with her husband, and moved to the open door, but stopped, turned, and asked: "Are you sure this Rusk will be at this tavern? It is quite early in the day, is it not?"

"Not for a Texian." John Clutter laughed.

The tavern did not fit the description of those Tom had seen or heard about from England to Illinois, not even those nests of heinousness he had passed in Chicago and wild, rambunctious Missouri. Saddled horses swished their tails in a round pen, while a man in duck trousers and a muslin shirt sat on a stump, drinking from a pewter stein. He stood, wiped foam off his mustache, and stared as Tom eased the roan down the lane.

This nameless public house consisted of three hewed log walls, maybe six feet deep and twelve feet wide. A ripped, dingy canvas tarp hung in the front, with an opening slit toward the left side. It flapped constantly in the wind. Maybe thirty feet off to the west, Tom spotted a still, smoking, the flames hot underneath, with two men of color and a white man with a wild, red beard overseeing the production of the liquor to be served here.

On the eastern side of the log-and-canvas structure, a carcass sat on some sort of spit, roasting the pig over hot coals. Two men squatted around the meat, while another stoked the flames in a nearby pit that provided the coals to cook the pig.

Stopping his horse, clearing his throat, and, remembering the sore-eyed man and his pitiful wife and children, Tom suddenly suspicioned that those good Clutters, like the vagabond Tom and Malone had met in the piney woods, had played Tom for a fool and sent him here as some sort of Texas jest.

No, John Clutter might have found a joke to be in order, but his wife would never have allowed it.

"Salutations, my good man." Forcing a smile, Tom nodded at the man standing in front of the stump. "My name is Tom C. Ponting, a cattle drover from Illinois, and John Clutter, that good chap, said I might find one C. W. Rusk here. I inquire to hire him to assist me in buying some of your fabled Texas longhorns."

The man blinked. Mayhap he was deaf.

Then the aroma reached Tom from the roasting pig. His stomach growled and his mouth watered. He had tasted pork many times, but never had anything smelled this divine.

The man at the stump cleared his throat. Tom forgot about the pig, and studied this wild-looking apparition. Tom waited. The man just blinked. Tom glanced at the opening in the dingy canvas. Looked at the men preoccupied with the still. Stared at the roasting pig. Turned back toward the mute with a pewter stein who tugged on one earlobe.

The man took another sip, lowered the drink, and said, "Say that ag'in."

Tom blinked away confusion. The man waited. "I am seeking—"

"Uh-uh." The man shook his head. "Start with that salutin' stuff. Just exactly the way you spoked it that first time."

His head started to ache. He wanted desperately to massage his temples. "Salutations . . ." he tested.

The man smiled, nodded, and motioned with his free hand for Tom to continue.

He forgot what he had said. "My name is Ponting. Tom Candy Ponting. I seek the countenance . . ." That wasn't the right word. "I come from Illinois." He felt completely flummoxed. "John Clutter." He pointed down the lane. "He said I would find a Mr. Rusk. C. W. Rush. Rusk, I mean. I am in Texas to buy cattle. Malone . . . I mean, Clutter. John Clutter. He told me . . . I am a cattle drover. I was hoping to have an interview with this Mr. Rusk. About buying not an insignificant number of Texas cattle. To drive to . . ."

The man spat, shook his head, and drank more of whatever the stein held. "You said it prettier the first time. Where you hail from, stranger? You sure do talk funny. Funny. But it's real pretty. It ain't Irish. I knowed some Irishmen."

"Why, Tom Ponting hails from Illinois," a voice called from behind the canvas. "Moweaqua, Illinois." A figure in buckskin britches and a

284

yellow-and-white ticking shirt stepped out of the tavern. He wore a battered black felt hat, and Tom saw two holstered guns on his hips, the one on the right butt forward, the one on his left with the butt facing the rear. The revolvers were Dragoons, Tom recognized, weapons meant to be carried in a saddle pommel, not on a man's hips, even a man shaped like a bull.

The man smiled. "Howdy, Ponting. I am C. W. Rusk."

That wasn't the name Tom knew him by. The last time Tom had seen this man had been north of Chicago, when he, favoring his right arm, was helping his outlaw partner toward the shores of Lake Michigan. The beard was gone, the hair no longer slick with grease, but wild and long, however the mustache remained the color of the finest ruby. And the eyes hard, frigid, and blue.

Chew. The Milwaukee bank guard and bandit.

He brought a tin cup to his mouth with his left hand and sipped. "Step down. If you want to talk beef." He turned slightly toward the oaf at the stump. "Whip. Take care of Ponting's horse." He laughed. "Looks like the same nag you was ridin' last time we run into each other. Come on inside, Ponting. We gots some catchin' up to do."

Reluctantly, Tom stepped down from the roan, handed the reins to the man called Whip, and walked to the canvas and log tavern. Chew, or

C. W. Rusk, opened the flap wide with his left hand, and Tom went inside. He found no chairs. No tables. The bar was a long rough plank nailed atop two crates turned on their sides. The back bar was a series of kegs, jugs on the top, except the one on the right. That was another keg, with a spigot plugged into it. Stamped black letters in the center read:

ALHAMBRA & OYSTER SALOON
Indianola, Texas
Stout Porter

But above that, in whitewash, someone had crudely written:

SToID fRom

A tin pail sat behind the bar, filled with water and empty tin cups or pewter steins.

He saw no bartender. In fact, the place was empty. Releasing the flap, Chew stepped to Ponting's side. The empty cup in his right hand now, still at his side, and his left arm wrapped around Tom's waist, the fingers tapping Tom's side. He guided Tom to the bar, released his hold, ducked underneath the plank, and turned around.

"You've lost weight," he said, those blue eyes shining as he nodded at Tom's waist. "What'll you have?"

"Coffee, Chew."

The head shook.

"First, it ain't Chew no more. Since I got back to Texas last fall, I've been C. W. Rusk. It fits me for now. I might keep it for a spell. Second, no coffee."

"Water then."

Chew swore underneath his breath, but took the cup from his right hand, which hardly moved, squatted by the pail, and filled the cup with water. This he set in front of Tom before he turned and went to the kegs. He found a jug, shook it slightly with his left hand, and returned. The right arm still hung at his side.

Noticing this, Chew smiled. "Right arm don't work so good no more. Not after your pard busted my shoulder practically in half."

"Where's *your* partner?" Tom asked. He made himself pick up the cup, held it up as in toast, and took a sip. He expected it to taste soapy, but if that pail served as a washing basin, it lacked soap.

"Powell?" Crew removed the cork with his teeth, spat it onto the bar, but spit too hard and the cork bounced off and landed on the dirt floor. "Dead." He took a sip from the jug, which he placed in front of Tom's tin cup.

"That's too bad."

"Not for me. He was gonna stove in my head." He shrugged. "Done him a favor. Rot set in after

287

you practically cut off all them digits on his right hand. They taken his whole arm off up to here." He motioned at the elbow. "At Fort Smith in Arkansas. He wasn't much good for nothin' except gettin' drunk after that. And a mean drunk he was."

"Well, Chew . . ." Tom made himself sip more water.

"Not Chew. Remember that, Ponting. The name's *C. W. Rusk*." He grinned, those blue eyes sparkling. "Now state your business. Milwaukee get sick of Illinois beef? You gonna drive some mossy horns all the way to Wisconsin?"

"Not Wisconsin," Tom said evenly, finished the water, and turned to look at Chew—rather, C. W. Rusk. "Illinois. Then on to New York City."

C. W. Rusk's eyes did not blink. The jug came back up, but he lowered it before it reached his lips.

"How far was it from your spread in Illinois to Milwaukee?"

He did not see any point to this charade, certain that he would be shot dead as soon as this amusement played out. But as long as he still breathed, he might find an opportunity. After all, C. W. Rusk had only one good arm, and both revolvers remained holstered.

"Roughly three hundred miles, though in all likelihood not quite that far."

"Well, by my reckonin', we rode nigh a

thousand from here to there." This time he took a couple of swallows from the jug. "How far would you guess you come from Illinois to here?"

"Not as far as one thousand," Tom answered. "*By my reckoning,* more than seven hundred miles."

The Texian grinned. "And then how far from your Illinois *hacienda* to the stockyards in New York City?"

He did not know the meaning of *hacienda*, but he still matched the man's smile. "Eight hundred. Nine. Maybe a thousand. It depends on the route we travel."

Rusk whistled between his teeth. "You're talkin' 'bout herdin' Texas longhorns, say, sixteen hundred miles? Maybe more." He shrugged. "Coverin' a lot of country, some of it not exactly peopled with friendly folks."

Tom answered with a smile, but he found the Texian's arithmetic impressive.

"And you ain't drunk?"

"Not in thirteen years."

C. W. Rusk backed away from the bar, eyes still hard on Tom, who turned and stared hard. He would not be shot in the back. He would look death and his killer in the face. To Tom's surprise, the leathery man knelt, picked up the cork with his left hand, and stepped back to the plank. He jammed the cork into the jug, and faced Tom again.

"How many head you plan on takin' to this New York City?"

Tom shrugged. "I desire to have seven hundred, maybe more, in Illinois. Then we shall take as many as we can . . ." He thought. ". . . one hundred and fifty or more on to New York. Or perhaps more. But not all. I should like to test the reception of Texas beef in that city first."

"*If* . . ." Rusk paused for a few seconds. ". . . you can even get them to Illinois." He leaned against the crate and planking. He studied Ponting, and Ponting did not blink as he watched Rusk. "Can that be done?" the Texian asked after a long silence.

Tom laughed. "As far as I know, no one has even attempted to make such a drive . . . yet."

Rusk reached for the jug, but pulled his good arm back. He smoothed his mustache, thinking for several long seconds.

"How many owlhoots you got hired for this job?"

He considered Washington Malone. Then he wondered if his partner were still alive. Tom prayed he was. He studied C. W. Rusk, once a bank guard and brigand called Chew. Still a brigand. But maybe he was something else, too. An adventurer? A dreamer? Or might he just remain that cold and ruthless killer and thief, playing Tom along, like a cat before it grew bored with the mouse.

"I have yet to buy any cattle," he said.

With that, Rusk whirled, strode to the canvas, and held open the flap. "Come on, Ponting," he said, and stepped outside.

He had moved to the side of the tent when Tom exited. After nodding at Tom, Rusk brought his left hand to his mouth and whistled, then waved his good arm at the cookfire. Tom stepped behind him and saw a man rise. Instead of walking the fifty feet or so, the man grabbed the reins to a palomino, swung into a saddle, and galloped the distance, sliding the horse to a stop.

"Ponting," Rusk said. "This here is Santos. But don't let the name fool you. He ain't no saint. Santos, meet Ponting. Tom C. Ponting. He ain't no *vaquero* like you. Calls himself a drover. But he knows beef. And he wants Texas beef. What he don't know, *amigo*, is longhorns. Let's you and me show him some."

"It will be my pleasure." He spoke perfect English with just the trace of a Spaniard. Or was he a Mexican? Santos bowed slightly in the saddle. Spanish or Mexican, he dressed like no one Tom had ever seen. The silk shirt, blue and collarless cotton, was the only plain thing about this Santos. His black hat was wide brimmed, flat crowned, sitting on a dark face that featured a thin nose, the darkest eyes Tom had ever seen, a well-trimmed mustache, and a scar just above the chin that made him appear as he had two sets of smiling lips. A darker blue sash wrapped around his waist, and he wore tight buckskin britches, the color of winter wheat, with long fringed sides, stuck inside tall black boots with the biggest spurs on the heels that Ponting could ever imagine.

Spinning around, Rusk looked until he found Whip, back at his stump, drinking from the pewter stein.

"Whip," he said. "Watch the place. Me and Santos. And even Mr. Tom C. Ponting. We'll be back this evenin'."

Whip nodded. "I like the way that fellow talks," he said. "Talks pretty. Real dandified. Don't let him talk hisself out before y'all get back for supper."

Rusk was already headed to get his horse from pen. "Gather your horse, Ponting." He glanced back with a wide smile underneath the mustache. "You got some learnin' to do this fine day."

# CHAPTER 25

When he somehow managed to climb down off the roan at the round pen near Rusk's tavern, Tom held tightly onto the saddle horn. What was that number of miles he had told Rusk? How far had he and Washington Malone traveled? Seven hundred miles? His thighs felt chafed, his hindquarters raw. Now that he was out of the saddle, he did not expect he would be able to sit in a chair for months. Luckily, he remembered that the tavern had no places for a man to sit.

To his surprise, Rusk and Santos left their horses in the corral and strode not toward the log-and-canvas structure, but toward the cookfires. Again, the smell of pork grabbed Tom's attention. He had not eaten since breakfast at the Clutters' place. His mouth watered. He gambled that he could stand even if he released his grip on the horn.

And he did.

"Come along, Ponting," Rusk called out. "Let's see if this chuck is passable."

They squatted or lounged around the fire, and Tom gently found a patch of thick grass that did not prod the bruises or irritate his chafed flesh. He had been smart enough to bring his whip along with him. Not for striking anyone, but he might need the hard handle to get back to his feet.

Whip bent down with a plate of smoking food and a steaming mug of coffee, and slid both in front of Tom.

"Thanks," Tom said wearily, "Yank."

"Yank!" Whip shot to his feet. "Yank? Do I look like a Yankee?"

Tom lifted his eyes. He had meant no insult. "Yankee," he explained softly. "As in *Yankee Doodle Dandy.*"

"Your voice don't sound so pretty no more, redcoat. I be a native Texian. Born in Georgia. Best remember that." He spit to the side. " 'Yank,' he calls me." Whip must have been talking to himself. "Calls me that again, I'll bust a cap on him, certain sure."

A few men chuckled, but most wolfed down food. Tom dragged the plate to him, hardly looking at his supper, and quickly reaching for the coffee. Suddenly, he felt thankful they were eating outside. Had he gone into that tavern, he might have consumed all of that stolen porter, or what was left of it, and anything in any jug that came within his reach.

After finishing half the coffee, he dragged his plate closer. No forks. No spoons. No knives. But the meat was sliced—no, jerked—in long strips, and the bread was . . . He praised God. It was not cornbread, but biscuits, hot, steaming, and smelling of sourdough. He shoved hot pork into his mouth. And thought he had entered the Kingdom of Heaven.

Rusk came over, squatted beside him, wiping grease and bread crumbs from his mustache with the sleeve of his shirt. He brought two cups with him, and slid one in front of Tom.

"You understand me now?" the Texian drawled.

Tom found the cup, nodding his thanks. He would not have to get up or crawl or drag his body to the big pot of coffee hanging from a tripod over a small fire. "I see what you mean."

"We're talkin' sixteen hundred miles. I've heard tales of men drivin' beeves to the gold camps in California. Never heard of no other drives exceptin' to New Orleans or Shreveport. Heard tell someone taken some beeves to Missouri oncet, but nobody ever told of the details. And Missouri and Louisiana—that ain't no sixteen hundred miles."

Tom blew on the cup.

"Seven hundred head?" Rusk asked.

"At least," Tom said. He found another piece of pork, and chewed on it, feeling saliva and grease roll down his chin and drip onto his shirt, and not caring one bit. "Maybe eight hundred. Depends on what we can buy."

Rusk nodded. "So . . . after what you seen Santos and me do today. You reckon you and your partner—yeah, I know he's with you. Seen it in your eyes. You reckon you two and maybe one more fellow can handle that?"

"I was told that a lead steer . . ."

Rusk laughed. "Yeah, you was told. Well, a good lead steer is mighty important. But let me put that question to you again. Do you reckon you and your pard . . . ?"

Tom wasn't sure how he managed to shake his head.

"Now you're wisin' up." Rusk sipped coffee, swallowed. "How many men did you need to get your cattle to Milwaukee or Chicago?"

"Just Malone and myself, and one, maybe two others."

"And you was herdin' . . . three hundred head?"

"At the most."

"How'd y'all eat?"

"We stopped along the way."

"Well, Ponting, there ain't no places to stop at much along the way. And even longhorns gotta eat. Grass. You need a cook."

"I have already thought of the necessity of hiring a cook. And I know roughly of the trails we must follow. We shall need to go through the Indian Nations, and follow the Military Road while paying tolls in beef or cash to Choctaws and Cherokees. Then we must find the trail to St. Louis. After that we are in Illinois, where I am familiar with the roads—and where there is tall prairie grass and shocked corn to feed our herd."

"If we get there before winter." Rusk sipped coffee. Or was that whiskey in the cup? "If we get there at all. And me and the boys don't eat grass. Let's talk about that cook you know you need. Got one hired?"

Tom shook his head.

"Then that's your job. Get a cook. And make sure he can hitch a team and drive a wagon. Here's mine: I get you a crew to nursemaid seven, eight hundred head. So far there's you and me and your shoulder-bashin' pardner."

*If Washington lives.*

"That makes three. Santos. He'll handle the horses."

"Horses."

Rusk grinned. "Pard, I've seen that roan of yours. You're lookin' at sixteen hundred miles. Maybe two thousand. Who the devil knows? That Illinois hoss you ride, he might be fine for nurse-maidin' farm cows and whatever you're raisin' up yonder. Tame critters. But these are longhorns. They get a notion, they follow that notion. We'll need three horses per rider. Three times four is . . ."

"Twelve." Tom wanted to let this Texian know he was no idiot.

With a nod, Rusk said, "Santos handles the remuda."

Tom guessed that the remuda was a string of extra horses.

"And four men might do it," Rusk continued. "*Might* do it. Handlin' the cattle. If I thought you and your cripplin' pard was good enough. But I ain't rightly sure of that. Maybe I'll have a better notion if you two are still breathin' by the time we get to St. Louis. If any of us is still alive at St. Louis."

Those cold eyes bored into Tom, who reached down and pulled up the last strip of pig meat.

"There's one more item you should take into consideration," Tom said.

Rusk breathed in hard, and let it out with a curse. "Let's have it."

Tom held up the strip of pork.

"We will drive hogs as well as longhorns."

"Hogs?" Rusk flung the rest of the coffee into the crumpled grass. "Are you daft, man?"

"I have been herding hogs with cattle for years."

Rusk stared. Turned, spit, wiped his mouth, and looked back at Ponting. "How many pigs?"

"Three hogs for every two steers has worked satisfactory for me in the past."

Tom waited, wondering if Rusk could figure out that mathematical equation. The Texian was working on it, but Tom already knew the answer.

"That's gotta be more than a thousand pigs," Rusk said.

Tom smiled. "One thousand, one hundred and twenty-five. If we have seven hundred and fifty head of longhorns."

He spat. "How you gonna feed them hogs?"

The smile widened. "The droppings, Mr. Rusk. The droppings."

"Droppings?"

Tom laughed. "Surely you know of droppings. The cattle eat the corn, or in this case, grass. What passes through the cattle, drops to the ground. The hogs pick up the droppings."

"Gol durn." Whip had walked over with the rest of the men. "I heard tell that you Yanks was skinflints, but I never thought you was so cheap you'd try to fatten hogs on the same feed as you fatten up your cattle on."

Rusk stared, mouth open, before his head shook.

"You'll be in charge of the hogs, Whip," Rusk said.

"Now, you wait just a—"

Rusk silenced the man with a hard stare before he turned back to face Tom. "How many men you figure it'll take to handle a thousand hogs? I ain't no pig drover."

"We called them hoggards back in England." Tom touched the scar over his eye, and shook his head, remembering. He saw the hard eyes on him and said: "The hogs generally follow cattle just fine."

"I see. But what I don't see, Ponting, is a thousand hogs to be found in this part of Texas. You might have to adjust that ratio of yours."

When he laughed, those blue eyes brightened. "Might have some hogs that'll be heavier'n gold. Win a pretty ribbon at that Wisconsin Agricultural whatever it was called." He frowned again. "And here's somethin' to know. Cattle drovers ain't particularly fond of herdin' pigs." He spit again. "I might bring along one or two more men. Just to be safe." Turning, he nodded toward the north. "Ain't so worried about cuttin' through the Nations. But Missouri could be ticklish."

He drained the coffee and waited.

Tom said nothing.

"Now let's talk pay," Rusk said.

Tom was ready for that. "Two bits a day."

"Not hardly. Fifty cents for every man I hire. You and that pard of yours, I'm figurin', don't draw no pay. You both get paid off after we sell those miserable beeves—and your fat hogs—and you don't get paid off till me and the boys get paid off. And I draw a dollar a day."

"No," Tom said.

"Then finish your grub and ride off. And best of luck to you, Ponting."

He turned, started walking.

"Seventy-five cents a day for you," Tom said after Rusk had covered twenty-five paces.

Rusk stopped, but did not turn around. "And a twenty-dollar bonus," Tom called out. "If we sell them for more than twenty-five a head in New York City."

"What about my men?" Rusk still stared at the pen.

Tom thought, inhaled, did his calculating, and said, "Thirty cents a day." He smiled at Whip. "For cattle and pig drovers alike."

Only Rusk's head turned. "Like as not, we'll be winterin' somewhere long before we ever see New York City."

"My stock farm. In Christian and Shelby counties."

"Big enough for seven or eight hundred cattle?" He snorted. "And a bunch of stinkin' swine?"

"I have already arranged leases from neighbors."

"All of us hired men still drawin' time?" Rusk asked.

"Cattle and hogs have to be fed and cared for in winter, too," Tom said. "For any of your boys who do not get homesick. If they pull out, I pay them what they are owed and send them home with a handshake and thanks. And a map if one is needed."

Now Rusk turned back and studied Tom.

"I shall draw up a contract by tomorrow morning," Tom said.

Rusk's face never lost that stern, wary look, but he walked over, knelt, and lowered his hand. "Out here, we take a man at his word."

"You will have a contract in addition to my word." But Tom took the hand and liked the hard grip. "A lesson I learned years ago."

"You'll learn more lessons." Rusk stood, now smiling. "Startin' tomorrow."

"I will be here at first light."

"Good." Rusk walked toward the canvas-and-log tavern. "But wear that fancy belt of yourn. The one that kept your guts from gettin' spilt on the road to Chicago." He laughed, and never breaking stride, shouted back: "Unless you'd like me to get your seven hundred head my way. But I won't never be hanged for rustlin' pigs. That's your department." He smiled at Whip. "And Whip's."

May 29, 1853

My dear Tom,

The quilters gathered today, and I assisted Mother. Mrs. Nilsson says her husband has gone to Springfield but she never misses him because he had a likeness made and it sits before her every evening so that she looks at him and sometimes talks to him. She can even hear his voice during those imaginary conversations.

I had to bite my bottom lip not to laugh at that old biddy's ridiculousness. For I need no likeness to talk to you. I need no daguerreotype to see you break into one of your smiles. I close my eyes, and there you are.

302

Sometimes I need not even close my eyes.

Mrs. Nilsson brought the likeness of her Bengt—what strange names some people have; I prefer the solid simplicity of Tom (and I know that is your true name, not Thomas)—with her. I gasped and said, "What a handsome man he is in this likeness, as he is in real life," when what wickedly ran through my mind was: "I would have nightmares if I knew a monster like this was on my night table as I slept."

Mr. Prescott has married. He and Mary Taylor were united three days ago. Father says it is the first wedding in our village's history. Perhaps, I think and do not blush, it shall not be Moweaqua's last.

It is long past bedtime, so allow me to bid you good night, and I guess I shall have to put you out of sight—but I pray you will appear in my dreams.

Good night, sweet Tom, and may God bless you.

Ever yours,
Margaret Snyder

# CHAPTER 26

He wondered if C. W. Rusk had sent him all the way down to Hopkins County as a joke. Forty miles, and he hardly passed a soul. At a cabin, though, two women pointed Tom down a narrow lane, saying he probably would find a Mr. Hart at a cabin about eight miles northwest. At least, they believed that was the man's name. The sisters and the youngest sister's husband had only met him once. They were new to the area, hailed from Louisiana, having crossed the Sabine last fall. The husband was out hunting. No, they didn't own any cattle. Didn't even have a cow. They were going to try farming. They asked if Tom would like some cornbread they had baked two days ago, but Tom declined. Sure was a lovely day, the older one said, wasn't it? The younger one giggled at Tom's accent. The older one told her sister not to be rude, that a man can't help how he talked, and that this stranger sure sounded more educated than the simpleton Sissy had picked for a husband. Sissy told her kid sister that if she took better care of her teeth and thought before she spoke, she might have found a beau in Logansport. They would have talked Tom's ears off, or come to blows, had Tom not explained that he had better find this Mr. Hart. So he had thanked them again, and kicked the roan into a trot before they thought of something else to talk or fight about.

Eight miles later, Tom found a cabin, surrounded by a split-rail fence, a barn, and cleared land. The door opened, and a tall man with a lean face stepped outside. Friendly enough, since he held no weapon. He reminded Tom of Abraham Lincoln.

"Good evening, sir," Tom called out, holding up his right hand. "My name is Tom Ponting. I am buying cattle. I was told to seek out a Mr. Hart. Are you that gentleman?"

"Who'd you say?" Stepping out of the doorway, he spit tobacco juice into the grass. He did not sound like Lawyer Lincoln.

"A Mr. Hart." Tom ground his teeth. He could not recall the man's first name; usually, his memory was excellent.

The head shook. "Don't know him."

Tom sighed. "Might any of your neighbors know of this cattleman?"

"Neighbors." The man spit again, wiped his mouth with the back of his hand, and swore. "Got too many of 'em. When I built this place, had the whole country to myself. Now I got two ol' biddies and another fool down that way." He pointed down the path. "And a family that way"—he pointed to the northeast—"that breeds like rabbits." He shook his head and cursed. "All crammed within twenty miles of me."

Tom grinned, waited for the man to smile at his joke—before realizing it wasn't a joke.

The man waved him toward the cabin. "Step down. Gettin' dark. You rid this far, might as well feed you supper."

He helped the man grind corn on a steel mill. The man fried salt pork, then made a kind of corn pone in the grease, warmed-over coffee that tasted like it was a week old, and that was their supper. He pointed to a bear skin by the fireplace. "That'll be your bed," he said. "See you in the morn."

At daybreak, Tom boiled the coffee, filled his host's cup, and they drank their breakfast before Tom followed the tall man to the barn.

Walking in the morning dew, the man said, "Might it be a Merida Hart that you was inquirin' about?"

Tom's face brightened. "Yes," he said, perhaps too loud for this time of day. "Yes. That is the name. I remember it now."

The farmer stopped, turned, nodding. "That's me. I'm Merida Hart."

"But . . . ?"

The man shrugged. "There ain't no *Misters* in this country, stranger. Don't know no *Mister* Hart. But I am Merida Hart."

Merida Hart wanted too much for the thin longhorns he owned, and Tom rode away.

• • •

Hart caught up with Tom later that morning.

"Follow me, pilgrim," he said. "You want cattle, there's a man you might want to meet."

It was farther than twenty miles.

Bill Coman had plenty of cattle, and his prices were lower than Hart's. Hart didn't seem to care one bit. Coman said he was rich. So rich he didn't need beef to eat. He even served his meals on fine china. Brought out cubes of sugar to drop into tea. And served stale bread and dried beef for supper.

Hart commented as he walked with Tom to the corral. "If that's how the rich eat, I'll stay poor."

Tom smiled, and they waited for Coman to step outside and show them his herd.

He herded twenty-five steers to Honey Grove, left them grazing by a creek, and returned to the Clutter place. Mrs. Clutter opened the door with a broad smile. That lifted Tom's spirits, and when he stepped into the cabin he saw Washington Malone. When Tom dropped his hat and rushed toward his partner, Malone held out his hand and said, "Don't come any closer."

Tom stopped, drew in a deep breath, and waited. Behind him, Mrs. Clutter giggled.

Sitting on the hearth, Malone offered no explanation. He dropped his head onto his chest, and cursed himself, and Washington Malone rarely used oaths.

Turning back to Mrs. Clutter, Tom found the woman now laughing hard. She had to make herself stop, sniff, and straighten. Then she laughed again. "He rode out this morning," Mrs. Clutter finally managed. "He had improved so much, and hearing that you were seeking cattle to buy, John thought that Mr. Malone might be able to find some for sale at the Fentons'. They are beekeepers mostly, but they do have some cattle."

Malone groaned.

"Were you stung?" Tom asked.

"No," Malone shouted. "They invited me into their home. It was awful, Tom. Just awful. There was honey everywhere. It covered the chairs. It covered the table. By thunder, it was in all their children's hair. Now it is all over my hands, my fingers, my boots, my hair, my clothes. As God as my witness, I shall never eat honey again."

Malone set in the tub, filled with hot soapy water, in the barn at the Clutters' place, cringing as he combed his wet—"sweetened," Tom called it—hair. But now the conversation had turned as Tom explained this alliance he had formed.

"With Chew," Malone said flatly. It was not as a question, but the look in his eyes made Tom explain.

Tom nodded. "But do not call him that. His name is now C. W. Rusk. He knows cattle. He knows the country. He knows where we can find cattle to buy."

"Surely you cannot trust that fiend." When Tom seemed to think over that statement, Malone straightened in the tub. "He will murder us and take the cattle for himself—if he gets the chance. You have seen what that villain is capable of."

"You might have reformed him."

"Balderdash." Malone fought down the curses, found the bar of soap and scrubbed his hair with it, let the soap drop into the water, and pointed a suds-covered finger at Tom. "That man is—"

Tom finished the sentence. "A spirituous and base scoundrel." He waited. Malone's lips remained flat. "But I shall state these facts again. He knows cattle. He knows other men who know cattle. He knows this country better than we do. We need him."

"He shall murder the both of us in our sleep," Malone whispered.

Tom smiled. "Not if we even the odds."

Malone looked up, unspeaking.

"I am in charge of hiring the cook. And the pig drovers."

"Pig drovers?" Malone leaned forward. "We never hired pig drovers. The hogs merely followed the cattle."

"True." Tom's head bobbed. "But we aren't in Illinois anymore. We are in Texas, and thus must abide with Texian peculiarities."

• • •

The Clutters brought Malone and Tom to a camp meeting that Sunday, where the sermon was mostly brimstone and the songs out of key. But as hands were shaken, the weather and just exactly what was Governor Bell doing for northern Texas were being discussed, a short woman with blond hair and blue eyes, wearing what had once been a white dress approached Mrs. Clutter. Tom noticed a short man with a hat in his hands, head bowed, who had been standing behind the yellow-haired woman, but Tom was called to join a conversation about how a North Texas spring compared to Illinois's. That took five minutes, and when the conversation returned to the current Texas governor, Tom eased back.

"Mr. Ponting."

Tom turned to see Mrs. Clutter and the blonde.

"This is Aretha Perkins," she said. The woman curtseyed, and Tom removed his hat. Mrs. Clutter nodded to the man who still held his hat and kept his head bowed. "That is her father, Mr. James Byers. They both hail from your neck of the woods."

"Greene County," Aretha Perkins said, before expanding: "Greene County, Illinois."

Tom tried to place it. "Western part of the state," he said without certainty.

"That's right. Two-day ride north of St. Louis. Pa yonder. He'd like to go back home. Pa come up from North Carolina with Ma. Ma died years ago. Then, us bein' Southerners, we moved down to Texas two year back. Pa wants to go back home. Ma's buried there. Me and my husband, Jim Bob, we ain't goin' back. But we hear tell you're headin' north."

Tom and Malone glanced at the man who still had not raised his head, and rarely lifted his gaze.

"Well . . ." Tom thought how he could state with sincerity and kindness that he was herding cattle, not forming a wagon train.

"Pa's a right fine cook." She turned, looking past her father, whispering something that would have offended the preacher and did cause Mrs. Clutter to step back, and then yelled: "Jim Bob. Bring your lazy self over here." A tall man in denim britches and a cotton shirt pulled away from a group of boisterous men in their twenties, slapped a cap over his thick brown hair, and hurried toward Aretha Perkins. "Bring the bacon, you simpleton," she barked. He slid to a stop, turned around, and ran to a canvas sack.

Facing Tom and Malone again, she shook her head apologetically, sighed, and went on: "Pa wants to go with you. I want Pa to go with you. So does Jim Bob. Pa cooks fine. Better than I do."

Tom shot a glance at James Byers, who shuffled his brogans in the grass. The husband arrived, panting, holding the canvas sack.

311

"There's some bacon. Pa cured it. That's one thing we will miss about Pa. He cooks real good."

Malone leaned closer, and whispered, "We do need a cook."

Tom smiled, but kept his eyes on the talking woman, and whispered back, "We need a cook who can handle—"

He stopped, cleared his throat, and when the woman paused for a breath, asked, "What was that you said, ma'am? My apologies. I just don't think I heard you clearly. About the late war in Mexico?"

She did not like the interruption. "Something about the Fourth—"

"The Fourth Illinois. He fought all over with that regiment. Pinned some medal on him at Veracruz. But he traded that for some rotgut whiskey." The last words came out as a shout and she marched over to Tom and Malone, waving a finger. "And that's where you two Yankees got to promise me. He don't get no liquor. You don't give him a sniff of liquor. Not beer. Not wine. Not nothin'. That you got to promise me before I let you take my papa back home." She lowered the finger she had been waving, and took a step back.

"Your terms are acceptable," Ponting told her. "Please introduce us to your father."

With a curt nod, she went to fetch the timid old man.

"We are going to New York," Malone reminded Tom.

"We have to get to Illinois first," Tom said.

He watched the woman, saying something not quite a whisper, but not loud enough for a shout to her father. A familiar aroma reached Tom's nose, and he saw the woman's husband handing a slice of bacon to Malone. Jim Bob broke off another piece and extended his hand toward Tom. "Pa smoked this bacon. Always liked it best of anything he ever cooked for us. Smoked it with maple wood. Try it. Make you think you died and woke up in heaven."

Tom accepted the piece and brought it to his mouth, which already watered. He bit into it. Quickly, he turned and watched the blond woman leading her father toward them. Tom chewed, swallowed, wiped his fingers on the sides of his trousers, started to ask Malone a question, when he quickly turned to Jim Bob.

"I say, sir, but . . . do you have hogs for sale?"

# CHAPTER 27

Santos worked his lariat like a magician while riding the palomino at a lope, hurled a loop over the long rack of horns on this running, twisting, turning steer, wrapped the rope around the saddle horn, and pulled the horse to a sliding stop, jerking the longhorn to the ground. When the animal tried to stand, Santos spurred the horse, pulling the steer to the crackling fire where his brother, a leathery man named Izan, waited.

There, Izan and a lean man called Bounce took charge. Within seconds, the hard-muscled Izan pressed his right knee against the brindle-colored beast's neck, while Bounce pinned the steer's kicking hind feet.

That's when Whip rose from the fire, and brought a long iron rod with a "T" shape at the end. With gloved hands, he pressed the "T" over the animal's showing left hip. The longhorn bellowed. As smoke rose, Tom smelled the burning hide. It was over in seconds. Izan stepped back, removing the rope, while Bounce rolled away from the legs, and Whip grinned at his artistry.

Yes, artistry. Tom marveled over the efficiency. How everyone worked together.

Sitting on his horse, left leg hooked over the horn, while sipping coffee with his good hand,

C. W. Rusk called out to Tom. "Sale brand. You brand your beeves in Illinois?"

"Some do," Tom answered. "There has been talk in the legislature to make it a law."

Rusk nodded. "Every rancher in Texas and Mexico has a brand." He chuckled. "Except that softhearted—and softheaded—Sam Maverick way down near the coast. He don't like to hurt his cattle. Or so I heard." Another rider, Zachary, dragged a new longhorn to the fire. "Sale brand marks it as yours." He nodded at Malone. "Figured a 'T' was easier to make than a 'M.' "

Malone shrugged.

"What is your tally?" Tom called out.

Rusk glanced down at James Byers, who held pen and paper in his hands. The man spoke too softly for Tom to hear over bawling beeves and snorting horses. The wind didn't help much, either.

"Three hundred and four," Rusk called out. "But we ain't much more'n half done." He sipped more coffee before pitching the empty cup into a tin pan. "How many pigs you bought?"

"Thirty-four," Tom answered.

He could see the grinning teeth beneath the man's ruby mustache. "Them's gonna be some real fat porkers eatin' the droppins of seven hundred longhorns. You best get to pig-buyin'."

"I shall," Tom said. "But please do not brand my hogs."

"Ain't gotta worry 'bout that," Whip said. "Don't mind cow dung. But ain't nothin' worser than pig—" A steer being branded bawled.

"That's the Red River." Rusk let the reins drape over the sorrel's neck. "Beyond that, the Indian Nations."

Tom breathed in, looking upstream and downstream, and at last exhaled. "It was not that wide at Fulton, Arkansas."

"Expect not. Likely deeper, though. Wintertime, you can ford it here when it ain't dangersome deep. You'll have to swim a bit right now. Always, you gotta watch for quicksand." He chuckled, spit between his teeth, and turned to Tom. "Can hogs swim?"

He did not answer. "It must be six hundred yards across."

"For the time bein'," Rusk said. This time he pointed northwest. "But if it has been rainin' upstream, well, I have seen this river spread out four miles. Heard tell of it bein' as wide as five or six. Never seen that, but I don't think that's some big windy. We got us right around six hundred head of cattle. You got us a hundred pigs. I know that ain't the ratio you want. So what do you want to do, boss man?"

"In your estimation, do you have enough men?" Tom asked. "I have found no hoggards as of yet."

Rusk grinned. "You got Whip. And if you

316

want to know the truth, I've found it hard myself to hire many men who want to push beef all the way to Illinois, and then maybe on to New York."

Tom counted out loud. "You, Washington, myself. Santos and Izan. Zachary and Bounce."

"Nope. Zach and Bounce said they'd help with roundin' 'em up and gettin' 'em branded." Rusk grinned. "I told 'em what you was payin', figured that started with the gather and all." He swished away a massive fly that became fascinated with his ruby mustache. "They'll draw their time when we've got that done. They got family." He snorted. "Got good sense, too."

Five then. "Whip."

He laughed. "If you count Whip, I reckon that makes six."

"Mr. Byers as our cook."

"Well, you have six hundred head—thanks to that Merida Hart." He nodded in approval. "Good fellow, that Hart. Come in handy. I guess we can wait till you buy the rest of your beef. See if you can add to your drove of pigs, too. Cross the Red then."

"No." Tom's voice was stern. "We cross what we have today."

"Ponting, the men we got figger to be drinkin' and payin' for my rotgut and porter. They won't—"

"We cross today. That's a lesson I shall not

317

forget. When a river can be crossed, you cross it. You don't tarry."

Rusk picked up the reins with his left hand. "If you cross here, you're in the Choctaw Nation. They are what we call civilized, but they are also what I call greedy."

"They have the right to negotiate a proper and fair lease." Tom was already turning around the roan. "And I shall meet their price."

Two of Rusk's hires agreed to mark for the crossing, taking their horses across the Red, finding the best path and marking that by keeping their horses at spots on the far bank.

"Try to keep 'em between Zach and Bounce," Rusk said, pointing. He turned, watching the sun begin to sink. The horse was up to its flanks in the water, and Rusk was maybe fifty feet from the muddy flats on the Texas-side bank. "Whip," Rusk shouted at the leathery cowhand who sat in his saddle at the rear of the herd. "You fall off that horse, you remember, grab the buckskin's tail. If you can't reach 'em, snag ahold the closest steer's tail. But don't try to grab no pig's tail, boy."

Laughing, he whirled the gelding around, spurring it into and through the shallows, and reined in hard in front of Tom and Malone.

Now Rusk grinned. "You boys fall off your horses, that gold'll take you straight to the bottom.

You'll be feedin' catfish." He turned sideways in the saddle and nodded at the Red. "River gets deep two hundred yards in. And the current can be tetchy. And stronger'n Hercules. Take one or both of you all the way to Fulton where you crossed her the first time. Lessen you get hung up in some driftwood. Or quicksand sucks you down." Sighing, he shook his head. "Nasty way to die. Many a man has just disappeared in these cold waters. No grave. No marker. No nothin'. If I was you, I'd give 'em fancy money belts to that drunk cook you hired. Let'm take all 'em yellow coins 'cross this devil of a river in his wagon. That'd be my plan anyhow."

Tom smiled back. "We have a different plan, Mr. Rusk."

The Texian frowned, spit, and pushed the brim of his hat up. "And what's that?"

Malone answered first. "Not to fall off our horses."

The wagon crossed first, but not until big trunks of elm trees had been strapped to the wheels on both sides to make sure the wagon would float. Izan swam his buckskin alongside Mr. James Byers, who used a whip to keep the team of oxen moving through the mud and muck and then into the deep part of the Red.

Rusk was right. The bottom appeared to drop off after about a tenth of a mile. Only the neck and head of Izan's horse could be seen as it swam through the middle of the wide river, and the two oxen almost disappeared, while Izan appeared to have kicked free of his stirrups, and was gripping the saddle horn with both hands.

Then hooves found muddy bottom, and finally solid ground, and Santos's brother simply eased his legs back around the buckskin's side, and his feet slid into the dripping stirrups. Another tenth of a mile the horse pushed through water up to its flanks, then to the hocks, and finally the shallows the last fifty yards.

Tom patted his horse's neck. The roan had always been a good swimmer.

On the northern bank, Izan tethered his horse to the roots of an uprooted tree and helped Byers unfasten the makeshift floats. Zachary stayed mounted on his bay, smoking a pipe.

"Let's get 'em movin'," Rusk called out. "Whip, I'll dock you a dime for ever' pig of Mr. Ponting's you let drown."

Tom nudged the roan. Behind him, he heard Whip singing—well, not exactly singing—and Santos joined in, putting the lyrics into Spanish. Santos had a beautiful voice. Tom tried the first song that came to him:

*Kathleen Mavourneen the gray dawn*
  *is breaking*
*The horn of the hunter is heard on the hill*

*The lark from her light wing the bright*
  *dew is shaking*
*Kathleen Mavourneen what slumbering*
  *still*

The singing stopped when the water reached
the roan's hocks. A moment later, the water filled
Tom's boot tops, and the weight of the money
belt seemed to triple. The sinking sun felt hotter
now, but the water turned freezing.

Water reached the roan's shoulders. Tom looked
at myriad horns nearest him, water dripping from
the tips, the bawling animals swimming.

He realized the roan was bigger—a full hand
taller—than the mustangs Izan and Santos rode.

Hooves lost contact with mud, and Tom, who
never had learned how to swim, held his breath.

*Next river crossing, let someone know you can't
swim and have him ride near you. Next time, let
James Byers carry the money belt in his wagon.*

But after a long panic, the roan found muddy
bottom again. Tom could breathe. Water reached
Tom's waist now, and the gelding snorted,
lunged, and Tom figured he was safe. Unless the
horse stepped into quicksand.

Turning quickly, he looked for Malone, finding
his partner and the chestnut a few feet ahead of
him. Tom twisted, spotted and heard Whip yelling
at pigs and cattle. Tom's eyes swept downstream.
No cattle. Just the slow-flowing wide river,

bending south about three hundred yards east.

For yards, horses and longhorns slogged through shallow water, then sunk, slugged, and negotiated reddish mud, and at last reached the dry banks of the Indian Nations. Up ahead, sitting on his dripping-wet horse, Rusk pulled off his hat and pointed it northwest.

"Good graze about a quarter mile," he said.

Reaching the Texian, Tom eased the roan away from the drove, reined up, and turned the horse around.

Suddenly Tom giggled.

Rusk turned, staring hard, shook his head, and barked, "Whip, how many pigs you lose?"

"Nary a one," the gleeful cowboy sang back. "They swim better'n you do."

Tom laughed harder.

Rusk turned around. "What the devil's got into you?"

Tom shook his head. "That . . . that . . ." He pointed at the trailing herd and the massively wide Red River. "That . . . it was simply . . . exhilarating."

"You think so?" Rusk pulled his hat down tighter, then swung down, flipped a stirrup onto the seat, reset the saddle to center it, and began tightening the cinch, hard to do for a man with one good arm, but Rusk worked with quickness and efficiency. "Wait till we reach the Canadian River. See how exhilaratin' that feels."

Tom emptied water from one of his boots as Rusk pulled his horse to a stop.

"As far as Santos and Izan can figure, ever' pig, ever' head of beef made it across." Rusk stared. "We got lucky."

Tom threw the boot closer to the fire next to the other one, then worked on pulling off soaking socks.

"Your pal Hart is supposed to bring in thirty more head tomorrow." Whip drifted over, squatted by the fire, and tilted the coffeepot, allowing it to fill a cup with steaming black liquid. He moved closer to Rusk and held the cup.

Barely even considering the lanky cowhand, Rusk took the cup and sipped.

"Santos and me can bring 'em across tomorrow," Rusk said.

"What about me?" Whip asked.

"Hart didn't say nothin' 'bout bringin' no pigs to sell."

Whip pouted, turned around, and let his bowed legs take him to the wagon, where Byers was whipping a wooden spoon in a big bowl that rested on the wagon's tailgate.

After pitching his socks near the boots, Tom sank onto the grass.

"And that will give us . . . six hundred and thirty beeves?" He wanted to make sure.

"Roughly." He must have seen the disappointment in Tom's face. "Don't fret, Ponting. You can fill out your herd in the Nations. These injuns know the value of beef. Also . . ." He tilted his head in a northerly direction. "It's too early right now to start trailin' the herd."

"It is not too early in Illinois," said Malone, also barefoot and sockless, and sitting a few feet away from Tom.

"Case you ain't noticed, you ain't in Illinois." Rusk kept his eyes on Tom. "Need I'm guessin' two more weeks. Let the grass grow some more. That'll give you time to fill out your herd, too." He pointed the coffee cup. "Armstrong's Academy is up there. You should ride over, iffen it suits you, look up a fellow named Thompson."

"Armstrong's Academy?" Tom asked. He set his cup on a rock.

Rusk nodded. "School." He snorted. "Teachin' injuns to read and write. Teachin' 'em to become white. Like they could ever get that red off 'em." He spit. "Thompson. He'll know if anyone around here might be lookin' to sell some cattle. He's a white man. Hails from Tennessee. And I'll bet my bottom dollar, that he'll sure want to have a parley with you."

"Why?" Tom asked.

"Well," Rusk drawled. "Thompson knows what this land's worth. Since this pasture's his. I figure he'd like to tell you how much he'll be collectin' from you." He laughed. "Pard, you was the one who insisted on crossin' the Red. Yes, sir, Thompson, that man sure knows the value of grass."

He leaned forward in the saddle. "An' speakin' of value, I'll owe Hart eight bucks a head."

Tom pushed himself up to his knees. He untucked his shirt from the wet britches, and fingered the money belt. His eyes remained on C. W. Rusk, who watched as Tom opened a compartment, and began fingering out the California slugs. Finished, he pushed himself up, and picked out a path as he went barefoot to the man on horseback.

Rusk pitched the empty cup to the earth, and held out his gloved left hand. Slowly, Tom dropped five octagonal coins into the deerskin.

"Got more heft to 'em than I figured." Rusk closed his fingers around the coins, then opened them again and stared. He brought the money closer.

"You'll owe me ten dollars," Tom said. "But I'll just mark that in my ledger. Deduct it when I pay you off in New York City."

# CHAPTER 28

Two miles south of the Fort Towson–Fort Washita Road, young boys, hoes in hand, dug holes, dropped in seeds, covered holes, moved on. An army, all dark-skinned and dark-haired, worked the fields, while others sat on the roofs of log cabins, patching holes.

It made Tom glad that he had never been a farmer.

"Good day, Brothers."

Turning in the saddle, Tom found a man in black pants and coat walking from another cabin. "Welcome to Armstrong's Academy, founded by Captain Armstrong not yet ten years ago."

Tom nodded. "Are you the Reverend Potts?"

Smiling, the man shook his head. "Alas, Brother Ramsay has been called to meet with the preacher at another church. Likely you saw it while riding up." He pointed. "They teach Choctaw boys there, but, alas they use the Choctaw tongue. Here, we speak English. We teach these young boys to speak, read, and write the way God intended." Pride filled his face. "We take pride in the orthography and chirography of these once heathen, but now semi-heathen boys."

Tom pointed at the field. "You teach them to farm, too, I see."

"Yes," he said proudly. "We strive to be efficient. As you might know, getting funds from Washington City or the Indian Mission Society of the Baptist Church is tantamount to asking for a miracle." He chuckled. "But we make do." He turned and looked at the Indian farmers.

"Twenty acres of wheat, more than fifty acres of corn, five acres of potatoes—Irish and sweet—and around two acres for beans, peas, beets, and melons. We had a good harvest last year. The year before, drought." He shook his head. "The Lord tests us. My name is Royster. Latimer Royster."

"Tom Ponting." He introduced Malone.

"You are English," Royster said.

"Till '47. I live in Illinois now. My partner and I are driving cattle north. We crossed the river yesterday, and I seek a Mr. Thompson to secure a lease to graze there for two weeks or so. And to buy cattle if he has any for sale, or knows of where we might be able to buy around one hundred head."

Royster's face changed.

"Oh" was all he said.

Tom waited. The man blinked. After glancing at Malone, who gave a slight, uncertain shrug, Tom looked back at the man in black. "Is Mr. Thompson here?" he asked.

He had to wait, as Royster decided what he should say—even though, the way Tom figured, all he needed to say was yes or no. Royster moved closer to the roan, put a hand on Tom's thigh, and said in a hushed voice, "Sir, as an obviously educated man from England, I should warn you that, well . . ." He looked across the saddlebags at Washington Malone.

Tom bent lower, whispering: "My partner is better educated and more civilized than I am, Reverend Royster."

"Oh." Royster straightened. "I am not ordained."

Tom feigned surprise.

"I am a humble assistant to Brother Ramsay and a servant to Christ our Lord." He moved back. "But as I was saying, just a word of caution to you both. Thompson he . . . he married a Choctaw woman. Well, she is only one-third Choctaw, but speaks that heathen tongue. So does Thompson." The last sentence came out as pure disgust. "Just a warning, sir." He smiled at Malone. "His ranch is on Boggy Creek, but he comes here often. Today, however, you will find Mr. Thompson at the Choctaw church I was telling you about. Hail the size of apples struck us two days ago. They are repairing the roofs at that heathen church, while our boys fix their dormitories. The roof of our church, God be praised, was spared."

After thanking Royster, Tom turned his horse and led Malone back down the trace to the military road that linked the two posts. But he reined up before they entered the woods, twisted around in the saddle, and looked back at Armstrong's Academy.

Malone turned his horse around, looked, waited, then studied Tom.

How long he sat there, watching the Choctaw boys plant their seeds and patch their roofs, Tom did not know. Only when the roan snorted and pawed the earth did he grip the reins and glance at his partner.

"Do you know anything about the Choctaws?" Tom asked.

"Just that they're Indians," Malone answered after a shrug.

"Yes."

"Civilized," Malone added. "Like the . . ." He had to think. "Cherokees. Creeks." Marney had mentioned the Creeks. "And . . ." But other tribes he could not recall.

"They once lived in some of the Southern states," Tom said. "I cannot recall the exact one or ones. Along with other tribes, President Jackson, I believe, had them relocated here." He shook his head. "I have never visited the states of the South, but from what I have read about and seen drawings of, the country is far different than these lands."

Malone made a noncommittal grunt.

"And now," Tom said, "we are teaching them . . ." He looked at his partner. "What was it Rusk said yesterday evening? *Teaching them to become white.*" He sighed, tightened his grip on the reins, and kicked the roan into a walk. "We should take notice of all we see. Like these Choctaws, they might vanish before our eyes. Disappear from our history."

"Not sure that would be a bad thing," Malone said. "Even back home, I've heard horrible tales about the Black Hawk War. And Tecumseh. What he and those Shawnee wanted to do. Came close to doing. If the Army had not won those fights, you and I would not be driving those Texas cattle back to Illinois and on to New York City."

Tom let his head bob, but with a sad smile, he turned and stared at Malone.

"And that is another thing." He spoke softly. He had not expected quite this emotion. A sense of foreboding, of loss. "All those canals. And these railroads that are beginning to connect towns and cities, states and territories. Who is to say that a cattle drive like this which we have conceived and, by luck and the grace of the Almighty shall see through, will ever happen again?"

He liked what he saw at the Choctaw church. The Reverend Ramsay Potts sat on the rooftop, working alongside two copper-skinned men and a Negro in chaps and boots. On the ground, another dark-skinned man lifted a sack toward the roof. The Reverend Potts—it had to be Potts, as he was the only white man here—took it, handed it to one of the Indians, then dangled his long legs over the side—though a ladder leaned eight feet away against the side of the cabin—and dropped to the ground.

The workers glanced at Tom and Malone, but kept working. Tom and Malone rode their horses to the cabin where the preacher smiled and waved.

"Welcome," he said as the horses stopped. "You're just in time. Mighty neighborly of you to ride over to help us replace some hail-busted shingles."

Laughing at his joke, he came and shook Malone's hand first, then Tom's. "I am Ramsay Potts."

"Reverend." Tom liked the firmness of the preacher's grip. He introduced Malone and himself, then said, "We were told by your associate at your fine school that we might find a Mr. Thompson here."

The dark-skinned, dark-headed man spoke. "My name's Thompson. David Thompson."

Tom stared like a schoolboy, unable to hide his surprise. But, yes, this man was white. His skin was deeply tanned, not coppery, and beard stubble covered his face. He wasn't Indian. He just looked like one.

"You are the man we seek," Tom said, and he started explaining.

. . .

It was, he decided, a successful trip. David Thompson's terms were generous, and the food his Choctaw wife prepared before they left was satisfying. He liked conversing with the reverend much more than he did with his assistant at Armstrong's Academy. The Baptist preacher invited them back for a tour of the school on the morrow, and Thompson said if Tom could give him a few days, he would draw a map to an Englishman's ranch who likely had cattle for sale.

They reached camp shortly before suppertime.

"What," Malone said, "is that wonderful aroma?"

Tom's mouth watered. Whatever the boys were cooking, it did not smell like beans and salt pork.

At Rusk's order, Whip hurried to the fire and returned with a tin plate filled with white meat with a golden battered crust. Fish, Tom deduced, and he broke off a piece with his fingers, held it under his nose, then put it in his mouth.

Granted, he had been eating beans and pig meat pretty much since he had arrived in Texas, but this was . . . he had trouble finding an adjective. Glancing at Rusk, he asked, "Mr. Byers cooked this?"

Everyone laughed.

"Come here," Rusk commanded. "Catfish."

He did not recognize this strange young man in Mexican denim pants and a homespun shirt. The lad, dark-haired and dark-eyed with a bronzed face and smelling of Red River mud, water but, mostly, fish, could not have seen more than twenty years.

"Howdy, Mr. Ponting," the boy drawled. "My name's Hennessy. Jim Hennessy. Live down in the piney woods near Louisiana."

"He just got hisself graduated from college." Whip slapped the boy's back so hard he almost fell to his knees.

"I recall, back in Somersetshire, reading of culinary schools—Queen's College in Birmingham was one, if I am not mistaken. But I thought such universities or courses were reserved for the weaker sex."

Laugher exploded all around him. Even this young Hennessy grinned.

"Shucks. They didn't teach us nothing about cooking and eating. They had me reading and learning about ancient languages and what they call philosophy and books and a lot of that math nonsense."

Tom tried to translate what the boy had said.

"Santos found him fishing on this side of the Red. He had a string of catfish that weighed nigh thirty pounds. He brought him here. Now he wants to join up with us."

Washington Malone was eating the fish left on

the plate that Tom had not gotten to taste. "It is quite good," he said with his mouth full.

Tom studied the boy for a moment, before telling Rusk: "We will be pushing seven hundred head of cattle ten miles a day. At times in land where water is scarce. How do you propose that this collegian catches enough fish to feed the multitude in our camp? Is this like the gospel story of five loaves and two fish supplied by a boy? This is not—"

"He's a hand." Rusk slapped the kid's shoulder. "Those piney woods produce good, tough stock. He got hisself educated and now he wants to see new country. That's what brung him up to the Red River. And Byers is quittin' us in Illinois."

Rusk leaned closer, lowering his voice. "But he might keep an eye out on that drunk Byers. And if Byers finds some John Barleycorn and gets roostered, maybe this boy here can feed us after a day's work."

"We are in the Indian Nations." Malone did not speak softly. "Where can Byers find—"

Rusk cut him off. "Ever had Choc beer?" He laughed. "Boys, whiskey is the easiest thing to find in the Nations. But, well, you're in charge of hirin' the cooks and the pig drovers, Ponting, so you make this decision." He took the plate from Malone's hands, and walked away. "You . . ."

He stopped, pitched the plate toward Byers, and put his good hand on the nearest .44-caliber Dragoon.

Two men led their horses into camp, and Tom recognized both men. The Cherokee and a Negro who had been working with Thompson and the Reverend Potts at the Choctaw church near Armstrong's Academy.

But now, all around Tom, came the sound of weapons being drawn from leather holsters, and that quiet but deadly metallic sound of the hammers of revolvers being pulled to full cock.

# CHAPTER 29

"Do not be alarmed," Tom said. Somehow he recalled the names. "It is Yargee and Colton Greene."

Whispering a savage curse, Whip began to raise his revolver, so Tom bulled his way past Rusk and latched on to Whip's forearm. "You mind that," Tom yelled, pushing the uncocked gun down. He turned around, stared hard on Rusk. "I boss this outfit," he said. "Remember who pays you."

That, he later thought, might not have been the wisest choice of words. Rusk could have shot him dead, killed Malone—and the two visitors. But at that moment, Tom scarcely had time to think. He stepped in front of Whip, raised his right hand, and approached the visitors.

"Hello there, gentlemen," he said. "You have arrived just in time for supper. Do you like catfish?"

The Indian just stared. Greene said, "Reckon so."

Rusk, Whip, and the hands squatted around the fire, eating fish and beans, drinking coffee. Mr. Byers and young Hennessy sat on the gate of Byers's wagon, the older man puffing on a pipe while the young, dark-headed youth told some story.

Underneath a shade tree on the far side of the camp, Tom glanced at Malone after the two visitors had finished talking.

Saying nothing, Malone studied the men at the fire. He swallowed, and looked back at Tom. Their eyes held for a moment before Malone faced the Cherokee and Negro.

"You understand where we plan to take this herd?" Washington Malone sounded incredulous.

"New York," the Cherokee answered.

"Wintering in Illinois," Colton Greene added.

"Can you comprehend that New York is more than a thousand miles from here?" Malone asked.

Yargee's chuckle held no mirth, and his eyes went cold. He sipped the coffee Jim Hennessy had poured him, spit it out, and leaned closer. "Do you understand that my father walked twelve hundred miles to get here? But it wasn't his idea."

Tom let the words, and the hardness in the man's eyes, sink in. Malone's mouth opened, but this time closed without asking another question.

"This happens to be my idea," Yargee said. "Mine and Colton's."

Colton Greene set his coffee cup on a rock. "I'm a freeman," he said. "That's supposed to mean that I can go anywhere I please. *Supposed to.* Freeman. Not freedman. I was born free. But sometimes I have to wonder if any man with black skin is born free. So you might not understand this, Mr. Ponting, but I've been here long enough to know that I'd feel a whole lot freer in New York. Hope so, anyhow."

Tom glanced at Malone, but his partner silently studied Rusk, Whip, and the crew.

"I've driven cattle." Yargee spoke evenly. "Two years back, I rode with an outfit that pushed a herd all the way to Hangtown. That's in California. Nobody told me how many miles that was, but my backside reckons it was farther than it is to New York. And the country we crossed wasn't quite as civilized as your Illinois or Ohio."

Added Greene: "I've worked more'n three years for Mr. Thompson. Working cattle. Not fixing Choctaw churches. Drove forty beeves to Fort Washita last year." He grinned at his Cherokee partner. "Not as far as Californy. But I bet you didn't have no twister scatter your herd from here to sundown."

"Tom."

Malone tilted his head, but by then Tom recognized the heavy steps and knew who it was without looking. He turned back to the visitors, focusing on the man now towering over Tom, Malone, the Cherokee, and the freeman.

"C. W. Rusk," Tom said, "meet Yargee and Greene." He stood, and stepped closer to the Texian. "They are joining our drive." He turned to stare into belligerent eyes.

"I pick who works this drive." Rusk spat out the words. "We agreed to that."

That's when Tom grinned. "But you told me, said it bold as brass, that I hired the pig drovers. Remember?" He stepped closer, no longer smiling. "They're hired. And if that does not suit you, you can take your men and cross the Red River back into Texas."

Rusk's left hand swept toward the butt of the massive revolver on his right hip, but stopped. His eyes locked on Tom's, and slowly turned to Yargee and Greene. The hand moved away from the Colt.

"Whip," he shouted. "Fetch your horse. Take this colored boy and this injun to the herd. They can take first watch." He looked back at the newcomers. "All right, pig drovers. It's your funeral."

The herd of longhorns totaled, by Santos's count, six hundred and thirty-seven, but Mr. Thompson had not returned with either a map or the name of a potential rancher willing to sell cattle—and they had been camped here for ten days. That morning, the last of the hogs had been floated across the Red on a makeshift raft.

"Whip," Rusk yelled. "Get them stinkin' pigs with the other ones, and be quick about it."

Fat hogs squealed—two started fighting—and the brutes scurried every which way on the river's edge, leaving stinking manure for boots, brogans, and moccasins to find.

Jerking his hat off and spitting tobacco juice, Whip wiped his mouth, found Rusk, and yelled: "That Cherokee and that darky—you said they was the pig drovers."

"They been promoted."

Santos and Izan, who had worked the raft, joined Rusk in laughing. Rusk squatted by the fire and refilled his mug with coffee.

"I'll help you, Whip."

Tom watched Jim Hennessy, now called "Catfish" by the entire crew, leave Byers's wagon and sprint toward the bank.

Lounging in the shade, Yargee and Greene glanced at one another. "Come on, pig drover," the Cherokee said as he pushed himself to his feet. Greene shook his head, but grabbed his lariat, while the Cherokee removed his oil cap, slapping it against his thighs.

"*Soo-ie!*" Catfish yelled, slapping his thigh.

"Come on," Tom told Malone.

His partner looked up, confused.

"Lend Whip a hand." Tom started to join the cook's helper, the Negro, and the Cherokee to help Whip manage the new additions to the Ponting-Malone herd.

"*Soiee.*"

"*Soiee. Soooo-iee.*"

When they reached the scurrying hogs, the

340

two Mexican brothers glanced at each other, shrugged, and stopped dragging the raft into the bushes. In moments, Tom, Malone, Izan, Santos, Catfish, Greene, and Yargee were helping Whip herd the stinking, snorting beasts to the makeshift pen Whip had built.

*"Soooo-iee."*

It brought back memories, some pleasant, some painful. Of those pig farmers in Somersetshire. And some rough, tough Irish hoggards in London.

*"Soiee."*

C. W. Rusk and Byers were the only members of the crew who did not help, but Tom understood why; Byers was preparing supper, and Rusk was a jackass.

When Malone slipped and fell in the mud, Tom stopped to help his partner up. Smiling, he nodded at the scene before them.

"We have a crew," he said. "Look at them work together. For the first time, my good friend, I feel that I might just win my bet."

The next day, while Catfish helped James Byers clean cookware and dishes, and Rusk explained the trail they would travel to pick up the Missouri road, two riders appeared at the edge of camp.

Whip reached for his rifle, whispering, "They both look like injuns to me."

Tom stepped away from Rusk, and looked. One

of the men held up his right hand and called out, "Hello, Ponting. Mind if we come in?"

"Leave the rifle," Tom told Whip. "It's Thompson."

"Who's with him?" Rusk asked.

"I do not recognize the gentleman," Tom said as the riders eased their mounts toward camp.

"He ain't no gentleman," Whip said. "Looks like a half-breed."

"You ain't far of the mark, Whip." Coals sizzled and smoked as Rusk emptied his coffee cup into the fire and pitched it into the tin tub of dishes. "If I ain't mistaken, that's Jesse Chisholm."

Chisholm had to be close to fifty years old. Or maybe he was nearer seventy. His hair was white, his mustache more silver than black. The skin was dark, but the eyes a cold blue, and when he spoke, Tom thought he detected a trace of Scottish. The surname, of course, was Scottish. Tom remembered his grandfather speaking of a drover named George Chisholm from Hawick in the southern region of Scotland. Thick, dark eyebrows definitely looked Scottish.

"Jesse's father-in-law ran a trading post on the Little River," Thompson said after introductions had been made and coffee poured. "Now Jesse has his own post on the Canadian. He's a big man with the tribes. Served as an interpreter for President Polk back in '46 for one of those treaties."

Chisholm looked uncomfortable.

"Well." Thompson sipped coffee. "Turns out, Ponting, that Jesse knows a fellow with cattle for sale."

That interested Tom far more than the trader's biography and exploits.

"Englishman like you," Chisholm said. "Calls himself Pussly. Good ranch. Good beef. Texas cattle like you got here. Fair man."

Tom waited for more information, but none came. Chisholm seemed unlike most merchants and traders Tom had known. Certainly, his manners bore no resemblance to Michael Snyder's in Moweaqua.

"Jesse can get you to Pussly's ranch, but . . ." Thompson did not finish the sentence.

"Creeks and Comanch' want something settled," Chisholm said. "Holding a council on the Canadian. I got that to tend to first. If you want to come along, I'd admire the company."

"Never heard of no Comanch' holdin' no council," Rusk said. "All I ever knowed them bucks to do was rape, murder, and steal."

Chisholm did not take his eyes off Ponting, but he answered Rusk. "Fine people. If you treat 'em right. Love a good joke. Love their kids and their horses. Reckon they don't mind Creeks so much since it wasn't the Creeks' choice to get put on what was once Comanch' and Kiowa land." He brought the cup to his lips.

June 1, 1853

My dearest Tom,

A copy of the Alton Weekly Courier, dated Friday Morning, May 27 of this year, arrived at Father's Store, and has caused quite a row. The headline reads "Gold in Texas," and while this report, from the 21st inst., says no official confirmation of any such gold strike has been received, but a man named Taylor, the newspaper stated, who was passing through the city, said that reports are true, even though he has not been to those "diggins," which are located about 100 miles above Austin between the Colorado and San Saba rivers. Are you near there? Have you heard of gold?

Father has told customers that it would be just like you, to stop this pursuit of wild cows and take off to the gold fields, and abandon your bet with him.

I say that you have no interest in gold or any precious stones, and that you will return this summer with cattle that will be worth more than all the gold in Texas, or California.

Then, tonight, just moments ago as I lay in bed and began penning this brief note, I reached underneath my mattress, and clutched the precious coin you gave to me before our sad departure.

I sleep with it every night under my pillow. I dream of you, and our future together, and I know, even if this report of a gold strike is true, that you will return soon.

I dream of that day.

Farewell, my prince, till this letter finds you happy and in good health in Springfield, Missouri, on your way home.

Ever yours,<br>Margaret Snyder

# CHAPTER 30

"Sorry you come?" Chisholm asked.

Tom had not really considered the risk. First, they needed more cattle. Then, a council would be peaceful, he figured, and, as he had told Washington Malone, he wanted to see all of this American frontier that he could. How much longer would these wild aborigines be part of this new country?

Now it struck him that it might be the last thing he ever saw.

The short, heavyset man rode a black-and-white pony faster and better than any equestrian Tom had seen. Shirtless, he wore a breechclout decorated with shells, and his hairless chest was painted blue, red, and yellow. His legs were bare, except for the tanned moccasins. His hair was darker than the wing of a blackbird, braided on both sides, wrapped in otter skins, with an eagle feather stuck into the scalp lock at the back of his head. He carried a long, feathered lance in his left hand, and jerked the hackamore with his right, pulling the pinto into a sliding stop.

As the dust settled, his black eyes bore through Tom.

Tom saw the scars. Recognized the signs of smallpox, and other healed wounds from battle,

Tom guessed. Then the man smiled, and turned his head sharply away from Tom and spoke guttural sounds to Jesse Chisholm. While they spoke, their hands and fingers moved, far too fast for Tom to remember.

When they paused, both men nodded, then began the mix of strange words and rapid hand movements, and soon, Tom turned toward the Canadian River. The country, lined with red-and-white dirt, short green trees, rugged grass, and a village of buffalo-hide teepees—just as he had imagined—fires, more horses than he could count, and he heard the songs, and the beating of drums.

Downstream, huts and lean-tos rose above the plains. That must be the camping ground of the Creeks.

Drums beat rhythmically, while songs by men and women sang out from both camps. Dogs barked.

No, he wasn't sorry. Especially now that the hard-riding Indian was talking to Jesse Chisholm.

"Ponting."

Tom turned quickly.

Chisholm's hands rested on the horn of his saddle. The Comanche, still holding the lance in his left hand, glared.

"This is Matzóhpe." Tom could barely understand the name. "Means 'Wildcat.' "

The name fit. Tom nodded, and raised his right hand.

"Show him your watch."

Tom looked. The watch had belonged to Tom's father. Surely, Jesse Chisholm had not offered to trade the watch for . . . whatever.

"Show it to him. Tell him how it works. In English. I told him in my best Comanch' and sign. Tell him. I told him you would know exactly when tomorrow begins. At midnight. Said you are right powerful among your tribe. That watch is your *puha*. Your power."

He pulled the watch from his pocket. It was nothing fancy, just open-faced, the silver tarnished, no chain since the bow had been ripped off. Never came with a seconds dial. Came from Pennington, if he recalled correctly, from London, though his father had taken it as payment for cattle. When Tom and John had left for America, his father had given John, the oldest, a new watch. Tom got this one.

Holding it out for the Comanche to study, Tom tried to explain how the watch worked.

When he had finished, Matzóhpe held out his free hand, palm up, and with a sigh, Tom gently placed the heirloom in the rough hand.

The Comanche hefted it, quickly brought it to his right ear as Tom held his breath, smiled at the ticking, and shook his head before returning the watch to Tom. He spoke that strange tongue, and Tom looked at Chisholm.

"He says you must be stupid. The stars and the

sun tell him the time. But since the Creeks are stupid, too, it is good I brung you. Says I'll be good to speak for his people, and you can speak for the dumb Creeks."

Tom blinked.

"It's a joke, Ponting. Comanches like a good joke. Laugh with me."

"Why'd you come along with me, Ponting?"

They sat in a lean-to the Creeks had built for Chisholm. The Comanches had agreed to send a woman over to cook supper for the two white men. That way everything remained fair.

Chisholm ate with his fingers. Reluctantly, Tom picked up a piece of greasy meat out of a handsome earthen bowl. He had been given a cow's horn for a spoon, but he did not see how one ate meat with a spoon. What kind of meat it was, he did not know. It tasted like liver. Cow liver . . . horse liver . . . cat liver . . . dog liver . . . it did not matter. He swallowed and decided that he was not hungry.

"I need cattle. You said you would take me to this Pussly after your affair with these aborigines."

The trader wiped his lips with a filthy shirtsleeve.

"Could have drawed you a map."

Tom found the cup of coffee, sipped it, and looked across the lean-to. "I come from an old country," he said. "My ancestors came to England in the eleventh century. Before anyone even knew of this America."

Comanche women sang. It soothed him, though the words sounded harsh to his ears and he knew nothing of what the song meant.

"When I was but a lad, I helped a drover take fifty-three bullocks—steers—to London. More than a hundred miles. And I remember passing all these buildings, old, ancient cities, and graves." He shook his head. "I would even go to cemeteries, back home in Kilmersdon, the nearest village to our stock farm. Trying to find the oldest year of birth on a gravestone, or the oldest year of death."

He sipped more coffee. "This is a new country. But it shan't always be new. I would like to see everything I can, take in all that I can, remember all that I can. Before it is all forgotten."

Chisholm licked his fingers. "That why you left the Old Country, come to America?"

Now his head fell, and shook. "Sickness struck our stock farm. And the farms of many throughout England. We lost many cattle. I had brothers and sisters, a grandfather. Though I had dreamed of coming to America, my father came to the understanding that it would be in the best interest for John, my older brother, and me—and for my father and my mother, my grandfather, and my sisters and brothers . . ." He stopped.

"Fewer mouths to feed," he said after a moment. "Food was scarce."

Chisholm nodded.

"What time does that watch of yourn say it is?" he asked.

Tom found the Pennington. "Eight forty-nine."

"Best get some shut-eye. Could be a long day tomorrow. And don't forget to wind that watch. You want your *puha* to be strong tomorrow."

He never quite understood exactly the cause of the dispute between the two tribes, but they did find common ground. A young Creek named Chitto explained that his people had been driven out of their home country. Burned out by white men. Survivors of one battle said their noses still breathed in the odors of burning flesh, and the screams of their babies still rang in their ears. The fierce Matzóhpe reminded the Creeks that when Comanche leaders, fathers, uncles, grandfathers rode into the *taibo* city of San Antonio, assured of a peaceful assembly, they were shot down in the streets.

The Creeks agreed to let the Comanches hunt buffalo. The Comanches agreed to pay the Creeks in horses. Laughing, Matzóhpe said they had stolen too many horses anyway, that feeding them would be hard if the winter proved harsh. A pipe was passed. Chitto even let Tom smoke, and when he coughed, gagged, and came close to vomiting, Creeks and Comanches laughed. The Comanches named Tom "Green Face." It was a fine name, the Creeks agreed.

The meeting was over that afternoon, and Tom and Chisholm saddled their horses, thanked their hosts, and prepared to ride to Pussly's ranch.

Matzóhpe stopped them at the river crossing. He pointed across the wide Canadian at an ox. A Brahman cow, white with patches of black as though a drunken painter had swung his brush at her. Probably did not weigh a thousand pounds now, but Tom could tell the cow had been trained in harness. She wasn't wild, and had that determined look.

The Comanche spoke rapidly, his hands and fingers doing that strange translation that meant nothing to Tom.

Once finished, he sat back on his horse, smiling, nodding, and crossing his arms over his chest.

Tom smiled back.

"He says you are a good *taibo*," Chisholm translated. "And he wants to give you that ox. Says you must take her. You will need her. She will help you on your journey. It became clear to him last night. But he did not understand the meaning until after the parley with the Creeks."

"Tell him—"

Chisholm cut him off. "I'm telling him you accept his offer with gratitude."

Tom turned to the trader.

"You don't insult a Comanch'. Besides, it ain't a bad-looking cow. He probably got her in some raid. But giving her away is a big honor."

Tom sighed, and nodded.

"You have to give him something in return," Chisholm said.

Tom studied the hard face of the Comanche, and then he knew exactly what Chisholm meant. He looked back. Chisholm nodded.

"This was my father's watch."

The trader shrugged. "Like I said, it's a good-looking cow. And you got a long ways before you're out of Comanche country, with or without any cattle."

Tom's fingers dipped into the pocket. He looked at the old relic. Well, it never kept that good of time, even when his father first got it. He showed how to wind it, how to set the time, tried to explain it. Chisholm translated. The Comanche's black eyes brightened. "Tell him not to wind it too tight. It'll stop working."

He watched Matzóhpe's right hand swallow the watch. The Indian nodded, then sang out strange words, turned his horse around, and galloped toward the teepees.

"He said," Chisholm translated, "that if you meet him on the prairie, do not fear him. He is your friend and he will not hurt you."

"It's good to have a friend." Shaking his head, Tom sighed.

"Ponting," Chisholm said.

Dust swallowed the vanishing Indian, and when Chisholm said nothing else, Tom turned.

"If he finds you alone on this prairie, he'll kill you for nothing more than your coat and your scalp."

Tom blinked.

Chisholm kicked his horse into a walk. "He's Comanch'. You're a white man. And this is his land. Best fetch your new ox. Got a long ride to Pussly's."

# CHAPTER 31

Miserable.

No, there had to be a stronger word.

Tom, the roan, and the ox-cow had covered much territory since parting ways with Jesse Chisholm at Mr. Pussly's ranch. Rarely had Tom seen such fine cattle country, good graze, good water, and a surrounding plain that must have stretched twenty miles in all directions. Tom had slept on buffalo robes for the first time in his life, and the cattleman showed him longhorn steers that all weighed, Tom guessed, at least twelve hundred pounds. Pussly and Tom settled at nine dollars a head.

But then Pussly had mentioned that some Shawnee Indians had cattle for sale, so Tom took Pussly's directions and rode out that evening. He got lost in thick woods no one had warned him about. Well, Pussly and his son, and two of Pussly's slaves had urged Tom to wait until dawn, but Tom was in a hurry. He was supposed to meet the herd at the Canadian River crossing in three days. He wound up in a pigeon roost. In fact, he had never seen so many pigeons—even in London. When they settled in the trees, he thought his eardrums would rupture. The wings, branches, the entire forest rattled like thunder.

So many pigeons flocked into the trees, branches collapsed.

He got no sleep that night, then had to pick his way around falls of branches and tons of pigeon droppings.

The Shawnees would not sell him any cattle.

Rain hit that evening.

He hoped to make twelve miles a day. He made six, by his guess, the following day, never seeing the sun, and as soon as one cloud passed, another poured.

Still, Pussly had sent one of his slaves with Tom to help him get the steers to the Canadian River crossing, where Tom and Rusk had agreed to meet. If Tom reached there first, he would wait. If Rusk arrived before Tom, the herd would keep pushing on toward Missouri, and Tom could catch up.

He and Joe, the slave, needed their lariats to pull the ox out of a mud bog. They made only five miles that day. At least they herded cattle on the north side of the Canadian, one river Tom wouldn't have to cross again.

The sun appeared the next morning, disappeared that afternoon, but the clouds had rained themselves out. The next afternoon, Tom and Joe let the cattle graze and rest on the Canadian's northern banks at the crossing. He stared at the wagon, the longhorns, horses, men—on the southern bank. The river must have risen nineteen feet.

"Malone," Tom yelled. "Washington Malone."

He heard no echo. There was little in this country to bounce around a voice.

"You sure that is your crew, boss?" Joe asked.

"What do you smell, Joe?" Tom saw a man being helped to his feet, lean against the wagon wheel for support, and bring a hand to shield his eyes.

"Smells like fish, boss," the slave said. "Fried fish."

Tom's head bobbed. "Catfish," he said. Besides, who else would be herding longhorns through this country?

"Tom? Is that you?"

He recognized Malone's voice.

"Yes." Tom felt himself grinding his teeth, but he breathed in and out, fighting down the anger. "How long have you been here?"

"Three days."

He bit off a curse that wanted to flash out of his mouth.

"There are Indians all around us, Tom."

Tom kicked a stone into the high water. *Scared.* He wanted to—Well, anger would do no good. They had forgotten his orders. When you reach a river, cross it while you can. Yet he also remembered what it was like to be scared. Driving the drove through the streets of London when he was fifteen years old. Or even the other night, with those pigeons flapping their wings and that horrible cooing noise they made. Or riding across that vast plain with Jesse Chisholm, feeling minuscule and all alone.

"We thought you were done for."

That wasn't Malone's voice. C. W. Rusk croaked out a belly laugh. "That we'd never see you—'cept maybe your scalp, danglin' from some buck's war shirt."

Tom shook his head. A hog squealed.

"Joe," he said softly, turning to the slave. "I can manage the herd till my men cross this river." Tom extended his hand. The man stared at it until Tom, finally understanding, let it fall to his side. "Your . . . your . . . Mr. Pussly will likely think you have either been killed by the elements or an enemy." His right hand disappeared underneath his shirt. He fiddled with the belt, fingered out a coin. It was a two-and-a-half-dollar piece.

"Here."

Joe stared, first at the coin, then at Tom.

"Take it," Tom said. "You have earned it. It probably is not enough payment, but . . ."

The Negro's head shook.

"No, sir. Can't take nothing from you, sir. I'd get flayed so bad, wouldn't be able to wear a shirt for two weeks was Mr. Pussly to find that money on me, sir. No, sir. Can't take no money, sir." He walked to his horse, gathered the reins, and returned to the river's edge.

"Who's that with you?" Rusk called across the Canadian.

Tom ignored the question. He looked at the slave.

"Can I ask you a question, boss?" Joe asked.

On the far bank, Whip shouted that it's too bad Tom Ponting couldn't swim a lick, otherwise he could cross the river and enjoy some of Catfish's supper.

"Of course, Joe," Tom said.

"Is it true?"

"Is what true?"

"That where you come from, that they got rid of slaveholding."

Tom nodded. "In my lifetime, though I do not remember really ever even seeing a slave. Parliament—that is our governing body— abolished the dreadful practice in '33." He sighed. "Twenty years ago."

Their eyes held. "Oldest boy," Joe said, "he nineteen." Joe turned to his horse, and pulled himself into the saddle.

"Maybe someday," he whispered, clucked his tongue, and turned the horse west.

On his second morning on the Canadian's north bank, Tom saddled the roan, stepped into the saddle, and guided the horse into the river. He guessed the width at a fifth of a mile. The current had slowed, but the depth surprised him. One of the men—either Izan or Santos—mounted a horse and uncoiled his lariat. Just in case he had to plunge his horse into the water and save Tom from drowning.

Fifty yards later, the roan's hooves touched bottom. Some of the men cheered till Rusk shouted: "Hush up. All that fooforaw might get that horse to buckin' in the current." He yelled to make sure Tom heard the rest: "Hate to lose all that gold."

*It's not as much gold as it was before I left Illinois, partner.*

Once on the bank, Tom dismounted, let Santos take the roan to the remuda, and accepted a cup of coffee from James Byers while most of the men returned to their breakfast.

Malone brought a biscuit that had been halved and filled with small slices of bacon. He handed that to Tom, who accepted it with gratitude.

"We really thought you were gone for good," Malone said.

Tom ignored the concern. "I thought you would be past Fort Gibson by now."

Malone looked across the river, sighed, and turned back to Tom.

"This territory makes me uncomfortable. All these . . . savages."

Tom washed down the bacon and biscuit with coffee.

"The Indians I have met have been kind and honest," Tom said. "One of those was a Comanche." He frowned, remembering his father's watch.

Behind him, Rusk roared: "Whip, if it takes you that long to saddle a fool horse . . ."

"Makes you think about who we call savages," Tom said.

Malone looked at the dirt. He sighed again. "I am sorry, Tom. I have let you down."

Tom finished the coffee and walked to Malone, clapped his back. "Do not thrash yourself over such a trifle." He heard the boots and hooves coming toward him. That would be C. W. Rusk. "If you had not delayed, you would be north of Fort Gibson, and I would be herding those ornery beasts just to catch up."

He turned to smile at the unsmiling C. W. Rusk.

"I got Whip saddlin' a buckskin for you. If he can get'r done before Christmas. The buckskin's a good swimmer. That roan of yours ought to rest a few days. Lessen you question my judgment."

"Never did. Never do. Never shall."

"Lyin' ain't your strong suit, Ponting."

Rusk shook his head, reached into a pocket, and pulled out a plug of tobacco and bit off a large chunk.

"How many head you get?" Rusk asked, nodding across the Canadian as he worked the tobacco with his teeth.

"Eighty steers," Tom said, then drank a healthy swallow. "And an ox."

"An ox?"

Tom shrugged. "We'll tie it behind Mr. Byers's wagon."

"Could just put him in with the herd. Meat's meat and beef is beef."

Tom shook his head. "You never know when you might need a good ox. And a Comanche says this ox will be our savior."

Rusk shook his head and swore.

# CHAPTER 32

"I remember back in Illinois," Washington Malone said after a long sigh, "when I thought rain was always a blessing."

He stared through misting rain at the Arkansas River.

"In this country, *patrón*," Santos said with a smile, "rain is always a blessing. In your country, you measure rain in inches. Here, we measure in drops." He sighed. "But, *sí*, it does make crossing rivers harder."

Rusk spit tobacco juice into a puddle. "I've seen the water higher."

Tom guessed the river's width at a quarter mile, but islands of sand might make crossing easier. Horses and cattle could rest on the sandbars. But the hogs? The rough current would drown more than a few.

"We'll need to build a—" Tom stopped. Rusk and Izan were drawing their revolvers.

Tom turned around.

He saw the Indians. Maybe a half dozen. One raised his right hand high, and Tom exhaled. "It's all right. They are Creeks." Recognizing the leader from the Canadian River council with the Comanches, Tom waved his right hand and called out, "Chitto." He hoped he came close to the correct pronunciation. "It is good to see you again."

The Creek answered in English. "It is good to see you, too, Green Face."

Working together, Tom's men and the Creeks manufactured a raft out of driftwood and timber, while Yargee, Colton Greene, Whip, and Catfish kept the herd back, and Santos managed the remuda. By noon, they had the raft complete, and James Byers stepped into the driver's box, used his whip, and got the two oxen to pull the wagon onto the raft. The spare ox would swim the Arkansas with the herd.

"You ready, Mr. Byers?" Ponting asked.

The cook chuckled. "Weigh anchor."

On horseback, two Creeks and C. W. Rusk pulled the raft out of the shallows. Tom held his breath as the logs sank from the weight of the oxen and wagon, but the raft held together, and while it did not look seaworthy, the raft drifted slowly. Byers began singing a bawdy tune.

"Are you sure that man is sober?" Malone asked.

Rusk and the two Creeks tossed the lariats into the raft, and guided their horses into the current.

The raft got stuck on the third sandbar, but the two Indians picked up their ropes, wrapping them around the saddle horn, and let the horses pull. Rusk dismounted, leaving his blood bay gelding on the sand, and pushed from behind with his left arm. Freed, the raft continued to float. Fifty yards later, it touched the other bank.

The hard part was pulling the raft back across the river.

No, the hard part, Tom soon learned, was getting one hundred hogs onto the raft. Then Yargee rode to the bank with a bawling calf cradled across his thighs, and a bellowing mother cow coming right after him. Whip laughed, shook out a loop, and let it sail over the cow.

Rusk had reached the bank by then, and he gleefully tormented Tom.

"Thought you said mixed herds was bothersome. Looks like you got hoodwinked. Someone sold you a cow."

Squatting by the fire, Tom refilled his coffee, stood, and looked at the sweating, river-soaked Rusk. "I recognize that cow as one you bought."

"Like . . ." Rusk shook his head and laughed.

Yargee dismounted, put the calf on the ground, and laughed as the animal scurried to its bawling, snorting mother.

"Whip," Rusk yelled, "turn loose that mama and get to your pig-drovin' duties. Get them hogs on that raft."

Whip was already removing the loop from the cow. He shook his head, spit out curses, and climbed back into the saddle while Rusk led his horse to the picket line before joining Tom by the coffeepot. Rusk found a cup, filled it, and squatted.

"We'll have to kill that calf," he said. "Won't be able to keep up with us. But that'll give the boys some real food to eat. I'm sick of fish. And beans."

"No." Tom dropped his cup in the tin basin, and rose, trying not to groan.

"That bawlin' calf ain't—"

"We have to pay these Indians for helping us. We shall pay them in a calf and give them the mama cow, too."

"Payin' an injun. You're loco." Rusk tossed out the coffee and stood. "I paid twelve dollars for that—"

"I paid twelve dollars for that cow," Tom said. "Now, let's get the rest of this herd across that river."

The hogs were ferried across easily. Those Creeks, Tom observed, knew how to handle rafts, horses, and swine. Chitto accepted the payment of cow and calf, and Byers served them leftover fried fish, biscuits, and coffee. Once the Creeks left, Santos drove the extra horses across the river, then the rest of the crew pushed the longhorns into the Arkansas.

Yargee rode his horse alongside Tom, for which Tom was grateful. He held his breath when the buckskin had to swim, and sighed with relief when they climbed out onto a sandbar. A few longhorns took advantage of the islands, too, but Yargee kept their respites brief, and when the Cherokee spurred his dun into the river, Tom followed.

Another short swim, another sandbar, and then a brief bath before the horse found its footing on the river bottom, and the wet, tired men, horses, and cattle breathed easier on wet, but firm, land. The misting rain stopped, and a ray of sunlight peeked through the clouds. Tom swung off his horse while the last of the longhorns swam toward dry land.

"Trouble!"

Tom reached for the reins, but the horse shied from his hand.

"Colton!" Yargee screamed.

Spinning around, Tom found a horse splashing west of the last sandbar. Saw the empty saddle. A hand came out of the water, followed by a head. Both disappeared.

Head and outstretched arm reappeared. It was Greene. He went down again. Izan, already across the river, spurred his horse, but reined it hard to a stop. He was on the east side. He would have to cross the river to an island, cut over. Or lope around the long line of cattle on this side of the Arkansas to a pasture a half mile north. Either way, it would be too late.

Rusk, still mounted on the bank's western

side, swore. Then he stood in the stirrups and bellowed, "Whip. You fool!"

But Whip was there, letting his lariat sail, and Greene somehow saw it when his upper body came out of the water. He reached. Grabbed. Missed. Started to go down, but his arm slashed out again. This time, he found the rope.

*"Hiyaaaa!"* Whip's hand flashed as he made three dallies around the horn, leaned forward in the saddle, and the horse moved. Greene disappeared underneath the water, but the rope tightened, and then he surfaced, like some fast-moving ship. Whip's buckskin reached the sandbar, and the cowhand kept the gelding moving till he was at the end, some forty yards to the east.

On his knees, Colton Greene slogged onto the sandbar, bent forward, coughing, gagging, shaking his head, cursing while simultaneously thanking God.

"How 'bout thank me?" Laughing, Whip began dragging the lariat back toward him.

Tom realized he wasn't breathing. He sucked in air, wiped sweat from his forehead. The horse that had thrown Greene reached the banks. So did the last of the cattle.

"You got less sense than a turnip, boy," Rusk yelled at Whip. Leading his horse to the picket line being set up by Byers and Catfish, Rusk shook his head and muttered as he passed Tom,

"Riskin' gettin' drowned to save a no-'count darky's life."

Having seen military posts on the frontier, Fort Gibson was what Tom expected. The town around it, however, took him back to London and 1840.

A plump redhead stood on the hitch rail in front of a picket building, gripping a post that held a lantern. "Howdy, Slim." Grinning, she used her free hand to pull down the flimsy and filthy piece of calico, exposing her left breast. "Drop in, and for four bits, you can see the other one!"

She laughed so hard, she fell, but two buckskin-clad men caught her. Another woman held up a whiskey bottle, yelling, "Mine's bigger and softer."

Across the street, a man strummed a banjo and shouted that Capt'n Bill dealt the fairest faro in the Nations, and the whiskey—

"Will blind you before you've had your second swallow!" a man in front of a canvas structure yelled. "Over here, we got pure Kain-tuck bourbon."

Another woman came out of a tent, removed the cigar from her mouth, spit out tobacco, and smiled at Tom. "Howdy, handsome—ever seen a public woman before?" She did not wait for a reply. "Well, you can't—lessen you show a doll like me four bits."

Tom reined the roan toward an adobe store.

They had followed the Texas Road along the banks of the Grand River to Fort Gibson, leaving the herd a ways back. Yargee drove the wagon, with Washington Malone sitting next to him. Byers remained back in camp fixing supper for the rest of the crew.

"*Asgahni*," Yargee whispered.

"What's that?" Tom asked as he tethered the roan at a hitch rail.

"Sin. Wicked. Evil." The Cherokee climbed off the wagon. "My people hate this town. This fort." He spat. "I wish we did not stop here."

Tom wished the same, but they needed flour and coffee, and Tom had letters to post.

He left Yargee outside. Otherwise, vermin on the street would probably steal the roan and the wagon. The sutler did a good job of stealing with his prices. On the ride back to camp, Malone said, "Rusk will be itching to visit this Sodom."

Tom nodded.

"How can you stop him?"

He let Santos take the roan when they reached camp, and saw C. W. Rusk leading his saddled horse straight toward Tom. At least the Texian didn't have the whole crew backing his play. Yet.

Rusk stopped a few feet in front of Tom.

"I'll be headin' into Fort Gibson. See if it's fit for the boys."

"It's not fit for lice," Tom said.

The man grinned. "You can't stop the boys. They've worked hard. Deserve a good drunk. And you sure can't stop me."

Tom looked over Rusk's shoulder, saw every man by the fire staring, waiting, anticipating.

Tom stepped closer, and Rusk, still holding the reins, lowered his left hand toward the nearest Colt.

"You touch that pistol, I will knock your head off," Tom whispered. Rusk froze, shocked. Tom kept coming, stopping when he was close enough to Rusk to smell the tobacco and sweat. "You made a bad error. You can't drop those reins and pull that heavy pistol before I drop you to your knees."

Rusk blinked.

"I will leave you unconscious, and you know I can do it," Tom continued. "I will shame you so badly, your men will lose all respect for you." He smiled. "Whip, that lad you abuse so, he might not fear you when he sees you bleeding and sniveling on the ground. Would he?"

The Texian's neck and face turned crimson.

Now Tom changed his tone. "You and all of these men have done good work. Hard work. And you and these men will be rewarded. But not here. You would be cheated. Infirmed. Possibly murdered." Nodding, he unballed his hands. "I am not such a hard man, C. W. Have you ever been to St. Louis?"

Rusk appeared to have been struck dumb.

"There are more saloons and gambling parlors than you can count. Some of them are honest. And, while I have no expertise in this matter, I warrant you will find a brothel to your liking." When he raised his right hand, Rusk flinched, but Tom just smiled and put his hand on the cowhand's left shoulder. "St. Louis. Not here. St. Louis, and we are just a wide river from Illinois. St. Louis, and I will pay for every bottle you and all these fine lads finish."

He extended his left hand, but kept his eyes locked on Rusk.

"Except for Mr. Byers," Tom said as they shook hands. "I must keep the promise I made to his daughter."

As they followed the Texas Road between the Verdigris, then the Grand rivers, the country changed. The hills turned higher, the woods thicker—Tom tried to recall the last time he had seen dogwood trees—the rivers became turquoise, and the clouds filling the blue sky were white. The rain was gone. Good water. Good grass. They averaged twelve miles a day.

Malone feared Indians, though they rarely saw any other than Yargee. In fact, they hardly saw any other travelers heading north or south. Tom worried about stampedes, though the cattle had become, as Rusk put it, "trail broke." Even the hogs settled into a routine.

Tom knew they had crossed into Kansas when they stopped at a well-used camping ground with two springs surrounded by hard, red mud. Osage Indians, Yargee told them, traveled down the Black Dog Trail here to drink the water to cure them of sickness. Others bathed here for the springs had healing powers.

Rusk laughed and called that "injun twaddle." But everyone filled his canteen with water from the springs, and Malone, Yargee, and even Mr. Byers soaked in the water that night before they put the cattle, hogs, and horses back on the road and turned east. Tom bathed, too. By his reckoning, they had been on the trail for just more than a month. He washed the shirt he had been wearing since crossing the Red River, and put on his spare.

Nerves settled down, even Malone's. The cause, Tom knew, had to be that they were out of Indian territory, but part of him liked to think those springs had worked their magic.

Before they stopped for their next camp, they had crossed into Missouri. A crooked sign nailed to a tree told them as much.

U aR in Mizzaru
onles sumbode
Movd this synn
2 kanses

June 3, 1853

My dearest Tom,

I must stop reading newspapers. Today I happened upon a horrible story about these most ghastly depredations committed by red Indians in Texas. My heart pounds, and tears blind me.

Please, Tom, tell me that this upper Brazos River and Fort Belknap are nowhere near you. Wichita Indians, the paper reports, are becoming more hostile and daring in their frontier depredations.

I fear for you, my love.

Oh, tears pour, my heart aches. Please write me that you are well when you reach the Springfield post office and find this letter waiting for you.

Yours truly,
Margaret Snyder

# CHAPTER 33

This part of the Texas Road was new to Tom.

Having turned south after Springfield with Malone, Marney, and those hundred mules when they came through Missouri in the spring, Tom decided to scout ahead that morning, so he saddled the roan, and rode out after one cup of coffee.

The country, forty, maybe fifty miles west of Springfield, was rugged but green, moss on the rocks, the timbers thick with cottontails, squirrels, even a few white-tailed deer. He had met no travelers. Then he saw the pole that crossed the road, and a bearded man sitting in a rocking chair on the lane's left side fanning himself with a battered brown hat, a jug on the dirt to his right, and a long rifle across his lap.

Tom reined in briefly, wet his lips, studied the hills on both sides of the road, then kicked the roan into a walk. The man kept fanning himself. The crooked pole had been set in to crudely V-shaped bars on each side of the trail.

A tin pail rested on the right-hand side. The man on the left kept rocking.

Tom reined up a few feet from the man, who stopped fanning himself, leaned forward in the rocking chair, and set the hat atop his dark head.

"Mornin'," the man said.

"Good day, sir."

"Headin' for Springfield?"

Tom nodded.

"Well, it's ten cents for horse and rider. Pitch the coin in the pail yonder."

A moment passed before Tom could speak.

"I do not believe what fell upon my ear, sir."

"You talk funny. But see how this falls upon your ear." He eared back the hammer of the rifle. "Ten cents, for horse and rider."

"But this is a public road."

The man, still rocking the chair, nodded. "And I'm the public." He grinned black teeth. "I like to hear the sound of coins hittin' that tin. When I hear that music, I take down that gate. Don't like to get up till I hear that music. Don't move 'round so good no more. Broke my back five year back. And got buckshot in the back of this knee." He patted the right thigh.

"You are a dastardly blockhead, sir. I shall not pay your ransom."

The man stopped rocking, and leaned forward.

"You ain't from Missouri, mister. I can tell by 'em ten-cent words spittin' out your mouth. But here, we don't take kindly to insults. Most folks ride this way, they just pay the toll, make no fuss. But ever' now and then, some uppity jackass decides to raise a ruction. We bury him."

Tom straightened. The rifle still laid across

the man's lap, cocked, but the brigand merely chuckled and resumed his rocking.

"You heard that *we,* I take it. Yup. Ain't just me. Got two boys in the trees up yonder for skinflints like you. They each got one of 'em newfangled revolvers, and both of 'em is capped for service."

"I shall report this brigandry to the local constabulary, sir."

The man nodded, kept the rocker going, and hooked his left thumb behind him.

"That'd be Carthage. Nice little town. Good folks. Got some lead mines. That's where we get our balls for 'em new-fangled, fast-shootin' short guns." He patted the stock of the rifle. "And Miss Mena here."

Tom scanned the trees in the hills, looking for any sign of two gunmen. Maybe the man was running a bluff.

"County seat, Carthage is. Jasper County. Sheriff's name is McCoy. Max McCoy. Honest as the day's long, but a bit of a sorehead. So you go right ahead and find Sheriff Max. Tell him Cornelius says to ride up and pull a cork with him next Saturday.

"After you pay your ten cents fare." He hooked the thumb again. "Cutoff to Carthage be 'bout a mile and a quarter east."

The noise came from behind. Twisting in the saddle, Tom looked west. The green trees, the dark hills, the long road—it felt just like staring into a tunnel. Hooves clopped on the hard-packed trail, the bell rang from that cow-ox's neck, leather creaked, drovers cursed, steers bawled, and someone—Whip, most likely—sang.

*Now way down south, not very far off*
*A bullfrog died with the whooping cough*
*And the other side of Mississippi*
*As you must know*
*There's where I was christened*
  *Jim Along Joe*
*Hey, get along, get along Josey*
*Hey, get along, Jim Along Joe*

Tom waited till the rider appeared. Breathing easier now, he turned back to the road agent. He feared Mr. Byers and Catfish would be leading in the wagon, letting the steers follow that ringing bell, but Rusk must have put the wagon in the rear. The road was too narrow for one to be riding along the trail. At the point rode Santos and Rusk. That was even better.

He could not think of two better men to back him in a fight. But what he really wanted this road agent to see was the massive horns of seven hundred Texas steers.

"By thunder." The man pushed himself out of the chair, leaned forward. "By thunder."

Tom turned back to the petty thief. "I am not alone. As you can see."

"Boys." The man looked up the hills. "Boys. You best get down here now."

"Uncle Cornelius, we best stay up here. Keep you covered from up here."

"Bybee. You an' Alva get down here right now. Show 'em we Bozarths . . ."

Tom looked up the hills, saw no movement, but Uncle Cornelius turned back, brought the long rifle up, but not aiming it, just keeping it against his chest. The hammer remained cocked.

The old man still ran his bluff. "It's three cents for ever' bovine, horse, or mule. Ten cents a wagon."

Tom leaned in the saddle. "Ever seen a man trampled by seven hundred head of cattle, *Uncle Cornelius?*"

"You wouldn't dare." Beads of sweat popped up along the ridges of his forehead. "You'd get kilt, too."

Tom straightened. "I am well-mounted, sir."

"Alva." The voice had gone up a few octaves. "Bybee."

Santos spurred his chestnut ahead, reined to a stop alongside Tom.

"And my friend here will shoot you dead. That will start the ball. And the stampede." He stared hard at Uncle Cornelius.

"There are two up in the hills," Tom told Santos softly, and looked down the trail. Rusk rode his horse back and forth of the leaders, stopping the herd for now.

"*Señor.*" Tom heard the hammer click on Santos's Navy Colt. "*No más.*" The chestnut blew hard, then began urinating on the road.

"Shall I kill this man, *patrón*?"

Tom looked back, first at Uncle Cornelius, then up at the ridges.

"Let's see what kind of deal he wants to make us first," Tom said.

"Well." The old man smiled, held the rifle out far from his chest, and made an effort of showing how he lowered the hammer, then stepped off the road and leaned his long gun against a bush. He glanced up the hill and said, "You boys, don't do nothin' foolhardy. Let's welcome these foreigners to Missouri. Show 'em how kind we is to strangers and wayfarers. You hear me, Bybee?"

No answer.

"Alva?"

Tom thought the two nephews, or whatever they were, had flown the coop.

"Yellow sons of . . ." Uncle Cornelius limped to the north side of the road, grunted as he raised the poll, let it fall in the dirt. He nodded, grinned at Santos, and crossed the lane. "Yes, sir, boys, yes sirree. We like to welcome foreigners to our fine state. Mighty fine. Mighty fine indeed. Good place. Good weather. Good people."

He raised the poll off the other "V," dropped it, bent with a crack of both knees and a curse, picked up the poll, and dragged it off the lane into the woods. "Good roads, too. You boys have a safe trip."

Then he ran—if one might call it running—and vanished among the briars, brambles, and bois d'arcs.

June 6, 1853

My dearest Tom,

Father scoffs at my letters. How will he act today since I posted my last letter to you just Saturday?

Mr. Woods said after Sunday Meeting yesterday that he heard from a wayfarer of a mail party that passed a large number of droves of cattle, all bound for California, and that many drovers suffered tremendous losses of cattle in consequence of stampedes during hailstorms.

I discern from Mr. Woods's telling that these droves were passing through the Ty. of New Mexico, but I take pen—the very fountain pen you gave me before you left on this adventure for you, but a heartache for me—in hand to pray that your travels have not been marred by hailstorms and stampedes, and that we soon will be reunited and can find some nuts to gather in the woods.

Ever yours,
Margaret Snyder

# CHAPTER 34

Four days later, they reached Springfield.

They bedded down the herd outside of town because Tom advanced the men two-and-a-half dollars and allowed them to, in groups, head into town for a bath, shave, and meal. "I will hold you to your word that no intoxicating spirits will be consumed," he said.

He didn't hold out much hope, but two dollars and four bits would not leave anyone in serious trouble as Tom could not recall any gambling establishments or hearing of any brothels when he and Malone had been there last spring.

Catfish rode into town with Tom. They headed straight for the postmaster, where the young cook's helper planned to mail a letter to his parents.

"This'll be only the second letter I've ever mailed," he said excitedly as they trotted into town. "First one was that one you posted for me. The one I wrote my folks saying I was hired to work this cattle drive and wouldn't be home till next year."

Tom said something in response. But he had no memory of what he had said.

"What made you do this, Mr. Ponting?"

"Have my post held?" Tom grinned. They were

getting closer to his destination. "It is a common practice—"

"That's not what I mean," Catfish said. "And you know it. What made you want to bring cattle and pigs all this way?"

"Oh," Tom said, "I would list my reasons as a foolish dream, an even more foolish wager, and a young lady."

The boy laughed.

"What's funny?" Tom asked.

"That you didn't call the young lady *foolish*." He pushed back his hat. "I guess she's the real reason."

A half mile later, Tom reined up. Numbness overtook him. Carpenters were tearing down the charred timbers of what had been Springfield's post office.

"Burned down Tuesday."

Turning in the saddle, Tom recognized the man crossing the street. Mr. Law, who owned the mercantile, held up his right hand, smiling. "Mr. Ponting. I was not certain I would ever lay eyes on you again." They shook. "I trust your endeavor in Texas proved rewarding."

"We shall see, Mr. Law. We shall see. But I have a drove of Texas cattle and hogs and we have made it this far." Somehow, he had forced out those words. Now his stomach turned, and he gestured at the ruins behind him.

"Postmaster Holland . . . is . . ."

"Holland." The man chuckled. "He's not postmaster anymore. Got a new one, just this week. Ingram. Archibald F. Ingram."

"So . . . the post office has . . . moved."

The merchant laughed. "Well, it's moving now. Archie rode down to the Piney. Be back on the morrow, I warrant. Some fire. Thought my store might go up with it. Archie and the marshal and the mayor and we all agreed it was spontaneous combustion. On account we didn't find no ashes within fifty feet of the cabin. And hot as it was, there wasn't no fires going within a hundred feet."

"The mail?" Tom asked hopefully.

Law shook his head.

"Blaze spread with great rapidity. Archie had to go out a window. Wonder we managed to save what we did, including the whole town. Archie lost ninety dollars in postage stamps, too."

"Is it possible to get a letter mailed from here?" Catfish asked.

"Oh, sure. Archie showed me how. I let him set up in a corner till we can find him a new place. Mail won't go out till Archie gets back anyhow. Come into the store. Sit a spell. I got some crackers y'all can eat. I'd love to hear all about your adventures."

Tom let Catfish do the talking. The boy stayed there three hours. It seemed that everyone in town wanted to hear about Texas. A few years ago, people longed to hear tales of California and the gold fields. Now they wanted to know of Texas. Catfish Jim Hennessy was glad to tell them.

Tom sat on the porch, half listening, staring at the ashes, the blackened wood, wondering if Margaret had written anything at all.

He stuck his letter in the back pocket of his trousers, bought paper, pen, and envelope from Mr. Law, and penned a new letter. He would save this old one for when he saw Margaret again. If he saw her again. Maybe he would even finish it.

Barring any fraudulent tollkeepers, they had eighteen days to go before they would reach St. Louis.

He brought the cup of coffee to his mouth, then lowered it. Tom stared blankly at Mr. Byers, turned, looked at Santos, who was so focused on his breakfast, he did not even notice Tom's look.

Turning, he saw Malone, writing something in the ledger opened upon his knees.

"Washington," he whispered.

His partner looked up.

"What day is it?"

The man blinked. He started to answer, but stopped, and looked over at Rusk as though the Texian might have the answer. Rusk just spit tobacco juice into the fire.

Malone looked back at Tom. "I . . ." He seemed bewildered. "Don't you know?"

"It is not Tuesday," Tom said. *That is the day the post office burned.*

"Well." Malone closed the ledger. "It's . . . it's . . ."

"It's just another damned day in the damned saddle on this damned road to hell," Rusk said with irritation, and, grunting, he pushed himself to his feet, stared hard at Malone, then turned and glared at Tom. "Ain't it?"

This road, he knew. He remembered the stops, the creeks, the crossings. Yet there were no turkeys to be seen on the Gasconade, and nobody desired to soak in the Meramec. In Union, Tom was forced to buy a new shirt and burn an old one. The sutler also sold kegs of rum. Tom felt the temptation, but walked out in his new shirt, mounted the roan, and rejoined the drove.

Leaving Malone and Rusk in charge, Tom reached St. Louis in midmorning. He got directions to the Pacific Stockyards from a boy selling the *Daily Missouri Democrat* on Locust Street, and found the place quickly.

Tom made the arrangements. The stockyards' landlord agreed on the price, and Tom met the drove on the city's outskirts and helped bring cattle, hogs, and horses to the stockyard grounds.

"You may sleep in the house, and your men in the barn," the landlord said.

"Thank you," Tom said as he paid the fee in advance, "but we understand our livestock." He chuckled. "And, on occasion, they understand us."

"Golly."

Whip's word was the first spoken as they gazed across the Mississippi River.

"It looks like an ocean," Catfish said. Then he giggled, ran to the bank, pulled up his duck trousers, and sank his right foot in the muddy water. "I touched 'er first," he called out.

Whip was second. Izan third. When Tom joined in, the others followed, even C. W. Rusk. All except James Byers. The cook just stared upstream, tears welling in his eyes.

They left Byers there. He returned to the stockyards fifteen minutes later.

That evening, Tom gave each man five dollars, and wondered how many he would see again that night and how many he would have to bail out of jail.

Mr. Byers cooked the supper on the other side of the gate. Catfish and Washington Malone stayed behind.

The sun set. Night settled upon them. The fire crackled. Coffee simmered.

"Want to make a bet?"

Tom blinked, thought he must have been

dreaming, but he saw Washington Malone smiling.

"Since when do you gamble?" Tom asked.

"Well, the sun has been baking my brains since we left Illinois."

Mr. Byers and Catfish straightened and leaned closer.

"Who is the first to return?" Malone said.

Tom laughed. "That's your idea of a wager?"

Catfish called out, "Yargee." Then he thought to ask: "How much are we betting?"

Malone shrugged. "Two bits."

"Done." The boy reached deep into his pants pocket.

"Mr. Byers?" Malone asked.

The cook just shook his head.

"Well?" Malone looked at Tom.

"Whip," Tom said. *That fool will be broke before he knows it.*

Malone said, "I shall go with Santos. Are we agreed?"

Everyone nodded.

"If anyone else arrives first, drunk or sober or in a policeman's custody, no one wins and no one loses. Agreed?"

More nods.

Two hours, fifteen minutes later—according to the new lever watch Tom bought that afternoon at S. C. Jett's store on Main Street—the gate squeaked open. Catfish was already dead asleep, and Tom must have been dozing, for his head jerked off his chest.

Washington Malone let out a heavy sigh.

Blinking sleep out of his eyes, Tom heard boots, spurs, and a grunt. He stared in disbelief. C. W. Rusk squatted by the fire, brought a half-full bottle to his mouth, and drank.

"This city . . ." Rusk made some vague gesture, and sank back onto his buttocks. He took another swig. "Well, it sure ain't Texas."

June 11, 1853

My dearest Tom,

The arrival of your letter of the 21st ult. filled my heart with elation to know at last that you have been on the trail for more than a month. Mr. Armstrong brought it from the post office in Decatur. Perhaps one day Moweaqua will have its own post office.

To be reunited, to continue the long conversations we have had when we have been left together fills my heart, for of late I have had little to occupy my mind but crooked needles as I have forced myself to commence a cordon of sewing. You should try to count this multitude of furbelows I have ruined.

My mind rarely functions at all, thinking

of our reunion that must come soon. I close for now, but know that always you shall be in my heart and soul.

Ever yours,<br>
Margaret Snyder

# CHAPTER 35

"*¿Un momento, señor?*"

Tom stopped at the gate, and turned toward Santos.

The *vaquero* and his brother stood a few feet away. Sitting on the fence's top rail, C. W. Rusk did not look down as he whittled the top wooden rail next to him with his pocket knife.

"Of course, Santos." Tom had been feeling fine. He had sold the entire herd of hogs for four dollars a head. He was ten days or thereabouts from reaching the end of this leg of the journey. He would be home, where he could sleep under his own roof in his own cabin on his own stock farm. He would see, feel, and smell all the beauty that was Margaret Snyder. He would still have a chance of winning a thousand dollars off Margaret's hard-rock father. And now . . . ?

"It is not that we do not wish to join you, *señor*," Santos said. "But Izan and I talked last night, after we found a priest to hear our confessions, and our conversation contintued this morning." He breathed in, exhaled. "For months, we have journeyed with you. It was my wish to continue, but Izan, he misses our *madre*, our *padre*." Santos jutted his firm jaw toward the wide river. "He fears if he crosses this, he will never return home."

Tom made his head move up and down.

"And what of you, Santos?"

The young man smiled, then shrugged. "He is my brother, *señor*. I must see him home. See that he returns to our parents, our country, safely. You may not understand—"

"I understand completely." Tom extended his hand.

After they shook, Tom reached underneath his shirt, and started to laugh. "I've lost weight, it appears." He fingered out two coins. "Good thing I sold those hogs." He turned his palm over, and nodded at the two California slugs.

"*Señor*." Santos shook his head. "That is too much."

"It's not enough. We never would have made it this far without you two . . ." Tom wasn't sure he could pronounce the word right, but he tried: ". . . *vaqueros*."

Rusk stopped whittling. "You two bean-eaters supplied your own mounts. Take 'em. Cut out a couple of spares, too. We don't need 'em. Sure don't need two quitters."

He tossed the wood behind him, folded the blade, and slipped the knife in his pocket. "Never mind. Me and Whip'll catch up your hosses." He jumped down from the fence, spit to the side, jabbed the knife blade into the fence post, then held out his left hand.

Smiling, Santos shook it. "I shall see you

393

when you return from this adventure, *mi amigo.*"

Rusk turned with a grunt and moved back to the gate. "Doubt it. They'll have strung you two horse thieves up by the time me and Whip mosey back to Texas."

Thirty minutes later, the two brothers rode west.

That afternoon, a flatboat captained by a Frenchman named Le Claire took the first load of cattle across the Mississippi. The waters were rough, but the toughest part of the job, Tom quickly learned, was keeping the longhorns from falling into the river, balancing the herd so the massive boat didn't tilt to one side. Once the boat touched Illinois ground, Catfish, his face a sickly white, staggered off ahead of the cattle, fell to the right, out of the way of the panicking longhorns, crawled to the bank, and vomited. He kept vomiting. An oarsmen said he had never known a body could hold that much liquid, especially a kid that puny.

Slapping hats against their thighs, Malone and Tom herded the rest of the cattle off the boat.

Mr. Byers, Yargee, and Colton Greene arrived in better condition than Catfish, but equally exhausted.

Whip and Rusk manned the last boat, Rusk cursing between vomiting, and Whip waving his hat, laughing, and singing:

*I'm salted down in great big lumps.*
*They curse my eyes and pick my bones,*
*And throw the rest to Davy Jones.*
*Poor . . . old . . . horse!*

Tom, Byers, and Whip were the only ones in good enough condition to return on the third flatboat to bring the horses into Illinois.

Leaning on the railing, looking north, he remembered the letter—still unfinished, by thunder, barely started—that he had been penning to Margaret. He reached into his pocket, pulled it out, unfolded it, and stared at that scrawl of his. When they reached St. Louis again, before herding the remuda onto the boat, he could find a post office and—

The wind caught the letter at that moment, he opened his mouth but did not speak, did not even curse, and barely sighed.

The paper flew, sailing, not high—like a bird skimming over the waves in the river, looking for an unsuspecting fish too close to the surface, floating carrion, or something some ferryboat passenger had lost. Like a letter.

It hit the dark water, and he lost sight of it.

*Well, most folks would not even call what I wrote a letter.*

Byers made coffee and tea that night, since few had any appetite. He warmed both over the next morning. Malone and Tom were the only ones awake as the cook gathered his sack of clothes and personal items, and the heavy Mississippi Rifle.

Reaching down, Tom grabbed the string to the pouch, lifted it, tossed it and caught it, the coins jingling, and held out the leather bag.

"You are welcome to a horse," Tom said.

"Thank you, no." He took the pouch, did not bother counting the money, and dropped it into a pillowcase. "Greene County is but a stretch of a soldier's legs from here."

"We would gladly have you stay with us, Mr. Byers," Malone said. "The rest of the journey should be easy, sir, as we have crossed into civilized country."

"Then you have no need of an old warhorse like me." Byers grinned, but a moment later he drew in a deep breath and let it out. "I shall much miss our fellowship, but you have a good cook." He smiled down at the sleeping young Jim Hennessy. "The lad can handle a team, too."

"So," Tom said softly, "this is farewell."

"Yes. I must see my wife."

"Give her our . . ." Malone's face paled as he remembered, but he finished the sentiment anyway. ". . . best."

Byers extended his hand to Malone first.

"Tell the boys, especially the lad, that it has been a pleasure." His eyes locked on Tom. They shook without another word, and Byers started walking along the river's edge.

"Mister Ponting? Mister Malone."

Looking up into Yargee's face, Tom smiled wearily. "Yargee. You slept through the morning, but Catfish is still asleep. We figured we'd rest and push on toward Moweaqua in the morning." He couldn't think of anything else to say, or anything that would delay what he read in the man's face.

"I been watchin' that ferry downriver." The Cherokee paused. "Back and forth. Back and forth."

"Yes." Tom stood and glanced down the Mississippi. "One day there will be a great bridge linking Illinois and Missouri. I wish to live to see that, for I have had my fill of boats, ships, and ferries."

"Reckon so."

Malone sat quietly, not even looking at either man until Colton Greene walked over from the river's edge. Then Malone sighed, as if he, too, knew what was coming.

Yargee turned to Greene, but several seconds passed before he could tell Greene: "Reckon I'll be riding back."

Greene's mouth opened.

The Cherokee looked back at Tom.

"Reckon I'm drawing my time, sir."

"Yargee . . ." Greene whispered. "We said . . ."

"We said lots of things." The tall Cherokee again faced his partner. "I believed them for a spell. But I've been watching families cross that big river. Some going east. Some heading west. But they were going . . . as a family."

"Your family, Yargee. Your people." Greene held his breath, trying to come up with the right words. "They are in their homeland. The Cherokees you told me about. The ones who escaped that roundup. The ones who . . ."

"My family's on Pecan Creek. Back in the Cherokee Nation. The family I know anyhow. That's where I belong. That's where I'm going. I don't know nobody in those mountains. I was four years old when we got forced west. West is what I know. So I'm going back. Back home. Hope you understand."

"I understand, Yargee." Tom extended his right hand. "I am proud to have made your acquaintance."

The leathery man looked at the hand, then into Tom's eyes. He took the hand and shook it hard twice before turning back to Colton Greene. "I hope you find what you seek, my friend."

Greene barely blinked, but after a long silence, he said, "I'll catch up a horse for you."

"Criminy." C. W. Rusk tossed the coffee Catfish had just poured him onto the coals. "You let another quitter go."

He threw the cup into the tin basin, put both hands on his hips, and spit, shook his head again, and stared hard at Ponting. He yelled, "Anybody else want to give up?"

"I sure won't be quitting." Catfish jumped back from the bacon grease popping in the skillet. "I aim to see the city of New York." He eased closer to the fire, and used the big fork to pull the cast-iron skillet off the red coals. "There's this Exhibition of the Industry of All Nations going on there beginning in May of this year. I aim to see everything I can."

"It's already July, boy," Rusk said. He frowned at Tom: "Who we got left?"

"I ain't quittin'," Whip said with a big smile.

Rusk's head shook. He opened his mouth, but Tom cut him off.

"We do not have the hogs. The cattle are trail broke. You have said that yourself." He kept speaking, quietly, and with confidence. "In ten days, maybe fewer, we shall be in Moweaqua, where we will have nothing to do but feed our cattle shocked corn for the rest of the summer and all winter, then drive them to New York City in the spring."

Rusk shook his head. "I never should have signed on for this fool enterprise." He spit again and stormed away from the camp.

"Me, neither." But Whip found a plate and

brought it over to where Catfish was burning bacon.

July 10, 1853

My dearest Tom:
Your letter from Springfield arrived, and while learning of the loss of all those letters shattered my heart as I felt your tears on the paper I held, I realize that the blaze that consumed all I had written is our Lord's way of saying that all that matters is our love.

This letter, and every letter that I write from now till I see you in the flesh, will not burn—as I shall save them under the mattress with a beautiful gold coin.

When we are happily reunited—at least till your journey continues with the coming of the next spring—I will give this and other letters for you to read.

Ever yours,<br>Margaret Snyder

# CHAPTER 36

At best, the corn would turn up short. With so many ears already twisted, Tom doubted if the fields would produce more than half an average yield. Some farmers had already given up, leaving the crops to dry. Wheat and oats might make out average, if a decent rain fell soon, but potatoes would likely be small.

And to think that back in Texas and through the Indian Nations, Tom had wondered if he would ever dry out from all that rain.

Maybe, when they turned northeast along the Kaskaskia, the country would green up. You never could tell about the weather.

Two oxen pulled the wagon, the spare ox-cow still tethered behind, Catfish working the lines, and Washington Malone, his back, shoulders, and hips shot again by heat, wind, and miles, sat next to him. That was an improvement over the past two days, when Malone lay on his bedroll in the wagon bed, next to the dwindling supply of food, hay, and oats.

Down the line of cattle, about a third of the length, Whip rode, slapping his thigh with his lariat, singing a soft ballad that the wind brought down the trail.

*Roll on silver moon*
*Point the traveler this way*
*While the nightingale's song is in tune*
*I never, never more*
*With my true love will stray*
*By the soft silver beams, gentle moon*

That drover's voice when he sang to cattle always surprised Tom. He turned, looked down and across the herd to where Rusk rode on the other side, then made out Colton Greene riding drag, almost hidden by the dust.

They had been traveling four days. No, this was the fifth. They would swing past Vandalia, where the National Road petered out from the east, turn north. Five more days at most and they would be home.

He wondered how far Santos and Izan had traveled. And Yargee. Surely Mr. Byers had reached his home by now.

*Ah me ne'er again may my bosom rejoice*
*For my lost love I fain would meet soon*
*And fond lovers will*
*Weep o'er the grave where we sleep*
*'Neath thy soft silver light, gentle moon*

He remembered London. At a tavern with John, after they had visited the House of Wax. A woman, a soprano, had been singing that song.

Men wept. Even those who had been engaged in some terrible row of fisticuffs over some slight, real or imagined.

Dust blew, cattle lowed, the left rear wheel of the wagon squeaked, Tom's roan snorted, and the hoofbeats sounded evenly on the trail. Tom turned again. Colton Greene appeared to be asleep in the saddle. Reins draped over the gelding's neck, C. W. Rusk kept slapping the coiled rope in his left hand against his leg. Tom adjusted the neckerchief that covered his mouth and nose, and thought about singing along in the final verses of the last chorus. But another voice reached him.

*I never, never more*
*With my true love will stray*
*By the soft silver beams, gentle moon*

C. W. Rusk had a fine singing voice, too.
Again, Tom wondered: *What day is it?*

He nodded at the man standing on the roadside, holding tight to the reins of a sorrel mare.
"Ponting."
Tom looked at the sky, hoping for a cloud, and again feeling disappointment.
"Ponting."
He blinked. Then he reined the roan off the road, pulled him to a stop, and looked down the

pike at the man with the mare. The longhorns kept moving along, paying no attention to anything but the steers in front of them, or the ass of the ox behind the wagon and the ringing bell tied around the cow's neck.

Tom pulled down the silk, or what once had been silk, from his face.

The man nodded. He appeared to smile. "I thought it was you. It *had* to be you." He laughed, and started walking toward him, pulling the sorrel.

Tom opened his mouth, closed it, watched the man walk toward him.

"Allow me to be the first to welcome you home."

Tom looked down the trail. Colton Greene kept the drag moving north. C. W. Rusk stared across the longhorns. Behind them, dust blended in with the sky as it had been for days.

Alfred C. Campbell raised his right hand. "It is good to see you. You have lost weight. But your cattle, they look good and fat."

The farmer was being polite. He should have seen this herd before it crossed the Red River into the Indian Nations.

Tom let one hand slide away from the reins, and felt a farmer's grip.

"By thunder, just look at those horns," the man was saying, "I never would have believed . . ."

Finally, a broad smile cracked the dust and

grime that caked Tom's face. "Captain Campbell" was all Tom could say.

*When was the last time I had a conversation of more than one or two sentences?*

"John's took right good care of your place, Ponting," Captain Alfred C. Campbell said. "Corn did better than most. Been a dry summer here. But you'll have something to feed these cows, though, well, glory, I sure didn't expect to see you with this many. Welcome home, Ponting. Welcome home."

Tom stared at his gloved hand.

*When did I last shake the hand of a neighbor?*

"You might win that bet, Ponting. You got more cattle than I've ever seen except in a Chicago yard."

Tom swallowed. "Captain?"

Campbell waited.

Tom tried to laugh. "How far away are we?"

Now the captain let out a roar of laughter that spooked his horse slightly, but Tom's roan and the passing longhorns paid no attention. "Five miles, Tom. Five miles. You'll be at your place before dusk."

He wanted to thank Captain Campbell, but it hurt just to speak that much. Still, he swallowed, worked up a bit more spit, and sent that down. His voice came out as a hoarse whisper, but the captain heard.

"Do I know what day it is? Why, yes, Ponting, I

surely do. It is Tuesday, the twenty-sixth of July. And it's still the year of our Lord, eighteen and fifty-three."

This time, he did not need the help of a stump, rock, or ditch bank to climb into the saddle. He kicked the roan into a fast walk and Tom caught up to the wagon.

"We're five miles from home, boys," Tom said. Catfish grinned. Malone just blinked.

"Washington, I need you to get our herd to the pastures. It will be dark then, but we are too close to stop. Can you see this done?"

"Of course."

"I must ride to Moweaqua. I feel certain there shan't be enough food, coffee, and tea at my place. I will fill my saddlebags and be back at the cabin tonight. Later, we can return for necessities."

"Moweaqua," Malone said.

"Yes. I will be there as fast as possible." He kicked the roan into a trot.

After he had gone fifty yards, Malone called out: "Flat Branch likely has cheaper prices." And followed with a cackling laugh.

He turned down the lane to the Snyder home. No one would call him a coward now, not riding up here, bold as brass, waiting for that German braggart to step outside and laugh and say, *No,*

*I am having my supper and I shall not open the store for anyone. Come back in the morning.* Certainly, there would be no offer to step in for coffee, no request to share some tales of Texas and those beastly longhorns, and Margaret would be confined—*imprisoned*—in her room.

But it was worse. Much worse.

In the dusk, Mrs. Snyder stopped sweeping the porch and stared, her cold eyes burning just as Tom remembered.

"Good evening, Frau Snyder," Tom tried. "I know the hour is late, but I was hoping to have a word with Herr Snyder and . . ."

"We heard you were back," she said. "Five men stopped to tell us of all they had seen on the road. Those cattle you bring sound like *monster*." She laughed. "You look . . ." Then she laughed harder.

Tom couldn't blame her.

"Go." She nodded, and Tom couldn't blame her for that, either. What had he been thinking? He was filthy, tired. He looked more like any monster than his longhorns.

But Frau Snyder pointed toward the village.

"Herr Snyder wait for you. Go. Maybe you buy *seife*."

Moweaqua had grown in the months Tom had been gone, and if the door had not been open, bathing the gloaming with yellow light, and if Michael Snyder's carriage not been out in front,

Tom might have given up looking for the cabin and ridden back to his place.

"Ah." Michael Snyder looked up from behind the counter. "Ponting. Welcome home. I hear you have many Texas cattle."

Tom nodded. "Yes, sir." He saw a sack of flour, a side of bacon, and miscellaneous items already stacked on the countertop.

"You need food?"

Snyder's English had improved, too.

"Just enough to get us through a day or two. I have a few men with me."

"How many cattle?"

"Around seven hundred."

Snyder's eyes widened.

"We have not done a tally."

"You push on to New York?"

Tom shook his head. "We could not make it until fall. So we shall wait out the winter, and move out come spring."

"If spring comes." Snyder laughed. "You surprise me, Ponting. You made it here with more cattle and faster than I believed possible. But still I think I will win my bet."

Snyder waved at the items he had laid out. "Take. Do not pay now. Your credit is good." He chuckled. "At least until you pay me one thousand dollars when I win our bet."

Tom looked at the items on the counter. That would tide him and his crew for a few days. Of course, it wasn't all he wanted, or really why he had ridden to the village, but he would not see Margaret tonight. So, this was Tuesday. Maybe he would come to Sunday's church meeting.

"*Ach.*" Snyder stepped back, laughing. "I did not think. You need soap. Much soap. I will find some."

He carried the bacon and the flour outside, tied them atop his bedroll behind the cantle, turned, and was heading back when a voice called from the shadows.

"Tom."

Margaret stepped forward.

"I wanted to see you," she whispered.

He stopped, looked in the doorway, swallowed. "I wanted to see you," he said.

She had crept out the window, climbed down the tree, and run all the way. Her brothers would not betray her, although they thought it was ridiculous that Margaret would do this for a man she had not seen in months.

As Mr. Snyder busied himself inside the store, Tom stared at Margaret, just a few feet away, her back against the logs. He wanted to wrap his arms around her, but he also thought: *Soap. I need soap.*

"I got your letters," she said. "Both of them."

The one from Springfield. Which mentioned

the fire at the post office. That wasn't much of a letter. Nor was the one he had posted right before they crossed the Red River.

"I started another one," he said. "Just never got around to finishing it. Pulled it out of my pocket while we were crossing the Mississippi." He sighed, shook his head, and said, "Wind caught it. It flew like a dove for, oh, two hundred yards, then the river caught it."

"Oh, Tom."

Her father came out of the storeroom, put something on the counter, nodded, went back to the storeroom.

"I wish . . . all those letters I wrote," Margaret whispered. "That fire. Oh, Tom."

Inside, Mr. Snyder began whistling.

"Tell me," she asked softly, "what you wrote in that letter."

He looked at his boots, then inside the store. Mr. Snyder stared over the counter. "Ponting. Here is your soap. Some clothes, too. And matches. So you can burn what you wear this night. I bring to you now."

Margaret backed away.

"No, Herr Snyder," Tom called out, and stepped onto the porch. "You've done enough. I'll get them."

One more step, and he would be inside.

"I better hurry home," Margaret whispered.

"You need wash clothes," Mr. Snyder said.

"And towels. I have some. Good linen." He disappeared underneath the counter.

She hadn't left, and the light from the door illuminated her face.

"I wrote," he said, " 'My love for you is boundless.' "

Then she stood next to him, wrapped her arms around his waist, and pulled him to her. She kissed his filthy, dirty, bearded cheek. "That's so beautiful," she whispered, "I might cry."

"I smell like horse sweat and cattle," he said.

"Yes, you do." She giggled.

Mr. Snyder came up, started stacking more items on the counter.

Margaret quickly slipped into the darkness.

"Come, Ponting. I have one more thing for you. Good cramp and pain killer. Cures dysentery, colds, toothaches, chills, fevers, piles. Good medicine. Mrs. Osborn highly recommends."

"I am sorry your letters got burned," Tom whispered as he stepped into the store.

"Don't worry," he heard her quiet reply. "I remember what I wrote. And we have the rest of the summer, and all through autumn and winter for me to tell you."

# PART IV
## 1854

A fine lot of nearly 100 head of cattle, from Texas, were sent over the New York Central Road on Wednesday, for the New York market. The high price of beef in all the eastern markets still continues, and the whole country is ransacked in order to supply the demand. Cattle can be purchased in Texas at almost a nominal price, and forwarded to New York, via the Mississippi river and northern railroads, so as to leave a good margin for profits at the present high rates of selling. We understand that more will soon follow.

—*Buffalo* (New York)
*Daily Republic*,
June 30, 1854

# CHAPTER 37

Tom had enjoyed wide celebrity in this part of Illinois, but not as much as Catfish, C. W. Rusk, and Whip. Colton Greene, by the color of his skin, was more a curiosity, but most people in Christian and Shelby counties seemed interested in those longhorn cattle.

Over that fall and into the winter, which, thankfully, had been mild, Tom and Malone sold a few. Even Michael Snyder bought one.

They had moved the herd from lease to lease, farm to farm, pasture to pasture, paying fees in cattle. More farmers arrived, more timber fell to axes, but now that spring came, those farmers would want their fields to plant their corn, their oats, their potatoes and barley. The grass was beginning to green up, and Tom had made up his mind.

Catfish opened the lid covering a cast-iron Dutch oven, revealing steaming hot biscuits, and Whip grabbed a plate and fork.

"When you have finished dinner, I want you three to cut out two hundred head," Tom said. "The best two hundred head we have."

Whip spun around. "You mean . . . ?"

"Take those two hundred to the south pasture. Let them graze there."

"Just two hundred?" Rusk asked.

"I have to get one hundred and fifty to New York City by the Fourth of July. Do you expect us to lose more than fifty?"

The Texian stared over his cup of coffee. "Can't say. Never drove no beeves to New York before."

"All I can say," Whip put in, "is that I'm glad I get to climb into a saddle again. Ain't fittin' for a man of my stature to spend all winter shockin' corn to feed to them dumb critters."

"We all going?" Catfish asked.

Tom smiled. "Unless anyone wants to draw his time and head back to Texas."

He swung down from the saddle, ground-reined the roan, and walked to the shade tree where Washington Malone sat on a chair, his lower body covered with a quilt. He did not stand to greet Tom.

"It's spread down to my knees," Washington Malone said. "Could hardly bend the left one this morning. Even Doctor Allcock's Strengthening Plasters did not help. It's better now, but . . ."

"How did you manage to make it out here?" Tom asked.

Malone laughed. "Sometimes, I can be as mule-headed as you." The smile fading, Malone shook his head. "I'll be ready for the drive. Don't you worry about that."

"I am not worried, but you shan't be coming with us to New York."

The eyes burned. "Now, listen here . . ."

"Calm down. Your counsel has always been wise and well thought out, so let me tell you my plan and hear your thoughts."

Malone started breathing easier.

"I am cutting out two hundred head to push to New York. We arrived here with six hundred and seventy-one. By Whip's and my count, we are down to six hundred thirty-three. Lost a few during the winter. Sold the others. That leaves us with four hundred thirty-three. Our pastures will feed two hundred and fifty. Do you find that accurate?"

"Yes."

"I daresay no farmer will give up his corn crop for cattle, so we must find something to do with one hundred and eighty-three longhorns."

"Chicago," Malone said, his face brightening. "When this rheumatism lets up, and it shall because the weather turns warm now, I will take a drove. Captain Campbell's son has the making of a fine drover. I shall ask the captain if I might hire John for the journey to Chicago. We shall see what the Illinois markets think of Texas beef."

Tom grinned. "You have read my mind."

With a wink, Malone added: "There won't be many savage Indians to frighten me on the road to Chicago."

Tom held out his hand. "You showed your fighting spirit the last time we were on that road. I shall never be able to thank you enough for that."

They talked about the weather, the Snyders, recounted a few stories from last year's drive, and shook hands. Tom grabbed the reins, mounted, and nodded a farewell to his partner.

"Want to lay down a wager?" Malone called out after Tom had traveled a few yards.

Tom turned, waiting.

"Five dollars that I get a better price in Chicago than you do in New York City."

Tom laughed. "I might not have five dollars to my name when I return from New York." He nodded, then put the roan into a trot.

Weeks had passed since he had last ridden into Moweaqua—or had seen Margaret. The sawmill buzzed with activity, axes chopped, hammers pealed, men whistled, women beat rugs with brooms, children played. Tom reined in the roan and watched masons lay bricks.

"Ponting."

Turning from the construction, he saw Michael Snyder standing in front of the store, waving Tom over, then resuming a conversation with a lanky man with a mustache and a tall silk hat. Several other men gathered around. Tom recognized Zeke Prescott and the two dice rollers he remembered from last year, Gilbert and Nye.

"Meet John Middleton," Snyder said once Tom reined up. "John, this is Tom Ponting."

The two greeted one another with nods.

"Middleton and his son will take over my store." Mr. Snyder pointed at the masons. "Brick store. W. G. Hayden is building it. Bricks are strong. This store will last forever."

"Good luck to you, Mr. Middleton," Tom said, and looked back at the big, grinning German. "What are you going to do now, Herr Snyder."

"In a few months, Ponting, I will be busy counting one thousand dollars. Maybe I will invest it all in the Illinois Central Railroad Company. I know how to make money. Not lose it."

"Reckon he does," said either Gilbert or Nye— Tom never could tell those two apart. "Much as he charges for tobacco."

Everyone, even Snyder, laughed. Tom found himself chuckling, too.

"Ponting," Snyder said, "I will do you a favor. This foolish bet of yours. You have no chance of winning. You will never reach New York City. So, here is my offer. You pay me one hundred dollars. We call off the bet." He nodded his own approval. "Agreed?"

Tom shook his head. "No, thank you, sir."

Snyder's smile widened.

"Fifty dollars."

Tom's head shook again.

"Oughta take that, Tom," Prescott said.

Snyder stepped off the porch and approached Tom slowly. Tom took a firm hold on the reins in case the roan startled, and the big German looked up, his eyes no longer laughing.

"Be smart," Snyder whispered. "You cannot win. Fifty dollars . . . is nothing."

Tom glanced at the men on the porch, then leaned down.

"Herr Snyder," he whispered, "if I took your fifty dollars, you would know—*and I would know*—that I would not be fit to court your daughter." The big man stepped back, still staring up at Tom, who pulled the roan around, nodded back at the porch loafers, and said, "You boys can buy some good Texas steers at Washington Malone's place."

"I hear it tastes like boot leather," said Nye. Or was that Gilbert?

Tom just smiled as he kicked the horse into a walk back to the road.

"Tom Ponting," Snyder called out.

Tom reined up and turned. The big merchant had not moved, but his face had changed.

"Come to my house this evening. Six o'clock. My wife, she cooks fine schnitzel. You come. Six o'clock. Bring all your . . . men . . . We feed them good. Even bring the colored boy. We feed you fine before you leave." He wet his lips. "You come?"

The last two words sounded like a plea.

"Margaret. Daughter Margaret . . . she will help cook." Snyder swallowed.

"I shall be there," Tom said. "And on behalf of my drovers, let me thank you and Frau Snyder— and Miss Margaret. Six o'clock."

He nodded again at the merchant and the rest of the men before kicking the horse into a trot.

Tom couldn't call it a victory, but he knew he had at last won Michael Snyder's respect.

And he would get to see Margaret before they rode off in two days.

He would have to carry that memory all the way to New York City. All nine hundred miles.

# CHAPTER 38

Tom had never seen the Sangamon that low.

They had decided to take only one extra horse per rider, with drag rider Colton Greene pulling that string behind him. Two hundred head of cattle, Tom and Rusk agreed, would not be as hard on horses as seven hundred. Tom wanted to make fifteen miles a day. What no one had counted on was that it took them three days to reach the Sangamon, eighteen miles from Tom's stock farm.

Because once they left Shelby and Christian counties, the country dried up.

Slowly, they kept the herd moving northeast, following the banks of the Sangamon, but the farther they traveled, the drier the country turned. Winter in Christian and Shelby counties had been mild and short, but Tom wondered if this part of Illinois had gotten any rain or snow.

While passing a hardscrabble farm south of Monticello, a young girl stepped out of a shabby cabin and walked down the lane to the main trail. Tom recalled Washington Malone's comment outside of St. Louis, where people stopped to point and gawk and hold out their arms trying to guess how far those horns spread. "If I had a nickel for every time . . ."

But when he saw the girl, Tom reined the horse off the road and stopped. The trail-broke longhorns, with a wagon-track road to flow, kept plodding along.

Her hair was blond, or had been. It had not been combed or washed in days, possibly weeks. She looked so gaunt, Tom didn't know how she had managed to walk the fifty yards from her house. She was dirty, pale, wearing a dress that might have once been white. The green eyes had sunk deep under her forehead, and she kept raising her right hand to her mouth, over and over.

"What's your name?" Tom asked.

The cracked lips remained open, but no words came out. Just the hand came up and down, up and down, begging for food. Tom could not guess how long it had been since she had eaten. Standing in the stirrups, he looked at the hardscrabble farm. A mule lay in the corral and did not move. He neither saw nor heard chickens. The corn in the field was dead, old, the stalks lying on the ground—and not many stalks for about eighty acres cleared for plowing.

"Where are your folks?" Tom asked as he sat back into the saddle.

Only the hand moved to the mouth. But those hands . . .

Burst blisters and scratches covered palms and fingers, the tips of which were soiled with black soil, dust, grime. They would need cleansing, or infection might set in and she could lose her hands, maybe even her arms.

"Child, where are your folks?"

He wasn't sure if she even heard him.

Tom turned, found Whip riding on the other side of the herd. He called out, then waved toward the leaders. "Stop the herd. Ride up to the leaders and stop them. Let them graze."

Not that there was much grass to feed anything.

Whip spurred his chestnut into a lope, and Tom turned down the trail, waved Rusk to come ahead, then he dismounted. He took the canteen, opened it, and held it out to the girl. She blinked, then motioned to her mouth again.

"Ma'am . . ." No, not *ma'am*. He wasn't used to children. "Child . . . I just . . ." He pulled out a piece of dried beef. She stared wide as though he held a chocolate cake. The way her teeth looked, brown with pale gums, he feared the tough jerky would pull them out. But it was all he had. He let her take it, shove it into her mouth. He expected her to cry, but she just grunted.

"Just let it sit on your tongue." He was on his knees now, putting both hands on her shoulders. "Just suck on it. Do not try to eat. Just suck. The juice. Just swallow the juice."

Tom rose as C. W. Rusk pulled his gelding to a hard stop. The wind took the dust toward the dead crops.

"God a'mighty," Rusk said, and dismounted.

Tom stepped toward the longhorns, which now had stopped, and milled about, searching for grass. The young girl sobbed without tears, but kept sucking on the jerky, her Adam's apple moving up and down as she swallowed juice.

Cupping his hands, Tom yelled at Catfish, coming up the wagon. He waved him forward, and the boy turned the two oxen to the side of the road.

"When Catfish gets here," Tom said, "have him . . . fix . . . I do not know . . . just . . . soften any biscuits left over in water. But do not let her eat too much."

"Kid ain't nothin' but skin and bones. What . . . ?"

Tom was already walking to the cabin. "Stay with her," Tom said. "Till Catfish gets here. Then I shall need your assistance, I fear." He kept walking, but said softly, "I think you'll . . . need to . . . bring . . . the shovel from the wagon."

The mule in the corral was dead, but not for long as no buzzards circled overhead. The wind picked up, batting the door to the privy open and shut. It was blowing away from Tom, and when he reached the door to the cabin, he was thankful. He turned, spit, coughed, spit again, and pulled the bandana over his nose and mouth.

Whip worked the pickax. Rusk used the shovel. Catfish sang to the girl, who sipped the tea he had brewed, softening the stale pieces of biscuit by dipping those into the cup before putting one in her mouth. She still had not said a word. Just off the road, Colton Greene circled the herd and spare horses that grazed, lay down, or rolled in dirt and dried grass.

Stepping out of the cabin, Sheriff Cass Adair pulled down his bandana, and spit. Wiping his mouth with the back of his arm, he drew in a deep breath and walked over to Tom.

"Well, that's . . . that's . . ." Adair shook his head, and spit again. "Good thing you came along," he told Tom. "Thanks for sending the boy in to fetch me."

That boy, Whip, and Rusk were digging three graves—ones the girl had started.

"How old is she?" Tom asked, still staring at the girl.

The sheriff looked up, shook his head. "I don't even know her name. He pa was Deitch. German, I think. Bought eighty acres from Bill Ingersoll two years ago. Didn't come to Monticello but once or twice a year. Guess he wasn't much of a farmer. How do you figure it?"

"Figure what?"

Adair shrugged. "You found them."

Tom closed his eyes and sighed. "She must have stabbed him while he slept. Dropped the baby in the privy. I'm hoping the little boy was dead before she did that. Went back to the rocking chair at the fire and . . ."

His mouth was dry but he tried to spit anyway.

"Yeah. That's about how I see it, too." The sheriff also spit, as if anyone could ever get rid of that smell and taste. He looked up the lane.

"Where'd you say you got those cattle?"

"Texas." Tom listened as the shovel and pick struck the land.

"Never seen horns like that. Good thing you came along."

"We never would have stopped if the girl had not . . ." He drew in a deep breath, and slowly exhaled. He looked away from the gravediggers and back at Cass Adair. "What happens to her?"

"Captain Godfrey's wife might take her in for a spell. When I get back to town, I'll ask the captain. You reckon she'll ride back in the buggy with me?"

Tom had no answer.

"I'll have the Doc Heimlich look at her hands and see what all he can do for her," Adair said.

"No offense, Sheriff, but you have not answered my question." Tom nodded at the girl.

"Yeah. I don't know if anyone in the county needs another mouth to feed. I got six kids myself, and Mildred's expecting another in July. So, most likely I'll write my sister in Chicago. She's always begging for money for the Ladies' Orphan Asylum Association. There's a Protestant orphan asylum there. My guess is the girl'll wind up there."

Tom nodded.

"Look at that dirt," the sheriff said, nodding at the graves. "Black dirt like that. Hard to believe a man couldn't grow enough corn and potatoes to keep his family fed."

Tom felt no need to respond.

"Reckon, I'll be headed back to Monticello," Adair said. "If you can stop by on your way through town, I'll have you sign a statement, and we will just call this murder and suicide. Besides, folks in town would surely love to see your Texas cows. Don't get many circuses through Monticello."

The sheriff walked away, and Tom turned to Catfish, and nodded. The young Texian, still singing, picked up the girl and carried her to Cass Adair's buggy. He found a piece of jerky in his pocket and handed that to her, then stepped back as the sheriff found his whip.

"Sheriff," Tom said, and waited for the lawman to look his way.

"Do you have a butcher in town?"

"Got two," Adair replied, lowering the whip. "We're the county seat, you know."

"I am willing to sell twenty head, ten to each butcher. What I get for those cattle, I shall give to you if you will send the money to your sister for that orphanage in Chicago."

"Well, that is fine and dandy with me if Wolstenholm and McGregor will go for it, but what's your price? Keep in mind that Monticello isn't Chicago or St. Louis."

"I paid eight dollars a head in Texas."

"McGregor's a skinflint, but that would likely suit him. Karl might even give you ten or twelve, it being for charity. I'll see what they say and meet you in town. Sorry it had to be under these circumstances."

When the buggy was raising dust down the wagon track, C. W. Rusk shoved the shovel into the dirt, climbed out of the grave he was digging, and found a canteen. He took a few swallows, wiped his mouth, pitched the canteen to Whip, and stared at Tom.

"For what you paid a head in Texas, Ponting, you lose money on this deal. I thought you was a savvy businessman, but you is just a fool."

Whip slammed the pickax into the mound.

"For once," he said, and waited for Rusk to turn around. "Just shut up and help me finish diggin' these graves."

He stared at the whiskey he had poured into a tin cup, and then at the bottle he had bought at the trading post on the outskirts of Monticello. Leaving the herd—minus the twenty they had left at the corrals behind two butcher shops—on the other side of town, agreeing to the lease price of one steer to be left with the pasture's owner, Tom had ridden back to town, dictated and signed the paper for Sheriff Cass Adair. The last butcher, McGregor, told him about Ekman's post. Ekman said it was genuine and pure Cincinnati rectified whiskey. Tom said he didn't care.

A shadow darkened bottle and cup, and Tom raised his eyes to find a smirking C. W. Rusk. The Texian turned, found an empty keg, dragged it over, turned it upside down, and sat, then pushed up the brim of his battered hat.

"That sheriff, he galled me, too." Rusk picked up the bottle, and drank. "That's a city man for you. Talkin' 'bout how all that black dirt, how come someone couldn't feed his wife and kids. Like he ever worked the land."

Tom inched his hand toward the cup.

"I ain't gonna stop you, boss man." Rusk brought the bottle over, and added a splash to the whiskey Tom had already poured. "You deserve a snort. Deserve to get roostered. Hell's fire, we all did, doin' what we did today."

But that wasn't why Tom sat here. He remembered all that talk he spouted out last year, about the starving people in New York, how bringing cattle to the market might save some lives. But that had never been the reason. New York wasn't hurting for cattle, and never would. He just wanted to see if he could do it. And then there had been that foolish bet with Michael Snyder. It was the challenge that had appealed to Tom. Just like the challenge all those years ago of seeing if he could cut it as a drover in England. It was the adventure. The newness. He wasn't yet thirty years old, but he wanted to see everything he could. That's why he had ridden off with Jesse Chisholm to that Indian council.

Rusk muttered something, shook his head, brought up the bottle again, and drank.

"Ain't all that familiar with Illinois, but I seen Chicago. And seein' how far behind we is, you ain't never gonna get these longhorns to New York by the Fourth of July. So if you wanna turn the herd and take 'em to Chicago, that's fine with me. You won't owe Whip and me as much as you would iffen we was to go all the way to New York. And then you'd be the quitter I knowed you to be all along."

Tom looked up. He pulled his hand away from the bottle.

Grinning, Rusk drank again. "The way I see it, it's like this: I brought two greasers into this job. Izan and Santos. And they quit on us. You brung on that Cherokee and the cook. Yeah, and your pard, Malone. He quit. You just give him that idea to take some cattle to Chicago. Maybe he will, but I doubt it. So that's two quitters for both of us. I ain't countin' ol' Byers since all along he was just plannin' to go back to see his dead wife. So we got two quitters each. That kid, Catfish, and that darky. They's your hires. We'll see if they got enough gumption to finish this job. I

431

doubt it. But me and Whit ain't quittin'. Till you call it quits."

Tom felt a smile crack his face. Catfish was actually Rusk's hire, but no matter. He slid the tin cup toward Rusk, then stood.

"I'll see you at camp," he said. "And I'll see you in New York."

Rusk nodded at the bottle and the cup.

"It's yours. Though you might save some for Whip and Greene."

"That ain't likely," Rusk said.

# CHAPTER 39

It took them five days to reach the Middle Fork of the Vermillion, and two days later, Catfish and Whip got sick. Bad water, Rusk figured, from a spring. He thought it had been impregnated with sulfur. That cost them two more days. After six days, they found the ferry on the Wabash River across from Attica, Indiana.

The ferryman seemed excited. One wagon. Three oxen. Four saddleless horses. Four horses and riders. And one hundred and eighty Texas longhorns.

"Horse and rider, ten cents," the bearded man said. "Fifteen cents for the wagon. Three cents for each cow and extra horse. So that comes to . . ."

He stopped, spit out tobacco juice, and locked his eyes on Colton Greene, who rode up pulling the string of horses. "That Negro with you, mister?" he asked, not taking his eyes off Greene.

"He is."

The ferryman fingered the tobacco from his cheek and pitched it into the river.

"I can swim my horse across," Greene said casually.

The man did not look away, but Tom guessed that this man wasn't about to lose ten cents for a horse and rider, no matter the color of the rider's skin.

"Mr. Greene is a freeman, sir," Tom said. "We are not slaveholders, and he is not a slave."

Now the ferryman turned. "It ain't that, mister. It's just. Well, we got us a new constitution. Passed a few years back. No nig— . . . no coloreds can settle in Indiana, and that includes mulattos."

"I am all Negro, sir," Greene said.

"I'm just lettin' you know the law." The ferryman would not take his eyes off Tom. "They can't live here. And I can't even hire me one to do this backbreaking work without gettin' fined."

"Sir," Tom said, "we have no intentions of settling in your state. Ever."

The clouds cut loose as the oxen and wagon came off the ferry. The boatman collected his fee, and told Rusk and Tom how to get to the ravine outside of town. "Good a place as any," he said, "to keep them till the rains let up—if they ever let up—and there's enough shelter to keep some of this wet off you. And the springs got good water." He looked up at the pounding rain. "Not that you need water now."

Weeks ago, they would have loved this rain, and it felt cleansing now. But if the storms continued, the creeks and rivers would be harder to cross. They would not be making fifteen miles a day in this weather.

When the rain slackened that morning, Tom rode into town. Attica looked . . . rich.

He passed three carriage shops, lost count of the warehouses, two fine hotels, a saloon that would impress C. W. Rusk, factories, stores, and beautiful homes built on hillsides, surrounded by trees. But he did not stop until he saw the canal.

He knew of canals, had traveled down one to Cleveland, but that had been on a packet. He had paid scant attention to ships that carried goods.

A boy in his teens, Tom guessed, but of stout bones and strong muscles, unharnessed a team of mules that pulled a colorful boat, almost flat, painted green, yellow, and brown. Another mule was brought from below the deck, and it took four workers to get it over what resembled a curved ladder that served as a bridge, connecting the boat to the towpath where mules pulled the barge. Once the mule was off the boat, workers began hauling bags from two heavy wagons parked alongside the towpath, across that strange bridge, and disappeared below the deck.

"Impressive, is it not?"

Turning to the voice, Tom found a brown-bearded man with a bronzed face. He wore white knee britches, a buttoned blue coat with brass buttons and white and red piping along the sleeves and a black hat with gold lace looped around the cockade.

"She's mine," the man said, pointing at ship. "The *Veronica Ashley*. Finest line boat on the Wabash and Erie Canal. I'm Schauinger. Captain Walter Schauinger. At your service."

"Tom Ponting, sir. I am a cattle drover from Illinois."

The captain grinned. "Nay, lad. You are a redcoat." Then he laughed. "Ah, but the war— no, two wars—are history. Unless there comes a third, I am your servant, sir. It is good to meet you, Ponting. Do you have items you need shipped? We head up the river once this grain is loaded. You say you ship cattle?"

"Yes, Captain. But I do not—"

"By grab, sir. You are the one I heard about. You arrived yesterday with a string of beastly creatures some men called cattle. Horns the size of . . ." He stretched out his arms as wide as he could.

"Yes, sir."

"It is an honor to meet you. You drive this herd to Cincinnati, I assume. Well . . ." He stopped. "By your face, sir, I see I am mistaken."

"New York, Captain. The city of New York."

For a while, Captain Schauinger stared. He did not blink until one of the mules brayed.

"Mr. Ponting, do you wish to trust your . . . drove, I believe you called it . . . to the care of the *Veronica Ashley*?"

Tom blinked. Then, chuckling at the captain's joke, Tom nodded at the boat. "She could not hold—"

"Sir, I can carry seventy-five tons of grain below. I can travel sixty miles in a day, God willing, no failed locks and no Covington scoundrels rolling logs into the channels. I can have you to Toledo in . . ." He straightened. "Do you think I jest, sir?"

Tom shook his head. "No, sir. But I have had few pleasures on the water."

The captain laughed again. "By thunder, sir, nowhere along the Big Ditch reaches deeper than four feet. How many head of cattle do you have?"

"One hundred and seventy-nine." Tom's curiosity increased.

"How much does one beast weigh?"

"A thousand to twelve hundred pounds."

"Well, sir, I could not take that many, but hear this: I can take half. And my brother, Tobias, will be here tomorrow with his line boat, the *Ingrid and Ilsa*. The Two Eyes, we call her." He laughed. "We can make a deal. Tobias can handle what I cannot. Bring in your cows. They can stay at my brother-in-law's corrals on the edge of town. He'll cut you a deal on the fees. We will charge you five dollars a head. A deal, sir. A deal I cannot believe I offer you, a Brit and a stranger to my eyes. And I will—"

"Rob you wholesale."

A younger, thinner man with powerful arms and shoulders stepped off the towpath, and put his hands on his hips, the light eyes sparkling.

"No line boat yet has carried livestock on these waters, sir. The only honest thing Schauinger has said—"

"Confound you, Brackeen—"

"—is that his brother-in-law owns those stables. He'll charge you for keeping them overnight, and the good captain—"

"This brigand—"

"—will be between Lafayette and Fort Wayne."

"—is not only a Covington man, he is Irish, by God. A scoundrel and—"

"If his brother-in-law does not tell you your cattle were stolen, rustled in the night. Ask any of those men loading grain. Or any—"

"—the devils of Covington are jealous of Attica, sir. They are brigands—and he—an Irish pig—"

"—who will gladly knock you into the canal just as I did last time, you Hun son of a—"

"I shall have nothing more to do with either of you. You are both scoundrels. Be careful, Ponting. You being a redcoat and him a dirty Irish pig, your throat may be cut before the morrow." He turned, barked an order at one of the sack carriers, and stormed away.

· · ·

He bought Brackeen a porter while he took his cup of tea in the tavern. Hooking their right boots on the brass railing, they leaned against the mahogany bar. The Irishman drank half the pint down, set the glass on the bar, and said, "You are not a fool. You would have discovered the scheme."

"I am not sure, Brackeen—"

"Call me Michael."

"Michael." Tom set his cup on the bar. "Desperate men act desperately."

"You have nigh two hundred head of cattle—"

Tom laughed. "It is a long story. But I need to have those cattle in New York by the Fourth of July."

Michael Brackeen finished his beer. When he laid the empty glass on the bar, he wiped foam off his mustache and studied Tom. "You are the one who should be drinking, sir. And not hot tea."

When Tom shrugged, Brackeen waved at the bartender, who filled another tall glass with beer, and brought it to the Irishman. "And bring a shot of Irish for my friend. This one is on me, English." He flipped a coin at the bartender, who caught it.

"I cannot drink the whiskey."

Brackeen grinned. "Which is what I hoped. I shall take care of that. And then we will go find a fine restaurant I know."

Tom stared at the man, and slowly smiled. Brackeen leaned closer. "The canal is not the answer," he said. "But have you considered the railroad?"

Tom laughed. Another joke from the Irishman. "From what I read in the newspapers—"

"I have laid tracks for three railroads. If the people of Attica grow smarter, they will see that the future of this new country lies in railroads, not canals. What Schauinger did not tell you was that his fine beauty of a ship, the *Veronica Ashley*, was supposed to be here last month. She couldn't. The aqueduct at Sugar Creek was damaged by flooding. Stopped all navigation up and down the Big Ditch."

Tom finished his tea. The whiskey looked tempting when it arrived, but Brackeen picked it up and downed it, chasing it with half his beer.

"Where do you go from here?" Brackeen asked.

"Indianapolis. Maybe follow the National Road."

"No." Brackeen finished the beer. "Go to Indianapolis, yes. Find Union Station. It opened in September last. That will convince you about railroads. And then . . ." He bit his lower lip, eyes staring at the smoke caught by the punched-tin ceiling, and finally smiled and looked at Tom. "Muncietown. Aye, make haste for Muncietown. Look up Marcus Smith. About your age. Tell him I sent you."

"Muncietown?"

Brackeen shrugged. "Well, some folks are calling it Muncie these days. Muncie, Muncietown. We called it Mud Hole Town. When you ask, 'Where is Muncietown?' you'll know you're there."

# CHAPTER 40

The Irishman from Covington was right.

Tom guided the buckskin gelding out of the way of the wagons, coaches, and other horsemen, and stared at Union Station. Five tracks moved through tunnels that went through a brick building that must have been more than four hundred feet long. One ugly locomotive coughed smoke as it emerged from the second tunnel, pulling tinder, three passenger coaches and caboose. He watched the train curve around to the north and cross a wooden trestle over—what was it someone had told him? Pogue's Run. South of the station, Tom spotted two more trains, but those were freights. The tracks that went through the building carried passengers.

Six railroads, seven tracks, one station. Instead of moving from depot to depot, rail line to rail line. If nothing else, it looked convenient and efficient.

He rode down the street and reined up beside a man standing on the corner, reading a newspaper.

"Excuse me, sir," Tom said. The man looked up.

"Do you know which train runs to Muncie-town?"

"The Beeline," he answered, and looked back at the paper.

"One more question, sir?"

Sighing, the man raised his eyes but not his head. "Yeah?"

"Since you have a newspaper." Tom attempted his politest smile. "Could you tell me what day it is?"

Marcus Smith picked up the gold coin, and leaned back in his chair. His eyes locked on Ponting.

"How many head did you say?"

"One hundred seventy-nine steers. Three oxen. A wagon. Five men."

"And how far?"

"New York City."

He turned the slug over and over, watching it glitter, before he looked up at Tom. "I can get you to Cleveland, Ohio, by June twenty-second."

Tom's sigh must have sounded louder than the steam hissing from that Cuyahoga Steam Furnace engine on the tracks outside.

"It's not that bad, sir," Smith said. "Once you're there, the Cleveland and Buffalo Railroad can get you to Buffalo. Or Dunkirk." Smith flipped the coin, caught it, and smiled. "And from either of those cities, mister, if you have more of these gold coins, you'll have no problem finding a train to New York." He pushed himself out of the chair. "There's just one thing we got to figure out."

Tom waited.

"What kind of cars we can put all those cows on. And how to get them on those cars."

They sold the horses. Even the roan. Tom headed away from the pens, but returned, climbed through the rails, and walked back to the horse that had been carrying him . . . he couldn't count the miles.

He rubbed the gelding's neck in a circular motion, the way Grandfather Theophilus had taught him. The horse snorted. Tom should have brought him a sugar cube, an apple, maybe a carrot. All he had in his pocket was a piece of jerky. He leaned closer, and whispered: "Maybe your next owner will give you a name." He had never seen any use in naming a horse, but that came from his father, not Grandfather Theophilus.

When he walked away this time, Tom did not turn around, even when he heard the roan following him all the way to the pen's edge.

The ends of two railroad ties leaned against the freight cars, with planks nailed to the ties, forming a ramp. A brindle steer took a tentative step. Colton Greene slapped the tough hide with a lariat. The longhorn started up, and into the car. A second steer followed. And a third.

Fifteen steers per car. Twelve freight cars. The oxen and wagon on a flatbed car. Two trains, one pulled by the Cuhahoga, the trailing train led by a new Niles and Company 4-4-0.

"The danger," Marcus Smith yelled over the belching locomotives, "is in the closed freights. If a steer goes down, it'll likely get stomped on. Or those horns might gut another."

Tom frowned.

"None of my men is willing to risk getting gored to death, or stomped to death," Smith shouted. "And freight trains have no place for passengers."

Tom nodded. "Three of my men and myself will ride with the cattle." He wasn't about to put Catfish in an enclosed car with fifteen Texas steers. That boy would stay with the wagon and oxen, hobbled and tied down, on the flatcar. Smith started to protest, but Tom stopped him by raising his hand. "I take full responsibility. If a steer goes down, we'll have to get it up. Now . . . is it possible to get from one car to another?"

Smith shook his head. "Don't try it. Even experienced railroaders get killed doing that. Just stay high in the car. Don't go to sleep. And for God's sake, don't fall."

It wasn't the best plan. Eight cars—roughly one hundred and twenty steers—would have no one looking after the cattle.

Tom shook the railroader's hand.

"I sent a note with the conductor on the express to Cleveland. With luck, Peter Moody with the Cleveland and Buffalo will meet you at the station." He stepped back. "Good luck."

"I shall need it," Tom said, and he pulled himself into a car crowded with sharp-horned animals.

The last steer jumped out of the car and onto the sand, and Tom, drenched in sweat and covered with dust, eased himself down. He needed to shield his eyes from the sun's rays after being boxed inside a wooden car for some ungodly amount of time.

"Is that the ocean?"

Tom recognized Catfish's voice.

"It's Lake Erie, son," a stranger answered.

Tom squeezed his eyelids tight, slowly opened them, and saw a thin man wearing a city hat. "Ponting?" The stranger held out his hand. "I am Peter Moody." He laughed. "Those are the wildest cattle I have ever seen."

The grip was firm.

"They are tame now," Tom said. He looked around. "Whip." He wet his lips with his tongue. "Can you find me a canteen?"

"Yes, sir."

Tom tried to smile. "Otherwise I might drink that lake dry."

Tom shook his head. "Why cannot we unload the cattle when this train stops in Dunkirk?"

"Because of the schedule," Moody said. "You stay on the train from Dunkirk to Buffalo. The cars will be uncoupled. Another engine will back up to those cars and take you back to Dunkirk."

Tom felt like cussing. "We pass through Dunkirk on the way. It is a waste of time for—"

"No, it's not, Ponting. We don't have the time to unload cattle and a wagon when we stop in Dunkirk. That's for water only. And even if we had time, you would still have to wait till the New York and Erie train arrived to take you to Hornellsville."

One hundred ninety miles to Buffalo. Then back fifty miles over the same tracks to Dunkirk. Tom wanted to punch someone in the jaw.

"Mr. Moody, this is utterly ridiculous."

"Welcome to the railroads, Mr. Ponting."

It was dark when the train finally slid to its final stop at Dunkirk, but the skies were gray in the east, and Rogers Lansing of the New York & Erie Railroad was ready. He had ramps to unload the cattle, even if the longhorns were still on a Cleveland and Buffalo train. Tom followed his fifteen head out, shook hands with Lansing. Torches brightened the yards, and Lansing pointed.

"Our station is that way. Two blocks. Can you get all of these cattle there? My men will bring our ramps."

A loud report from a freight car caused Lansing to jump back. Another followed.

"Were those pistol shots?" Lansing asked.

Tom was already walking to the car. More men with torches moved in. So did a policeman. When the door was opened, and the ramp placed in, C. W. Rusk stepped out. The policeman started to bring a whistle to his mouth.

"It is all right, officer," Tom said. He stared up at Rusk.

"Two dead," Rusk said. "When we stopped hard. Nothin' I could do." He slid the smoking Dragoon into a holster. "I'll push these others out."

The policeman just stood there—until the first longhorns came down the wooden ramp. Then he backed away until darkness swallowed him.

"One of our butchers will buy those dead cattle," Lansing said. "Sherwood will pay a good price for—"

Tom cut him off. "Is there an orphan's asylum in town?"

The railroader stopped, thought a moment, and shook his head. "No, but there's one up in Buffalo."

"Can you have the meat shipped there?"

Lansing thought for just a moment. "Yes, sir. Yes, I shall see that is what happens."

Lansing pulled open the door to the new railroad car and climbed inside, then bent and offered his hand. Tom was not too proud to accept the boost into the car.

"Andrew Dickinson came up with the plan. He's out of Hornby. That's north of Corning."

Tom studied the racks that stretched from one end of the boxcar to the other, capable of being lowered, then legs folded out and fitted to the flooring, keeping one animal confined, unable to move, unable to gore another steer.

"Other railroad companies haven't been smart enough to have figured this out," Lansing said. "But, by grab, they don't know how to ship sheep or hogs. What do you think?"

"It is a start in the right direction—"

"I know," the railroader interrupted. "But Dickinson never figured on having a steer with a set of horns spanning eight feet. Maybe nine. But it's the best we can do for you."

"I appreciate this, sir. Very much so."

"But there's one problem. We only have three cars like this." He shrugged. "That'll hold forty steers. Maybe forty-five, forty-seven if we can get the smaller ones in here. The rest will have to travel the old way. But I might be able to get you another one of these new cars to Hornellsville. Dickinson doesn't live that far from there. Then it's one easy train ride to Bergen Hill. And a ferryboat into New York City."

They squeezed forty-five steers into the three newfangled livestock carriers, crammed the rest in eight boxed cars, and loaded the oxen and wagon onto a flatcar. This time, Tom let Catfish into one of the boxed cars, the one that held the fewest animals, the one closest to the caboose. Tom climbed into a middle car, but not until he watched the other doors. Whip took one closest to the engine; Colton Greene pulled himself into one a few cars back; Rusk climbed into the car behind Tom's.

Tom reached up, found a slat, pulled himself up, and breathed in the stink of cattle, hay, wood, and Lake Erie just before the big men removed the ramp, closed the door, and locked it from the outside.

# CHAPTER 41

Darkness. How late Tom didn't know. He kept shifting his legs, moving his arms, alternating which hand gripped a wall slat and which one swung freely. One day, a drover would not have to ride in a freight car staring at wicked horns.

Even in the confines of a car crammed with steers, the night air felt cool as the train weaved through hills and valleys. He reached up with his left hand, grabbed hold of a slat, and his right hand had not let go of the slat when the iron wheels screamed, the car lurched, cattle bawled in panic, and then felt a jarring crash as if the train had run straight into a mountainside.

He fell. No dying thoughts. No last words except *Ommmmph.* He hit belly-first on a bawling steer's back. Saw horns slashing, then he was on the ground. A hoof stomped his left ankle. Tom screamed. Rolled out of the way of another longhorn. Rolled again. Right or left, he wasn't sure. Rolled himself into a ball. Made himself as small as possible. Another hoof grazed his ribs. He hit something solid. Not flesh and hide, but wood. His right hand shot up, found a hold. Somehow, the cattle near him moved to the other side of the boxcar. He felt off balance. Realized why. The car listed to this side. On his knees now. Glimpsed the point of a horn. Sucked in as much breath as he could. His shirt ripped, but the steer's head turned right, and was gone. Grabbed another slat with his left hand. Pulled himself up. Again. Again. Till he was above the cattle. At least for as long as he could hold on.

"Hey." He coughed, tried to shake clarity into his brain, crawled underneath a bawling steer, made it to the closed door, and coughed out, or maybe prayed, "Get me out of here."

A black head and torso appeared, illuminated by the lantern in a big hand. Tom could breathe again.

"You hurt, mister?" the man asked.

Tom raised his head. Took advantage of the lantern, and looked around the car. No steers down. And, by thunder, he was alive. Relatively unhurt.

The man of color helped Tom sit up. "I'm all right," Tom whispered.

"Good." The man pulled away, took the light with him. "We need every man we can out here, sir. It's a god-awful tragedy."

Filling his lungs with outside air, he grabbed wood and leaned outside, readying himself to jump to the ground. Then he looked down the tracks.

"Dear God," he whispered, and leaped to the dirt.

"What happened?" Tom asked the Negro with the lantern.

"Not sure. Looks like the express had pulled into a siding for water. Must have pulled out too far. We hit her. You sure you're all right?"

Tom didn't answer. He felt sick. At least two cars ahead of him were overturned. The one just behind him was leaning this way, off the tracks like Tom's and the car before him. Other cars appeared to have remained on the rails.

A strange light shined on the ground at the head of the train, and slowly Tom realized that it was another locomotive. Must have been that express the man had mentioned. The engine that had been pulling this train was off the tracks, upright, but now a smoking mass of smashed metal. The tender rested on its side on the right side of the rails.

That's when he recognized those other sounds. Babies crying. Screams of men and women. He had been thinking about cattle, his cattle, when up ahead, men, women, and possibly children were badly hurt. Dying.

A voice cried out behind him.

"Whip? Whip? Whip, where are you, boy?"

Torches were being lighted all along the rails. The brakeman ran forward with another lantern. C. W. Rusk staggered near the rails. The Black man with the lantern who had opened the door to Tom's boxcar tried to help Rusk. Rusk shoved him to the ground.

"Whip!"

Tom spun now, remembering. Another door was pulled open, but this time a man flew out, hit the ground, rolled over. Then a longhorn jumped out. Tom reached the man who had jumped out of the car. Other longhorns leaped to the ground. Train crews, and Colton Greene, scattered out of the path of the frightened cattle.

Rusk roared past him. "Whip? Whip?" He didn't seem to notice the longhorns in front of him.

Tom started after him, stopped beside Colton Greene. "You all right?" he asked.

"Think so," Greene whispered. "Think so."

"Mr. Ponting?"

Turning, Tom cursed himself. He had forgotten all about Catfish. But the lad ran toward them, and now he sighed with relief.

"Look after Colton, Catfish," Tom said, turned, and staggered after Rusk.

"Help me. Help me. Oh, God A'mighty, somebody please . . ." The voice from inside the overturned freight car let out a gagging cough.

"Hang on, Whip," Rusk yelled through the crushed wood. "Hang on." He came off his knees, and looked up. "Give me a boost," Rusk said.

Tom put his hands together, bent forward. Two men came to help. Must have been from the express car, dressed in suits and ties. Rusk reached up with his left hand, then fell, cursing as he rolled over, screaming savagely, pounding the dirt with his good hand.

Straightening, Tom drew in a breath. "Help me up there," he ordered.

One of the men bent to help Rusk. Another shouted, pointing at the longhorns, and ran back toward the wrecked express. Colton Greene and Catfish came into the light.

"Help me get up there," Tom told them.

He didn't know how long it took him to get to the side of the car, now facing the stars and moon, but once he pulled himself up, he rolled onto his stomach. Hung his arms below. Rusk just cursed and beat the ground with his fist.

Inside the car, Whip coughed and cried.

"Colton," Tom cried.

Greene stepped forward, extended his hands. Tom pulled, Catfish pushed, and Greene slid onto the wood beside Tom.

It took two other railroaders, and another passenger from the express, to get Whip out of a car littered with dead longhorns. Onto the side of the tracks. Then lowered in blankets onto the ground. Tom didn't know how Whip could still be alive. But he was when Tom dropped from the cattle car and moved into the torchlight.

"Whip." Rusk rocked the boy in his arms. Tears poured down his cheeks. "Whip. Whip."

Blood poured out of the cowhand's mouth. He

coughed. The lips moved up and down, but no words came.

"Whip," Rusk cried. "Whip."

No one said anything. Not beside the freight car. But up the tracks, people wailed in agony and anguish.

"Whip. Oh, God, Whip. Stay with me, boy. Stay with me."

Shuddering, Whip sighed. Then closed his eyes.

"We are fewer than two miles from Hornellsville." Tom waited. Wasn't sure if C. W. Rusk even heard him, just sat there, Whip's head on his lap, smoothing the dead man's hair. "Wagons are being sent from Almond, which I'm told is just a mile from here." He pointed. "One will take Whip—"

"His name was Roosevelt," Rusk said hollowly, still stroking the hair, slowly rocking back and forth. "Roosevelt Dupree." He laughed suddenly, shook his head. "Mama always said that was a name for a president."

Tom could not speak.

"I give him the handle Whip." Rusk's laugh sounded hoarse. "On account of how much I loved to whip up on'm." Then he lifted the stiffening corpse to his breast, wrapping that one good arm around poor Whip, not caring about the blood. He wailed harder than anything Tom had ever heard, and swung the right side of his body

456

until Rusk's bum right arm landed on Roosevelt Dupree's back.

Words died. Tom started to put his right hand on Rusk's shoulder, but stopped. He stared into the dawn. The express's conductor kept shaking his head, talking to someone, probably one of the volunteers who came to help.

He felt the presence behind him, and slowly turned. Catfish, his face still pale, waited.

"They . . ." Catfish stopped, shook his head, and apologized as though he had wrecked the train. "They don't know how many cattle we lost, sir."

That did not surprise Tom. He opened his mouth, then closed it. A good man lay dead because of a stupid bet, Tom's arrogance, and the dead lad's brother sat there grieving. How many lives had been ruined? Tom wanted to run to the edge of the woods and throw up. He wanted to be back in Somersetshire. Or Ohio. Milwaukee. Anywhere but here.

Tom reached up and put his hand on Catfish's shoulder, steadying him. Though Tom didn't know he had managed even that.

"Wasn't our fault," the freight train's brakeman said. "It was . . . God's will."

"You want me to . . . ?" Catfish started, but Tom shook his head, silencing the young Texian. He started to tell him that it was all over. They were quitting. For all he knew, the railroad would want to take the cattle as payment anyway, maybe blame the steers for causing this disaster. He wanted to send the boy back to those Texas piney woods where he could fish as long as he wanted. But he heard C. W. Rusk—no, he heard Roosevelt Dupree's older brother sobbing without control. Then he heard another voice. It sounded clearly, so clearly.

*When ye take a job, see it done. See it done no matter the cost.*

Edward Jardine, that great cattle drover. Speaking to him on a fork in the road southwest of London. Fourteen years ago.

"Where are the cattle?" he suddenly asked. "The ones that can walk."

"Most of the cars stayed on the tracks," Catfish said. "Those that didn't." He dropped his head.

"Yeah."

"Weren't all our cattle." Colton Greene walked up. "The dead ones. Saw some Jerseys. Hogs. Sheep, too. But we lost aplenty."

The conductor of the express stopped a few yards away. His eyes met Tom's.

"You did good work, Catfish." When the boy looked up, Ponting gestured toward Rusk and his dead brother. "Think you can look after Rusk?"

The Adam's apple bobbed, and Catfish nodded. "What do I have to say to him?" he whispered.

"There's nothing to say." Tom nodded at Colton Greene, and they walked to the conductor.

"It shall take days to get these tracks cleared," the conductor said. "I have been told that most of the cattle are yours, and are being delivered to New York City . . ." He stopped. "Well . . ." He cleared his throat.

"There is no urgency," Tom said.

"Be that as it may, if you can manage, with your men, to get the cattle to Hornellsville . . . Well, sir. You have a wagon. And we have . . . dead." He swallowed. "The train in Hornellsville will be held."

Tom sighed. Then the voice came to him again. *When ye take a job, see it done. See it done no matter the cost.*

Roosevelt "Whip" Dupree's blanket-covered body lay on the wagon's bed. So did the engineer's from the express, or what remained of him. The fireman said he had leaped from the cab when he realized what was about to happen. Just didn't clear the tracks. A porter. And three passengers. Tom and Colton Greene helped Rusk into the back. Whip's brother used his good arm to put his right one atop Whip's body.

Catfish tied the ox-cow up behind the wagon, then climbed into the driver's box.

Men, women, and children from the area came to help, or watch. Some sang hymns. A preacher prayed, and two stock farmers gathered behind the longhorns.

Holding his whip, Tom stood on the left-hand side of the road across from the wagon.

Catfish looked at Tom, who nodded. "Go ahead, son. Take them to Hornellsville."

The boy swallowed, clucked his tongue, whipped the lines. The two oxen pulled the wagon. The tethered cow-ox started walking behind, the bell hanging from her neck ringing. Ringing. Ringing.

Excitedly, Catfish turned around and watched.

The leaders moved slowly after the trailing ox, the bell chiming. Steers started following. Tom knew they would. The bell kept ringing. Some women pointed. Young kids cackled. C. W. Rusk stared blankly.

Catfish laughed, then turned around to watch the road.

"Look at that," a farm woman cried out. "Look at how those cattle just follow that bell."

Ten longhorns went past Tom.

Another twenty.

He stopped counting and waited till the stragglers plodded on.

"I wish to hell we had been doing it this way," Tom said softly. "The whole time."

# CHAPTER 42

Steam hissed from the 4-4-0 Taunton at the Hornellsville station as C. W. Rusk led a black horse toward the last cattle car. Tom waited. The Texian still wore two belted Dragoons, despite stares from everyone in town, including one nervous constable.

"You win the bet, Ponting," Rusk said after stopping. The horse tugged at the reins before Rusk tugged back.

"What bet is that?" Tom asked.

"I'm quittin'. You still got the college boy and the darky. You win."

"How much did we wager?"

Rusk spit tobacco juice into the sand. "I ain't takin' nothin' from you."

"I owe you wages. More than three hundred and eighty—"

"Forget it. You paid for a fine coffin. Undertaker said you paid for a marble headstone." He breathed in deeply, then let it out. "That's all I want from you."

A bell began ringing on the locomotive.

"I got some clippin's of Whip's hair. I'll be takin' one of those down to Hard Labor Creek. Give to my mama. Ain't seen her in years."

"I'm sorry . . ."

"Nah." He shook his head. "Don't be. Like ever'body's been sayin'. An accident. Anybody to blame, it's the engineer on that express. You get your cattle to New York. Get roostered if you make any money. For me. Me and Whip. You and Catfish . . ." He snorted. "Even Colton."

"You'll need money," Tom said. "It's a long way to Georgia."

"How'd you know that we hailed from Georgia?"

Tom smiled. "Whip. When we first met. He said he was a native Texan. Born in Georgia. That amused me."

"You got a memory, Ponting."

Tom bowed his head. "Sometimes I wish I didn't."

"Yeah. Well. I best be ridin' out." He turned, grabbed the horn with his good hand, and pulled himself into the saddle.

"I still owe you money," Tom tried again.

"I won't take it from you. Besides." Rusk, Crew, Dupree, whatever his name was, tried a grin. "You know I got ways of gettin' money. How you reckon I got this horse?"

Tom made himself laugh.

"I won't shake your hand, Ponting. Just because . . . because . . . well . . . I'm ornery. Won't wish you luck, neither. Because I still recollect how I got crippled." He tightened his grip on the reins. "But I'll say this about you. You're a man to ride the river with."

Clucking his tongue, he turned the horse around, and spurred it into a lope.

The bell rang from the monster 4-4-0, and Tom walked to the freight car with the side door still open.

They unloaded the cattle on a Saturday afternoon in Bergen Hill, New Jersey, and let them graze in a pasture and drink from the Hudson River. Long before sundown, people were taking the ferry back and forth just to see these strange cattle. Tom paid two cents for *The Brooklyn Daily Eagle*, only to learn that the boy selling the newspapers had robbed him. The price of the *Eagle* was a penny.

*"Never have I seen cattle like that!"*

*"My, my, my, look at the size of those horns."*

*"Must be from Iowa."*

*"What makes you say that, Chester?"*

*"Long horns. Have to come from the West. I say Iowa."*

Tom finished the newspaper late that night, let the paper fall into the fire, and pushed himself to his feet and made his way to the ferry office.

"Does this boat run all night, sir?" he asked.

The man looked up, and stifled a yawn, and pointed his cigar. "See that city across the Hudson?"

"It is hard to miss, sir."

"That's New York. It don't know midnight from

noon or Christmas from any regular Wednesday. You wanna cross?"

"I do, sir."

"How many cattle you got down there?"

Tom shook his head. "Not near as many as I started out with, sir."

"How many?"

"Sir, you misunderstand me. I have a wagon pulled by two oxen, and an extra ox. Three riders."

"You mean you gonna just leave those nasty-looking brutes here? Mister—"

Tom laughed off the very thought. "Sir, my good man, no, sir. Not at all. Especially considering the fee I have been charged for a few hours of grazing."

"Buster, cattle don't ride this boat for free. Now." He stopped. He must have seen something in Tom's eyes.

"The cattle will swim behind your boat, sir."

"Are you crazy?"

"Most likely. The last passenger, Mr. Greene, will cross separately. Just to make sure all of our cattle leave Bergen Hill safely. Now, what is your fare for one wagon, an extra ox, and three passengers?"

Tom let out a ragged breath when the ferry pushed away from New Jersey. He reached over to the ox-cow tethered behind the wagon, and rang the bell. Catfish stood up in the wagon box.

With the cattle, Colton Greene slapped a steer's hindquarters with a lariat, stepped back. Tom heard the bawling cattle. Then one stepped into the river.

Tom tapped the bell again.

A dark steer followed. Another. Another. Colton Greene started yipping like a coyote. No, he was laughing. Catfish joined him. So did the ferryboat operator. And the people in New Jersey who watched the strange beasts with long horns move into the Hudson and swim behind the ferry, chasing the ox and the bell.

He remembered that night, all those years ago, in the dark, waiting for that signal. In London. With fifty-three bullocks to take to the Smithfield market. Tom shook his head. Another scene came to him. The cattle of several droves bellowing in the darkness, behind him, in front of him. But here, in a city bathed with yellow light from windows, from carriages, and the lanterns that lined the ferry, reflecting off the Hudson. The cattle lowed—Tom's cattle, not Sydney Ivatts's, not Edward Jardine's drove—Tom C. Ponting's steers, branded with a "T" to prove his ownership. And they were all behind him.

But the nerves still came. He was sweating, but this was July. And New York City baked in July.

In London, they drove the cattle at night. In

New York, he waited. He just wanted to be across the Hudson before the people started flocking in to their jobs, their shopping, by thunder, even their crimes. He pulled a paper from his pocket.

*Allerton's Washington Drove Yard*
*4th Ave & 44th St*

He could see the light above the tall buildings. Dawn would be here soon.

Tom turned the paper over.

Latting Observatory
42nd St and 5–6th aves.

That was the tallest structure in the city. Three hundred and fifteen feet. They had built it for that Exhibition of the Industry of All Nations that had started up last year. Look for it. He'd be able to find the cattle yards.

"All right, Catfish." Tom climbed out of the driver's box, squeezed the young Texian's shoulder, and moved to the open tailgate. "Let's see if we can find that exhibition you were so excited to see. Look for a tall needle pointing above all the other tall buildings."

When he sat down, letting his legs dangle over the street, the wagon lurched forward. The cow-ox lowed, the bell tied around her neck rang. The longhorn steers started to follow.

Something else chimed.

"Hold up," Tom whispered urgently, and he felt the wagon slow, stop.

A loud, deep chime. Another. Another. Church bells. Ringing throughout the city. It was Sunday. Sunday morning. Sometimes he thought nothing sounded better than church bells on a Sunday. And he wasn't what most would call religious.

But he didn't want those cattle to be nervous. So he started talking.

"Easy, boys. Easy." The brindle and the dark one stared at him. "You boys are all right. Been a good herd. Trust me, partners, I cannot say that about every drove I ever had. Just a bit longer. Listen to that. They sound real pretty. Real pretty indeed." He laughed, shook his head, and nodded at the lead steers. "Boys, I mean to tell you something that I never noticed. I looked at the back ends of you boys for so long, what, eighteen, nineteen, maybe twenty-one hundred miles. All that time, I never really saw just how handsome you gents are. Yes, sir. You boys are the most handsome steers—bullocks we called you back in England—not that it matters. I bet some people call you that in these United States, too. But you are handsome. Coming from an ugly cuss like me, that is one high compliment."

In the driver's box, Catfish chuckled.

The bells stopped, the echoes dancing off buildings, trees, hills.

"Move on, Catfish," Tom said. He reached over and tapped the bell hanging from the ox-cow's neck.

Hackney coaches pulled to the side of the streets. Men stepped onto the streets, then retreated when they realized what they were seeing. Mothers raced out to wrench their sons' arms as they pulled them, screaming in protest, back to the safety of sidewalks.

"Is that it, Mr. Ponting?"

Tom turned and saw where Catfish pointed. The Stars and Stripes, maybe the biggest flag Tom had ever seen, flapped in the wind from a long pole that rose from a towering point that rose well above the dingy, dark, tall buildings lining the streets.

"Has to be," Tom said. "Head that way, Catfish. And keep a lookout for Fourth Avenue or Forty-Fourth Street."

Fifteen minutes later, the wagon turned a corner, Tom jumped from the tailgate, and waved his hat, pointing the lead steers into the gate men began dragging open.

For a moment, he stood there, after the last steer had been herded in by the drove-yard workers, and felt a great emptiness. It was over. All those miles. More than a year's work. All those cattle. The crossings. The sickness. The owlhoots and rapscallions they had encountered. And the good men and women they had met. The Indians. Jesse Chisholm. Mr. Byers. Yargee. C. W. Rusk. Santos. Izan. And poor Whip. He wondered what Washington Malone was doing right about now.

A strange voice shouted: "Those your beeves, mister?"

Tom turned, finding a slim man with sandy hair and a thin mustache running across Fourth Avenue, cursing at a hackney driver who cursed back, then almost trampling a woman, not even apologizing as he stumbled, straightened, and came into the drove yard.

"These your cattle?" the man asked again.

He didn't look like a buyer, but Tom was new to this market. "Yes."

"My name's Sturbin. John Sturbin. But call me Sturb. From Iowa, I hear. Not me. I'm from New York. Greatest city in the world. I mean, I hear the cattle came all the way from Iowa—wherever that is."

"Well." Tom couldn't lie to a buyer or broker. "Texas actually."

"Texas. That's even better." He found a pencil above his ear, and pulled paper from his pocket.

"Mind if I ask you a question?"

"Not at all," Tom said.

The man must have asked forty. But never how much Tom wanted for them. Then this Sturb looked at his watch, let out a blasphemy, turned, and bolted across the street, again exchanging curses and gestures at a driver of a freight wagon.

Moments later, Tom felt the assault as butchers and stockmen circled him. Those who couldn't get close enough to him closed in on Greene and Catfish. They guessed at where the strange steers came from—Iowa. Arkansas. The mountains of the moon. The gates of hell. Tom felt he had been caught in a stampede by the time most of them left to get closer looks at the longhorns.

"They can wear you out."

He turned to the voice.

"James Gilchrist. Cattle broker."

"Tom Ponting." He held out his hand, liked the firmness and quickness of the man's shake.

"Any offers from that crowd?"

Tom laughed. "If I were a drinking man, I would be dead drunk. They all wanted to stand me to a drink."

"Texas cattle are new to this city."

Tom stared. He had told only that strange man, John Sturbin, that the cattle came from Texas, and Sturbin had raced off into the canyons of the metropolis without a goodbye.

"I'm come from Ohio."

"Illinois," Tom said.

"That's what I would have guessed. We Western men know cattle. I have read about Texas cattle, but these are the first I have seen. Shall we talk a little business?" Gilchrist nodded at Greene and

Catfish. "I'll stand your drovers to breakfast." He nodded at a tavern across the street.

Tom put his arm around Catfish's shoulder, and they looked at that tall structure, Latting's tower, but this part of the city seemed abandoned. A policeman leaned against the door, smoking a cigar. Wind howled around the corners, bringing papers and trash and dust with it.

"Reckon we missed the big show." Catfish sighed. "Shucks."

Tom shrugged. "It does not appear to be open. But this is Sunday." He looked up. "But there's a sight, son." He pointed.

Above them, that giant flag of the republic waved over the city of New York.

"Hmmmm" was all Catfish said.

"I'm glad this place is closed," Colton Greene said. "I wouldn't want to go up that high."

"Catfish," Tom said. "I bet the exhibition is open tomorrow. When we sell the cattle, we'll come back. Ride all the way to the top if you want." He looked over at Colton Greene. "I am sure Mr. Greene can find amusements at the Crystal Palace."

The grin widened across Greene's face. "Yes, sir. I bet I sure can."

"Let's find a place to eat," Tom said.

"Mr. Ponting."

Tom waited. Catfish stared at his feet, kicked

a peanut shell into the gutter, sighed, and finally looked at Tom. "Well, I was wondering. Maybe. It might not be open today either, but, well . . ."

"Go on. We have a few days in this city yet."

"Well, there's this place I heard about in the drove yard. Barnum's American Museum. Fellow said General Tom Thumb's there. You can see him. Tiny as he is. Smallest man in the world. Not more than twenty-eight inches tall. They got a giraffe, too. A live one. I mean, I reckon it's alive. And a lady. A real lady. With a beard."

Greene slapped his thigh, tilted his head back, and laughed.

"Man said it cost just two bits," Catfish continued. "Unless you want special seats. Those cost fifty cents."

Tom smiled. "I think we shall have an excellent day tomorrow. And a fine Fourth of July the day after."

# CHAPTER 43

After reining in the zebra dun, Tom shook his head. He would have to get reacquainted with Moweaqua. The brick building was finished. People Tom didn't recognize came in and out of the store. The sawmill whined. He looked over at Cowle, Shay, and Goodwin's flouring mill and saw those black letters, clear as day.

*This mill erected in 1851*

Behind the cabin, men worked with shovels and tools Tom didn't recognize, making a path, he figured, for a railroad.

Tom clucked his tongue, kicked the gelding, and rode to the cabin. He swung down, ground-reined the dun, and moved to his saddlebags. A minute later, he lugged two pouches into the cabin. For once, Snyder's place was empty except for Michael Snyder, who pored over a ledger. The big man looked up with a smile Tom thought would vanish as soon as the merchant recognized Tom. Instead, the smile widened, and Snyder slammed the ledger closed.

"Ponting. It is good to see you. Welcome home."

Tom nodded, crossed the floor, hefted the pouches, and laid them atop the counter.

"This belongs to you, Herr Snyder. A thousand dollars. In California gold."

Snyder's smile vanished, but the eyes looked hungrily at the leather. He nodded, and looked back at Tom. "You made it to New York I hear."

"Yes, sir." And Tom had made it home. Traveled by train with Catfish all the way to Indianapolis, after leaving Colton Greene in New York. He paid Catfish's stage fare to someplace called Nacogdoches, Texas. The boy said he could walk from there to his home, but Tom had forgotten the name of that town. Tom had found a stagecoach to Decatur, where he bought the zebra dun.

"With a hundred and thirty head."

"Then I owe—"

"No, sir." Tom interrupted. "I lost the bet. The bet was one hundred and fifty head to New York by July fourth. Got there, got the cattle sold on the third. Day early. But twenty head short."

"That is close—"

"No, sir." Tom shook his head. "This is yours. You won the bet."

The head shook, but the fingers pulled on the rawhide string, and a big hand reached inside, came out with one of the octagonal coins. Snyder whispered something in German then, letting his fingers close around the coin, and laughed.

"Maybe you take cattle to New York next year?"

"No," Tom started answering before Snyder had finished. "Not New York. No, sir. Too far. Too big. But I thought . . . well . . . maybe Canada."

"Canada." Now the German howled. "That is funny. You learn. You learn. You learn not to bet against me," Snyder said, enjoying himself now, coughing out laugh after laugh.

Tom made himself grin. "I have to get back home, sir. Just wanted to pay my debt." He got only four steps before Snyder called out his name.

"You come, Ponting. Come work for me. I pay good wages. You stop this fool cattle business. Work with me. You won't go broke."

Smiling now, Tom eased back to the counter. "Broke, sir? Oh, no, Herr Snyder, I am not broke."

The German looked suddenly confused.

"One hundred and thirty head of Texas cattle were sold, by me, in New York." He patted one of the pouches. "Cattle I paid twelve dollars at the most, they sold for a lot more than that in New York City. *A lot more.* Now, granted I lost a few on the way. Gave some to help out a few orphans. Used others to pay for leases and the like. And I figured my expenses totaled, oh, two dollars a head from Texas to Illinois, and with the trains and ferries, seventeen a head from Muncie to New York." He smiled again. "No, sir. I am far from broke. Even after paying my partner his share, I am not broke. Not rich, but far from broke." He patted the pouches. "This money I lost. Well, that is the chance you take when you gamble. Maybe I will learn my lesson someday. But it was money I could afford to lose. Or I would not have bet it."

He nodded. "Be seeing you." And walked away again. This time, he made it to the door.

Again, he turned when Snyder called his name.

"How much?" Snyder was excited. The German was more apparent. He even stuttered. "H-h-how much they pay . . . f-for those cows? H-h-ow much . . . in New York?"

"Eighty dollars a head was the lowest. One hundred dollars a head was the highest." Tom nodded again. "And Washington Malone is on his way to Chicago with his drove. I do not expect him to get as much as that, but I figure, well, three dollars or more center weight, he will make out just fine. *We* will make out just fine." He walked outside.

Tom was about to swing into the saddle when Snyder called out his name again. Snyder stepped away from the cabin, stopping a few feet from Tom and the zebra dun.

"You come to supper," Snyder said. "You come tonight. Six o'clock. My wife. We will roast a fat pig."

Tom smiled. "Well, sir. Frau Snyder cooked the last time I was there. How about if I provide the meat this time? Beef. I have plenty of beef."

Snyder nodded and took a tentative step forward. Then he held out his hand, showed off the fifty-dollar slug, flipped it up, caught it, flipped it again, and let it slide into his pocket.

"Maybe we make another wager. A thousand dollars. You get money back. Or I get more money."

"Oh. I am not sure about that." He put his hand on the stirrup and looked over his saddle. More trees had fallen to axes. Moweaqua was practically wide open now. A man could see a long ways.

"Canada." Snyder slapped his thigh. "I bet you never get cows sold in Canada. Impossible. Too far north."

"Canada, eh." Tom dropped the reins to the dun, kept his hand on the back as he walked around the gelding. He stared. "North to Canada."

Michael Snyder coughed out laughs again.

"*Dummkopf*. That is west."

Tom didn't answer. He could see Margaret, just as beautiful as he remembered, and he sure had a lot to tell her. She looked like she was running toward him. Tom started her way.

"Let me think that over, Herr Snyder," he said.

Folks who were in Moweaqua that day said they thought Tom Ponting moved at a pretty good lope himself.

# EPILOGUE
# 1907

Tom C. Ponting is easily the best and most widely known citizen of Moweaqua. They know him all the way from England to San Francisco, and they have a good word to say for him every step of the distance. He has been known by three generations and he may outlast one or two more.

—(Decatur, Illinois) *Sunday Review*,
June 9, 1907

He felt every one of his nigh eighty-three years when he stepped out of the house, pail in hand, and limped toward the barn. He made it halfway, without his cane, when the most god-awful commotion he ever heard had the dogs barking, the mule braying, and one of the cows kicking its stall.

The screen door opened, and Tom turned, shot a glance at Margaret, who stood behind the screen as one of those horseless carriages—folks called them automobiles these days—came bounding over the potholes, smashing the cow patties, and smoking like a chimney. Didn't have a roof. What would that fool driver do in the rain? Not that it would rain this morning.

Cowards that they had always been, the four dogs scrambled under the porch, growling. The man in the automobile sawed that wheel, grabbing one of the levers before the velocipede slid, sputtered, coughed, and died. Chickens kept squawking. The dogs still growled. Margaret started to close the screen door. Maybe she would fetch the shotgun. Because the man looked like he might have just come from the moon, with that muffler, leather cap, and those dirty goggles.

"I say, but I hope this is the Ponting residence." The car hissed.

The goggles and scarf and hat came off. Fellow looked like a regular human being now.

"My name's Ponting." Tom shot another glance at Margaret, who must have decided that no firearms were needed at the moment. "Tom C. Ponting."

"Excellent." The man climbed onto the side rail and hopped into the dirt. "It is a pleasure to meet you, Thomas. My name—"

"No, sir." Tom shook his head. "My name is Tom. Spelled that way in the Bible back in England. My folks figured I would never learn how to spell Thomas. So they named me Tom."

"My apologies, Tom. My name is Ethridge. Henry T. Ethridge. Editor of *The Daily Review* out of Decatur."

"That yours?" Tom pointed the pail at the still-hissing car.

"Yes, indeed. Just bought it. A Buick Runabout. Paid twelve hundred bucks for it."

"I paid twelve hundred dollars for a bull once," Tom said.

"Indeed." Mr. Henry T. Ethridge sounded excited.

Tom nodded. "Indeed."

"Well, sir, I know that the readers of the *Review* would be delighted to hear about all of your adventures. Your life story as it is."

Tom laughed. "Did Bill Gilbert put you up to this?"

"Sir?"

"Bill Gilbert. Sounds just like something he would do."

"No. I do not know a William—a Bill—Gilbert."

"Mac McLaurin then."

"No." Before Tom could guess another name, the editor started explaining. "I talked to Dorothy Kautz last week, sir. Her father's bank is one of our best advertisers. She told me you have been dictating your autobiography to her. She says you have lived an exemplary life. And I know from going through our morgue—our old newspapers, sir—and talking to some old-time . . . our *leading* historians that you are, shall we say, a visionary, a man whose story should be told to every Illinois citizen. If not these entire United States."

"Rob Evans. Robbie we call him. How much did old Robbie pay you to do to this?" Tom chuckled. "I should have guessed Robbie . . ."

"Honest, sir. I come on my own volition. After talking to Miss Kautz."

Tom tapped his leg with the pail.

"This is no jest?"

"It is no jest, Mr. Ponting. We would like to publish a series of articles about your life, your adventures. I have been told that you were the first man to drive a herd of Texas longhorns all the way from the Lone Star State to New York City."

The screen door squeaked, banged shut. Margaret had stepped onto the porch.

Now Tom frowned. "That book I been telling Miss Dorothy what to put down. That is just something for my kids and my grandkids. So they would know something about Margaret and me when we are gone."

"My publisher is willing to help you get that book edited and published." He smiled. "All twenty-five copies. But we would like to run a series of articles in our Sunday papers. So more people might become aware of all you have done in this extraordinary life."

Tom shook his head. "I bought and sold cattle. That is all I have ever done."

"Your story should be told. You are telling it, sir. For that book for your heirs. I would like you to tell it to me, so that I may tell my readers."

Tom stared at the man with the fancy, noisy automobile. "Last time I talked to a reporter, that I recall anyway, was in New York City in eighteen and fifty-four, and he never even told me he was a reporter. Sturbin was his name. He asked me all sorts of questions that I figured he was wanting to buy some longhorns. Then he wrote all this stuff in his newspaper and never even mailed me a copy of the blessed article." Tom frowned.

"I have told you that I am the *Daily Review*'s editor. And I promise to send you a stack of newspapers."

Tom stared at Margaret.

"They call you the Cattle King of Central Illinois," Ethridge said.

"They called me lots of other things, too." Chuckling, he faced the newspaperman again. "I had a partner. Good man. Washington Malone." He frowned. "He died too young. Thirty-one years old. God took him Home in '62."

"And you have also known Buffalo Bill Cody. Horace Greeley. P. T. Barnum. The Swans of—"

"Barnum . . . now there's somebody you ought to write about."

"Much has been written of Barnum already. Little has been written about you."

"For good reason." Tom shook his head. "And probably more lies about Buffalo Bill—that he told himself." His head tilted back as he howled.

Regaining his composure, Tom looked at this Henry T. Ethridge. "I met Jesse Chisholm once. He got a cattle trail to Kansas named after him, and you want to know something? Far as I know, that trader never took a herd of cattle anywhere."

"That is the type of stories I desire."

Tom stiffened. "Do not get me wrong, mister. I have never wanted a trail named after me. And Chisholm was a mighty big man with the tribes. That Western country could have used a lot more men like him. Rather than Chivington and Custer and the likes."

The newspaperman nodded.

Encouraged, Tom continued. "Took a herd to Canada. And to Denver, Colorado. I did more than just bring some stupid longhorns to New York City. That was . . ." His head shook. "That was probably the least important thing I done. Would not be worth mentioning except for one fact." He looked at Margaret, puckered his lips, and blew her a kiss.

She pretended to catch it, and brought her hand to her heart.

Tom smiled. God, how he loved that woman.

"I knew Abraham Lincoln."

Ethridge laughed. "Everybody in Illinois born before 1865 knew Lincoln, sir. But this article is not about—"

*"I knew Abraham Lincoln."*

"Tom," Margaret cautioned.

The newspaperman started talking again. "I do not doubt you, Mr. Ponting. But this article is not about the men you have known. It is about you."

Tom looked at Margaret again. She nodded. And blew him a kiss.

"Well." Tom turned back to Mr. Ethridge. "You want to start this here interview right now?"

"That would be wonderful. I have notebooks and pencils in the other seat. If you'd allow me . . ."

Tom shrugged.

"I have a creed," Tom said as the man bent over his Buick. "Had some cards printed up. I can give you one if you . . ." He stopped. Ethridge paid no attention.

"This story will tell people the opportunities America gives her children," the editor said while picking items out of the spare seat, "and those who choose to live in America. And Illinois."

Straightening, Ethridge looked at Tom. "You were saying something about a card with your creed."

"Oh." Tom waved his hand. "It—"

"It's a beautiful sentiment," Margaret sang out. Tom glared at her, but she dismissed him with a wave of her hand. She recited the back of the card:

> *There is so much bad in the best of us.*
> *And so much good in the worst of us.*
> *It hardly behooves any of us.*
> *To speak ill of the rest of us.*

"That's revelatory," Henry T. Ethridge said.

*Revelatory. Re-ve-la-tory. I shall look that word up in my Webster's after this jasper has gone back to Decatur.*

"There's much more," Margaret said, " 'Do not keep the alabaster . . .' "

"Aw, hush up, Margaret." He felt his face flushing, which would make the white mustache and goatee reveal just how old Tom was.

"Perhaps we can reprint your card and your creed with one of the articles," the newspaperman said as he bent back to get more reporting supplies. "We have that technology these days as you have seen if you have read our newspaper lately. The greatness of our country shines through our inventions but more so through men like you."

Tom studied Henry T. Ethridge as he stepped away from the Buick Roundabout with pencils over both ears and notebooks sticking out of myriad pockets. "America is great," Tom said. "I could not have done half of what I have done back in England."

He regretted that statement. Made him sound like he was running for office. And then memories swelled through his head and heart. The slaves he had met in Texas and the Indian Nations. He thought about men he had not remembered in years. Colton Greene. How had he made out in New York? Yargee. Did he make it back to Pecan Creek alive? What had become of young Jim "Catfish" Hennessy? And Santos and Izan? Old James Byers. He sure hoped Byers lay beside his late wife in Greene County.

And he felt a sudden pain when he pictured one-armed C. W. Rusk. He tried to recall the man's real name. Did he ever know it? Then he remembered poor Whip, choking to death on his own blood, after being hauled out of that smashed railroad car. Roosevelt Dupree. Who could have been president of these United States.

Tom felt like calling the absurd interview off until he looked back at Margaret, who gave a reassuring nod.

The editor stopped a few feet from him.

Tom blinked.

"Is that a . . . milk pail?" Ethridge asked.

Tom looked at the rattling piece of tin. "Well, yes, sir, of course it is."

"Can you milk a cow?"

Tom nodded. Then, insulted, he straightened. "Yes, Mr. Ethridge, I can milk a cow. I have been milking cows all my life. Let me tell you—"

Margaret laughed so hard she fell against the screen door. Tom and Ethridge turned to stare.

Still laughing, Margaret shook her head, and had to bring the apron up to dab her eyes.

"Yes, Mr. Ethridge," she told the newspaper-man. "Yes, he can milk." Laughing that musical way that Tom had always admired, Margaret looked straight at Tom, but she spoke to the newspaper editor with a fancy horseless carriage:

"But he is a good deal better at *driving* cows."

# AUTHOR'S NOTE

"Don't quote me in your term paper," I have often explained to readers. "I make things up." While some of my novels follow history as closely as I can keep it, *Longhorns East* falls more into the "inspired by" category. Yes, the basic story is fairly true. Tom Candy Ponting was a transplanted Englishman who became a noted cattle dealer in Illinois, and in 1853 drove cattle from northeastern Texas to Moweaqua, Illinois, wintering the herd there before continuing to Muncie, Indiana, then used the railroads to get his cattle to New York City in July 1854. Ponting's memoir, *Life of Tom Candy Ponting*, first published in 1907 and reprinted in 1952 by the Branding Iron Press in Evanston, Illinois, was my primary source, along with some 1907 newspaper articles out of Decatur, Illinois. But neither went into great detail, so I embellished. While *Longhorns East* is ostensibly a cattle-drive novel, I set out to write a journey novel and paint a panorama of America in the 1850s. While Ponting and his men might not have run into crooks and experienced a train wreck, Jesse Chisholm's cameo appearance is based on Ponting's memoir.

Most of the supporting players are fictional.

According to Ponting, he made the drive from Texas to Illinois with help from his partner, Washington Malone, and the cook, James Byers. Byers left the drive after crossing the Mississippi River into what is now East St. Louis. There was no bet with Ponting's future father-in-law, though Ponting did finish the drive by rail from Muncie, Indiana, to New York. Newspapers reported the arrival of longhorns. Other than Byers, the cowhands came out of my imagination and cowboys I have known.

In real life, Tom's bride-to-be, Margaret Snyder, was younger than she is depicted here. While I understand that women sometimes married at much younger ages back then, having a man almost thirty years old wooing a girl thirteen or fourteen felt way too creepy.

Other sources included: Haydn Brown's article "Drovers: Scotland to London Via Norfolk!" (NorthfolkTalesMyths.com, April 21, 2018); David Dary's *Cowboy Culture: A Saga of Five Centuries* (Avon, 1982); Frank Webster Farley's 1915 thesis for the University of Illinois's College of Agriculture, *History of the Beef Cattle Industry in Illinois*; Diana K Reeves Phipps's *Tom's Trail: In the Footsteps of the First American Cowboy, Tom Candy Ponting: A Story Told by His Great Niece* (self-published, 2019); *Chronology of Illinois History, 1673–1954*, compiled by Margaret A. Flint for the Illinois

Blue Book, 1953–1954, reprinted by the Illinois State Historical Library in 1955; *Moweaqua Sesquicentennial 1852–2002 Souvenir Program*; Arthur Andrew Olson III's *Forging the Bee Line Railroad, 1849–1889: The Rise and Fall of the Hoosier Partisans and Cleveland Clique* (The Kent State University Press, 2017); Elbert Waller's *Brief History of Illinois, Third Edition* (Galesburg, IL: Wagoner Printing Company, 1910); J. Wesley Whicker's *Historical Sketches of the Wabash Valley* (Attica, IN: self-published, 1916); and James W. Whitaker's *Feedlot Empire: Beef Cattle Feeding in Illinois and Iowa, 1840– 1900* (Ames, IA: The Iowa State University Press, 1975).

I pored through articles and advertisements from 1840s England and 1850s America on NewspaperArchives.com and Newspapers.com.

Debby Adams Arnold and her husband graciously made me feel at home in Moweaqua, while guiding me on a tour of Ponting country and letting me sift through the records at the Moweaqua Historical Society and Moweaqua Public Library. Vauna Stahl did the same at the Christian County Genealogy Society and Historical Museum in Taylorville, and Abe Lincoln likely would not have made a cameo in this book without her stories. Donna Lupton pulled out countless books and sources at the Shelby County Historical and Genealogical Society in Shelbyville.

Susan M. Smith, archivist at the Minnetrista Museum & Gardens in Muncie, Indiana, dug up plenty of tidbits and helpful information, while Chris Flook, author of *Lost Towns of Delaware County, Indiana* (Charleston, SC: The History Press, 2019), provided useful information via e-mail.

So did Robert Good, his wife and staff at Muncie's Delaware County Historical Society, and Robert drove me around Muncie. The staff at Muncie's Carnegie Library, including Sara McKinley, was quite helpful—although they did leave me to my own devices during that weekly test of the tornado warning sirens. We aren't familiar with such Midwestern quirks in northern New Mexico, and when you look up while sirens wail to find yourself alone in an unfamiliar library wing, you wonder: *Surely, someone would let me know if this is the real deal . . . right?*

Brittany Hays, director of the Attica Public Library, and her staff provided much information, as did Lee Bauerband, the delightfully charming local historian who answered questions and showed me some important spots in Attica.

And I certainly can't leave out Mama Chan for the great Thai food in downtown Moweaqua.

Tom Candy Ponting died on October 11, 1916, at age ninety-two at St. Mary's Hospital in Decatur, Illinois; Margaret would follow in 1922. A few days before he died, Ponting told his son,

Wayne: "I might not get well, and if I don't, for God's sake tell the preacher to cut it short."

Sounds like a man I would have enjoyed knowing.

Johnny D. Boggs<br>
Santa Fe, New Mexico<br>
September 15, 2022

**Center Point Large Print**
600 Brooks Road / PO Box 1
Thorndike, ME 04986-0001 USA

(207) 568-3717

US & Canada:
1 800 929-9108
www.centerpointlargeprint.com